EVERY WORD UNSAID

Books by Kimberly Duffy

A Mosaic of Wings
A Tapestry of Light
Every Word Unsaid

EVERY WORD UNSAID

KIMBERLY DUFFY

BETHANYHOUSE
a division of Baker Publishing Group
Minneapolis, Minnesota

© 2021 by Kimberly Duffy

Published by Bethany House Publishers
11400 Hampshire Avenue South
Bloomington, Minnesota 55438
www.bethanyhouse.com

Bethany House Publishers is a division of
Baker Publishing Group, Grand Rapids, Michigan

Printed in the United States of America

Library of Congress Cataloging-in-Publication Data
Names: Duffy, Kimberly, author.
Title: Every word unsaid / Kimberly Duffy.
Description: Minneapolis, Minnesota : Bethany House Publishers, a division of
    Baker Publishing Group, [2021]
Identifiers: LCCN 2021031570 | ISBN 9780764235658 (trade paper) |
    ISBN 9780764239366 (casebound) | ISBN 9781493433858 (ebook)
Subjects: GSAFD: Christian fiction.
Classification: LCC PS3604.U3783 E94 2021 | DDC 813/.6—dc23
LC record available at https://lccn.loc.gov/2021031570

Scripture quotations are from the King James Version of the Bible.

This is a work of historical reconstruction; the appearances of certain historical figures are therefore inevitable. All other characters, however, are products of the author's imagination, and any resemblance to actual persons, living or dead, is coincidental.

Cover design by Jennifer Parker
Cover image of young woman running by Ildiko Neer / Arcangel

Author is represented by the Books & Such Literary Agency.

Baker Publishing Group publications use paper produced from sustainable forestry practices and post-consumer waste whenever possible.

21 22 23 24 25 26 27   7 6 5 4 3 2 1

To Ellie.
Everyone should see life through your eyes.
Beauty abounds. Excitement is only a daydream (or book) away.
Stories are waiting to be captured and told. And there you are,
camera and pen in hand, on the precipice of a grand adventure.

And in memory of Pandita Ramabai Sarasvati.
"A life totally committed to God has nothing to fear,
nothing to lose, nothing to regret."

"I once was lost, but now I am found,
was blind, but now I see."

—John Newton

1

August 1897
Deadwood, South Dakota

Nothing brought Augusta Constance Travers more joy than slipping away. And nothing frustrated her more than the companion meant to keep her from doing so.

Gussie slid back from the building's corner, drawing Dora Clutterbuck farther into the alley.

"What are you doing, Miss Travers?" Dora shrugged Gussie's hand from her arm and placed her fists on hips that could use a Scott three-piece bustle pad. Perhaps Gussie would gift her one. There was little she could offer that might soften Dora's expression, but her figure was another matter entirely.

Gussie craned her neck around the building and saw the man pacing the boardwalk outside their hotel's front door. She flattened herself against the wall and pressed a finger to her lips. "We've been caught."

Dora didn't even try to stanch her smile. "Praise God." She made for the street, her hand already lifted in a wave.

Gussie grabbed her. "You cannot ruin this for me." She made

sure the strap of her camera bag lay securely over her chest and then marched toward the back of the hotel. "I'm not ready to be found."

Dora huffed and scurried to keep up. "Miss Travers, it is time to shake the dust of Deadwood from our shoes and return to civilization. I'm not sure how much more of this I can take."

Gussie paused when they reached the back of the hotel, searching for an entry. A door stood propped open by a large rock. She was safe. For now. "I hardly think your duties a heavy burden. Indeed, except for this last month, every trip has been made first class."

"This last month has undone anything Mr. Pullman could offer on his trains," Dora muttered.

Gussie chuckled. Dora often cast a cloud over their adventures, but she did own an amusing proclivity toward overstatement.

Something shifted near a pile of rubbish, drawing Gussie's attention. She caught sight of the little scamp, trousers too short and shirt too large, who had taken to following them around. A smattering of freckles spilled across his nose. She'd always been partial to freckles, even though her own skin remained untouched because of Mother's violent insistence that Gussie carry a parasol everywhere she went.

She reached into her pocket and fished out the coin she'd tucked in there before leaving her room a couple of hours before sunrise. "Don't spend it on something practical."

The boy snatched it away, a grin lighting his grubby face.

"You darling boy."

"Why do you bother with urchins?" Dora stepped away from him, and Gussie herself resisted the urge to wrinkle her nose at his scent. "You've given too much of your pay to vile creatures since we left New York, and it's wasteful, I say."

Before Dora could launch into her tired lecture, Gussie pinched the boy's chin and gave him her most brilliant smile. "Every child deserves to be seen. No matter their station. No matter . . ." She glanced toward Dora, whose scowl seemed a much nastier thing than the boy's filth. "Well, no matter anything."

A familiar cough echoed from the street, and Gussie glanced over her shoulder. They would soon be discovered.

She skirted a pile of vegetable scraps, stepped through the hotel's back door, and entered the kitchen's chaos. A red-faced woman wearing a calico dress and a stained apron shouted at the collection of young women and children unfortunate enough to be employed by her. Kettles shrieked, pots bubbled, and a dog with one eye and suspect bare patches around his tail gnawed on a bone.

"Come on." Gussie glanced behind her to see that Dora followed, and they took the servant's staircase. "I hired you specifically because you said you had a thirst for adventure. Have I not given you that? Have there not been many adventures?" Their echoing steps punctuated her questions. Gussie mentally ticked off some of the trips Dora had accompanied her on. Nearly a month traveling the Ohio River, ending in a whirlwind tour of New Orleans; a few fun days exploring the delights of Coney Island; a boring week at the Greenbrier Hotel in White Sulphur Springs, West Virginia. That had been an apology for dragging Dora through the Midwest after the Ringling Brothers Circus. "Do not flag on me now."

"*You* didn't hire me. Your father did."

They reached the Bullock Hotel's third floor, and Gussie stuck her head out the door and looked both directions down the length of carpeted hall before darting from the stairwell. She'd taken a room here as restitution for the month-long trek she'd arranged through the Badlands, thinking Dora would enjoy the luxury, though Gussie couldn't imagine time in a dull hotel being more interesting than the marvels outside it. What photos she had been able to capture!

In their room, Gussie set her bag on the narrow brass bed she'd claimed and pulled out the smaller satchel protecting her Folding Pocket Kodak. She'd been given a model before it was available to the rest of the country and had been traveling and taking photos with it to send back to New York. Everyone now wanted the machine Miss Adventuress carried around the world. She patted the satchel, then removed the journal she'd kept this trip. She always kept one during her travels, scribbling snippets of thoughts and descriptions of America's natural beauty. They were a handy reference when she wrote her regular column for *Lady's Weekly*.

Gussie skimmed the notes she'd taken that morning. They were unlikely to make their way into a column—too serious, too introspective—but they would still serve a purpose when she was back in New York, trussed up like a Christmas turkey and suffocating beneath expectations. They would remind her of wild freedom.

Waking early that morning had been worth the inconvenience. They had walked down a deserted Main Street, through Chinatown and Elizabethtown, and then, after only a mile more, Gussie had been met with incredible vistas. The Black Hills rose above them, pine trees and jagged rocks framing a sunrise so vibrant it brought tears to her eyes. A photo couldn't do the scene justice, of course, but her words would spin pictures. And Miss Adventuress's description would take her readers away. Away from household duties and crowded cities and dull routines. To South Dakota and a rough frontier town and experiences one could only dream about.

And read of in *Lady's Weekly*.

Gussie set the book aside and rested her chin in her hand. "Where should we go next?"

"Chicago."

Gussie sighed.

"You've been gone long enough, and if your parents have sent *him* after you, it means you must return to your aunt in Chicago." Dora poked one priggish finger into the air. "It is *time*."

Gussie rolled her eyes and slapped her hand against her knee. "Very well. Back to Chicago you shall go."

Dora gasped. "Truly? And then home to New York? Is this interminable madness over?"

Gussie ignored her and pulled a carpetbag from the bottom of the wardrobe across the room. She set it on the bed and began unbuttoning her jacket.

Dora eyed her with suspicion. "What are you doing?"

"The train leaves in sixty minutes. You must be on it." Gussie removed her jacket and set it aside, then let her skirt puddle around her feet. "Thank heavens I had the foresight to hire a woman my size."

"Your father hired me." Dora's voice was as acerbic as an unripe persimmon.

Gussie grinned and waved her hand toward Dora's serviceable rust-colored bodice. "It's an awful color for me, but it will suit. And you *think* Father hired you."

Gussie had experienced two wonderful years of freedom, traveling as *Lady's Weekly* photographer and columnist Miss Adventuress, before she was asked to write weekly. It meant more travel. More exciting destinations too. But also, according to her parents, more opportunity for a ruined reputation. Dora was a compromise, but that didn't stop them from sending a Pinkerton after her when she left unexpectedly. Of course, it also didn't stop her from continuing to leave without informing them.

She couldn't bear their negativity and pronouncements of certain social doom. She'd had enough of it from Dora too.

"Well—" she huffed when Dora just stood in front of her, still as a statue—"undress. We haven't much time."

Dora's face fell. "You aren't planning to be on that train with me, are you?"

"You must know me better than that by now." A year together, and Dora still seemed surprised when Gussie acted like the independent woman she was.

Dora's brow wrinkled. "I can't leave you here by yourself. It will ruin you. Your parents will, at the very least, release me without a reference."

"I won't allow them to." Gussie patted Dora's shoulder. "Don't fuss. I'll leave Deadwood on the morning train. And I'm only making one stop—there's a waterfall outside Sleepy Eye I wish to capture. The train pulls through there twice daily, so I'll be on my way to you and Chicago only a day later."

"But you will be alone. On the train. For two days."

"So will you. Women travel alone now, Dora. It isn't unheard

11

of. Nellie Bly traveled the world on her own almost a decade ago."
Gussie lifted her skirt from the floor and draped it over the edge
of the footboard.

"Your sister's wedding is in less than two weeks."

"And we will be there in plenty of time. Just Sleepy Eye, Dora.
Two days in Chicago, and home we shall go."

Dora still stood unmoving, her thin lips twisting.

"I can contact Mr. Smart if you think I need someone to accompany me."

"Don't you dare," Dora squeaked. She began to disrobe.

Gussie went to the wardrobe and removed Dora's few items.
She hid her triumphant grin before returning to the bed, arms
full. Dora had detested the man Lillian Clare, Gussie's editor and
friend, had hired to guide them through the South Dakota wilderness. Gussie had no qualms about Mr. Smart—he'd kept them
fed and safe as she took photos of buttes and candy-cane-striped
rock formations. He'd led them through the Black Hills for an
additional two weeks and deposited them safely in Deadwood,
pocketing the money Gussie handed over in a velvet pouch and
leaving without a backward glance.

Which suited Gussie just fine. She didn't feel as strongly about
his propensity for spitting fat wads of chewing tobacco at their
feet as Dora did either. Gussie could put up with a lot, as long as
she was afforded the opportunity to breathe. There was a lot of
air and space around Deadwood. Just her, her Kodak . . . and her
uptight companion.

Gussie dropped the clothing atop the bed and made a show of
folding a few pieces before scooping the rest up and dumping the
whole pile into the bag. She whirled and lifted her hands, as sup-
plicant a posture as Dora would ever witness. "These are our only
options—either I travel back to Chicago and Aunt Rhoda alone,
or I travel in the company of an uncouth man who couldn't care
a whit about my reputation."

"Or you can come home with me." Dora went to the window
and peeked past the curtain. "And him."

Gussie snorted and held out her hand for Dora's skirt.

Dora clutched it to her chest. "I could stay here with you, I suppose." She said it so mournfully that Gussie considered agreeing, if only to reward her companion's acting ability.

"No. You must go. I need to evade him for another couple of days, and you are the perfect diversion." Gussie plucked the skirt from Dora's grip.

"Your aunt." Dora buried her head in her hands. "She's going to be so unhappy."

"Aunt Rhoda is routinely unhappy. Let's at least give her a reason."

Gussie stepped into the skirt and draped the fabric so it fell neatly over her bustle pad. "Hurry. Retrieve my traveling gown. We don't have much time. The train leaves soon, and I need to be sure our ruse works." She wouldn't be caught this soon.

Dora went to the wardrobe and donned the navy wool skirt and jacket. Gussie sighed, her fingers itching for the velvet trim and large buttons. What a shame. She would have to give the traveling suit to Dora, of course, as restitution for this latest escapade. And Gussie did so love it.

"What a lovely figure you have, Dora. That outfit suits you." It did too. Gussie didn't know why Dora sought the most unflattering colors and fabrics for her gowns.

Dora's fingers paused their fumbling, and her shoulders stiffened. "Do not flatter me, Miss Travers. Everyone is sure to be angry with me. And if you meet some unfortunate end, as you seem so driven to do, they will hold me responsible for your death."

"Oh, don't be so cross. We've had a great adventure."

"One I'm glad is nearly at its end."

"Not entirely. Don't forget that my readers wish for waterfalls."

Dora whirled, her eyes protruding in such a fashion that Gussie considered suggesting she see a doctor. "I will leave you for good, Miss Travers! And then where will you be?"

"Stop fussing. It will all come out in the end. It always does." Gussie pulled the pins from her hat and transferred it from her head to Dora's, tugging down one of the large white feathers so

Every Word Unsaid

that it hid her profile. "Perfect. Once you're settled in your berth and he's boarded the train, I'll escape through another car." Gussie grinned. How she loved this game. She went back to the bed and snapped the carpetbag closed. "Now, we must go. I will carry your bag to make a show of it."

"Miss Travers, your aunt isn't—"

Gussie shoved her own bag into Dora's arms. "If you're that worried, just get a room when you arrive in Chicago." She snagged her lip between her teeth and went to the bureau where she'd hidden her reticule. Dora appreciated nice things. Gussie handed her enough money to cover a week at the Palmer House. "A fashionable one."

Dora counted the bills, and her mouth went slack.

"Aunt Rhoda need never know you left me in Deadwood. I'll be on the Saturday morning train. Meet me at the station, and we'll return to her house together, gather my things, and go straight to New York."

Dora wrestled a sigh too heavy for someone only two years older than Gussie's twenty-five. But it signified victory. "Very well."

Gussie pressed her hand against Dora's back and ushered her from the room. "Once the train departs, he'll likely only show his face at stops to make sure you don't disembark. Have a steward bring you meals and try to stay in your berth until you reach Pierre, where you switch trains. It won't matter then if he discovers our duplicity. Now, let's dupe the detective."

And if Gussie's luck held, he wouldn't catch up with her until Chicago was within sight.

14

2

The next morning, before Gussie had even finished her morning toilet, a telegram was slipped under her door. She padded toward it on bare feet, and her heart did a little zing—the surest sign of imminent adventure—when she saw her editor's words typed out across the card.

Luisa Corsetti at Niagara Wednesday. Can compare waterfalls east and west. Readers will love it.

Gussie counted the days to her sister Phoebe's wedding on her fingers. Oh, why had she ignored Spearfish Canyon during her trek through the Badlands? It was positively overrun with waterfalls.

She tugged her hair from its braids. No matter. Niagara Falls was only a few hours from home. Once she gathered Dora from Aunt Rhoda's in Chicago, she would depart, spend only a night on this little detour north, and be home by the next evening. Plenty of time.

Dora would be livid, of course, but Miss Adventuress lived only as long as readers were satisfied. Or so Lillian liked to remind Gussie.

She didn't give her companion a single additional thought until she had seen Redwood Falls and was back at the Sleepy Eye station, waiting for the train that would take her to Chicago. Sitting on the uncomfortable bench inside the depot, she reached for her notebook, wanting to capture the sights and sounds of her excursion before they slipped from her thoughts. But her patting fingers encountered only her camera and a pen in its leather case.

She pulled the bag near her face and squinted into its dark recess. It was large, specially made to carry everything she needed for her work. She shifted the camera to the side, and her brows pinched.

And then she remembered.

A pile of clothing tossed atop her mattress. Atop her notebook. Everything bundled and thrown with haste into a carpetbag.

Dora had her notebook. All of her notes, snippets of articles that would later be filled out and mailed to Lillian.

Gussie groaned. Dora had better keep that book safe, for it not only contained weeks of work, but also, tucked between its pages, receipts from *Lady's Weekly* payments, and those contained both her real and assumed names. If Dora was careless with it . . . if anyone happened upon it . . .

Gussie leaned against the wall and closed her eyes. Father had threatened to disown Gussie numerous times. And, bother and bluster, if her reputation were ruined and it damaged any chance of the Traverses climbing into Mrs. Astor's Knickerbocker set, he might make good on it.

Gussie's parents tolerated her work only as long as it remained anonymous. Not many people knew Gussie Travers was the daring Miss Adventuress. Her nearest relatives. Her childhood friends Gabriel and Catherine MacLean. Her editor, of course. And Dora, the country's best-paid companion.

Gussie pressed her fingers against her eyes, and when she released them, stars spotted her vision. Dora could be cantankerous and unbearable, but she wasn't careless. Her journal would be safe.

She reached for a discarded piece of notebook paper. "It better be," she muttered. The thought of being disowned didn't pinch as much as it should have except for the fact that she wasn't quite ready to support herself on her paltry wage.

Shaking free of those worrisome thoughts, she filled one side of the paper with everything she could remember about the notes she'd kept over the previous week, then flipped it and scratched out the beginnings of her next column. She had been mailing them as she traveled west, and this one would make it just in time to be printed in next week's Wednesday issue.

When one travels west, past Cincinnati and Chicago and Des Moines, the cares of all those things that come with living among throngs of people slip away. You no longer worry who wore what. No longer think the latest gossip should enjoy preeminence in one's thoughts. No longer wonder if Frances will wed Franklin. All that is left is God's smile on mankind—the beauty and majesty of this untamed country—and you want nothing more than to imprint its picture on your mind so you never forget.

She reread her work and nodded. Her readers enjoyed when she wrote as though speaking directly to them. They loved Miss Adventuress's easygoing manner, and *Lady's Weekly* often received letters from people who felt they were friends with Gussie. She was careful to give them what they wanted, for they had placed so much trust in her.

They expected greater things from Gussie than her own family, who only wanted her to marry well. To do her part in raising the Traverses' station, much the way Father had raised their standing at the bank. Her readers were a sight easier to accommodate.

"Every lady must embroider. It isn't that hard. Why can you not manage a simple sampler?"

"Oh, really, Augusta. If you cannot sing, try at least to become proficient at the piano."

"No. I will not dance with you again, for my toes cannot bear it. How hopeless you are."

17

Gussie's fingers clenched, sending painful spasms over her knuckles. She massaged them, her thoughts kidnapped by long-ago memories. Stiffening her spine, she focused again on her work. There was little she could do about words flung in heedless negligence, but she could spin her own. And they might drive the others away.

"Ma'am? Train's loading." The man behind the counter jerked his chin toward the door, and Gussie smiled her thanks. She gathered her bag and read the column's final paragraph as she followed the porter onto the train.

Dear readers, think more distantly than your own cozy homes today. Dream of barren landscapes and lush forests and waterfalls that sparkle as brightly as any jewel ever did. It is your dreams that keep me moving toward the undiscovered.

Gussie stepped into the train car and stretched her neck, easing the kinks. Minnesota and South Dakota weren't exactly undiscovered, but one may as well be the Arctic, and the other had only become a state eight years prior. They were as far from her readers' lives as the moon. And Gussie aimed to provide a peek at other places. Places to dream on. Places to wish for.

After she followed the porter to her berth and watched him settle her bags on the bed and draw the velvet curtain, she made her way to the dining car, eager for a decent meal and a few moments with her book.

She ordered lobster salad and a glass of chardonnay, then set *A Lady's Journey East* on the white tablecloth and ran her hand over its light blue cover. She traced the gilt title with the familiarity of one who had spent a decade reading the words contained in its pages. The author, Cordelia Fox, was the heroine of Gussie's youthful dreams. While other girls yearned for princess castles and knights in shining armor, Gussie only wanted to explore the beaches of Cyprus, ride an elephant through India's forests, and climb dunes in Morocco.

Gussie opened the book, its binding worn and cracked, the pages stained from adolescent exploits. Here a smudge of golden paint from when she was banished to her room for playing Midas. Her sister Lavinia hadn't appreciated the effort it took to paint her parakeet. There the remains of the contraband holiday gingerbread she'd stolen the night before Christmas. She'd eaten half of it and spent the entire next day groaning and clutching her stomach while Mother sadly shook her head and Father took all her gifts to a poor family from church.

She swiped at the brown stain, again feeling her parents' disappointment. That had never gone away. Not really. And over the years, it had only grown.

Gussie shook her head and flipped the pages, filling the empty places of her heart with Cordelia Fox's adventures. With romance and excitement and thrill.

Some people had dime novels. Gussie had travel memoirs. Written by women who had cast off tradition and expectation and stepped into places unknown. Women who not only were changed by their experiences but had, in turn, changed the world.

Nellie Bly had proven herself capable and that women were equal to any task. Cordelia Fox had taken all she had learned during her travels, settled in China, and launched one of the country's first rural teacher training facilities. And Pandita Ramabai Sarasvati . . .

Gabriel MacLean, who had always been called Specs on account of the spectacles he'd worn since early childhood, had sent Gussie a copy of Ramabai's book a couple of years earlier. It was leather-bound and much underlined, and Gussie loved the story of the Indian woman traveling to England and the United States, telling the world about the terrible plight of widows in her country.

She has earned my highest regard, Specs had written.

After that, Gussie sent him and Catherine clippings of her columns with trepidation, knowing she could never measure up to Ramabai. Knowing her own work lacked in comparison.

She turned her attention back to *A Lady's Journey East*. There was no use in thinking on such things. Her columns would likely never change the world, but they changed moments, at least.

A waiter delivered her meal, and she continued to read as she ate, occasionally turning to look out the window and watch as the never-ending plains disappeared into darkness. This was a terrible land. Unforgiving and inflexible. But it tugged at her. She thought that if she threw herself from the train, it would catch her . . . then consume her. And something about that drew her forward until her nose touched the window and she saw past the reflections of the other diners. Saw the shapes and shadows of prairie grass and clumps of stunted trees.

She could lose herself here. Get off at the next stop and become a product of reinvention. Anyone she wanted to be. Who would she choose? Who was worthy of her thrumming heart? Who deserved the blood pulsing through her veins and throbbing in her ears? Who would measure up to all those female explorers and world changers, pressed together and compounded?

A chill swept over Gussie's limbs, and she reached for her wine glass, eager for warmth. For the tangible reminder that she didn't live in a book. That, despite their inability to understand, her family still loved her.

Just before her fingers touched the cool, smooth glass, she saw his reflection.

Sitting across the table from her, his steady gaze watching. Waiting.

A smile curved her lips.

She dropped her hand to her lap, pulled away from the window, and looked at him. There was a beat of silence occupied by a moment of mutual respect. They tipped their heads in honor of the game they played.

And then Gussie lifted her fork and speared a bite of salad. "Well, hello, nanny. What took you so long?"

Uncle James raised his brows, then reached into his coat pocket and withdrew a battered letter. "One might think you would show a little gratitude toward your personal mail carrier."

Gussie gasped and snatched the envelope. With no idea where she'd gone, her parents hadn't been able to forward Specs's and Catherine's letters once she left her aunt's house. She slid her finger beneath the flap and tore at it, too eager to feast on her friends' words to care about such little things as decorum or neatness.

She pulled out the single piece of paper, and her eyes went to the bottom of the sheet, where Specs's signature declared a greater boldness than he ever could in real life. She skimmed the letter— more details than she cared to note about the infirmary in some tumbled area of Poona, a garden party badminton game, and the efficacy of a plague vaccine—then peeked into the envelope.

"Nothing from Catherine again," she said.

Uncle James watched her, his placid expression hiding thoughts she'd soon discover.

"Ah well. She did just marry a Brit with what I can only imagine is a delicious accent." Gussie lifted her fork and stabbed it into a piece of lobster. "A well-deserved bit of joy after she and Specs lost their parents, wouldn't you say?"

He didn't take the bait. "Imagine my surprise when I discovered your trip to visit Rhoda was a sham."

"I'm surprised it took you so long to realize it." She took the meat into her mouth and chewed, slowly and deliberately, then tapped the tines to her lips. "You're becoming slow in your old age."

He sat back against his chair, his fingers lifting to smooth the lines from his forehead. "Your aunt waited a week before contacting your parents. She is mortified. And furious. She doesn't care to be played, Augusta."

Gussie set down her fork down and sighed. "In truth, my visit was well-intentioned. I didn't think to set out west until I arrived at the station and saw how far the railroad had gone. I'd intended to do some local travel around Chicago, but how could I resist towns called Deadwood and Sleepy Eye? It was almost too exhilarating to be true. And Lillian loved the idea."

"Of course she did. The more outrageous your trips, the more money the magazine makes."

Gussie shook her head. "You make it all seem very base. Lillian is invested in my success."

"I hope the success your trip brings is worth a broken relationship with your aunt. She said to take you straight home without stopping in Chicago. She might well write you out of her will."

"Your sister knows me not at all if she thinks that will motivate me toward a life of boredom and dreariness."

"Only the rich are afforded the luxury of not caring about wealth."

"I just spent a month crossing the most desolate places and sleeping in tents. I think I can manage without Aunt Rhoda's jewels and Flora Danica dinner service."

"Can you manage without your family? You push them too far."

Gussie waved her hand. "They care little what I do as long as I do it anonymously. As far as everyone else knows, I've been visiting with my aunt in Chicago."

"They care for much more than your anonymity. You disappeared. You were gone for over a month with no word to anyone but Lillian. We only had your articles in *Lady's Weekly* to reassure us you were well."

"Did you enjoy them?"

Uncle James gripped the edge of the table and leaned forward. "This is not a joke, Augusta. Phoebe, instead of focusing on wedding preparations, has been wringing her hands over your disappearance. Everyone else, as well. Lavinia. Your parents. Rhoda. They have all been worried sick. You push too far."

Gussie glanced away, her eyes drawn once again to the window, though now the darkness had fully enveloped the scenery, and clouds shrouded the moon and stars. His words, rather than convict her, teased open a tight bud of hope. The flower unfurled, releasing the scent of promise. Of past. Of memories.

"They were worried?" she asked.

"Of course." He scrubbed his hands through his hair, and the bags beneath his eyes seemed to grow heavier. "With all the celebrations surrounding the upcoming wedding, everyone knew that one misspoken word, one whisper of scandal in the papers, would mean disaster for Phoebe."

The petals withered and fell. Gussie's sigh drew Uncle James forward as he recognized the ambush bound up in his words.

His fingers touched hers. "They were worried for you too. You know that."

"I know nothing of the sort." She swallowed and stared at the remains of her dinner. Her stomach soured, and she sipped her wine. "I promised nothing after my trip to Florida." She'd disappeared without a word then too. Had come back to anger and the insistence she travel with a companion, at least. "They would have never approved of this trip west. But they knew I felt trapped. They know how unhappy I am in New York. This should have surprised no one. I cannot be expected to satisfy myself, and my readers, with safe jaunts around the Eastern Seaboard. Those trips must be broken up by the ones that make everyone else unhappy."

He grunted and crossed his arms over his chest. "Look at me."

She ignored his request for a moment, but Uncle James wasn't easily put off. Gussie knew he would sit there and allow her to stew until she heeded him. And when she did, she felt like nothing more than a recalcitrant child. She put her eyes somewhere above his left shoulder, not eager to see the disappointment in his gaze.

"Augusta, you have had advantages not offered to many. Not only because of your father's wealth and position, but also because your parents have allowed you a measure of freedom most people in your circle would consider ill-advised. Careless even. It would go well for you if you appreciated that instead of lamenting the things they cannot, in good conscience, give you."

"The house in Harlem."

"I'm sorry?"

"I want to go back to the townhouse in Harlem. Before Father made his money and Mother decided the best things for us were good marriages that raised her position. That's what I want. I want to share walls with Catherine and Specs again. I want my old life back."

She lifted her gaze and saw the stern lines of his mouth soften. The compassion lighting his blue eyes—so like her father's. So unlike them too. No one would ever believe she found the most security and acceptance with her uncle, James Travers, retired Pinkerton agent. Out of the three siblings, he was the least successful. The least refined and well-heeled. But Gussie most identified with him. Uncle James had been larger than life when she was a child. And his image had never tarnished.

"That's not how life works," he said. "You cannot turn back time. You can only make the best with what you're given today."

"Life at home . . . it stifles me. I feel as though I'm drowning in the tedium of it. I can't breathe there. Exploring and writing and taking photographs makes me feel alive." Her gaze dropped to her dinner plate, brilliant white china rimmed in gold. In New York, she suffocated beneath her parents' disappointment. Every moment she spent deflecting harsh words and scolding with a devil-may-care attitude that fooled everyone but her was another moment without air. Without life. "I know you understand," she whispered. "You were a Pinkerton. You chased outlaws across the country. And you loved it, didn't you? Can't you believe that same desire for the thrill courses through my own body? I'm not alone in this." She lifted her book and waved it at him. "Cordelia Fox felt it too."

"I know you're not alone. And I well understand your desire to explore. To set out to see the world and feel every exhilaration this life can offer. But you must work within the strictures of your social position. You have an obligation to your family. You may care little for your reputation, but it is inexorably tangled with that of your sisters. Your parents. Even Rhoda."

Gussie yanked her hand from his and grasped her skirt, twisting it between her fingers. "I took the companion Father hired. I didn't go off alone."

"And where is she now?"

"You know very well where she is."

Uncle James's eyes closed, a deep sigh raising his chest. When he opened them, Gussie stared at her book and pretended to focus on the type. "You have so far been lucky in your evasion of consequences. Your larks have gone undetected by your social circle. There are still, as yet, half a dozen men willing to make you their wife."

"I will eventually settle down to marriage and children, but until I meet a man who makes me wish to stay still, I see no reason I cannot continue on as I have for the last few years."

"But will it be too late?" He stood and leaned over the table to place a kiss on her temple. "One day your luck will run out. You will have alienated your family, lost your suitors and society's regard, and you might well be tired of running. Of disappearing."

He started to walk away from her, and she grasped his fingers before they slipped free. "Will you desert me, Uncle James? If I lose everyone and everything else, will I lose you too?"

His palm found her cheek. "Never. But there may come a time when I am not enough. You're right. My life has been exciting. I've lived more than any person I know. Experienced and seen more than I expected." His voice dropped, and with it, her heart. "But it's been a lonely life, Augusta. I want so much more for you."

After he left, Gussie picked at her dinner before pushing the plate away and returning to her berth. She drew the curtains tightly around the bed and lay her head on the pillow. Staring up at the embellished ceiling, clutching her book to her stomach, she ran over Uncle James's warnings.

He was wrong.

Maybe he had regrets—Gussie assumed she would one day, as well. Who could live life without them? But that didn't mean his would become hers.

The kerosene light flickering above her head shed a yellow glow over the pages of Cordelia Fox's catalog of exploits, drawing

Gussie's attention and daydreams. Whatever Uncle James thought, whatever he said, she knew her story would be different. And when it came down to it, she wasn't sure she could give up the thrill of adventure or of seeing absolutely everything for anyone or anything. Even if that meant she ended up alone.

3

Do you think Miss Clutterbuck went back to New York?"
Uncle James tapped his knuckles against his lips.

"I have no idea. Wherever she is, though, she's likely happier than she ever was with me." Gussie kept her gaze pinned on the window of Buffalo's Exchange Street station. She had ten minutes, at most, to board her train. She pinched her skirt, rubbing the fabric over the ticket she'd purchased while Uncle James had been directing a porter with their trunks.

"Are you not upset she has abandoned you?"

Gussie glanced at him. When they arrived in Chicago, Dora hadn't been at the station. Nor had she shown up at Aunt Rhoda's during the nearly two days Gussie and Uncle James were there. As far as she could tell, Dora Clutterbuck had endured enough of Gussie and her wanderings. "Not at all. It was Father who insisted I travel with her. Though it is frustrating in the extreme that my notebook disappeared with her. I can't possibly remember all the wonders I saw."

She tapped her foot against the floor, and her knee jiggled her skirt. Passengers were beginning to board her train. The one that would take her to Niagara.

"Are you well, Augusta?" Uncle James asked.

She nodded. "Anxious to get back to the city after my month of wandering the desert."

He grunted, and his jaw stiffened with well-deserved wariness. "You should have considered that before insisting on taking an absurd amount of time readying this morning. If we had left early, we would have caught the Lake Shore Limited and been nearly home by now."

She gave him a weak smile. If she didn't get on her train, the dawdling would have been for nothing, and she would be headed toward the wrong part of the state despite her false tardiness. "Uncle James," she said, catching sight of a distraction, "I think that woman needs help at the counter. The booking clerk is arguing with her."

He looked toward where she pointed and, ever the gentleman, went to assist. Gussie watched him cross the room, a twinge in her chest protesting her deceit. What an absolutely wretched thing to do. But she had little choice, and once Uncle James seemed entirely distracted, she crept from the station and darted across the platform. A porter offered her a hand, but she ignored it and fled up the stairs and into the car.

Falling into one of the plush chairs, she turned her face toward the window. Uncle James stood in the depot door, his head whipping around as he looked for her.

Gussie pressed her hands against her roiling stomach. He didn't deserve to be ill-treated. He had been kinder and more loving toward her than any other member of her family. She lifted her hand to the glass. "I'm so sorry, Uncle James."

He turned toward her as though hearing her whispered apology, his eyes locking with hers just as the train began to move. He darted after it, and Gussie lurched to her feet and made for the vestibule.

The porter had just put his hand on the door to close it, but Gussie's appearance stopped him.

"Augusta!" Uncle James was walking beside the train, his eyes on the end of the platform. "What in heaven's name are you doing?"

"Only a short trip, Uncle."

"Your sister's wedding."

The train was picking up speed, and Gussie saw the edge of the platform running to meet them. She gripped the doorjamb and leaned out, the wind whipping her hair free from its pins. "I will be home tomorrow evening."

Uncle James skidded to a stop just before running out of plank. "I am getting tired of chasing you, Augusta."

"Miss, it has become unsafe. Please allow me to close the door." The porter gently pried her fingers free and forced her away.

Even after the door closed, though, the wind still found its way through the cracks and crevices around it, wheezing with Uncle James's declaration. His frustration and disappointment. It followed her back into the luxurious Pullman Palace Car and wound itself around her heart.

Uncle James had never spoken to her in that way before. In the face of every one of her escapades, he showed only amused patience or concerned empathy. When she disappeared during a week-long trip to visit a distant cousin in Ohio, turning it into a twelve-day excursion to photograph the Michigan coast, Uncle James had easily caught up with her. It had been her first assignment for *Lady's Weekly*, prohibited by her parents, mocked by her sisters, and understood only by Uncle James.

Father had sent him as soon as he received a telegram from their cousin telling of Gussie's defection. And when Uncle James found her, his words had drawn her into a safe place—the first she'd known since being yanked from her happy childhood. *"You are the daughter of my heart, and I am proud of your courage. Your independence. You are a credit to your sex."*

He had then gone on to chastise her for being so foolish. For not seeing to her safety. For leaving without word to anyone and causing so much worry. But, after all was said, he pulled her to his chest, rested his chin on her head, and sighed. *"I cannot fault you too much. I well know the incessant calling toward the unknown. I know the boredom that comes from being too long in a place."*

Had Uncle James understood it was more than boredom that drove Gussie from home, he might have let her run unhindered. If he knew the things that chased her, threatening to wrestle her to the ground and pummel her.

He didn't, though, and since then, they had played a grown-up version of cat and mouse. She would flee to some far-flung town, usually one boasting an interesting name and an assortment of criminals, misfits, and hangers-on, and he would follow, a week or two behind, picking up the bread crumbs she accidentally, and sometimes purposely, left for him.

And when she was caught, she knew it was time to return home.

But this time, in Deadwood, she'd experienced too much liberty to *want* to return. It was the farthest she'd ever been from New York. The longest trip away. He hadn't found her trail fast enough—the Badlands didn't allow for good tracking—and time passed. Each day without social obligation, without fussing and primping and trying so hard—so very hard—and still not measuring up, was another day to push back the curtain a little more.

Once that curtain was drawn, revealing all the wonderful, lovely, beautiful things this world had to offer, Gussie was loath to let it drop again. There was so much out there. So much to do and see and share. So many people to meet. So many faces to photograph. So many places to just rest.

Gussie dug through her satchel and withdrew her camera bag. She unlatched it and slipped her fingers into the pocket sewn close to the leather. Withdrawing a clutch of photographs, she thumbed through them. They were not the landscapes Miss Adventuress was known for. No sunbaked canyons or chaotic cities sprouting out of gulches made desolate by lawlessness and God's neglect.

They were, instead, portraits. As useless to *Lady's Weekly* as the sober scribblings Gussie occasionally made in her journals. An old Chinese man sitting outside a restaurant, his mustache sweeping the ground. A tired young woman, her eyes bleached with too many years of hard work and dashed hopes. The owner of Deadwood's most infamous saloon—Dora had nearly perished on the spot when Gussie stopped to photograph him—Byronic with his flopping hair, velvet coat, silver pistol, and flirting, laughing eyes.

She shoved the photographs back into their hideaway pocket. These people, these places, had stolen from her the ability to be content with the everyday.

She rested her head against the window and closed her eyes, wanting nothing more than to allow the gentle swaying to lull her to sleep. But she only saw Uncle James's drooping shoulders and heavy frown imprinted on the back of her lids. Only heard his words. *"I am getting tired of chasing you, Augusta."*

She should be elated. Unless Father wanted to hire a private investigator unrelated to them—and she had doubts anyone with less experience and talent could find her as easily as Uncle James—and pay the exorbitant fee only to have her refuse to accompany the detective to New York, she would be left alone. Nothing stood in her way.

She had no notion of making a good match, despite Mother's intentions and hopes. She would happily settle for a perfectly ordinary husband, one who saw her as an equal. Who brought kindness and wit to the equation, but not the burden and responsibility of a great fortune. That was her wish. And she was more likely to meet him traveling hither and thither than at balls and among her mother's friends.

But even though she *should* feel untethered and liberated, she only felt a gnawing emptiness in her belly. It grew and spread, filling the neglected places of her heart and mind and soul. The places she didn't often look for fear of seeing ugly truths.

A place she didn't want to see now. For Niagara Falls waited, and Gussie intended to capture it.

The next day, Gussie rode an omnibus from the Clifton Hotel, where she had taken a room, to the Lower Steel Arch Bridge. She'd experienced the majesty of the falls the day before when her train stopped, allowing its passengers to spill onto the bridge and take in the enthralling view. For a few moments, Gussie had simply stood there, forgetting she even carried a camera. Before her, the magnificent falls spilled over rock, sounding as though the earth had given up all its water, spewing it here in this one place. Below her, wearing a shawl of mist, crashing white waves churned and danced in abandon. Her chest ached with the beauty of it.

South Dakota's Badlands had captured her imagination with their terrible, barren loveliness. They had caught her breath and stolen her voice.

But Niagara Falls captured her heart. It made her want to sing. To shout praise to the God who had fashioned such a splendid view. Her readers would love it. Bits of description, more poetry than prose, wove between her thoughts, and she wondered at the best angle to capture the splendor of it all.

Now, as she returned to the bridge to witness Luisa Corsetti's daring stunt, a crush of people filled the space between her and the gorge so that she couldn't even see the top of the falls. Gussie had never despised her height until that moment. If she were a smaller woman, she might push toward the front and have a commanding view of the event. Others would allow it because her head would pose no barrier to their sight. But as she stood taller than the average man, let alone woman, no one would be inclined to let her through.

"The trouble with being out of the ordinary," she muttered.

A passing woman, wrapped tightly in a thick cloak despite the heat, paused in her path. "What is this? There is no trouble with being out of the ordinary." She spoke with a lyrical accent and moved back toward Gussie with the spare steps of someone used to having their own way.

"I only mean that because of my height, I will not have the opportunity to capture photographs from the front." Gussie held up her Kodak. "I work for a magazine, and I'd hoped to share my experience watching Luisa Corsetti make history."

The woman's brows rose, and a smile played on her full lips. "You are a journalist?"

"In a way. I write about my travels."

"Then you will come with me, yes?" The woman took Gussie's arm and started in the direction opposite the bridge, toward a cluster of people.

"But I must see Luisa Corsetti. I have an assignment. I'd hate to disappoint my readers." *And editor.* Lillian could be intimidating when crossed.

"And see her you shall." The woman grinned, revealing a perfectly straight set of small square teeth.

Before them, the crowd parted. A tall, thin man wearing a floppy suit and a broad smile opened his arms. "Here is the woman of the hour."

Gussie frowned and looked at her companion.

With nimble fingers, the woman tugged the ribbon holding her cloak closed and let it fall from her shoulders, revealing puffed chiffon sleeves billowing from a corset-like bodice of red-and-white stripes. The short skirt was fringed in dancing cord and stood out from her hips as stiff as a platter. "It is I." She grinned and bowed with a flourish of her hands.

Gussie forced her gaze off the woman's muscular legs and met eyes that sparkled with as much animation as the sequins of her brocade costume. "Miss Corsetti."

"Please, call me Luisa." She led Gussie toward the edge of the gorge, where a thick steel cable had been tethered, and pointed toward an outcropping jutting over the river. "You will stand there, looking toward me and the bridge beyond. That is my wish. I want everyone to see how many came to witness Luisa Corsetti crossing the falls."

Gussie looked at the two-level bridge, the lower deck crammed full of spectators and a train stopped on the upper deck to allow passengers to watch. And across the chasm, on the American side, throngs pressed as close to the edge as they safely could.

"Do you know," Luisa said, her voice pitched low, almost

disappearing in the crashing sound of water, "the papers refused to share my story. Because I am a woman. And women are not supposed to do dangerous things. They are not supposed to be brave or"—she winked at Gussie—"out of the ordinary. But I think you understand, no?"

Gussie nodded. "I think I do."

"So you will make sure to take a good photograph with all this in the background, and I will give you an interview afterward."

Gussie grinned in agreement. She'd never done an interview before, but she could work quotes into the body of her column. "May I get a photo of you before you cross?"

Luisa, a showman at heart, strode toward the edge of the cliff and placed one foot on the rope that would see her safely to the other side, arms curved like a dancer.

Gussie had never considered interviewing any of the people she met during her travels, but this small, dynamic woman seemed a good person to start with. The entire world was full of interesting personalities. It would be a shame to ignore them in favor of sights and sounds.

She pressed the camera's lever, and as the daredevil crossed a thin line into history, Gussie wondered if maybe she could one day follow her.

4

Gussie had every intention of arriving home when she'd promised Uncle James, but things tended to go awry where she was concerned. An encounter with a thief who stole her favorite satchel—but luckily ignored the camera bag where she had tucked her money—had eaten up half a day while she sat in the police station. That, however, had proven less disastrous than her encounter with the falls while riding the *Maid of the Mist*, which resulted in a chilly night in the hotel, poking at the clothes she'd strung over every available surface in an attempt to help them dry. A delayed train then resulted in her entering her home the night before Phoebe's wedding smelling as though she had slept with a herd of goats.

She attempted to slip past the parlor, but Uncle James, who had met her at the station, gave a sharp shake of his head, the gas sconces flickering vaguely sinister shadows across his face. "They wish to speak with you."

Her steps were heavy as she crossed the foyer and tucked herself beside a large urn at the parlor doorway. Lavinia sat at the Knabe piano, fingers moving expertly over the keys in a way Gussie could never hope to emulate. She rubbed her hands, reminded of the pianist her parents had hired to mold her into an image of accomplished femininity.

"*You are hopeless.*" Smack. The thin leather strap he had kept atop the piano reddened her fingers. Smack. Pain exploded across her knuckles. Smack. The words had torn more than flesh.

"What is Lavinia doing here?" Gussie's older sister lived in a castle-like house across the city with her rich-as-Croesus husband. Had she come home only to attend Gussie's upbraiding? How very bloodthirsty.

"She's come to help Phoebe with preparations." Uncle James stepped into the room and glanced back at her. "Time to face the music."

"So very witty." She followed him, and the piano rang out a discordant note, which gave way to snarling and snapping.

"How could you do this to me, Gussie? And right before my wedding."

"What a selfish child you are. When will you grow up?"

"You're lucky you weren't murdered in some godforsaken saloon."

"You'll never find a husband if you continue to insist on behaving like a vagabond."

"That's my hope," Gussie muttered.

"Sit in the chair, Augusta." Father pointed toward her regular place of torment.

She flopped into it, crossing her arms loosely over her chest.

"Augusta, really. Have you lost your manners as well as your mind? Sit straight, please." Mother, arms gracefully resting across the armrests of her chair, tapped the curved wood with her fingernails. Eyes narrowed and gaze sweeping over Gussie, she looked for all the world as though she'd just stepped out of a fashion plate. Not a bit of worry made itself apparent on her face. "Where is your companion?"

"She seems to have absconded with my favorite dress and hat."

"If only you could have traded them for a bit of sense." Father paced the room before settling on the settee with Uncle James.

Gussie pressed her teeth together and shifted so that she sank even farther against the unforgiving chair, releasing a musty scent from her clothing that forced her nose to wrinkle. "I had every intention of being home two days ago, but unforeseeable matters came up."

"Unforeseeable matters always come up where you're concerned." Lavinia crossed the room and settled on a dainty chair that seemed ungainly in comparison to her graceful figure.

"I don't know how unforeseeable any of these matters are when she puts herself in these situations." Phoebe's smug words grated.

"Would you like to tell us exactly what you were thinking when you ran away yet again?" Mother never yelled, but her soft words couldn't cloak the sharpness of her displeasure.

Gussie cleared her throat and sat up straight, matching her mother and sisters' postures. She could be every inch the lady they thought she should be. At least for a time. "I was thinking that my readers wanted me to go somewhere exciting, and Deadwood seemed as good a place as any."

"You silly girl." Mother cast her eyes toward the ceiling. "With your silly words and silly ideas."

Gussie steeled herself against the insults. Against the numbness that stole into her chest and filled her limbs and made her arms and legs as heavy as lead. Against the knowledge that her parents didn't know her. Her sisters didn't understand her. Her family had sacrificed their previous happiness and cozy memories on the altar of social ambition. Her shoulders slumped, and she pressed her head into her hands.

"I really don't understand." Mother sighed as though all of life's disappointments could be explained by Gussie alone. "You were such a clever child."

Father stood and held his hand toward Lavinia and Phoebe. "I think it's time for you to go to bed. It's very late. You don't want to look haggard at the wedding tomorrow."

Gussie stood with them and then sank back down at her mother's sharp reprimand. "Not you, Augusta. Looking tired is the very least of your worries."

When her sisters had filtered out, Uncle James and Father scooted a few chairs toward Mother. Then they sat down in a row and faced her. A firing squad and a prisoner.

Before they could speak, Gussie did. "I'm truly sorry I worried everyone, and I really meant to be home sooner."

"It still wouldn't have been enough time to be fitted for a new gown." Mother crossed her arms, though she never looked belligerent when she did so. Only extremely disappointed.

"I have plenty of gowns. Half of them have yet to be worn."

Father cleared his throat. "Aunt Rhoda is very unhappy with you."

"I didn't go to Chicago with the intention of leaving. But when I saw how far the train went, I couldn't resist. My readers have been asking that I go somewhere more exciting for months, Father, and there is very little in Chicago they would find interesting. I owe it to them to—"

"You owe it to us, Augusta! You owe it to *us*," Father snapped. "You owe us respect and obedience. You owe us a month or two of peace. A month or two free of worry that everything we have built will be undone by your foolishness."

Gussie dropped her head and stared at her hands, fingers twisted together and white knuckled. Beneath her nails were crescents of dirt. Her skin was rough with calluses from riding for weeks straight. She lifted a finger to her mouth, teasing a hangnail with her teeth.

"Augusta," Mother warned.

Gussie sighed and shoved her hand beneath her leg. One word. That was all it took for the country's most intrepid female explorer to be reduced to childhood. Small and insignificant and never, ever enough.

Gussie glanced at Uncle James. He rarely said anything at these meetings, but he was always present. Whether as support for Gussie or her parents, she didn't know.

"Do you wish to die?"

"What?" Gussie asked, dragging her gaze back to Mother.

"You are constantly running toward danger," Mother said. "Running away from us. It makes me wonder if you care so little for life that you seek death."

"No. That's not it at all." Gussie thrust her finger into her hair and scratched at a bite. The Bullock Hotel hadn't been as clean as promised.

"Then why?" Father scrubbed his hand over his eyes and cheek. "Why do you seem to love living life at the very edge of propriety and safety?"

"How could you not know? Have you never read my column?" Father and Mother both turned red and avoided her eyes.

They hadn't. They had never read it. Likely they relied on Uncle James to keep them abreast of her whereabouts. She pinched the bridge of her nose to ease the burn of tears. They had preened with pride when Lavinia had been asked to dance a quadrille at one of Mrs. Astor's balls. And when Phoebe had caught herself the heir to New York's largest department store, they threw a dinner party. Her sisters were the pride of Mr. and Mrs. Travers. They were extolled and encouraged.

But for Gussie they had nothing but disdain.

She looked at Uncle James, his eyes drooping and sad, compassion dulling their color. That was what Gussie got: not her parents' pride but her uncle's pity.

They had stopped listening to her long ago. Stopped understanding even before that. "I do it," she said, "not because I wish for death, but because I wish for freedom. I am suffocating here, in this house." She looked at them until they met her gaze. "I am suffocating in this family."

Mother rolled her eyes. "This melodrama is beneath you. It is beneath us." She sniffed, and her gaze swept Gussie's soiled clothing. "You may leave."

Gussie stood.

"There are some newspapers in your room. I took the liberty of marking a few articles I thought you might find particularly interesting."

Gussie stared at her mother, who looked for all the world like a respectable, calm woman of wealth and position. Gussie wasn't deceived. "Very well."

Not wanting to give her family another opportunity for torment, she darted from the room and up the stairs.

She crept down the hall and pushed at her bedroom door with a finger. Peering inside, a shaky laugh scuttled from her lips. The curtains were drawn, and the setting sun, bathing everything in red light, displayed a room that looked as it should.

She was being absurd. What had she expected, for Father to burn her things in a fit of fury?

Gussie dropped her bag on the bed, sat on the edge of the mattress, and pulled the *Chicago Daily Journal* onto her lap. It was folded back on itself, a dark rim of ink circling the headline.

Adventure-Seeking Woman a Threat to Contented Motherhood

Gussie snapped open the paper and smoothed it atop the bed, leaning over to read the subtitle.

Miss Adventuress pens stories that shock and appall. Reckless behavior seeks to shade the zenith of feminine virtue in shadows.

Her heart bounced wildly against her ribs. As she skimmed the article, then went back to reread and more securely comprehend what was being said of her, Gussie's mouth went dry as wool. Her lips moved with the print, an occasional squeak making its way past them. And finally, to tie it all up, a phrase so horrifyingly uncomplimentary, Gussie wasn't sure whether to laugh or cry.

She decided on laughter, for nothing could be more ludicrous than the lies before her.

Miss Adventuress aims to share the world with our wives and daughters. Instead, she imparts a malignant desire for something wholly unsuitable for any woman of sound character: a yearning for what lies beyond the safety and satisfaction of home and hearth. *Lady's Weekly* and Miss Adventuress, whoever she may be, do a great disservice. They undermine all that is feminine and virtuous with immodest frivolity.

"Well, I never realized I had so much power." Gussie slapped the newspaper and stood, intent on shedding the layer of grime from her skin and printed accusations from her mind. Then she saw another paper. This one tucked between the mirror and a perfume bottle on her dressing table. Folded and marked. She crossed the room.

Magazine Advocates Women Abandon Home and Family for Life of Adventure

Gussie scanned the article, her gaze snagging on a particularly fanciful string of absurdity.

It is our duty as protectors of all that is good to refuse our wives and daughters access to this folly. And if it should be made known who Miss Adventuress is, there will need to be a reckoning.

Gussie rolled her eyes. "I do not care if I'm run out of New York with pitchforks." She stalked toward her wardrobe and pulled at the knob with a viciousness she wished she could use to wring someone's neck. "Stupid. Asinine. Unimaginative." She took a deep breath through her nose and exhaled, releasing the tension crawling across her shoulders and up her neck.

They could write whatever they wished. *Lady's Weekly* boasted more subscribers than all of New York's newspapers combined. And hers was its most popular column. What she wrote about, the photos she shared, captivated the modern woman. Others could fight against it, leverage attacks against her character, lie and cheat and have a fit of conniption, but it didn't change the truth.

People loved Miss Adventuress. And Gussie loved every moment of freedom Miss Adventuress gave her.

Phoebe looked beautiful, of course, in her white silk lansdowne gown, a train falling over the small bustle pad and trailing behind her as she walked up the aisle. With her slightly olive complexion, Gussie avoided wearing pure white. But then, her brown-blond hair—she'd never been able to pinpoint the color—looked particularly lovely against lavender or light blue, and Gussie was fond of any color found in the daytime sky.

She picked at her skirt, twisting the fabric and rubbing the pads of her fingers over the nubby silk twill. Mother's lips had flattened when Gussie appeared at the top of the stairs that morning, ready to join her family in following Phoebe to Trinity Church.

"I've never worn it, Mother. No one shall know."

"I shall know."

Gussie leaned forward in the pew and craned her neck to see past Lavinia, her brother-in-law, Father, and Uncle James. Mother sat, a bland expression on her face, eyes focused ahead. She could be watching her youngest daughter wed or the brilliant display of sunlight filtering through the stained glass. Who knew where she looked. What she thought. Only her sharp words betrayed any sort of emotion, and as she was separated from Gussie by a row of people, her lips remained closed.

Small mercies.

They didn't last long. As the bishop droned, Gussie noticed people whispering behind their hands, one to another, until the entire place rustled with the fervor of whatever gossip was deemed more important than the wedding of two of society's most privileged.

"What is going on?" Lavinia hissed when the sound became too great to ignore.

Gussie shrugged but then noticed those around her giving her sidelong glances, old ladies scowling and young men leering. She looked at Phoebe, whose hands were in her soon-to-be husband's but whose eyes were on her.

Gussie's scalp prickled, and the sensation shot a quiver through her belly. What could she have possibly done between arriving home after dinner last night and entering the church only an hour ago? She twisted in her seat, her gaze sweeping those in the pews behind her, and she met not one set of friendly eyes. They all revealed varying degrees of censure or, in the case of a few bold men, lasciviousness.

Her face burned, and she turned around, staring at the hem of Phoebe's gown brushing the polished floor. Before she could worry more about it, though, the whispers died down, and Phoebe once again turned toward her groom. The vows were exchanged, the couple marched out of the church, and Gussie hoped she wouldn't find herself in the middle of a scandal on today of all days.

Unfortunately, she had a tenuous history with luck, and hers seemed to have deserted her somewhere outside of Chicago.

As she followed the press of the crowd from the church, she sensed the eyes of dozens of people following her. Just before she reached the carriage that would take her home, someone grabbed her arm and yanked.

Gussie jerked her head toward her assailant. "Lillian, why on earth are you manhandling me?"

"Just come with me, Gussie. Your father and uncle are waiting for you in another vehicle." Lillian peered up into the carriage. "Mrs. Travers, your husband asked me to tell you that they will be following shortly."

Mother's jaw clenched. Lavinia leaned toward her husband and whispered something in his ear—likely nothing complimentary.

"Very well." Mother waved them away.

Gussie shook off her friend's grasp and marched down the walkway. As promised, Father and Uncle James sat inside another carriage, both looking handsome and much younger than their years in fine black morning coats and trousers. They also both wore grim expressions. Father's may have even contained a frisson of fear.

Gussie sat opposite them, Lillian beside her, and the horses took off with a clip-clop-clip of hooves. "What is going on? Why aren't we in the carriage with Mother?"

"Did you notice the disturbance you caused in there?" Nothing much fazed Lillian Clare, so Gussie didn't care for the tremor in her friend's voice.

"I did." Gussie looked at her father, but he just gripped his hair in his hands, his silk top hat tossed aside like a child's forgotten doll.

"You've been discovered, Gussie." Lillian held out her hand, and Uncle James placed a newspaper in her palm. She handed it to Gussie. "How did this happen? We were so careful to hide your identity."

Gussie held the paper off her skirt, afraid the ink would stain the fabric. "The *New York Daily News*? I didn't realize you read this horrid thing." She wasn't sure how the paper had survived its Confederate-supporting past, but it routinely printed stories disparaging feminists, with whom Gussie was certain Lillian identified. A woman couldn't edit a magazine without finding herself on the wrong side of myopia.

"I don't, but the newsie insisted I wanted to know the identity of Miss Adventuress. I agreed with him."

"Read it, Augusta, and stop this prattling, please." Father sounded tired. Tired and defeated.

Gussie took a deep breath, and the headline slipped from her tongue on a heavy exhale. "'The Misadventures of Miss Adventuress.'" And below, the tagline, "'Fall from Grace for a Society Darling.'" Gussie's mouth went dry, and she looked up at the other passengers in the carriage.

Uncle James nodded. "It gets worse. Keep reading."

Gussie pressed her hand to her chest, her heart thumping heavily beneath her palm. "'As half the country follows the adventures of globe-trotting Miss Adventuress, there have been whispers of scandalous behavior. It seems *Lady's Weekly*'s intrepid explorer has made some unsavory decisions, casting a shadow over her reputation.

"'From travels into the wilderness with naught but a knife-wielding, wild-eyed guide, to abandoning social obligation for the thrill of unsavory adventures, Miss Adventuress is far from a proper role model for our mothers, daughters, and sisters.

"'The *New York Daily News* has, therefore, taken it upon ourselves to defend our country's fairer sex. Having learned the identity of Miss Adventuress, we are loath to subject her to the scandal and ridicule exposing her name—and that of her family—will bring, but we feel we have no choice, given her salacious behavior.

"'Dear readers, Miss Adventuress is none other than Miss—'" Gussie dropped the paper and clapped her hands over her mouth. Her name slipped out, strangled by the tightening of her throat and weave of her fingers. "'Augusta Travers, member of the well-regarded Travers family of Manhattan.'" She anchored her gaze on her father's and uncle's shoes, polished and pointing toward her like condemning arrows.

"Yes, well." Lillian's hand crept over Gussie's, cold and not as comforting as she probably intended. "Cat's out of the bag. How shall we minimize the damage?"

Father made a sound in his throat that was somewhat like a laugh but much more like a growl. "Minimize the damage? It's well and good for you to play at caring now. You've gotten what you wanted, and the news will no doubt sell more copies of your precious magazine, if only because people are curious to see the downfall of one of New York's most well-regarded families. Why, Miss Clare, perhaps you leaked the story to the *Daily News*. You were, after all, the one to encourage her in this foolishness."

"Father, what nonsense. Lillian is one of my dearest friends and would never put my reputation at risk." Gussie had met Lillian at a society event four years earlier that would have been a fruitless waste of time had they not crossed each other's paths.

"Indeed not." Anger made Lillian's voice prim. "And Gussie approached *me* about writing a column."

Gussie nodded. "It's true." As Lillian rose to a position of prominence at *Lady's Weekly*, Gussie had seen a possibility. For purpose and relief from the boredom and a chance to be counted among her greatest heroes. "Do not hold Lillian accountable for this."

Father, elbows resting on his knees, raked his fingers through his hair, making it stand up straight. He would regret it later, when they attended Phoebe's wedding luncheon. He would have to retreat to his bedroom so his man could put things to rights again. "Then who should I blame? Who else knew? I can assure you, it was no one from the family. None of us would like the negative attention."

"No," Gussie said, certainty building within her, "but I know who did it."

They looked at her, expectation raising their eyebrows, dread drooping their lips.

"It was that awful Dora Clutterbuck you hired to keep my virtue intact while I traveled, Father." Gussie pulled at the fingers of her gloves, removing them one by one and laying them neatly on her lap. Sweat slicked her hands and threatened to stain them.

"That's ridiculous," Father said. "She was highly vetted. And I paid her to keep quiet."

"Yes, but money doesn't buy loyalty. Especially since it likely wasn't enough to keep me out of trouble. Perhaps, when I forced her to return to Chicago on her own, she'd had enough. And when I accidently packed my notebook with her clothing, she stumbled across the very thing that would prove her way out. The papers have stood against me from the very beginning, have they not? No doubt the *New York Daily News* paid a handsome sum for the revelation of Miss Adventuress's identity."

The carriage turned into their drive and ground to a halt just behind the one carrying Lavinia and Mother. Phoebe left her groom and the receiving line at the front of the house, running toward them in a cloud of chiffon. She met Mother with a shout of rage that very nearly rattled the windows.

"Mercifully," Uncle James said, and Gussie dragged her attention off the drama unfolding outside the window, "this didn't happen in time to prevent Phoebe's wedding."

The door yanked open, and Phoebe and Mother filled the space, both of them sporting hats askew and eyes that bounced wildly around. Phoebe's were red-rimmed, and when she opened her mouth, nothing emerged but a whimpering kind of stutter.

Mother, though, demonstrated no such inhibition. "You have not only destroyed your sister's wedding," she said, reaching forward and gripping Gussie's arm with pinching fingers, "but your life, as well. You are ruined. How could you go off into the wilderness alone with a strange man? Have you no thought to your future? To our future?"

"It isn't true, Mother. I did no such thing. Miss Clutterbuck either told a whole lot of falsehoods, or the paper took the truth and twisted it to fit their narrative."

"But you've been found out, have you not?" There was a note of hope in her mother's question that turned Gussie's heart heavy. She knew what it was to suffer from unwarranted optimism.

"I have."

Mother's entire face seemed to fall in on itself, turning her brilliant beauty into a rumpled parody. "And now?"

Phoebe found her voice and hissed, "She must be sent away."

"Surely not!"

"Where would she go?"

"And ruin whatever shred of respectability she has left?"

Everyone began discussing Gussie's future without thought for her own opinion. She sat there, staring around the carriage, almost able to see the swirl of confusion, anger, and fear that threatened to engulf the sanity of her family. One by one, they quieted, becoming aware that she spoke nothing for herself.

"I've already come up with a solution." Every head turned toward Lillian, who swiveled in her seat, knees bumping Gussie's.

"*Lady's Weekly* would like to sponsor a trip, paying for your passage and daily expenses. You would travel to a country your readers will most likely never see, writing and photographing as you go. It would get you away from New York, *and* it would grow your readership. Think of how exciting it will be to write of places outside the States. You would have to be gone six months at least, if not more, to make it worth the trouble. And by the time you return, some other scandal will have overshadowed yours."

"You mean she'll be gone for months, destroying what is left of her reputation." Father crossed his arms and sat back in his seat, glaring across the carriage. "I'm still not convinced you didn't organize this little controversy, Miss Clare."

Lillian rolled her eyes. "Why would I do such a thing? Gussie has been our most popular columnist since the inception of the magazine."

"Where? What country?" Gussie whispered, tamping down her excitement in deference to her parents' and Phoebe's distress. It wouldn't do to seem too eager for the opportunity.

"Absolutely not. You are not gallivanting off to some foreign country. And certainly not alone." Father clambered from the carriage, slammed his hat back onto his head, and stalked toward the house.

Mother took Phoebe's arm. "Come, Augusta. You must show your face and pretend this is all a lot of nonsense. We will decide what to do after our guests leave." Then they turned and left, not even offering a backward glance to see that Gussie followed.

Gussie looked at Uncle James, but he only shrugged and stepped down from the carriage. "The chickens have come home to roost."

"Finally." Gussie expelled a puff of air and turned toward Lillian. "They have gone, and now you must tell me—where shall I go?"

Lillian grinned. "I've considered numerous possibilities, but there is one place—a place so foreign, it would likely grow subscriptions wildly—that I keep coming back to. And not only

48

do I have contacts there who would ease your way, but you do, as well."

"India?" Gussie whispered. When Lillian nodded, Gussie's eyes slipped closed. She was going to see them again. Catherine and Specs. And with those names twisting around her thoughts came her dearest, sweetest, most wonderful memories.

Lazy summer days—as lazy as Gussie allowed them to be—and cozy winter evenings, and a history all knotted together and unable to be unwound. Lined up like mementos on a bureau, dust-covered but so precious.

A few minutes later, with a promise to stop by the *Lady's Weekly* offices to discuss details the next day, Gussie stood in the drive, waving as the carriage bore Lillian away. She pressed her hands to her heart, feeling as though she might have the opportunity to follow in her hero's footsteps. Cordelia Fox—world traveler, adventurer, and writer. Perhaps with a trip to India, Gussie would experience enough to fill the pages of a book.

The image unfolded in her mind like a flower untwisting its petals—slowly and with agonizing detail. Gussie Travers, camera and pen in hand, making her mark on the world.

Could it be possible? Could she change her life's story? Could she do something more than bungle things? Could she really *be* someone?

As the carriage disappeared around the corner, Gussie gave herself a little shake and turned to face the house. To face the comeuppance she was sure to receive.

She just had to make it through today. Make it through whatever torture her parents intended to inflict upon her in the guise of a handsome smile and a fat bank account. And endure the punishment they were sure to dole out with the exposure of her carefree persona.

But as she arranged her expression into one Mother would find suitable, all flavorless placidity and decorum, her thoughts scattered in countless scrumptious directions. She squeezed her hands together to keep from throwing them up in the air and forced her mind to focus on dull, tired things her parents would find wholly unobjectionable: Phoebe had looked beautiful. Gussie truly did need new nightclothes. She hoped Cook had made the little shrimp toasts she loved so much.

But her thoughts took flight anyway.

India!

5

G ussie paced her room, making a path along the carpet that went from bed to window to the chair where Uncle James watched as she lost herself to fury. "How could they do this to me? We don't live in the sixteenth century. They cannot force me to leave."

"When have you ever *not* wanted to leave?" Uncle James pointed out, his pragmatism inexcusably annoying.

Only hours earlier, Gussie had been hiding behind a potted plant —Phoebe had invited an obscene number of guests, which meant no real sit-down meal—eating toast piled high with shrimp and scallions with great crunchy bites that would have mortified her mother and sisters if they could see her. Which they couldn't, because they weren't looking for her. Unfortunately, a few curiosity seekers *were* looking for her. And they pounced with pointed questions and gleeful inquiry into the lies papering the city in black and white.

She'd only meant to defend her reputation. But the conversation turned heated and drew an even larger crowd that took attention off the bride.

An unforgivable turn of events.

Phoebe's tears and Mother's icy glare and Father's scowl.

Uncle James had been tasked with escorting her to her room, telling her they were planning to send her to Aunt Rhoda's indefinitely, and she'd been pacing and protesting ever since. How long could a wedding luncheon with no real lunch endure?

The door flung open, and her parents entered.

Gussie stopped her frenzied steps and stood in the middle of the room, her entire body rigid. "I'm not going to Chicago."

"You must leave New York. I have hope that, in time, the gossip will die down." Father stared at her as though studying proof of a decline in stock value. "But we cannot allow you to stay here and continue to harm your sisters' happiness. And Rhoda might succeed where we have failed."

Gussie jerked back as though he'd struck her. She wrapped her arms around herself and whirled away from them. Went to the window that looked out over the street, where a parade of carriages waited for wedding guests.

Mother neared. "This latest catastrophe has proved to be our greatest trial. You have never shown the slightest interest in doing what is best for this family. It has always been about what you wanted. It is time for you to settle down. There may still be a family in Chicago willing to take you on. A man willing to overlook your ruined reputation."

"I will not settle for a man 'willing to overlook my ruined reputation.'"

"You've wrecked every opportunity to make a decent life for yourself," Father said from his place near the door. "Settling may well prove your only option. And what else can you do if it is?"

"I can continue traveling. Outside of the state and our social set, no one cares about the *New York Daily News*. They've heard nothing of Dora Clutterbuck's vicious lies. I will work and no longer be a nuisance to you."

Father slashed his hand through the air. "No. You know as well as I do that other papers will reprint the story by the weekend. Do you take me for a fool? I won't indulge your lunacy any longer. I will cut you off, do you hear? No more allowance if you refuse."

His voice rose with every word. "You will go to Chicago and either allow Rhoda to guide you in becoming a suitable wife for someone—God, anyone—who will put up with you, or you will live quietly and devote yourself to good works."

Gussie reached toward the wall, needing something sturdy to rest against as the world spun around her. Father had never shouted at her before. He'd lost his temper, yes. Had snapped and made demands. But never before had he sounded so possessed of fury. "I won't do it."

"You will," Father said, "or you will be forced to rely on *Lady's Weekly* to provide your living. Do you believe that possible? How long do you suppose you could live on such a meager salary? And when society has cast you out, when you lose the interest of the public and your darling Lillian turns away from you—"

"She would never! Lillian is my friend."

"Lillian is a woman of business. Do not pretend you know more on that topic than I. She will not keep you if your columns no longer sell copies, make no mistake of that."

"Then I shall do something else." A moment ago, her hand against the wall had been sufficient support, but now Gussie leaned back, her entire body weak and failing. "I will write books. I will . . . I will marry someone of my own choosing!"

"Write books? Augusta, you may have found a modicum of success with your frivolous column, but do you really believe yourself capable of writing a book?" Father looked at her as though she'd sprouted wings and antennae. As though he wanted to stomp her beneath his shoe.

"And who will you marry, dear?" Mother's brows lifted almost imperceptibly. Not enough to disrupt her carefully arranged expression but enough to punctuate her question with astonishment. "Who would have you? Unless you're speaking of that silly proposal the MacLean boy offered when you were children?" Her lips tipped into a mocking smile.

"Don't be ridiculous, Mother. I haven't seen Gabriel MacLean in years."

"You will marry me for real when we're grown, won't you, Gussie?"

They had been playing at bride and groom, roses ringing Gussie's head, Specs wearing his father's cravat and waistcoat. His glasses slipped down his nose, and his expression was as sober as always.

"Don't be silly. Who else should I marry? Now, smile. You don't want the guests to think I forced you into this."

The "guests" were Catherine and an assortment of tin soldiers and porcelain dolls. But Specs had grinned, and Gussie had said "I do," and they were all supposed to live happily ever after.

But for the fire, accidently started by Mrs. Templeton, the MacLeans' housekeeper, who had fallen asleep with a cigarette everyone knew she wasn't supposed to have. That foolish choice had consumed the MacLean home. Had consumed the adjoined house that had once been Gussie's own. Had consumed Catherine and Specs's parents. Had consumed every last bit of happiness Gussie could claim.

The consuming of her own family, the one that made Gussie anathema, had been less dramatic. That had been set ablaze by a brilliant investment.

"You know nothing about the world." Father held his hand out for Mother, who turned her back on Gussie and readily joined him. "You are a child, Augusta, throwing a tantrum. And this is how we have always handled your outbursts. You will stay in your room until our guests have left. I don't wish to give them anything else to gossip about. It's unseemly that you should capture so much attention when it's your sister's wedding day. Next Thursday you will leave for Chicago. At Rhoda's, you will be kept beneath a watchful eye and not allowed to leave without an escort, for I do not trust you to resist whatever urges you to run away. In a year or so, Rhoda will begin to look for someone in Chicago society to take you on. Then . . . you will be your husband's concern."

Father turned to go but paused before disappearing down the hall. Gussie licked her dry lips, unable to resist the hope that fluttered in her belly. He didn't mean these things. Couldn't mean them.

"We will not allow you to ruin anything else."

Then they were gone.

Gussie slid down the wall, a tangle of limbs that refused to cooperate, and Uncle James was near her in an instant, gathering her to him, pressing a kiss against her temple.

"I always thought they might still love me, despite not understanding me."

"They do love you, dear girl. They are frightened for you. For your sisters."

Gussie pushed at his arms and pulled away. "Do not try to appease me. We both know I have always been the Travers family's black sheep."

He said nothing. How could he, in light of the things her father had said?

"Go. Leave me alone."

He did.

Gussie sat near the wall the rest of the day, moving only when the sky turned dark, stars spangling the view outside her window, and the chill forced her into a nightgown and beneath the covers.

A maid brought her water but no food, so Gussie, unwilling to join her family for dinner, found the Christmas candy she'd hidden in the back of her desk and took it to bed.

She chewed on Tootsie Rolls and pastel mints as she thumbed through her favorite travel books. Sucked on lemon drops as she flipped through story after story of adventure in far-off places. And when the room went dark, she lit the gas lamp, tore into a French Chew, and took a pen to the pages, underlining and circling and memorizing. Wishing the words of courage and adventure would suffocate the painful ones shouted by her father.

"I am not all they say I am," she said. "I'm not." But no matter how often she repeated it, the things spoken over her only flamed brighter.

Miss Corsetti, just before she stepped out onto that rope, told me the papers refused to write about her feats because she is a woman. And women aren't supposed to do dangerous things or be brave. They are expected to be ordinary.

Gentle reader, I am about to step out onto my own rope—one that stretches from America's golden shores across the wild waters. I cannot tell you now where I am going, but I promise I will be brave. And my adventures will be anything but ordinary.

I hope you join me in the journey.

Gussie leaned her chin in her palm and read over her work with a critical eye. She pushed back at the curls slipping from her sloppy chignon, her gaze skipping across the last column she would write stateside. With a decisive nod, she set down her pen, slipped the column into an envelope, and gathered everything she would need for the day's errands: the pile of photographs she'd culled from drawers and boxes and between the pages of beloved books, and the notebooks she'd chosen that best showcased her writing. After she tucked everything into the old satchel she stored in the bottom of her wardrobe, she crept from the house.

Father was at his office, Mother was out making calls, and Uncle James had returned to his own home, so there was little reason to creep, but she didn't wish for a servant to see her skulking about with a large bag and report to her parents. She would be home before they realized she'd even been gone.

She hailed one of the new electric hansom cabs that were beginning to vie with horse-drawn carriages for space on New York's congested streets and settled against the tufted leather seat.

At an unassuming three-story brick building, she stepped onto the road and took a deep breath, clutching the satchel. Perhaps, today, life would change.

Lillian grinned when Gussie walked through her office door. "There's my favorite columnist!"

Gussie settled into one of the hardback chairs on the other side of Lillian's desk. She removed her column from the satchel and hesitated only a moment before sliding it across the desk. "It's a little different from my typical fare."

Lillian raised her brows, but she dropped her head and read quickly, finger coming to her tongue as she turned the pages. When she finished, she pinched the bridge of her nose and took a long moment to rub at the corners of her eyes.

"You don't like it? I know you didn't ask for an interview, but I thought my readers would enjoy learning about the woman who demonstrated so much mettle."

"It's . . ." Lillian sighed. "It's not *bad*. It's only that you are so good at what you do." She blew a puff of air from her lips. "All right, Gussie. If you really want me to print this, I will, but don't make a habit of deviating from the norm."

Gussie took a deep breath. She'd enjoyed writing about Luisa and her fight for recognition, but she had bigger things to worry about than diversifying her column. "My parents are planning to send me to Chicago next Thursday. There is a passenger steamer— the TSS *Constance*—leaving two days later from Boston, and I need to be on that ship."

Lillian nodded. "You will be. It will take about a week to get to London and another three to travel to India. I will make all the arrangements in the next few days and see that your itinerary is delivered into your hands." She paused to shuffle through a few papers. "We want six months' worth of columns—twenty-four in total. While you're traveling, we will use up the columns we've yet to print from your trip out west and then print back issues until you begin producing. We're giving you about five weeks to get there, equip yourself, and start writing. I want your first few columns mailed to me by the second week of October. As it is, we won't receive them until mid-November."

Gussie gripped the edge of Lillian's desk and scooted toward the edge of her chair. "And I will have time to visit with Gabriel and Catherine?"

"If you manage it well. Spend some time around Bombay to acclimate yourself and get a few columns sent. Write some from

Poona, if you need to, but don't settle there too long. We don't want to bore your readers. If you are unable to complete your work in India, it will reflect very badly on *Lady's Weekly* and me. I wouldn't like that."

"I won't fail. You know I love nothing more than seeing new places. And I wouldn't do anything to disappoint Miss Adventuress's readers."

"Right. Well, most of my contacts are in the north of the country. If you wish to see the south, you will have to make your own arrangements. We will pay you half your six months' salary up front, in addition to a per diem that should cover your lodging, food, and travel, with the rest payable upon your return and your commitment met. Does that sound good?"

"Yes, except . . ." Gussie cleared her throat, attempting to release the frog that had swallowed the certainty in her voice. "I'd like to discuss the possibility of expanding my work."

"How so? We've no need of another columnist writing about travel or adventure. You've filled that role admirably. Perhaps if we hadn't just hired Miss Kirby to take care of fashion and gossip. . . ." Lillian shook her head. "The only open position is politics."

Gussie blinked. Politics? She didn't really care for the topic and knew very little about it. But . . . "I can do that."

Lillian's expression went blank. Then her laugh filled the room. "Oh, Gussie, you can't be serious." She searched Gussie's face and sobered. "But you are. You are serious?"

"I am. I'm perfectly capable of writing about politics."

Lillian waved her hand as though flicking away a bit of lint. "You don't write about serious matters."

"I could."

Lillian shook her head, a look of condescending amusement teasing her expression. "Stick with what you're good at. The world doesn't need another middling writer discussing dull things. Your photographs and playful banter are what make you stand out. Why muddle with that?"

Another middling writer? Was that true? Without her photographs and the peculiarity of being a female traveler, would anyone care what Gussie wrote? "My father has threatened to cut me off if I don't go to Chicago. I cannot survive on my income writing as Miss Adventuress."

A steely glint entered Lillian's eyes, and she sat back against her chair. "There are a million people in this city who not only survive but support families on the amount you are paid. If you consider a more modest wardrobe"—Lillian jerked her chin toward the hat perched on Gussie's head, which boasted a profusion of feathers and silk flowers—"you might be able to survive on your income."

Gussie's face flamed. She had no defense. She couldn't even say how much her hat cost, let alone how much one would need to put a roof over their head and food in their belly. She only knew how much she made from her columns. Pin money, she had always called it. Funds meant to be dipped into when she happened across a lace shawl or a collection of poetry and wanted to feel grown-up and independent. "Of course. It was a foolish thought."

Lillian gave a decisive nod. "I know it hasn't been easy for you—having Miss Adventuress's true identity revealed. But it has been good for the magazine. Subscriptions have jumped nearly ten percent since the news broke, and we've been flooded with letters asking where you're going next. You're a paradox—wealthy enough to have the kind of life most people can only dream of yet willing to toss it off for a tent and a shot of a desolate mountain. From *la crème de la crème* of New York society, yet utterly careless when it comes to reputation."

"I'm not careless of my reputation, Lillian. I've done nothing indecent or improper."

Lillian waved her hand. "It matters little. Not as long as you are producing the type of content readers expect and want. And what they want is Miss Adventuress in India. Just remember to keep the tone as light and airy as that confection atop your head."

Lady's Weekly wasn't far from Gussie's next destination on Bond Street, close enough that she decided to walk. Not close enough that she didn't regret her decision within two blocks. She squinted up at the sun beating down on New York's inhabitants and twirled her parasol.

She might as well get used to the heat. Catherine and Specs promised that Poona offered the occasional cool breeze and balmy day in January, but October would be warm. Thankfully, though, she would be leaving India before the summer months, which she'd heard were as hot as a kitchen fire.

Gussie sobered at the heedless thought. She would do well to consider her words and refrain from using such a phrase around her friends. Their parents' death in just such a disaster wasn't far enough distant that they would appreciate the metaphor.

She paused outside the offices of C. S. Epps and Company, pulling a handkerchief from the reticule hanging from her wrist and swiping at her brow. It wouldn't do to appear before one of the country's most powerful men in publishing looking disheveled and as disreputable as the papers made her out to be.

"Miss Augusta Travers?" the secretary said when she introduced herself and asked for an audience with Mr. Epps. His brown curls fell over his eyes in a most pleasing way, and Gussie decided he seemed the type to be impressed by money and connection. She had no problem exploiting her name if it got her what she wanted.

"Yes." She gave him a playful smile. "Of the Travers family. You have heard of my father, Mr. Thomas Travers?"

"Of course I've heard of Mr. Travers. I've also heard of Augusta Travers." At his leering gaze, Gussie's flirtation slipped away like the shrugging off of a cloak. His handsome face had exaggerated his charms in a most deceptive way.

"Do not believe everything you hear about people. It is most often untrue."

The secretary gave her a crooked grin, then shrugged. "I'm sorry I can't help you, but Mr. Epps rarely sees anyone without an appointment." He leaned his elbows on the desk, carelessly pushing aside a stack of papers. "And you do not have an appointment."

Gussie pressed her lips into a firm line. If she left this building without seeing Mr. Epps, it meant losing her only opportunity to secure the possibility of a future income that could support her, if not in the manner to which she was accustomed, at least in a manner that would see her fed and clothed. It was freedom from being forced to succumb to her parents' wishes. It meant the realization of a lifelong dream.

But she wouldn't sacrifice her pride and play the coquette for this odious man.

The office door scraped open behind her, and she turned. Her mouth dropped. "Uncle James."

The man behind the desk scrambled to his feet. "Mr. Travers."

"Johnny. Will you tell Mr. Epps that my niece Miss Augusta Travers is here to see him?"

"Certainly, sir." He shuffled away, and Gussie narrowed her eyes. "Are you following me?"

"Do you think your parents trust you just because you are in New York?"

"Why shouldn't they?"

He raised his brows. "Gussie, they do not want you disappearing before your trip to Chicago. Gossip will never settle down if you do. Why are you here?"

Her gaze skipped to the door through which the secretary had disappeared. "Trying to become Cordelia." At her uncle's furrowed brow, she continued. "You introduced me to Cordelia Fox and her lifetime of adventure. Don't you remember?"

Maybe he didn't. Perhaps it hadn't meant as much to him as it had to her. It was only a long-ago present of a book to a girl. An uncle gifting his young niece with a trifle. But the moment she saw the gilt title splayed across the blue leather, she pinned the memory to that dusty corner of her mind that hid away the loveliest of her recollections. It was the moment she knew she wanted to live a life of adventure. And write about it. He had given her that.

"I remember. You've always been single-minded in your devotion to your dreams."

"I never stopped wanting to write my own book," she whispered. "And now seems an opportune time to explore the possibility."

"Because you need money."

"Because I need affirmation."

He studied her, rolling the tip of his mustache between his fingers. He shook his head but smiled too. "Who am I to stand in the way of such a long-held aspiration? Especially when you can make the argument that I was the one to place it in your mind." He drew nearer at the sound of approaching footsteps. "And lucky for you, I'm acquainted with Mr. Charles Epps. He has hired me half a dozen times to deal with the various threats and scandals that seem to follow wealthy, important men."

The secretary, now meek and subdued, reappeared. "Mr. Epps will see you now."

"I will wait out here for you," Uncle James said.

Mr. Epps—older than her father and just as brusque—stood when she entered. "Miss Travers, please have a seat." He waved toward the chair opposite his desk and sat down when she did. "What can I help you with today?"

Gussie pulled her satchel into her lap and drew out the envelope containing her photographs, as well as her notebooks—catalogs of all she had seen and done over the previous few years. Then she took a deep breath and flashed him a smile. "I've long been a fan of the books your company publishes, Mr. Epps. Namely those titles by Cordelia Fox. I own every one of them, and they have become much-loved friends."

"How nice of you to say so."

She nodded. "But Miss Fox's last book was published twelve years ago, and C. S. Epps and Company has published no female travel narratives since."

"Well, that is because Miss Fox had the unfortunate bad luck of being bitten by a many-banded krait."

"Oh . . ." Gussie blinked at him. "I hadn't heard. I thought she was teaching in China."

"She was. And also writing a book for us on her work and travel in that country after her long hiatus, but her death preceded her deadline."

"How terrible," Gussie murmured, her heart twisting in a painful little dance. Cordelia Fox, dead by snakebite. No longer in the world. Never again to set her eyes toward adventure. "Although, for a woman as daring as she was, it does seem a suitable way to leave this earth. She never did anything the regular way, did she?"

Mr. Epps inclined his head, and Gussie gathered her thoughts. "I'm here, Mr. Epps, because I believe I may be what you are looking for."

"I didn't realize we were looking for anything in particular."

Gussie gave a decisive nod. "You are in need of a female writer willing to travel to distant places. And I happen to be one. I'm also a photographer." She pulled out her photographs and placed them on the desk. "Which only makes my work more appealing."

Mr. Epps began to sift through the photographs. "These are very good. Do you have any examples of your writing?"

She passed over one of her notebooks and glanced over her shoulder, making certain the door remained firmly shut. "All of my work, thus far, has been focused on the United States, but I'll be traveling to Asia soon and can promise you many humorous anecdotes and cheerful observances."

He grunted, and his thick thumbs flipped through the pages of her notebook. After a few minutes, he closed the book and settled his hand atop it. "Miss Travers, while I admire your initiative and acknowledge that your photography and writing have merit, I cannot offer you the distinction of becoming published by C. S. Epps and Company."

Gussie stared at him, fingers fumbling the clasp of her satchel. "But why not if, as you say, what I do is sufficient?"

"Oh, it is more than sufficient—especially your photographs. They are singular in their composition and subject. It's only that what you do isn't what we do." He lumbered from his chair. "Here, let me show you."

She set down her bag and joined him at the wall of mahogany bookcases. He opened one of the glass doors and withdrew two books, which he passed to her. "These were written by my son and daughter-in-law." He smiled at her fondly. "You remind me of her—very determined and forward-thinking. They are entomologists and have traveled all over the world, documenting many species. Even discovering a few. They are in Sierra Leone currently."

Gussie ran her fingers over the type—embossed blue letters on red cloth. *Butterfly Diversity of the Western Ghats by Nora and Owen Epps. Illustrated by Nora Epps.*

The second book was larger, the cover made of tooled cream-colored leather that boasted gilt lettering. *Chasing the Insects of South America: In Search of Beauty.* The same names appeared below a delicate illustration of a large blue butterfly.

"If you read them," Mr. Epps said, "you will discover they contain nary a glib word. They are serious books meant for serious readers. We simply do not publish the types of things you write."

"But Miss Fox—"

"Miss Fox's books were all published more than a decade ago. Things have changed since then. Why, even her most recent book would have been a more serious look at her work in China. She would have written about her travels through that country, yes, but all within the framework of her many sober accomplishments."

Gussie looked down at the books in her hands. "You must be very proud of them. They've produced something beautiful that will impact many people."

"I am proud of them." He cleared his throat. "I'm very sorry to disappoint you, but your work just isn't right for us." He must have seen something in her face because the rigid lines of his jaw softened. "If you ever decide to write things of a more serious nature, I will be happy to take a look."

Gussie inhaled and handed the books back to him. "Thank you, Mr. Epps. I will keep that in mind."

But Lillian's words trailed her from the office.

"The world doesn't need another middling writer discussing dull things."

6

Less than a week after Gussie decided to upend her life, she found herself on a train bound for Chicago, Uncle James sitting beside her on the plush velvet first-class seat.

Gussie sent him sidelong glances as he periodically tugged at his beard, pinched the ends of his mustache, and gripped his knees with white knuckles.

"I don't enjoy this, Augusta," he finally said as they passed through the rolling hills of eastern Pennsylvania. "I just don't see any way out of it."

"I know."

Uncle James grew silent then, staring out the train window as Gussie mentally sifted through the satchel the porter had stored beneath her seat when she objected to him stowing it with the rest of the luggage. It contained her Kodak, a few rolls of film, a change of clothing, her journal, and a couple of Cordelia Fox's books. It was enough to see her to Boston.

All the money Gussie had, including the advance on her salary Lillian had given her, was hidden in the pouch she'd hung from a cord around her neck. Just the way Nellie Bly traveled when she'd taken her trip around the world. How amusing that Gussie's family had endeavored to accumulate ever more belongings while Gussie was able to fit all she really needed into an old leather satchel. She grinned at their lack of foresight. At what they had missed in underestimating her.

Uncle James shifted, and guilt pierced her impertinent thoughts. He didn't deserve what she was about to do to him.

"Uncle James?"

He looked at her.

"I want you to know that I love you. You, Catherine, and Specs are the only people who kept me from feeling lost my entire life."

A frown knit his brows. "No matter how far you go, Augusta, you will never be lost. And this hasn't been said enough." He held her gaze, and the back of her throat began to ache with all the things she wished she could tell him. All the things she needed to hear. And then, as though he'd pulled them from her thoughts with the skills he'd honed as a detective, he said them. "You are fearfully and wonderfully made. You are the daughter of my heart, knit from my own dreams and hope. There is nothing wrong with you. Nothing that makes you broken."

She bit down on her lip, tempted to tell him everything. But too much relied on her ability to slip away from him. Her commitment to Lillian and *Lady's Weekly*. Her promise to entertain her readers. Her future.

So she laid her head against the seatback and pretended to sleep.

When they arrived at LaSalle Station, Uncle James exited the train and held his hand out for her. She took a snapshot in her mind of the moment. Nestled the portrait of the dearest man in the universe deep within her memory. She didn't know when she would see him again.

Her fingers found his, and she stepped to the platform, then followed him to the baggage car and watched while he spoke to the attendant. A few seconds later, he turned to her. "They're having trouble locating your trunk. I'm going to help them."

Just as she'd planned.

It had only taken a whispered word and clinking coins to convince the porter to put her trunk on the train headed to Boston. There it would sit until she claimed it.

When Uncle James leaned into the baggage car, she slipped away, unhindered by nothing more troublesome than her satchel.

It took only five minutes to escape the crowded station and hail a hack. "Please, hurry. My train leaves from Central Station in"—she lifted the watch pinned to her jacket—"thirty minutes."

"Are you crazy, miss? You'll not make that one."

"I must." Against everything she wished herself to be—strong and capable and independent—tears filled her eyes. "Please."

At the sound of her choked cry, the driver's face filled with the sort of fear inspired by outlaws, natural disasters, and evidently weeping women, for he urged his horses forward and set them to a brisk trot. Thankfully the roads were clear of traffic, as darkness had descended hours earlier and was broken only by the regular gas lamps offering circles of watery light.

When they arrived, Gussie pressed money into the driver's hand and shouted, "Thank you!" as she dashed through the station doors and located the ticket booth.

Her heart hammering in her chest, arms cradling her satchel, she darted to the platform, ticket between her teeth.

"Best hurry, ma'am." A porter ushered her inside the car, and she fell into a seat just as the train's wheels and gears began to grind.

"I made it." She covered her mouth with her hands and took great gasping breaths. "I made it."

The woman sitting in front of her turned and gave Gussie a sour look. "You did. And they are about to lower the berths. I hope you don't talk to yourself all night long."

The woman whipped her head forward again, and Gussie stifled a giggle. She reached into her satchel and withdrew her longtime friend and encourager. Her best and dearest companion.

Cordelia Fox's words would offer her comfort. Only another female adventurer and traveler could understand how Gussie's pulse pounded. With each beat of her heart, she gave an ecstatic, though silent, shout. Closer and closer to her destination. Closer and closer to freedom.

Gussie ran her hand over the well-worn cover. Flipped through the pages until she reached where she had left off.

And found a piece of folded paper.

With clumsy fingers, she opened it and pressed the crease flat.

Did you really think to fool a Pinkerton? Seventy-two hours, Augusta, and then I'm coming after you. See you soon, darling niece.

Uncle James

Gussie's heart thrummed with the train's wheels clacking against the tracks, and she laughed. The woman in front of her turned to glare, and Gussie waved the note.

"The chase has begun."

7

October 1897
Bombay, India

Gussie had very nearly kissed the ground when her feet touched Bombay. Eighteen days onboard a ship had tested the limits of her sanity. But India wrapped her in its effusive, chaotic, wide embrace. It called her forward and outward, and she soon found herself entirely lost to its charms.

Lillian, with her never-ending supply of contacts that stretched farther than Gussie had ever dreamed, had given her a stack of letters of introduction meant to open doors to the well-heeled, well-connected, and welcoming. Gussie started with a few days at the home of an English poet who had absconded to India after her rich husband's death and taken refuge from her grief in the bubbling, exciting cauldron of another place. It was enough time for Gussie to visit a dressmaker and outfit herself for this new life in the tropics.

She spent a couple of days exploring ancient temples built into caves before heading north to a hill station that offered splendid views of mountains and lakes. Then she went south toward Alibag along the coast, stopping at little villages to eat curried fish and dip her toes in the warm waters of the Arabian Sea.

Gussie delighted at how India filled her yearning for adventure in a way no other place had. She'd thought the colors of a Dakota sunrise unparalleled until she saw the sunset settling over the Western Ghats like a stole. Her heart had leapt at the sight of the great Niagara plunging and crashing beneath a thin cord stretched taut beneath the steps of the world's most courageous woman. But then she wandered through a fort that resolutely clung to the sand, its stones tumbling into the Arabian Sea, her feet treading where maharajas had stood centuries earlier.

America, with its youthful zeal and brazen thirst, whispered a sonnet to Gussie's heart. But India sang, her voice a thunderous roar, to the percussion of drums. It reached inside of her and wrestled with the accusations that had chased her across the ocean.

When Gussie had photographed and experienced enough to fill a month's worth of *Lady's Weekly* columns, she poured everything she had seen and heard and tasted onto paper, but she withheld what she'd felt, for those things were too deep and solemn for Miss Adventuress.

After posting her work to Lillian, Gussie's heart turned toward Poona. Toward Catherine and Specs.

The six hours on the train seemed as interminable as the weeks she'd spent getting to this country. She hadn't seen her friends since the horrific fire the year they'd all turned fifteen. Catherine and Specs moved to Philadelphia to live with their aunt after their parents' death. Gussie had always meant to visit, but Mother never saw fit to allow her. By the time Gussie realized she could travel without her parents' permission, the MacLean twins had already left for India—Specs, having completed medical school, as a medical missionary working with a local doctor, and Catherine unwilling to be separated from him after losing their mother and father so violently.

Gussie bounced in her seat and stared out the window, admiring but unable to fully appreciate the mist-shrouded hills rising and falling in a kaleidoscope of emerald. Maharashtra's arresting beauty couldn't compete with the knowledge that the train brought her ever closer to her dearest friends.

Everything had happened so quickly that Gussie hadn't had the opportunity to write and let them know of her visit before leaving home. And then, when she arrived in England, she'd decided to surprise them. She leaned near the window, attempting to see past the tracks stitched ahead of them in a crooked seam. Catherine was going to be delighted—she'd always loved Gussie's larks. Specs, though . . .

Gussie blew through her lips. Specs disliked both surprises and larks. But he had written her so many fond letters, and their friendship spilled through the years like a ribbon unfurled. He couldn't possibly be dismayed by her appearance.

Still . . .

She tugged her lip between her teeth. Specs always had been a stickler for following convention and rules. He was a serious sort. Not entirely dour but definitely grave. She thought of his thin, solemn face, round glasses perched atop his long nose as he looked up at her—he had been an inch below her in height the last time she'd seen him. Gussie had inherited her grandfather's stature, whereas her sisters remained acceptably petite. There weren't many men she didn't match inch for inch, if she didn't stand over.

Maybe she should have sent a message and told them of her visit. It would be disappointing in the extreme if she arrived and didn't receive the reaction she hoped for. Could she bear Specs's disapproval?

Gussie rubbed the pebbled leather of her camera bag, which was strung across her torso and resting in her lap. She couldn't do anything about it now. Besides, even after her most disastrous childhood escapades, Specs eventually came around and forgave her. He would this time, as well. And Catherine's letters had spoken of her husband, John, as a kind spirit. He might have influenced Gabriel MacLean.

With her doubts and worries addressed and conquered, Gussie leaned her head against the seat and napped.

"Memsahib," someone said, jostling her shoulder.

She jerked upright and glanced around, blinking. The train had stopped, and outside the window, a wave of passengers fanned out over the platform. She squealed, thanked the startled porter, and leapt from her seat.

Out on the platform, Gussie looked around, recognizing nothing, and a laugh rose to her lips, spilling out to skip along the wild mass of color, babble of languages, and press of vehicles. Even when she'd traveled to the very edge of civilized America, there had still been a sense of familiarity. Nothing in South Dakota had reminded her in any way of her life in New York City, but she still understood it. Understood the language, the social structure, the manners, the context.

India, though, worked tirelessly to overwhelm her. To delight her. To surprise her. And below that thought, simmering in a place she'd never taken the time to poke around, there arrived a thought so outlandish, she wondered if her sleep-addled mind had yanked it from a half-remembered dream.

India felt like a homecoming.

She belonged here. In this place as scattered and audacious and *alive* as she was.

A barked command drew her attention, and she followed the sound to see a British man wearing a funny hat and an even funnier mustache waving over the train's third-class passengers. He motioned a handful of nurses in starched white aprons and caps toward a cluster of women and then began examining the men in full view of the other passengers. Gussie started when the doctor shouted for a soldier, who trotted over from his place against the wall and pushed an elderly gentleman into a wooden tub. The man began to twist and cry out, but the soldier ignored him and doused him with something in a bucket, giving little care to the man's mouth and eyes.

"Oh no." Gussie lifted her hand and took a few steps forward, but her progress was hampered by a parade of men carrying a pallet. Above them, lounging regally, as though he were surveying his kingdom and not bound by a jeweled collar and leash, was a leopard.

When the procession had passed, the poor mistreated man had disappeared and a grim, glaring one had taken his place. Ducking to avoid meeting the man's eyes, Gussie located a porter and directed him to her luggage, sending glances over her shoulder at the strange welcome Poona offered its poorest visitors.

Off the platform, a line of small carriages, carts, and palanquins waited along the street. Stopping at a two-wheeled cart, its horse swaybacked and tired-looking but not nearly so much so as its driver, Gussie asked, "Ganj Peth?"

The man flashed a bright smile. Everything about him was crooked save his teeth. "*Namaskara*, memsahib."

"I must be taken to Ganj Peth."

"Ganj Peth?" The driver's eyes widened, and he shook his head. "No, you don't want Ganj Peth. You want Ghora Chhavni?"

Gussie shrugged. "I want Mrs. John Archer and Dr. Gabriel MacLean."

His eyes brightened. "Doctor! You want doctor?"

"I do!" She offered the driver a triumphant grin and hoisted herself into the cart.

After the porter loaded her trunk onto the seat beside her, the driver snapped the reins and eased into the steady traffic. He looked over his shoulder. "Doctor move to Napier. Near cantonment. Not far."

As they rode, Gussie clutched her camera bag to her middle and peered from beneath the fringed canopy. Mansions and houses— Specs had written that they were called *havelis* and bungalows—of varying sizes lined the street, the edges of gardens peeking from behind them. Great flowering trees offered shade and color. Shops and restaurants, many boasting European names on ornate signs, beckoned with glittering display windows and doors thrown open to let in air. Business, however, seemed less than brisk, and as they ventured farther into the city, a sense of forsaken loneliness littered the streets like a playroom deserted by its grown-up occupants. Some buildings seemed abandoned, with *Gone to Bombay* splashed over shuttered windows in red paint.

"Where is everyone?" Gussie asked.

"Indians live here too. *Bangla-vargi*. Rich and educated, you understand? But they leave. Everyone who can, leave Poona."

"But why?" Gussie gripped the splintered edge of her seat. "Are Dr. MacLean and Mrs. Archer still here?"

The driver jiggled his head. "Yes, yes. They stay. For work. Doctor is needed."

Gussie exhaled her relief just as the cart stopped before a tidy bungalow wrapped by a deep verandah. Floor to ceiling windows lined the façade, each bracketed with green shutters. Butterfly bushes, spiky purple heads drooping beneath the weight of their flowers, softened the edge of the building and invited vibrant butterflies to land atop them. It was as pretty as a picture.

Gussie resisted the urge to pull out her camera. The house would be in its present state after she saw her friends.

Already someone had opened the front door. Stepped into the doorway and lifted a hand to shield his eyes. Catherine's husband? He stared at her as she climbed from the vehicle, took the steps two at a time, and smiled a greeting. Her smile faltered when he stepped onto the porch and she noticed his bare feet. Odd. She didn't think she'd ever seen her father's feet in all the years she'd known him.

"Hello. I've been told this is the residence of Mrs. John Archer and her brother, Dr. Gabriel MacLean."

He nodded and opened his mouth, then closed it quickly. She stepped closer, noting his height, at least two inches above her own.

"Why are you here? You shouldn't be here." He groaned and gripped his head. "I have too much already to manage. You are beyond my capacity."

Behind him came padding steps and a soft voice. "What is the matter? Who is there?" Catherine appeared, rubbing at a pair of spectacles with a cloth and looking much the same as Gussie remembered.

When she saw Gussie, her eyes widened, and she clapped her hands over her mouth.

Then she burst into tears.

Gussie's arms were around her friend in an instant. "Oh, darling, what is it?"

Catherine sniffed and pulled away but kept her hands on Gussie's sides, not breaking contact. "I'm so happy. So happy to see you. I prayed only yesterday that God would send me a friend, and look! He's sent the very best one I've ever had. I never dreamed—! But of course, I'm always doubting the good things he has for me."

The grumpy man who had opened the door cleared his throat. "She can't stay, Catherine. You know that."

Catherine's expression fell. "I know. I know. You must leave, Gussie. It isn't safe in Poona."

"What? I can't leave. I've only just arrived." She turned toward the man and frowned. "Are you Catherine's husband?"

He snorted and shook his head.

Catherine laughed. "Have you forgotten Gabriel? It has been a decade since you've seen him, I suppose, and he's changed very much. Hasn't he grown so handsome?"

Gussie's mouth dropped along with her stomach as her gaze swept over the man's face. Nothing about him reminded her of Gabriel MacLean. Not his height, for she'd always been taller than him, nor his athletic leanness that little resembled the skinny limbs of the boy she'd grown up with. Not even the auburn curls that had been brought into submission by an overzealous pair of scissors. Gussie distinctly remembered his hair being as red as a tomato.

Then Catherine handed over the spectacles, and he placed them atop his nose, putting everything into focus not only, Gussie presumed, for him but also for her.

And there he was.

"Specs!" She stood on tiptoe and slung her arms around his shoulders. "Have you given up on shoes?"

His hug, stiff but not unwarm, felt as unfamiliar as the city. Strange, since they'd once been as close as siblings. "In the house, yes. It's a filthy habit—walking around the floors and carpets, dragging all manner of things in from outside."

She pulled away and grinned. He might have grown into a man who bore little resemblance to the Specs she remembered, but he'd changed not at all.

She looked at the house and raised her brows.

"You may as well come in," Specs said. "You won't be able to return to Bombay until the morning anyway."

Specs motioned for the driver to deliver her trunk and laid a coin in his outstretched palm. Gussie watched him, tilting her head this way and that in an attempt to reconcile her memories with the man who stood in front of her. He looked at her, brows raised, and she shook her head.

"I won't be returning to Bombay for a couple of weeks at least. I want to spend as much time as possible with Catherine—and you—before I leave. Miss Adventuress has come to India."

The twins exchanged a look that did not bode well for Gussie's visit. But they led her down an airy, open hall toward the back room of the house.

"Come, sit near me." Catherine took Gussie's arm, and they settled onto a teak settee upholstered in blue and painted with swirling filigree. Specs took the matching chair opposite.

"This is a lovely home," Gussie said. The room was lined with windows, shutters flung open to allow in light and perfumed air. "I didn't realize a mission doctor could be so successful, Specs."

"This is my home." Catherine took Gussie's hand and licked her lips. "John's home."

Gussie clapped her hands. "And where is your wonderful husband?"

"There was an incident. You see, he worked with the Indian Medical Service, and two men unhappy with John's superior attacked. But John was with him. And he . . . he was shot, Gussie. Killed." Catherine's lips trembled, and her freckles stood out against her pale skin. "I never wrote to you of it, for I couldn't bring myself to put it onto paper."

"Oh no." Gussie wrapped her arms once again around her friend, squeezing her shaking shoulders as though she could hold Catherine's shattered life together by the force of her affection. "I am so sorry. So sorry you've endured such a trial. And so sorry I couldn't meet the man who stole your heart. He must have been extraordinary to deserve you."

"He was. He . . ." Catherine looked at Specs. "You tell the rest." She rested her hands over her stomach and looked at the floor.

"John was a gifted physician," Specs said. "He worked tirelessly on behalf of his patients. He also had a soft heart, and that, combined with his bullheaded determination always to do what was right, saw to his death. He was riding home from a ball at the governor's palace with the plague commissioner, who was not always determined to do what was right. His harsh methods garnered him many enemies. Brothers, inflamed by the injustice of these policies, attacked and killed them. John had been trying to convince the commissioner to ease up on some of the more extreme methods being implemented. He was caught between them."

Specs lapsed into silence. While he'd been speaking, a servant entered, setting a silver tea service on the table before them. Catherine poured Gussie a cup, putting in two cubes of sugar just like she'd always liked. She handed it over with a sniffle. "Gabe is right. You should leave on the first train out of Poona."

Gussie stared at her. "Whatever for? I'm not leaving you now. Not when you need the comfort of a friend."

"Did you not hear what he said?"

Gussie shook her head and looked between her and Specs. "Surely you don't believe I'm at risk of being attacked."

Specs's expression pinched, and he crossed his arms over his chest the way he always had when they were kids and she'd frustrated him by refusing to abide by his pragmatism and good sense. "Catherine's husband was walking home with the *plague* commissioner. Do you not know what that means?"

"The bubonic plague," Catherine clarified. "A quarter of the city's populace left when news spread that this particular epidemic was causing double the death rate. Though, now that things are under control, they are beginning to return."

"Does that have something to do with the way they were treating the third-class passengers coming off the train? Pouring something all over them?"

"They were disinfecting them," Specs said, his jaw tightening.

"In a very inhumane manner." Gussie shook her head. "But if things are returning to normal as you say, why should I leave? You're here." Gussie looked at Catherine. "And you stayed."

Specs sighed and rubbed at his forehead. "I remained because I'm a doctor. Catherine was grieving, and then, before she could go stay with friends in Pondicherry, she was beset by terrible nausea that made even standing impossible."

Gussie took Catherine's hand. "Are you well now?"

"Nearly better." She turned a pretty shade of pink and leaned close so only Gussie heard her words. "I was left with a gift before John died. I am pregnant."

"How wonderful! Now I have even more of a reason to visit for a while." Her friends fell quiet, so Gussie took the opportunity to sip her tea. "How very British of you, Catherine. Teatime. Do you remember when we read *Pride and Prejudice* the summer we turned thirteen? How we fell in love with those British men and their fine manners and lovely accents? You with Mr. Bingley and me with Mr. Darcy." She offered Specs a frown. "And you with no one because you refused to play along with what you termed our 'silly fancies.' Catherine, your John sounds very much like Mr. Bingley. Was he everything you'd daydreamed about?"

Catherine's smile turned soft, and she nodded. "He was. Thank you, Gussie, for not being afraid to speak about him. I sometimes feel as though people believe if they mention John or what happened, I will shatter and turn to dust." She sipped her tea, and when she set her cup back in the saucer, her face was positively radiant, casting the rest of the room in shadow. "Gussie, he had the most delicious accent."

They giggled as though they were schoolgirls again, huddled together beneath a tree in Central Park, reading Austen.

"This stroll through the past has been precious, but you really must leave as soon as possible, Gussie." Specs's words invited no argument.

She smiled. She loved a good debate. "I will not. You said yourself the disease has been contained."

"I said it's under control. That doesn't mean there is no more plague in Poona. It has been a highly contagious and deadly epidemic, spreading through the congested areas so quickly that officials are having trouble staying ahead of it. I have enough to worry about with my work and Catherine's safety. I do not have time to worry about you."

Gussie stood and crossed the few feet between them. She looked down at Specs, an advantage she could only claim because he sat and she didn't. "I thought you would be pleased to see me. I will admit to a certain amount of disappointment that you seem eager to see me gone when it has been so long since you left New York."

The harsh planes of his face softened. "I'm not eager to see you gone, Gussie. Of course I'm pleased to see you. But mostly, I'm worried for your safety. I'm worried for Catherine's safety, and she rarely leaves the house." He angled a look at her that said more than his words.

Gussie studied him and recognized the spark of fear in the shadow of his gaze. It had always been that way for Specs. And she remembered something he had said to her just before his parents died. *"When I'm with you, the anxiety that follows me around like a great, hulking dog is muzzled. Maybe it's because I can't hear it due to your endless prattling, or maybe it's because you are so fearless that I don't wish to seem timid in comparison."*

She touched his cheek, surprised by the stubble scraping the soft pads of her fingers. Gabriel MacLean had, indeed, grown up. "I'm going to stay. For now. Because I know, deep down, you want me to stay. I will not be bound by your fear. And I will not allow you to be bound by your fear."

"It is caution, pragmatic caution, that inspires me to send you away. Not fear."

"Mmm. It is good for us, then, that you have little sway over my decisions. If my parents couldn't convince me to give up traveling and Uncle James couldn't induce me to follow him home from Deadwood, you cannot make me go."

He lifted his hand to hers, which she still held against his cheek. An intimate gesture, for certain, but Gussie held Specs's heart as near as she would a brother's. "You never did listen to any sense," he said.

"No. Never. Sense is a dull companion."

8

The next morning, Gussie awoke to light pouring through the windows. She could see the sky from her bed, as vibrant and evocative as delftware. It called her forward, and she stretched her arms above her head, then tossed the coverlet aside. She'd burrowed beneath it when she saw, in the moonlight, a very hairy spider moving over the ceiling.

The perfumed air drew her to the window, and the birdsong and monkey chorus promised stories eager to be told. Sights ready to be forever immortalized on film. Gussie flung her arms wide as though embracing the whole of it. She never had taken small bites, and this day demanded a throwing off of hesitation. A greedy swallow.

With a whirl, she went to the rosewood wardrobe across the room, just barely taking note of its lovely pattern inset with contrasting teak, and removed her favorite ready-made. The lavender striped shirtwaist with its high ruffled collar and black ribbon referenced the Kodak Girl look everyone knew. The black jacket and white linen skirt were no-nonsense. The slightly puffed sleeves, jeweled belt buckle, and straw boater wrapped in silk ribbon were nods to femininity.

The ensemble made Gussie feel strong and capable enough to

take amazing photographs, if not fashionable enough to be in one. A shadow passed over her anticipation. A reminder of the family portrait lurking in her camera bag's pocket, waiting for an opportunity to taunt. Gussie set her jaw and went to the bureau, where she dug through a jumble of silk hose, supporters, and accessories until she located and withdrew a pair of lace gloves. Then she shoved the distressing memory inside and slammed the drawer closed upon it.

By the time she made her way toward the dining room, to which the most tantalizing scents drew her, she'd once again captured her bright mood.

Catherine smiled and patted the seat next to her. "Come sit by me. Karuna will serve you."

"Thank you," Gussie murmured when Karuna set the plate he'd filled at the buffet in front of her, and her stomach grumbled at the scent of spices she couldn't identify. At home, she managed meals with decorum, always remembering her mother's admonition to "eat lightly, as befits a woman." Whenever she indulged, Mother would warn her against growing as robust as a farmhand. But since arriving in India, she'd become accustomed to eating her fill. And she felt better for it.

She glanced across the table at Specs and watched as he tucked into his meal, taking hearty bites without thought. She grinned. "This looks wonderful." Then she matched him in filling her fork.

"As do you!" Catherine smoothed a finger over the smart buttons at Gussie's cuffs. "I've not seen anything so modern here."

"It is a good two or three miles to the Poona Boat Club. I will hail you a *tanga* after breakfast." Specs took a neat bite of food and smiled with closed lips.

"Boat club?" Gussie took a small scoop of what looked like rice, beans, and fish onto her fork and brought it to her tongue. Slightly spicy, redolent of the sun and earth and everything in between. No, she couldn't be expected to suppress her natural appetite.

Specs waved a hand toward her. "By the looks of it, you wish to go boating. The Mula-Mutha River offers beautiful vistas."

Gussie set down her fork and stared at him, brows raised, until she realized how much she must resemble her mother. "Gabriel MacLean, you have spent too much time with your dull medical journals. I am not going sailing today. This is the look of a modern woman. The New Woman. The Kodak Girl. This is the look of the future."

Having said her piece, Gussie lifted her fork again and took another bite. Her eyes slid closed, and she couldn't help the sound that tickled her throat. A sigh? Or perhaps it was a groan. She lifted her lashes and saw Specs watching her, trying to hide his grin behind a napkin. He patted at his lips until Gussie thought he would rub them away. Which would be a shame, because he'd always had such lovely lips.

His eyes lightened a shade, glimmering behind the lenses of his spectacles. He held up his hands in mock surrender. "If you don't wish to row, perhaps you shouldn't wear a sailing outfit."

Gussie sniffed as she swallowed her food. "I'm excited for the day to begin." She shifted her attention to Catherine and pulled at the strap of her Kodak bag, draped over her chest. "Where should I start?"

"Must you work right away?" Catherine asked. "I would love to introduce you to Ramabai, and she is only in town until tomorrow. This might be the one opportunity you have to meet her, for she spends a lot of time at Mukti Mission, which is near Kedgaon village."

Gussie reached for Catherine's fingers. "Pandita Ramabai? The one who wrote the book Specs sent me?"

A woman who had traveled more widely than Gussie. The first woman to be accorded the title *pandita*, a scholar of Sanskrit. A wise teacher. The woman who was changing life for women in India and inspiring others to do the same.

Catherine nodded. "You will want to meet her. She is a singular woman."

Specs cleared his throat. "She's bringing a group of probationers to Sassoon Hospital this morning and will likely return to the flat above the infirmary, where the girls have been staying with Bimla and the others, to see that it is clean. Would you like to see the infirmary where I work with Dr. Paul?" He stilled, then gave a self-deprecating laugh. "That probably wouldn't interest you. It offers no beautiful views or fascinating fodder for a women's magazine."

"Don't be uncharitable, Gabriel." Catherine shook her head, sending the red curls of her fringe dancing on her forehead. "Of course Gussie would love to see where you work. She is our dearest friend and has always shown an interest in our lives."

Gussie pressed her teacup to her mouth and ducked her head. Catherine had always been overly generous about Gussie's motives. It was Specs who had seen through her at every turn. Even now, he knew she would rather find a vista to photograph or stumble into an experience that would make her heart and pen race. She raised her gaze over the rim of the cup and met his. A challenge lay in his eyes, even while a smile played with the corners of his lips.

"I would very much like seeing where you work, Specs. And Pandita Ramabai is someone I should most certainly make the acquaintance of."

There. That would set him off his high horse.

"Good. Lucky for you, we don't see plague patients, and there hasn't been a case in Ganj Peth for some weeks. I just ask that you stay out of trouble this morning."

"Honestly, you act as though I'm incapable of having a perfectly ordinary day."

He snorted, and she glared at him, but he only held up his teacup in a toast. "I've never known you to have an ordinary day."

Catherine patted Gussie's hand. "It is only because you are such an extraordinary person. Why, you have accomplished so much, and Gabriel is just as proud of you as I am. He may pretend otherwise, but he enjoys listening to me read your columns and would be sadly bereft if you stopped sending them to us."

Gussie tilted her head and offered him a teasing smile. "Is that true, Specs? Are you secretly an admirer of *Lady's Weekly*'s feminist rhetoric? Or simply an admirer of me?" His face reddened, turning only a shade lighter than his hair, and Gussie laughed. "I am only teasing you, silly boy. Stand down."

Catherine gave her brother an indulgent smile. "Do you remember, Gabriel, when we were about ten and she made you play *The Light Princess*?"

Specs groaned. "No, do not resurrect that old story."

"Oh, but I must."

Gussie held up her hands. "I agree with Specs. What a terrible thing you're doing to us."

Catherine laughed and then covered her mouth with her hands, her eyes going wide. "I have not laughed like that since John died." She turned shining eyes toward Gussie. "You have brought joy back into this house." She gave Gussie a conspiratorial wink. "And now I will encourage it by recounting the story of New York's light princess."

"I will only defend myself by swearing to have never read the book." Specs covered his face with his hands and shook his head.

Catherine continued, ignoring him. "Gussie, you took the eponymous role, naturally, and Gabriel was assigned that of water. And because the light princess is not subject to gravity as ordinary things are, you hopped around the furniture, from your bed to a rickety table to your writing desk, to the chair in the corner, until you came to the middle of the room where—"

"Where I was lying on the floor, draped by that smelly moth-eaten cloak we found in the attic." Specs groaned. "And when the light princess reached the end of her journey . . ." He glared at Gussie and pointed toward his chest.

Gussie held up her hand, blushing at the memory. "She floated through the air to land gracefully beside the calm, glinting waters."

Specs rolled his eyes. "You floated as lightly as an anchor thrown off the New York Produce Exchange building. You nearly burst my spleen. And I will never live it down."

He dropped his head to the table with a gentle thud, and Catherine laughed. "Gussie, I will never forget how you flopped atop him with a decidedly inelegant grunt, and he was"—Catherine's laughter filled the corners of the room—"released of all air. For the rest of the year, you called him Wind until he practically begged to be called Specs again."

Specs raised his head and met Gussie's gaze. "And that is why I will never admonish you for assigning me such a ridiculous nickname. I know you are capable of far worse."

"You have no idea what I'm capable of." Gussie crossed her arms.

"Oh, I think I do." He tossed his napkin onto the table and stood. "I believe you are capable of nearly anything you set your mind to. Whether that is traveling to places best suited to cowboys and outlaws or ignoring basic physics or convincing a boy who had always been sensitive to the teasing of others to embrace a nickname that called attention to the thing he most despised."

He rounded the table and pressed a kiss to Catherine's temple. When he passed Gussie, he leaned down, and her heart thumped at the idea of his mouth against her skin. And what a ridiculous notion that was because he was *Specs*.

His breath whispered across her ear. "You are capable of nearly anything. I'm only hoping I won't be beneath you to break your next fall."

⁂

Gussie ended up at the boat club anyway. She and Catherine took a carriage there and watched British men in sailing whites cast off the docks in skiffs into the poetically named Mula-Mutha River. Then they walked the half mile to Bund Garden.

The garden was as well laid out as Central Park. It boasted an even greater assortment of tiered steps, grassy hills, and plants, and Gussie experienced a strange sense of knitting together. Home, which had never felt like home, and India, the place invading every hollow spot within her.

Before them, a set of curved stairs led down to a wide walkway flanked by potted plants and trees. Behind them, an arched bridge spanned the river, guarded by a Medici lion. It was all very elegant. Familiar, but in the best way possible. Novelty tempered with familiarity made for a marvelous experience.

Gussie pulled her Kodak from her satchel and tugged on the front of the camera, expanding the bellows. The sun was high and bright, eliminating all shadows, so she pulled the stop to its middle position and centered the view within the finder, straight out from her midsection. She pressed the lever and listened for the click of the shutter.

"I'm very proud of you, Gussie. And I know Gabriel teased you at breakfast, but he is as well." Catherine had never said a false word in her life, but her inherent sweetness prevented her from seeing anything but kindness in those she loved.

"Do you really think so?"

Gussie shouldn't care what Specs thought of her. And before that morning, if anyone had asked her about it, she would have vehemently denied giving his opinion a bit of notice. But for reasons she wasn't sure she wanted to understand, she always had. And when she thought he might find her wanting, something within her wanted to curl up and weep.

Gussie blew out a breath. Of all the ridiculous things to worry about.

She turned to Catherine with a bright smile and took her arm. "Let me photograph you."

"Oh no, I couldn't. Is it even proper? I'm only four months into mourning. And I'm expecting. It doesn't seem a suitable thing to do."

"What a bunch of piffle. It's not as though I'm asking you to dance a jig at a ball. Here, let me."

Gussie tugged Catherine until she stood before the handsome stone lion, the bridge stretching across the river behind her. With a more gentle touch, she took Catherine's hand and put it on her hip. Stepping back, she considered the composition, then nudged Catherine's arm so that her fingers cupped the very edge of her middle. The pose promised something more than was initially apparent.

"My featured work is always landscapes," Gussie said as she walked backward a few more feet so that she could capture Catherine's entire body, the lion, and a portion of the bridge. "But I do love taking portraits." She held the camera steady and grinned. "I particularly like people with an interesting look about them."

"You will surely be disappointed in mine, then."

Gussie took in Catherine's fair skin, bright hair, and severe clothing. And even though she yet grieved her mayfly husband, quiet grace and impending motherhood made her more beautiful than many women. "You are stunning."

Gussie pressed the lever just as Catherine's expression softened and a small smile peeked from beneath her propriety.

Gussie closed her camera and tucked it safely into its case. "Now," she said, taking Catherine's arm, "shall we go meet your friend and see Specs's workplace? I shall have to fuss over every stethoscope and vial."

"Don't tease him. He shouldn't like to be made smaller in the eyes of his patients. And I know he wishes to appear successful in yours."

"Poppycock. Your brother thinks me silly. He was only too quick yesterday to disabuse me of my arrogant assumption that I still hold a place in his affections." Gussie regretted the words the moment they slipped past her lips. She flushed and stared straight ahead, pretending interest in an ornate gazebo crowned by a tall, pointed finial. "That sounded petulant. I would only hate to think he no longer finds me amusing."

"He wants you safe, that is all. He would force me out of Poona if I let him. You know how he's always worried. And when our parents died, it only grew worse. He thinks if he works hard enough and is able to command everything around him, it will all be well. But I have learned that nothing you do or don't do has any impact on how long you might be given with someone." Catherine guided Gussie down a set of wide steps tucked between two potted hibiscus plants. "Gabriel has always been so competent. And I think all those years playing knight to your princess gave him an unattainable example to live up to."

"*Playing knight to your princess . . .*" Specs had always been there for Gussie. For every ridiculous notion she had that demanded an accomplice. For each harebrained adventure, even those that were poorly conceived and not at all planned. He had looked on her with admiration, even as he admonished her for never thinking before she jumped.

And then, when she refused to back down, he would jump with her.

She'd been easily distracted as a child, flirting with possibilities and flitting from one excitement to the next. But always—always—Specs had been there beside her. Sober and sensible and never wavering in support.

"I will not tease him today," she promised.

Catherine hailed a fine carriage, hired out by some rich merchant, she said, who turned every venture into coin. While they made their way through the city, she pointed out sprawling mansions in a mishmash of architectural styles—British, Persian, and Indian—that inexplicably created a harmonious whole. "Gabriel lived and worked in the old city before John died and he moved in with me. Ganj Peth is close to Sadar Bazaar and nearer his patients. They would never come to the camp area to see him and Dr. Paul."

"Why is that?"

"For one, it would pose a financial hardship. Their patients are unspeakably poor. That's why Etak—Dr. Paul—opened the infirmary in Ganj Peth to begin with. The people there can't afford most doctors, and the other mission hospitals are on the opposite side of the city. Plus, there are many doctors who will not touch someone of a lower caste, and these people are the lowest. When Ramabai suggested Gabriel move here after medical school, she already knew she would connect him with Etak. The doctor had more work than he could handle even before the famine and plague."

The streets narrowed, and if Gussie had reached out of the carriage, she could have touched the laundry hanging from sagging balconies like tropical birds on a branch. She could just see past screened windows where shadows played and told stories not yet fully written. The silvery sound of a flute threaded between the rattling wheels and the shouts of a man selling a kaleidoscope of birds flitting around in bamboo cages. Gussie leaned her head out the window for a better look but noticed instead an abandoned home, a red line splashed across the door.

"What's that?"

Catherine turned to look. "It marks the home of plague victims. They paint the door to let others know it's been contaminated. The occupants are moved to the plague hospital, and the building is cleared, fumigated, and whitewashed."

"Do they return home when they are well?"

Catherine's eyes followed the house as they moved past it, and her gaze grew distant. "Most don't get well, Gussie. Sixty percent die. And if they are lucky enough to survive, their homes are usually looted, their belongings lost or destroyed by officials who care little, and their family snuffed out by disease. Life is capable of great ugliness."

As they rolled on, Gussie saw an entire street of marked buildings. And she saw the bowed shoulders of the people plodding forward, stepping aside to avoid the piles of animal excrement that caused Specs to discard his shoes before entering the house. She saw clusters of nearly naked children, their ribs swallowing the shadows and standing in relief. And she wanted only to return to the Mula-Mutha River, where men called out greetings as they rowed over the water and women wandered down cleared paths.

But then she saw two young men, their gazes serious as they pondered the chessboard between them. One threw his head back and laughed, as melodious as the flute. There came the gentle sound from one of the screened windows of a woman singing to a crying baby. The sun, high now and warm against Gussie's cheeks, smoothed the rumpled lines of the city and blessed it with a kiss.

They stopped outside a two-story building boasting a second-story balcony and a heavy, recessed door set between columns. The driver helped them to the street, and they started forward.

Before they reached the door, though, Gussie tangled her fingers in Catherine's. "But also great beauty. Life offers that, as well."

Catherine smiled, and they ducked beneath the doorway. She tugged at the strap of Gussie's Kodak bag. "That is true. And I know you will do your best to capture it."

The room they entered was pierced by beams of sunlight filtering through the shutters and illuminating dancing dust motes. A few rickety benches were pushed against the wall, empty save for an old man who smiled up at them with a mouth devoid of teeth.

Catherine wiggled her fingers at him and poked her head into the room off the entry. "The office is empty. Gabriel and Etak must be with patients."

A wail pierced the silence, followed by the gasping cries of an infant. A woman, wrapped in the most delicious shade of green, appeared in the doorway that led to a hallway, clutching a baby to her chest.

Specs followed her and noticed Gussie and Catherine. "You've come."

"Did you doubt it?" Gussie asked.

He cocked his shoulder against the doorframe and crossed his arms. "I doubted you would miss an opportunity to run for the nearest deserted outpost the moment it presented itself."

Gussie smiled and pushed past him. She found herself in a narrow hall. A door opened into what looked to be a well-stocked pharmacy. Another revealed a wide-open space cut in half by a scarred table, one wall lined with sinks, and a stove boasting a bubbling cauldron. At the end of the hall, she entered a long room bearing a row of narrow cots. In the corner, wooden screens carved out a private examination area.

Two nurses, wearing white skirts, bodices, and caps, skirted cots and administered medicines. Nearly all the beds were full—men with bandaged heads and arms, groaning or watching Gussie warily, and children whose eyes burned with fever and fear. Gussie's arms tingled with the desire to hold them. To soothe and comfort. She hated to see suffering. Especially in those so young.

One of the nurses moved toward a screen and pushed it back, revealing a leather-padded medical chair boasting a frightening number of levers and moving parts. A doctor leaned over a patient, his hands prodding and his voice low.

When he straightened, Specs drew Gussie near. "Etak."

The doctor turned, and when he saw Gussie, his smile spread. "You must be Miss Travers. I am Dr. Paul, and I'm so very happy to meet you. I have heard stories of your youth and your traveling adventures for years." His hands were warm when he took hers. As warm as his voice and the joy dancing in his eyes. As warm as the Indian sun. "I have traveled extensively throughout India and England, where I went to school, but I have never had the fortune of going to your country. Dr. MacLean, though, has shared your columns with me, and through them, I feel as though I've been there."

Gussie glanced at Specs, her smile growing into a grin when his cheeks flushed.

"Dr. Paul likes to travel. I thought he might enjoy your stories." Specs coughed and hurried across the room to help a nurse struggling to bandage a patient's arm.

"He's an excellent doctor," Dr. Paul said as they watched Specs and the nurse engage in conversation. "I was grateful Ramabai convinced him to work with me."

"He's always been extremely disciplined and focused." Gussie watched as the nurse probed the patient's wound, and Specs leaned in to examine the area. His hair fell over his forehead, and he impatiently pushed it away. He stood and looked at Gussie, his brows drawing together and his mouth forming a quizzical smile when he saw her staring. Even then, she couldn't drag her eyes away from his. Couldn't stop herself from trying to figure out why this new Specs was so . . . appealing.

She shook her head as he finished his examination, went to a washbasin in the corner to rinse his hands, and then approached her. "What thoughts have you looking so twisted up?" he asked.

"Nothing." Gussie let her gaze sweep the room, as much to take it in as to keep him from reading her thoughts. "You never told me your infirmary was so large. It's quite impressive."

"It's not my infirmary. I only work here. It's Dr. Paul's infirmary."

"It is *our* infirmary. I couldn't do this work without your assistance." Dr. Paul lifted his hand in a mock salute, then crossed the room to see to a child who was scrambling away from a nurse attempting to administer medication.

Specs tucked his hands into his jacket pockets. "Do you really like it?" He stared at her, his jaw working to contain emotions she was sure he didn't want revealed.

She admired his restraint. She had so little of it. Had spent a lifetime saying and doing as she wished. She suddenly wanted nothing more than to win his regard. She'd always assumed she had it but had never deserved it. Not really. "I do. I'm honored to call you my friend."

She didn't know another man like him. Not one person of her acquaintance could claim half the charity Specs owned. After completing his education at the College of Physicians of Philadelphia a year early, he'd been offered a position at Philadelphia's most respected hospital and asked to teach at the Women's Medical College. He stayed in Pennsylvania only another ten months, giving up what promised to be a successful career to serve in India. Under another man's legacy. He gave and gave and gave.

Her eyes dropped to his shoes, scuffed and out of date, standing pigeon-toed the way he had when they were children and he was spouting some *amazing fact* no one else in the world could possibly care to know. But she'd always cared. Because he had cared for her.

Catherine joined them, and Gussie stood between her and

Specs, just as it had always been. His arm brushed Gussie's shoulder, and if she leaned just slightly, she could rest her head against it. Not many men were tall enough to enable such a thing. And it suddenly seemed as though they were made to fit together.

"I'm sorry for teasing you this morning," she said. "I was still a little hurt, I think, because you didn't seem happy to see me yesterday, and I wanted so badly to see you."

He patted her shoulder the way she'd seen him do to Catherine a million times. And for reasons beyond her understanding, it felt more like a slap than affection. "I only meant for you to be safe. I worry enough over Catherine, and she doesn't court danger."

"I know. I'll leave tomorrow, if you truly wish it."

Catherine took her arm. "No! Don't make her, Gabe. I want her to stay. She is safe enough from the plague. There have been no cases where we live. Only that one nurse at the plague hospital, but she was spit on by a patient. Right in the eye. Gussie has no reason at all to visit the plague hospital."

Specs's hand slipped from her shoulder and rested against the dip of her back, his fingers warm and firm, during Catherine's speech. Gussie's eyes slid closed, and she wondered at the sensation prickling her scalp, crawling down her neck, and shivering across her shoulders. It was only Gabriel MacLean, after all.

Dr. Paul joined them. "You know it's unlikely she will come down with it living with Catherine in the suburban municipality. And we don't see plague patients here. She's as safe in Poona as anywhere else in India." He gave Specs a curious sort of wink. "If that's what really has you worried."

Specs narrowed his eyes and dropped his hand. "Very well. I could almost never say no to Gussie when we were younger, and I don't suppose that's changed very much, especially with the two of you declaring your support." His eyes met hers. "You have to listen to my advice, though. No wandering into misadventures."

Catherine gave a trembly laugh. "She will be the very picture of decorum."

Specs snorted. "I look forward to seeing that."

"I used to live here," Specs said as Gussie and Catherine followed him up the narrow staircase to the second floor of the infirmary. "When I moved in with Catherine, our nurses took this apartment. They have a private entrance outside, but this allows them quick access to our patients. Dr. Paul lives on the outskirts of Ganj Peth."

Gussie didn't have time to question him, for a woman, her head and face nearly entirely swathed in a scarf, opened the door and ushered them inside.

"Hello, Bimla. We've come to see Amma," Specs said.

She dipped her head but peered out from beneath the hem of her scarf at Gussie. "Amma is rolling mats in the bedroom. She will be out in a moment." Her words rolled slowly from her tongue as though she were tasting each one before speaking. "I've prepared tea." She froze, and her gaze fell to the floor. Hesitation and uncertainty wrapped her, palpable and heavy.

"Oh," Gussie said, clapping her hands together, "how did you know? I'm absolutely famished and was just thinking how much I wanted tea."

Bimla gave a nod, and when she lifted her head, a small smile tilted the corners of her full lips.

"Yes, Bimla," another woman said as she came from the far room, "tea sounds wonderful."

"Amma." Catherine met the woman in the middle of the room, and they grasped hands. "How good it is to see you." She waved Gussie forward. "I want you to meet my dear friend Augusta Travers. Gussie, this is Pandita Ramabai Sarasvati."

The woman waved her hand. "Please, my girls call me Amma."

They settled in chairs and settees around a low table, and as Bimla began pouring tea, Gussie studied the two women. Though both wore white saris, the garments were only similar insofar as color and drape were concerned. Whereas Bimla seemed to disappear beneath the folds, only her black eyes visible as she pressed the scarf over her nose, Ramabai was framed by the fabric, her eyes snapping in contrast. Gussie had never been so drawn to do a portrait before. The two women together presented a striking composition.

Specs shifted beside Gussie and took the teacup Bimla held out to him. "I trust your stay has been restful and productive, Ramabai."

She inclined her head. "Productive, yes. Restful? Not this time. The probationers have been settled at Sassoon Hospital, and I am leaving for Mukti Mission in the morning. There I will rest." She turned the full brilliance of her smile on Gussie. "I hope your journey here was a good one. Did you set upon any storms over the Atlantic Ocean?"

Gussie shook her head. "No. All was as calm as church."

Specs pressed his lips together and lifted his cup, his gaze meeting hers over the rim and telling her he knew her thoughts. Knew she'd have reveled in a storm. At least a small one.

Ramabai didn't yet know Gussie's proclivity for peril. "When I went to your country a decade ago, I thought the ship would be overcome by waves."

"Did you enjoy your visit to the United States?"

"Yes, of course. And I also came to know your Dr. MacLean while there."

Gussie grinned at Specs, whose neck turned a vivid red. "Is he my Dr. MacLean?"

"Don't tease him." Catherine laughed. "Amma, Gussie is possessed of a singular desire to see my brother blush at every turn."

Specs found his voice. "My aunt, when she taught at the Women's Medical College, heard that Ramabai was coming to witness the graduation of India's first female medical school graduate, a relative of hers. I was hardly more than a child, but Catherine and I were invited to have dinner with her. It is she who encouraged my pursuit of a medical degree and who invited me to India when she heard of my discontent in Philadelphia."

"You were discontent after graduation? I never knew. Why did you not come home to New York?" Gussie tilted her head, a yearning for what could have been coiling in her belly. If he had returned, Catherine with him, how might her life have been different? Would she have found contentment in their friendship and acceptance? Would she have even wanted to leave and chase other things?

"I felt God calling me to something else, and I could never forget the stories Ramabai told us over that dinner about the struggles of women in India. About the child-widows and victims of famine and lack of any real opportunity for them to free themselves of the shackles forced upon them by virtue of their sex. And then there was you."

Gussie tilted her head. "Me? What have I to do with any of that?"

Behind his spectacles, Specs blinked, and she noticed how long his lashes were—nearly brushing the glass. A slow smile curved his cheeks, and wrinkles crept from the corners of his eyes. "You've always said your greatest desire was to free women from the bondage of respectability. That you thought your sex should shake off expectations and forge the path they thought God, not society, laid for them. And compared to those ambitions, mine—of a comfortable, safe life—seemed sad and limp. I knew you would use every talent at your disposal to pursue bigger things. I guess I didn't want to lose myself to small dreams."

Gussie's mouth had fallen open at the start of his speech and grown wider with each word. She snapped it closed. "I had no idea."

All the years she'd known him, Gussie had thought Specs possessed little passion and even less courage. He'd been her willing, sometimes crotchety companion, and she hardly ever gave a thought to his own desires and dreams. How wrong she'd been. She wiped her hands on her skirt and lifted the teacup to her lips, if only to distract herself from the cloud of confusion that had settled over her since discovering Specs had grown up.

"Miss Travers, what is it you are doing in India?" Ramabai asked.

"Call me Gussie, please." She forced her attention off Specs and onto the fascinating woman sitting on the settee across from them. "I'm a columnist and photographer with the magazine *Lady's Weekly*. I travel and take photographs and write about my experiences."

"Gussie's column is one of the country's most popular." Catherine preened like a mother hen.

"How wonderful." Ramabai glanced between them. "Would you consider spending some time in Kedgaon village with us? I have so wanted to have photographs taken to send to our supporters in England and the United States. They understand the work we do here in Poona, but Mukti Mission is new."

"Oh, that would be an adventure." Gussie would have to telegram Lillian and convince her that their readers would be interested in rural Maharashtra—at least for one issue. Having sent only four stories before heading to Poona, she didn't have much time before she needed to mail the next set of columns. It would be interesting to interview Ramabai in the way she had Luisa Corsetti, but she wouldn't even attempt to convince Lillian of the merit of the idea. It didn't seem likely that Ramabai's work lent itself to anything remotely light and airy. "I'm familiar with the work you do here in Poona with the widows, but what is it you do at Mukti Mission?"

"Mukti Mission is where I brought my famine orphans. I tried bringing them here, but the authorities insisted they go somewhere else, as there were hundreds of them. I obtained a working farm outside Kedgaon village years ago, and it seemed a good place to settle children who had lost their parents and health. They needed clean air and abundant food, and we've been able to give them that. They would enjoy meeting a photographer from the United States."

Catherine scooted to the edge of her seat and leaned forward, her eyes, so like her brother's, gleaming mahogany. "I could join you, Gussie. What fun we would have."

Beside her, Specs hooked his foot over a knee and tapped his fingers against his leg. "That's half a day's journey. How long would they be gone?"

"They could stay a week and return with me when I come back to Poona," Ramabai said. "My rest in the country is to be a short one, for I've work that must be done here."

Gussie clapped her hands. "I love this idea. Something new to see. Children to love. People to meet. It will be an adventure." She sent Specs a playful smile. "Whatever will you do to keep yourself occupied without me, though?"

Her attempt at teasing drew the strangest response. When he turned toward her, his expression spoke of so many things she'd never seen in him. Desperation and passion and a masculine energy that seemed incongruent on the face of the boy she had known as bookish and sensible and not tossed by human emotion.

Gussie swallowed hard, only able to speak past the lump in her throat because she forced herself to break Specs's gaze and focus instead on the threadbare carpet beneath her feet. "This sounds like a wonderful opportunity, Ramabai. I'd be honored to visit Mukti Mission."

It would give her space from Specs and the baffling, dreadful confusion he subjected her to.

9

The next day, they passed a pleasant eight hours in the carriage Ramabai had hired to take them to Kedgaon. Gussie sat beside Catherine, and across from them, Ramabai shared a bench with Bimla, who'd been given time away from the infirmary so she could address some of the health concerns plaguing the staff and children at Mukti Mission.

Something about Bimla drew Gussie's interest. Maybe because she was again draped head to toe in a white sari and made such an effort to hide behind the scarf she had tucked around her face and behind her shoulder. Bimla didn't speak. She instead looked out on the scrubby brush and scattered villages outside the window, but she kept an ear turned toward their chatter.

"You're very quiet," Gussie said with a laugh when their conversation dwindled. "I'm not sure I've ever gone so long without speaking."

Bimla turned from the window and pinched the fluttering edge of her scarf, pulling it more tightly around her face. She inclined her head.

"She is shy about her accent," Ramabai said, "though she has acquired English almost as quickly as she has her nursing skills. She has only been with me a year."

"I spoke a little English before. My father worked for a family in the cantonment." Bimla worried the pleats of her sari between long, tapered fingers.

"And you were trained as a nurse through Sharada Sadan?"

"Yes. I am a widow of five years."

"Five years! Why, you don't sound any older than I am."

"I am twenty. I was married at eight years old and went to live with my husband when childhood ended. My in-laws turned me out of the house when they grew tired of me, and I went to my parents' home."

Ramabai turned to Gussie. "She is being very modest. Her in-laws reside in Barsi, a hundred and thirty miles from Poona. It took her almost a week to arrive home. She had no shoes, no food, and only the water spared by kind people along the way."

Bimla dropped her head, a thick braid slipping past the hem of her scarf and revealing a cheek puckered by scars. Gussie's quick intake of breath caused Bimla to grasp the fabric and turn her head away.

"I'm sorry. I didn't mean to upset you. I was only startled."

Ramabai patted Bimla's knee and said something in Marathi, waiting for Bimla's nod and whispered response. "She said to tell you her story, for nothing will change if she isn't brave enough to share it. After her husband died and she returned home, her parents and brother refused to acknowledge her. She wandered the streets for weeks, begging, until a cousin took her in as a servant. But his wife was a cruel woman and beat her, often with rods. She took great sport in stabbing Bimla's face with her hairpins and cutting her with a kitchen knife. Bimla was beautiful, and her cousin had taken to forcing himself upon her, which riled his wife's jealousy. Many of her wounds grew infected, and they never properly healed. Bimla heard of Sharada Sadan, my mission in Poona, and took refuge with us, where she improved her English, learned to read and write, and studied to become a nurse. She began working with Dr. Paul and Dr. MacLean only a couple of months ago."

"I begged my mother-in-law to keep me, but she said I was unlucky. That even looking upon my face would cause hardship for the rest of the family. After I was cast out and I returned to Poona, I wept and asked my mother not to send me away." Bimla's fingers brushed the inside hem of her scarf, as elegant as any woman in Mrs. Astor's Four Hundred. "I only learned what it was to belong after I met Amma."

"There is injustice everywhere," Ramabai said. "Every country, every culture, shares in a history of victimization and cruelty. But so often those who suffer most are women and children. They are used and cast aside. God could have set me in any place, any era, and I would have had the opportunity to minster to the oppressed. But he set me here. Now. I will not waste it."

Ramabai only spoke of herself, but Gussie lifted her own work in comparison and found it lacking. She had stumbled into it, only seeking an escape from the vacuousness of life in a Fifth Avenue mansion. And it had distracted her enough, at first. It gave her something to look forward to. Something to *do*. But now, listening to Ramabai and Bimla, she wondered . . . all her work, her striving, her running . . . did it really mean anything?

Fortunately, they rumbled up a long dirt drive soon after Gussie's thoughts turned unaccountably dreary. A swarm of girls, swathed in threadbare saris and waving skinny arms above their heads, surrounded the carriage.

"Amma! Amma!" they shouted, their voices a choir of joy, when the driver helped Ramabai to the ground. She walked among them, touching their heads in blessing. Stopping to whisper in the ear of one, cupping the cheek of another.

Bimla pushed the scarf from her head, and Gussie couldn't look away from the joy and peace written on her face, transforming an act of violence into something that looked very much like love. "Amma has lifted these children from death. Offered them freedom and life. They will never forget that. She has impacted so many. Future generations will call her blessed."

Gussie's chest ached with longing. Had she ever felt such things for a person? Had she ever been loved enough for someone else to feel such things for her?

Never. The word, that hateful, twisting word, spun around her thoughts. Consumed them. *You will never learn. You will never manage it. You will never understand.*

Never.

An icy chill passed over her despite the sun's benevolence, and she swallowed against the memories threatening to choke her. Her fingers tightened around the carriage doorway, knuckles turning white as she looked out on the scene.

Ramabai returned and lightly touched Gussie's hand. "Come. They want to meet you."

Gussie disembarked, tripping a little over her skirts and feeling as though she were about to face Mr. Epps again instead of a cluster of children. In Marathi, Ramabai introduced her, though Gussie only understood her name, and when Ramabai said something of particular interest, the children cheered, easing the band around Gussie's chest.

Ramabai waved them silent. "They are very excited to have their photographs taken. Most of them have never even seen a camera."

"I'm happy to be here." Gussie looked out over the smiling faces and noted a few with interesting features, many with beautiful bone structures, one with deep dimples that made her heart dance at the girl's loveliness. Maybe she would make copies of some of the photographs. And one day, when she stumbled across one tucked between the pages of a forgotten book or opened a hat box to discover a far-flung memory, she would remember Ramabai and what great things could be accomplished by a single woman.

Catherine spoke, interrupting Gussie's thoughts. "All of these girls were early victims of last year's famine. They lost their parents. Had it not been for Ramabai, many would be dead. You should have seen them, Gussie. They were all so frail. Some of them wrapped in rags. They could hardly gather the energy to lift themselves from the carts as they were brought here. And now they are building this place."

"These shelters are only temporary," Ramabai said. "Very soon we hope to build more permanent structures."

Gussie looked out at the makeshift buildings scattered over the dusty space that had been cleared of brush and stomped down by hundreds of feet. It didn't look like much—Deadwood was luxurious in comparison—but Gussie could envision what it would become. "I am happy to have a part in the building of this place."

Brick by brick, photograph by photograph.

Four days into their stay, Gussie dug through her satchel. She sighed and pushed the bag off her lap. The cot beneath her—a *charpai*, Ramabai had called it when she first showed them their room—creaked. Catherine, who lay on the charpai beside her, removed her arm from over her eyes and looked at Gussie.

"I only have one roll of film left. Six photographs, Catherine. That's all. I don't imagine there is a studio in Kedgaon?"

Catherine laughed. "Likely not. There will be too much movement to capture anything today at the children's practice, so save it for the photographs you want to take of Amma with some of them."

Gussie loaded the remaining roll of film into her camera. "These children are so darling that I've struggled to moderate myself. I want to capture each and every one of them. Did you see the girl with dimples? The deep ones that show though she doesn't smile?"

"That is Anjali. I don't know much about her story except that Amma found her nearly perished from exhaustion. Everyone in her village had died of famine, and she was using her hands to dig graves for her family. She'd only managed to bury her baby brother."

"Oh." Gussie blinked away tears. "How sad. I had no idea these things were happening."

Catherine sighed and swung her feet to the floor. "All over the world. But today the children are safe and fed and are looking forward to sharing with us the stories and songs they have been practicing, so let's give them a captive audience."

Gussie took Catherine's hand, and they walked toward the area between the buildings that had been cleared in preparation for the academic event. In the distance, the Western Ghats peeked at them from behind a coronet of wispy clouds. Nearer, palms and trees heavy with fruit encircled Mukti Mission, lending it the feeling of being nearer myth than real life.

The shouts and chatter of over two hundred children disabused Gussie of the fanciful thought as they neared the gathering. She laughed as little girls surrounded them, touching their skirts and offering garlands of flowers. She bent to allow a child to lay one over her head.

Ramabai shooed the girls away, then motioned them toward a cluster of wooden chairs where she sat with Bimla and a few of the senior staff. Gussie took the seat beside Bimla and turned so she could scan the crowd for little Anjali, who had so captured her heart. Even more so now, after learning her story. Gussie had watched the child keeping to the fringes of gatherings all week. Doing nothing to bring attention to herself. Quietly taking in everything around her. She had waited while everyone else ate. Waited until Gussie found herself alone. And then she crept into the silence, slipping her hand into Gussie's and running her fingers cautiously over the Kodak.

"They are beginning." Bimla touched Gussie's shoulder, drawing her around.

Gussie swiveled and saw the first group of girls stepping forward, shy smiles giving way to sweet voices. "What are they singing?"

"It is a hymn by Hari Govind Kelkar about how the Bible offers us hope."

Gussie sat back and watched the girls with greater attention. That they could endure such suffering and still sing of hope denied power to the harshest experience. The harshest critic.

While the third group of girls recited a flurry of math drills, Gussie again turned in her seat and looked over the crowd of enraptured children. "Do you know where Anjali is? The quiet child with the dimples."

Bimla pulled her attention from the dancers and shrugged. "I assumed she would be with the others. She did not want to take part today."

"She's not here." Gussie inched forward in her chair. "Maybe I should check and see that she is well. Should I tell Amma?"

Bimla glanced at Ramabai, then shook her head. "No. The girls would notice if she left, and it would cause a commotion. I will come with you, and we will look for Anjali together and see if there is a problem."

They slipped away from the gathering.

"She sleeps over there." Bimla pointed to one of the shelters. "I am sure she is well."

Before they even reached the doorway, though, Gussie heard a whimper. She pushed at the rough wooden door and found herself in a one-room space, similar to the one she'd shared with Catherine all week, only longer and boasting two rows of charpais. "Anjali?"

Her gaze skipped over the puddles of light filtering from the open spaces between the roof and walls as she searched the shadows. On the far charpai, tucked into the corner of the room, a tiny curled form shifted.

"Oh no!" Gussie hurried down the middle of the room, her skirts brushing the cots as she passed. She touched Anjali's pale forehead and looked up at Bimla. "She is very warm."

Anjali murmured something, and Bimla made a soft sound in her throat. "She says she is sorry she missed the singing, but she lay down for a moment because she was tired, and when she awoke, everyone was gone and she felt ill."

"Oh, poor child."

"Sit with her. I will return with tulsi tea to help bring down her fever."

After Bimla left, Gussie sat on the charpai beside Anjali's, her knees bumping against the opposite frame. Anjali looked up at her with wary, fever-heated eyes.

"When I used to get sick," Gussie said, knowing Anjali couldn't understand but hoping she would be comforted anyway, "my nanny would sing me a song." Never her parents, though. No matter how often she asked for them. She could still feel Nanny's fingers, firm and tender, as she stood in the gap for those who should have been there. "'Lavender's blue, dilly, dilly . . .'" Gussie began.

She didn't sing even half as well as she played the piano, but Anjali's breathing slowed, her face relaxed, and she turned on her side and cupped Gussie's hands against her chest.

"I think she's asleep," Gussie told Bimla when she appeared carrying a tray and stack of rags a few minutes later.

"You like children." Bimla set the tray on the floor, careful to steady the clattering teacup. She knelt beside it and swirled one of the rags in a bowl of water.

"I do." Gussie lifted her other hand to brush back the sweep of hair hiding Anjali's face so that Bimla could lay the rag over her forehead. "They are everything lovely about the world. Innocent."

"I was married before I reached Anjali's age. There was no innocence. Not for me. Not for many of the children here."

"I suppose not."

"And your childhood? It was innocent?"

"Much of it. Until I turned fourteen."

"What happened then?"

"Nothing so terrible as marriage or famine, but that is when my parents acquired what they thought they wanted and when they realized they no longer wanted me."

Not good enough for a Travers. Try harder. Do better.

"They abandoned you?"

Gussie removed the rag that had grown warm with Anjali's fever and put it back in the water. "Not physically," she said as she wrung it out, droplets making music in the bowl.

Bimla got to her feet and sat beside Gussie. "The pain is the same, though." She traced circles on her sari. "I cried for my mother when I first went to my husband's house. Every minute of those first days. Then every hour. Then every day. Until I realized she would never come."

"*Nanny, I want Mother. Why won't she come?*" Gussie had thrashed on her bed, the fever filling her blood. Her thoughts. Her tears. Even then. Even during the years Gussie remembered as being touched by light and love, her parents had chosen other things. Other people.

"What do you do with that pain?" Gussie asked. "Sometimes I think it will consume me."

"I have poured it into nursing. I take my hurt and turn it into healing. It is a redemption." Bimla reached for Gussie's hand, their fingers tangling much the way their stories had. "And you, Gussie? What have you done with your pain?"

Anjali blinked her eyes open, and a scratchy moan crawled from her throat. Bimla stood and lifted the cup of tea. Steam still lifted from it, perfuming the air with something pungent.

As Bimla helped Anjali take a sip, Gussie considered the question. What had she done with her pain? She had buried it deep. She had run from it. She had dabbled in rebellion and filled her days with every type of adventure.

"I have done very little with it, I'm afraid," she whispered when Bimla set the cup back down and resettled beside her.

Anjali, her expression sagging with misery, spilled tears onto the thin rope cot that cradled her. Gussie cupped her cheek and murmured comfort.

"It seems you have done something wonderful with your pain," Bimla said. "You have turned it into love."

On her last full day before heading back to Poona, Gussie attempted to corral a group of the smallest children around the chair where Ramabai sat making clicking noises with her tongue. "These girls are so naughty."

Gussie laughed as Ramabai grabbed the arm of one who zipped past, pulling the child onto her lap and covering her face with a dozen kisses.

"Now I have you trapped. Quickly, Gussie, take it before she escapes."

Gussie knew Ramabai wasn't joking. Each photo she'd taken most likely included the blur of a child darting off. She centered the scene in her viewfinder and pressed the lever, grateful for the opportunity to capture images that only a handful of years earlier would have been impossible. It allowed her the opportunity to freeze time. Remember lovely things.

When she looked up, the girls scattered. Gussie noticed Bimla walking toward a large tamarind tree, the canopy wider than its height. She leaned against the trunk, staring up into its branches. Her movements were as lissome as a Degas ballet dancer.

Standing far enough away that she could capture the entire tamarind tree, its dried brown fruit hanging from the branches like clusters of arthritic fingers, as well as Bimla's draped form, Gussie readied her camera. Her last picture at Mukti Mission. She wished she'd packed more film, but how could she have known what beautiful things she would see here?

Most beautiful was the friendship that had grown between her and Bimla over the two days they'd cared for Anjali, sitting beside her bed and wiping her brow and feeding her buttermilk spiked with spices. Bimla was beautiful. More than that, she was a surprise. And when Anjali's fever broke, it seemed something had been knit between them.

Gussie smiled down at Ramabai, who watched her in silence. But there were questions behind her lovely eyes.

Gussie sighed and, heedless of the dirt, sat on the ground at Ramabai's feet. She didn't resist the tug of this woman. Who could? "Bimla has endured so much."

"She has," Ramabai said.

Gussie ran her fingers through the dust, creating patterns that meant nothing, and lifted her chin. The sky was clear and blue, great downy clouds traveling across it in a flock. "Yet I'm a little envious of her, despite what she's been through."

"Why?" Ramabai's warm hand found Gussie's head, and she knew why all the children gathered around her, clamoring for her attention. There was something in the press of her palm, the sweep of her fingers that made things seem right. It wasn't a thunderbolt. Nothing that spoke of power. It was comfort and peace and softness. It was compassion. It was the reflection of a broken savior stretched over a cross.

Gussie blinked, retrieving the tears that clung to her lashes. She wouldn't cry in front of this woman who had experienced so much, seen so much. She had no right to weep. Not when Bimla had suffered untold abuse. No right to feel scattered to capricious winds. Not when her life had been safe, and she'd been afforded so many opportunities. No right, at all, to wonder if she would spend a lifetime running toward something she didn't know the name of.

"There's purpose in her work, isn't there?" Gussie said. "She knows what she's doing, and she's good at it. She's needed."

"And you don't feel that way about your own work?"

Bimla pushed away from the tree and walked back toward the cluster of buildings, soon finding herself in a game of chase with a trio of skinny toddlers running between twisting laburnum trees. The sun was setting now, draping everything in amber and citrine.

"I like to think it does, but it all feels so empty. I love photography and writing. I tell myself I'm encouraging women to pursue their dreams. But nothing I do ever feels like enough."

"Who does it need to be enough for?"

Gussie turned away from the sky's fresco and looked at Ramabai. "For everyone, I suppose."

"Well, now, that might be the problem. You do not need to be enough for everyone. You do not even need to be enough for God. You cannot be. So your striving is in vain. Bimla has found purpose because she walks in the knowledge of that. There is no more *must* or *should*. It is all love." Ramabai slipped from her chair and knelt in the dirt beside Gussie. Together, they watched the sun make its final statement. "If you embraced that freedom, what would you do? Where would you find your purpose?"

Gussie thought of that day in Mr. Epps's and Lillian's offices. He would not publish the types of things she wrote. She didn't think Gussie capable of being anyone but Miss Adventuress.

But there were so many words waiting to be told. And they sprang up within her like water from a well. "I want to tell stories," whispered Gussie. "They are everywhere. I see them, and I want to share them. But more than the type I write now. More than the things I capture on film. I want to tell stories that *matter*. I want to share pictures of things that change people. But I have no idea what that could look like and . . . is it even enough?"

"Even Christ told stories, Gussie. There is power in them."

"I'm afraid I'll fail."

Ramabai smiled. "'Perfect love casteth out fear.' Stop running from the things God has called you to because you're afraid what others will think."

And Gussie let herself cry.

10

When they arrived back at Catherine's bungalow late the next afternoon, Gussie threw herself onto one of the settees in the sitting room and heaved a great sigh. "That was fun." She eyed Catherine's belly as her friend settled into the chair on the other side of the Agra carpet. "But children are exhausting."

Catherine laughed. "Especially two hundred of them."

"Memsahib, a telegram came while you were away."

Gussie pulled her arm from her eyes and saw a servant holding out a silver tray. She bolted upright.

"Who is it from?" Catherine leaned forward as Gussie slipped her finger beneath the envelope's flap and withdrew the message.

"Lillian." Gussie's eyes scanned the message, and her lips pinched. "It's a response to the message I sent her before leaving for Mukti Mission." Her shoulders sank as she scanned it. "She says no one wants to read about dull rural areas. That I have been paid half my salary upfront, and I must not disappoint her. Or my readers." She glanced at Catherine and lifted her shoulder in a nonchalant shrug that would fool no one, least of all her dearest friend.

Catherine rose from her chair and joined Gussie on the settee. She leaned over, her eyes traveling the length of Lillian's message. Gussie knew when she reached the most hurtful portion by her gasp. "'You are not the only person who can be Miss Adventuress.'" Catherine smacked the card, freeing it from Gussie's fingers, in a rare display of temper. "You have done nothing to deserve her scorn."

Gussie bent to retrieve the telegram. "I knew my questions might not be received well. There really isn't much at Mukti Mission that would excite Miss Adventuress." Augusta Travers was another thing entirely.

"Well, I think *Lady's Weekly* is lucky to have you. You could be writing any manner of things, and here she is, treating you as though you're expendable."

"What would I write?" Gussie laughed, but the sound was hollow. "*I want to tell stories. Stories that matter. Pictures that change people.*" She shook her head. She hadn't even known those desires had settled into her heart until they spilled at Ramabai's feet. She didn't know what to do with them now. "Besides, I've given my word. I've been paid, and I need to meet my obligations. Though I wish she hadn't been quite so harsh."

Catherine folded her arms, frost curtaining her eyes as she gazed at the telegram, and Gussie's nerves settled in the face of her friend's loyalty.

"I will need to write a few columns while I'm here in Poona. Would you help me decide where to go?"

"I suppose . . ." Catherine's arms fell to her side, and she bit her lip, eyes squinted at the ceiling. "How about we pack a picnic lunch and go to Parvati Hill? There's a lake and a temple. It's beautiful. Perhaps Gabriel can join us. He's worked every day for over a month."

A strange thrill zipped through Gussie that she did her best to ignore. She was only looking forward to an adventure, as small as it promised to be. It had nothing at all to do with spending the day with Specs. He was one of her oldest friends, after all, and more like a brother than an actual man.

But the next morning, Specs helped her into the tanga, and as she thanked him, he settled across from her, his eyes luminous as honey. She'd never noticed how they glowed.

She nearly dropped her camera bag when she recognized something startling. She did not think of Gabriel MacLean—at least not this new, handsome, so incredibly *charming* Gabriel Maclean—as a brother.

Except she was Miss Adventuress. Falling for her friend, settling in one place, and becoming a missus didn't fit into her plan. Even worse, though, would be falling for her friend and him not wanting her in return.

That seemed a more likely scenario. Gussie had a knack for wishing more than anything to win the regard of people who were not terribly impressed with her.

She stiffened her back and clutched her camera case, eyeing the lace spilling from her sleeves with a frown. She'd passed over her practical ready-mades that morning. Reached instead for this walking gown the color of the sky. Knowing it set off her blue eyes. Acknowledging how the Swiss waist enhanced her curves.

For *him*.

She set her gaze outside the tanga so she didn't accidentally meet his eyes and tried to ignore the tangible sense of calm that had settled over her when he'd climbed inside. How could she have let this happen?

"Are you all right?" Specs asked as the driver eased the cart into traffic. "You're pale."

He reached across the tanga and pressed the backs of his fingers against her forehead. They were warm, and his touch was softer than any man had a right to claim.

She leaned into it, and her eyes closed.

"You don't feel feverish."

Gussie jerked away, aware of how she must look. "It's only very hot here. I'm not ill."

He nodded, but behind his glasses, Gussie noticed a wrinkle between his brows. He looked so endearing. So completely adorable.

And she couldn't take her eyes off him the rest of the trip to Parvati Hill.

Could she tell him?

"You never do the right thing."

Would he want her?

"Who will ever want you?"

What would make her worthy of him?

"You will be the ruin of us, Augusta."

With every question came a rebuttal. A reminder of her failures. Of her inadequacy.

The moment the cart squeaked to a stop, she leapt from it and darted toward a large tree shading the banks of a placid lake.

Specs's laugh chased her. "What are you running from?"

She swept her arm around the tree trunk before she hurtled headlong into the water and swung her head around. He'd followed her. "From you, of course." From her suddenly inconvenient desire for him.

How far would she have to run to escape it? Would Udaipur be far enough? That was where she planned to go after leaving Poona. Or would she have to cross a continent? An ocean? She couldn't allow herself to be rejected. Not by him.

He grinned when he reached her and set down the picnic basket. "You're hiding something. What's wrong?"

Despite the futility, she again attempted to ignore his presence. "Your instinct grows irritating, Specs."

"I'm a doctor. I can't help it. Kind of like how you can't help gravity."

Catherine reached them. "Leave her alone, Gabe. She's entitled to her own thoughts." She glared at him, which was as threatening as a kitten yawning, but he listened.

"It's pretty here," Gussie said, desperate for a distraction.

Specs sighed and shifted so that he fully faced the lake. "It is. Peaceful."

"Magical."

"Charming."

"Enchanting." Catherine looked up from where she sat unpacking the basket, joining their childhood game.

Gussie bit her lip. This was familiar. This was how it was supposed to be. "Otherworldly."

"Oh, the writer is a show-off." Specs bumped her shoulder, and they stared in silence at the water that reflected the trees sprouting from a rocky island in the middle of it. At the boat bouncing against the island's shore and the three men who stepped from it, dhotis flapping as they took the stone stairs and disappeared into the brush. Above them, a barren hill rose like the hump of a sleeping giant from a cloud of mist clinging to the earth despite the sun, tamarind trees and footpaths clawing its banks. A complex of temples adorned the crest.

Gussie's heart settled into a tranquil, rhythmic beat, fear conquered. For the moment, at least. How strange. It seemed Poona had accomplished what her parents despaired of her ever possessing. It calmed her.

Catherine leaned back on her heels. "You should go nearer the water. I'll prepare lunch."

Specs's touch on her elbow compelled her forward, and they walked toward the lake, picking their way over stony outcroppings and dusty mounds sprouting clumps of grass. Specs didn't say anything at first, and Gussie allowed herself to rest in his presence. Enjoy his company and the quiet.

But then it felt as though she was enjoying it too much. Her breath rattled in her chest, and the *wanting* of him practically vibrated between her ribs.

She stooped to pinch a rock between her fingers. "I bet I can still beat you."

He snorted. "I haven't skipped rocks in years, and I think you might have been practicing for this moment of glory, so I won't argue."

She turned to look up at him, her fingers rubbing the smooth surface of the stone. His mouth quirked in that funny way he had when he was trying not to laugh, the sun casting his face in shadows and filling in the angles of his jaw and cheeks and throat. Her breath caught. How could she think to ignore him? How had she never noticed him?

She'd always thought him a little boring. Too thoughtful and bookish. Her heart had never raced around him. Shivers had never traveled her spine. He had never filled her dreams.

But now he stood there, so earnest and sincere, and that suddenly felt like more than enough. It felt like too much to contend with.

Gussie straightened and, with a movement as practiced as Specs had presumed, flung the rock toward the water, where it twirled and bounced.

Specs counted, his voice round with laughter. "One, two, three, four, five, six, seven, eight, nine, ten, eleven, twelve, thirteen, fourteen."

Then the stone sank beneath the water as though exhausted from its journey.

Gussie turned a triumphant smile on him. "Your turn."

He smirked and lifted a stone—too round and jagged.

"I win!"

"I haven't even thrown it yet."

"You don't need to. That stone will sink like a boulder."

He narrowed his eyes, set his body at an angle the way she'd taught him when they were eight—he hadn't forgotten all her lessons—and the rock sailed.

Then sank.

"I win!" She twirled, but before she could raise her arms in victory, she found herself lifted into the air.

"I'm going to try with something a little larger. And louder. Will you skip or sink, Gussie?"

She shrieked. "You better not. I will sit on you the entire way home, and you will be as wet as I."

Specs stilled, his arms tightening around her, and she touched his chest. Just to steady herself. Not to feel the pounding of his heart, nearly as fast as her own. Not to press against his shirt with fingers that had only a moment ago smoothed over the firm lines of a stone. Sinking. She was sinking.

His throat moved. "I . . . I'm not sure I would mind that overmuch."

A cough sounded behind them, and he practically tossed her to the ground.

"Lunch is ready," Catherine called, her words tripping over the water as though they were weightless. "And it seems you are too. Finally."

Gussie's eyes widened, and she looked up at Specs, but he was already striding away as though something a sight more frightening than an old friend were chasing him.

11

Gussie sat at the desk in her room the next morning, paper before her and pen in hand. She'd jotted down a few lines:

Parvati Hill rises above the city, colorfully painted towers poking into misty clouds. The city is dotted with temples, their golden domes reflecting the sun that is ever present. Ruined fortresses whisper tales of love and betrayal.

Their picnic lunch had been enchanting, made more so by the storybook setting and stirrings of romance. It would make for a sentimental column. Which had always been enough before but now seemed insipid. "Vacuous. Insubstantial." Gussie scratched her head with the tip of her pen and scowled at her words. "Jejune."

She'd come to India for adventure, but from the moment she'd arrived, it seemed as though the country had every intention of unwinding all the layers Gussie had wrapped round and round her heart.

But beneath the layers gilded by light lie shadows that promise all may not be right in . . .

Gussie blinked away the image of Bimla huddled in the corner of the carriage, shrouded in white, and read over the words she'd scrawled. She shook her head and slashed through them.

A sigh scraped its way from her throat, and she scribbled a title. *A Day in Poona: Queen of the Deccan.* Instead of shadows, she would focus on the city's green beauty, the crumbling forts that told stories of strength and defeat, and the manmade lake that set off a temple-studded hill the way a colorful scarf framed the face of a beautiful woman.

And then she had to leave. Because as much as she loved Poona, its charms wouldn't fill more than one column. Maybe two.

Perhaps it was for the best.

She tapped her pen against the paper, watching as ink sprayed. "Focus. Work."

India is like a thousand little countries connected not by language, religion, or custom, but by beauty. I have only seen a small part of it, but the promise of more is a siren call becoming impossible to resist. The trains crisscross mountains, plains, and cities, willing to deposit a visitor anywhere they wish to go for only a few coins and a spirited nature.

Gussie rested her chin in her hand, elbow braced against the desk, and stared out the window. She had coin. She possessed a spirited nature. She boasted motivation.

She needed to leave Poona. Needed to travel and see other parts of India because her readers had requested it. Lillian expected it. The coins clinking in the bag she'd shoved into the corner of the desk drawer demanded it.

And the thoughts she had been entertaining begged for it.

"All right. That's enough for now." She slapped down the pen and gathered her box of developing supplies from the bottom of the wardrobe, along with the rolls of film she'd exposed at Mukti Mission. Then she went in search of a makeshift darkroom.

"Where are you headed with all of that?" Specs peered at her from the library settee, where he sat reading some dull-looking journal as thick as a Tolstoy novel.

"I want to develop these photos and get them to Ramabai before I leave Poona. Is there a room without any natural light?"

He tapped his bare foot against the rug and tilted his head in that agreeable way that always made Gussie want to ruffle his hair and drag him toward adventure. "You could use the storage room at the back of the house. There are no windows in there." He laid his book on the cushion and stood. "I'll show you where it is. Do you mind if I join you? I've always wondered at the process of developing photographs."

Trapped in a darkroom with Specs? How completely foolish. "Of course. It will be like old times. Me interrupting your dreary studies to teach you interesting things."

"Just so," he said with a laugh and held his arms open. Gussie shoved her box into them, but before she could step back, he reached over his burden and pushed one of her curls off her forehead. "I'm very happy you ignored me and stayed. You have been good for Catherine. You have been good for—" His eyes darted toward the open door, but no one stood there, she knew. Catherine was resting in her room. "You have been good for me."

Her mouth had gone dry at his touch, and it turned positively arid with his words. It was almost as though he hadn't intended to touch her, hadn't considered the consequences of saying such things. It seemed a thing of habit, even though it had been so long since she'd seen him. Even though they were no longer children, and adults never did or said such things without a promise of something more than old friendship. Her thoughts zigzagged over troubling ideas. And delicious ideas. And ideas that sent shivers of confusion through her.

She pressed the back of her knuckles to her cheek. Could he see how her face burned? He was obnoxiously more observant than the average person.

"I'm glad I came and stayed as well." Then it all seemed too much. Too intense. Too serious. She hid the chaos of her thoughts with a flashing smile. "Lead the way."

She followed him through the house, snagging a servant's attention and requesting pitchers of water chilled with the ice Catherine used to stock the icebox, and into a small room that boasted only a low table and crates stacked against the walls.

Specs set her supplies on the table, and after the servant delivered her water and left, Gussie shut the door. She cast a critical eye at the light slipping from the crack beneath it before setting down the Kodak Candle Lamp. With the strike of a match, she lit it, and the room glowed with dull red light.

She held out her hand. "Give me your jacket."

"My . . ." He shrugged and removed it. When she went to the door and shoved it into the crack, he made no complaint.

She instructed him to pour the water from one of the pitchers into the tray she set before him, and while he did that, she added water from the other pitcher into the developing powder, mixed it with a wooden stick, and poured it into a different tray.

As Gussie worked on the film—removing the black paper backing, passing it through the clear water, then the developer, constantly moving the strip up and down, up and down, as the photographs took shape—she was aware of Specs's eyes on her.

He stood to the side, out of the way but near enough that she could smell his unique scent—dusty old books, the spiciness of the soap Catherine said came from the market, and the sweet scent of the carbolic acid he used to disinfect the infirmary. She continued to move the film through the developing solution and found the rhythmic motion of it combined with Specs's proximity caused her eyes to droop closed. Her breathing to slow. Her weight resting ever so slightly against her heels, moving her shoulders closer to his chest. Brushing the thin linen of his shirt.

"What do you want to do with your life?"

Gussie's eyes snapped open, and she righted herself and her thoughts as she studied the images coming to life before her. They still needed another few minutes of development. "I'm doing it now. I'm traveling and writing and taking photographs."

"For *Lady's Weekly*?"

"Of course."

"What about your book?"

She rubbed the itch on her chin against her shoulder. "What book?" How could he possibly know about her book? She'd told no one of her disastrous meeting with Mr. Epps.

"Gussie, you've been talking about writing a book since your Uncle James gave you *A Lady's Journey East* for Christmas when you were ten. It was all you spoke of for years. You were going to travel and write just like your hero, Cordelia Fox."

"How do you remember that?"

"It was important to you."

Tears pricked Gussie's eyes. It *had* been important to her. Yet her sisters laughed and her parents scoffed, and they all made little of her ambitions. But Specs remembered.

"I had a thought, just before I left New York, that I would write one about my travels here in India. It seemed a good place to start."

"You may as well. You're already here."

"I saw a publisher before I left." Her hands stilled, and the photograph's image turned wavy beneath the solution. "He said he won't publish the fluff I write."

"He said that?"

"Well, not in so many words but near enough."

"You don't write fluff. I've read every one of your columns, and they're full of humor. Beautiful imagery. They're subtle, unlike some of your escapades, but the writing is lovely. Your photographs are exquisite."

She laughed.

"They are. You have a gift. Of noticing things and capturing them—in words and photographs."

"You've always been single-minded in your devotion to my questionable abilities."

"I'm not just saying this because we're friends. I've known since we were children that you were destined for great things. That you would accomplish everything you set out to do. And more. I just needed to get out of your way."

Gussie withdrew the paper, pinching it between her fingers. "What a silly thing to say. You're the one who kept my feet on the ground. Who reminded me that I was neither a princess nor made of light."

"And I'm sorry for it. You were never meant to settle into a comfortable, still life. Not like Catherine, who bloomed where she was planted."

"Catherine only wants to be close to those she loves. It's understandable, given all she's lost."

"Yes, but still I wonder . . ."

She glanced over her shoulder when his words trailed off. "Wonder what?"

The shallow cleft in his chin deepened as he pressed his lips together. There was grief in his eyes. Grief and hope. "I wonder if it would help her to uproot and leave this place that has only offered her drought and pruning. What if she traveled with you when you leave Poona?"

Reality crashed against Gussie, and she whipped her head around so he wouldn't see what was likely printed across her face. She was *leaving*. Leaving not only Poona, this city that had somehow crept into her spirit and captured her heart, but also leaving Specs.

And he seemed not to care all that much about her departure.

12

The next morning, Gussie sat across from Specs and Catherine in a carriage, her eyes bouncing back and forth between them the same way the wheels bounced over the street—with jarring and bothersome frequency.

If she had known when she awoke that the twins would spend the entire ride bickering, she would never have asked to accompany Specs to the infirmary. But she wanted to visit with Bimla and give her the photographs from their trip to Mukti Mission.

"I will not leave you here alone, Gabriel. I've already said that." Catherine rarely spoke above an elegant rustle, like the whisper of silk skirts brushing together, but her voice had risen in volume during their twenty-minute ride through Poona, and now she sounded like a fishwife with an overabundance of trout to sell.

Specs's calm tone typically succeeded in diffusing arguments, but Gussie could catch the frayed edges of fear in it now. Fear, his old enemy. She wished there was something she could do to help him release it, but she could claim an entire family, as detached as they were, and he only had Catherine. "Now that you feel better, you should go stay with Morag in Jaipur, which isn't far from the places Gussie plans to see. In fact, Morag writes that Jaipur is a beautiful city, and there is surely enough to photograph to keep Miss Adventuress's readers happy. Travel with Gussie for a few weeks, and then settle somewhere the plague has not reached. We have friends and contacts all over India."

Catherine threw up her hands. "Would you have me moving endlessly around India? What if the entire country becomes afflicted?"

"Then perhaps you should leave the country."

"Leave India? You can't be serious. This is my home."

"Who is Morag?" Gussie asked as the carriage stopped before the infirmary.

"A longtime friend from when I taught at the Women's Medical College of Pennsylvania." Specs climbed down when the driver opened the door and held out his hand for Catherine. "Please go with Gussie. I worry about you constantly."

"I'm expecting," Catherine hissed. "I can't go gallivanting around the country."

"You're perfectly healthy. Traveling is much less a risk than staying here and being exposed to bubonic plague." Specs took a deep breath, and Gussie thought he sounded tired. More than tired—bone-weary.

"You know there have been only a few cases in the area where we live. I'm just as likely to contract it in Jaipur. And what if something should happen to the child? I want you near. What if something happens to *you*? What if you get it? Shouldn't I be here to nurse you back to health?"

"No," Specs said evenly. "I convinced a bacteriologist I know, Waldemar Haffkine, to give me the vaccine he's been working on the last time I was in Bombay. It's said to significantly reduce the risk of contracting the disease."

"But who knows if it's effective." Catherine stepped to the ground and put her fists on her hips.

Specs turned to assist Gussie down. "If I do become ill, I shall check myself into the plague hospital and have a nice relaxing holiday."

"As if you would spend a moment more than necessary in that awful place." Catherine poked at Gussie's back. "Tell him I must stay in Poona."

Gussie lifted her skirt and stepped over an open drain. "Why is the plague hospital awful?" She wouldn't allow herself to be torn between them.

Specs gave a weary sigh, and Catherine glared at her brother, but the question broke the tension.

"Dr. Hunter, the woman who runs it, has good intentions, but she is typical of most British doctors here—she believes the methods are justified by the results," he explained. "They contain the plague and slow the spread of it, but they are harsh and don't take cultural sensibilities into account. The plague committee, on which Dr. Hunter sits, has enacted abrasive measures. Troops force their way into private homes, and until recently, the women were subjected to examinations by men. There were accusations of terrible injustice. They have banned traditional medical practices. They destroy personal possessions. At the hospital, they don't allow visitors, and many people die alone. It's a terrible thing." He stared up at the infirmary and scratched his head. "It doesn't help that the death rate is so high and most who enter do not leave. People believe their loved ones are being killed there."

The heavy words settled over his shoulders and bowed his back. Catherine touched his arm. "Things are changing, though."

Specs gave her a wry smile. "Slowly." He stepped toward the door. "Which is how everything moves beneath Raj rule."

Grateful her diversion had worked, Gussie trailed Specs and Catherine into the infirmary and down the hall to the examination room. He would remain there, relieving Dr. Paul, who had sent word that he and the nurses had been up all night with a man who had nearly lost his leg in an accident.

Bimla and Dr. Paul stood opposite each other over a sheet-draped patient, so deep in conversation that neither noticed the group's entry. Specs crossed to the back of the room where a child adorned in a crown of bandages slept, and Catherine went directly to the staircase that led to the nurses' apartment, where she would wait for Bimla to join them, but Gussie couldn't take her eyes from her new friend. For, just as she'd done at Mukti Mission while seeing to the children, Bimla had removed her scarf and, without any timidity and completely unaware of how radiant she was, spilled love over her patient.

Without conscious thought, Gussie lifted her camera from its bag and took three steps to the left in order to take advantage of the sunlight streaming through the window, casting squares of light beneath Bimla's feet.

The shutter's click was as soft as Dr. Paul's murmured words, yet it drew Bimla's head around, and when she saw Gussie and Specs, a shadow settled over her face, and she drew her scarf up over her head.

"I didn't realize you'd come. I am finished here. I believe the other nurse will be down shortly. Amma has told me she will be coming this morning for a visit, so please join me upstairs." Bimla was all polite welcome, but Gussie didn't miss the wall that had been erected when Bimla raised the gauzy fabric now draping her face. It hid not only her scars but also the pleasure that had transformed her usual reserved expression into something snapping with vibrant joy.

Bimla ducked her head and crossed the room, and Gussie noticed Dr. Paul's gaze follow. "I don't believe she wants to be in photographs," he said.

Gussie glanced at the staircase, Bimla's steps still echoing. "I didn't consider that. I should have. I don't like to be in photographs either."

He looked at her, brows raised. "Why is that?

"I've never found a scene I thought I should knit myself into. I observe, Dr. Paul. From a distance. It is safer that way." She nodded at him. "Her face is in shadow anyway, but I won't develop the film."

She started for the stairs, but his soft words turned her head. "Or you could . . . develop it and give it to me. To keep safe." He rubbed at his chin, his gaze not meeting hers. "For a time when she might see herself the way the rest of us do."

Gussie chuckled and gave him a nod before turning back toward the staircase.

Ramabai was already in the apartment, settled on one of the settees in front of the doors that led to the second-floor veranda. Bimla and Catherine sat in cane chairs opposite her, their backs to Gussie. Ramabai waved her in. "How nice! I didn't realize I'd have the opportunity to see you again before you left Poona, Gussie."

Gussie held up the clutch of photographs. "I come with gifts."

Ramabai's eyes brightened with curiosity. "The photographs from your time with us?"

Gussie nodded and sat when Ramabai patted the cushion beside her. "They turned out beautifully."

She handed over the stack and pointed out her favorites as Ramabai riffled through them. Groups of smiling children. One of Anjali, head bowed over a flower still dangling roots and clumps of dirt. Ramabai and the women who staffed Mukti Mission. Redemption and hope stamped in black and white.

Ramabai paused on the photo of Bimla standing below the tamarind tree, hardly visible beneath the leafy canopy but still, somehow, managing to capture attention.

"Your supporters will likely not care for that one," Gussie said, knowing they would prefer to see details of the work they helped fund.

Ramabai stared at it while Bimla and Catherine waited curiously. "Probably not, but I think it's wonderful. How you've captured her . . ." She smiled and slipped it back into the stack before the others could see it. "I will keep that one. What a gift you claim."

For a moment—a spot of time almost inconsequential but for the pain—something malicious squeezed Gussie's heart. Her chest hitched, and she pressed her hand to it, trying to protect herself from the memories. The disappointment. The knowledge that her parents and sisters had never understood her love of photography as easily as Ramabai, a near stranger, did. That none of them appreciated the beauty Gussie could capture with leather and a square of metal.

"I only take pictures and tell simple stories. Anyone could do it."

Ramabai tilted her head. "No, it is more than that. Anyone can take a photograph, that is true, but not everyone can do so and retain the essence of a person, a place, or time. You collect memories."

Those words loosened one of Gussie's own memories, long interred.

"What is the point of all this absurd travel? Your silly dabbles. It reflects poorly on you. And on us. I don't understand why you cannot be like your sisters."

Gussie swallowed and looked at Ramabai. She couldn't look at Catherine because Catherine knew about the words that followed her. Knew that from city to plain, village to mountain waterfall, across oceans and over foreign places, they were ribbons that trailed after her, tying her to others' expectations and assumptions. Gussie would see sympathy and love in Catherine's expression, and her fear and doubt would be exposed. "I suppose that is why I do it, then." If it took a thousand rolls of film—a dozen trips across the world—she would replace the memories that haunted her like so many venomous keepsakes with ones that were beautiful.

Ramabai clapped. "I've come to share with you good news, Bimla. Savitri is getting married."

Bimla gasped and covered her mouth with her hands. "How wonderful."

"Who is Savitri?" Catherine asked.

"She is one of my widows. She came to us when her husband died of diphtheria, and she now works at Sassoon Hospital. She tended to a man last year—he had broken his leg in an accident—and he never forgot her. After six months, he returned to the hospital and asked if she would be willing to become his wife. They will marry next month."

"Perhaps you will marry soon, Bimla," Gussie teased, remembering how Dr. Paul had watched her. How he had asked for her photograph.

Bimla dropped her head, but not before her eyes flashed with longing. "No. It is uncommon for widows to remarry."

"But you are allowed now," Catherine said. "The Widows' Remarriage Act has seen to it."

Bimla shook her head. "Savitri's intended must be an uncommon sort of man. We are seen as bad luck. Used. Meant to be tossed away. Not many men would want us."

"Whyever not?" Gussie asked.

Ramabai sighed and put the pictures on the table between them. "Why is anyone treated poorly? There are always those who are reviled. Others cast all manner of fault on their shoulders in an attempt to make sense of life's hardships. The weak are despised. Those without the means to protect themselves, without the ability to provide for themselves, without a voice, must bear the burden of everyone's hatred and malice. That is why it is so important to speak truth when we have the opportunity. To reveal in the light what is hidden in the darkness." She was lit up like the flash of a magnesium lamp.

Gussie wished she could stay and learn from Ramabai the way her widows did. Stay and watch Catherine find joy in motherhood. Stay and discover if Bimla was wrong about marrying again. Stay and see if anything more would grow between her and Specs.

But *Lady's Weekly* and her readers and the leather pouch full of coins and her father's threat to send her to Aunt Rhoda conspired against this aberrant longing.

Heavy steps sounded outside the door, and Specs appeared. He glanced around their circle before his gaze landed on Catherine. "There has been another outbreak here in Ganj Peth. I have spent the last hour directing people to the plague hospital. We are not equipped for this. I wish you would consider going with Gussie."

Gussie recognized the pernicious thing behind Specs's ashen face and the way he drew his elbows tightly to his sides. He had always tried to make himself look as small as possible when fear twisted his thoughts.

Catherine sagged in the face of her brother's tension and anxiety. "Oh, all right. But I am returning home after we spend some time with Morag. I won't stay away from Poona permanently."

Specs flopped to the floor, legs crossed beneath him, with a relieved sigh. "I'm so glad. We will not argue about your return now."

"Would you consider coming with us too?" Gussie asked. He couldn't go. Wouldn't even if he could. She knew that. But she wanted to ask it, in case . . . in case . . . "It seems dangerous for you to remain here, even having had a vaccine."

Specs offered her a crooked smile. "So says the woman chasing trains and photos in the wilderness."

Oh, his voice did something to her insides. How had she never noticed how deep, how warm it was? Or had it changed somewhere between New York and India? Why had he gone and grown up so well in her absence? She would have much rather he stayed the same lanky, awkward boy she'd always known. That would be safe. And familiar.

"When are you leaving, Gussie?" Ramabai asked.

"In a few days. I hate to, as I've come to love Poona." *Love my friends. Love . . . Specs?* She nearly laughed at the absurdity of her thought.

Ramabai met Bimla's gaze, and a silent conversation passed between them.

"It would solve our problem. For the present, at least." Bimla's fingers kneaded the edge of her scarf, and she drew it more closely around her face.

Ramabai nodded and pressed her palms together. "Dr. MacLean, if I provide you with a newly graduated nurse, would you be willing to do without Bimla for a time?"

He shrugged. "We'd miss her expertise, of course, but yes, that would likely be fine."

Gussie was certain Dr. Paul would miss more than Bimla's expertise.

Ramabai turned to Gussie. "Would Bimla be able to join you on your travels? At least for a while? She would be a great help to you. This is her country. She speaks the languages and understands the culture in a way you aren't able to."

Gussie grinned. "I would love for her to join us."

"It won't cause any hardship for you?" Bimla seemed to sink into the chair, pulling her arms in and dropping her head.

"Of course not. From what Ramabai just said, I wonder how I traveled India at all without you. You shall be a help, I'm sure of it."

Bimla kept her tucked-in position, but Gussie could see a small smile creeping onto her lips.

"Hopefully this latest outbreak will calm down before your return." Specs's brows knit, and he jerked his head around to look at her. "Gussie, is this it? Will you be returning to Poona at all before you leave India?"

"Don't be silly. Of course I'll return." And if he continued to look at her in such a way, she might consider never leaving. Her legs twitched, and she crossed her feet, pressing her ankles together tightly. With a glance back toward him, she noticed he had removed his glasses. He held them loosely between his fingers, indents showing where the metal frames had rested on his nose.

"Good. I would hate to think I only had another couple of days with you. And I'm grateful for your generosity." He replaced his glasses and studied Gussie, looking up at her from his place on the floor the way he had when they were younger and she had three inches on him. And only platonic feelings.

She swallowed and sat back in the settee. It wouldn't do to spend too much time considering entanglements with a man who likely knew too much about her to find a romance anything but preposterous.

"Well," she said, looking at Catherine and Bimla, "it seems we're about to have an adventure. I can't imagine a better way of starting one than discovering it will not be the lonely variety."

"Why do you wish to join me at the infirmary today?" Specs scooped a bite of mutton and lentils onto the spoon he'd made of the fluffy bread a waiter had set on the table.

"I thought I might take some photographs of you and Dr. Paul before I leave." Gussie took a bite of her lunch. "And maybe the nurses too." He narrowed his eyes, and she pointed to the mutton biryani mounded onto a silver platter and studded with chunks of meat and fragile threads of saffron. "This is very good. I never much cared for mutton, so I commend the chef for changing my mind."

When she'd asked to join him at work that morning, she'd had no idea they would have lunch at his favorite restaurant—one of the only restaurants in Poona, he'd said—Dorabjee & Sons. Spending time alone with Specs over a meal only gilded her plan. Or would have if he hadn't insisted on being so skeptical of her motives.

"Do you think it's a bad idea to take photographs of your work?" she asked.

"No, but I wonder if your real reason for wanting to come with me today is a bad idea."

She tore a chunk of bread from the piece on her plate and shoved it into her mouth to stifle her nervous laugh. He always could tell when she was hiding something.

"Gussie."

"I can't imagine what you're—"

"I will not be dragged into another of your schemes."

"Specs!" She dropped the bread and hoped her feigned offense hid the unease underneath. Not that she had anything to feel uneasy about. She only meant the best. And it was a silly little thing, really. "You are being unaccountably mistrustful. When have I ever given you reason to worry?"

With one finger, he pulled at the rim of his glasses, sliding them down his nose, and looked at her over the frame.

She huffed. "You look like a schoolmarm, which isn't at all a satisfactory use of your appeal."

He waggled his brows. "You think me appealing?"

Her jaw dropped, and unable to capture any of the thousands of words that regularly filled her thoughts, she merely looked at her plate. She did, God help her. She truly did. And she hadn't wanted him to notice.

"You are impossible, that's what you are," she said. "Finish eating. We both have work to do."

Whether merely distracted from his original line of questioning or because he recognized her turmoil, he did, indeed, return to his meal.

When they left the restaurant half an hour later, he seemed to have forgotten not only his concern over Gussie's true purpose for joining him at the infirmary that day but also the strange disquiet his teasing had produced.

She didn't forget, though. It was all she could do to attend to their conversation. She was only distracted from her roiling thoughts when they stepped from the tanga that had brought them to Ganj Peth and a man sitting atop a carpet-draped stool unfolded himself and stood.

"Beautiful memsahib, you wish for nice perfume?"

Specs waved him off, but the merchant remained undeterred and thrust an open jar toward Gussie. She bent down to sniff his offering, and her eyes closed at the heady scent that brought to mind images as vividly as a photograph. "It's lovely," she murmured.

It was Specs.

She'd caught the scent of it whenever he was near, vying with the sharp odor of carbolic acid. This smelled like a walk in the woods. Like springtime and baking and the tightening of arms around her. It sliced through all the layers she'd packed over her heart as easily as scissors across nitrocellulose film.

Gussie had learned a long time ago to grasp anything that helped her remember good things. And Specs was a good thing. A lovely thing.

"I will buy it."

Beside her, Specs muttered beneath his breath and leaned over to sniff the jar. "It's only patchouli attar, Gussie."

He asked the merchant a question in Marathi, and the answer drew a volley of words that would have had Gussie reeling even if they'd been in English. She just lifted the jar to her nose and breathed in this keepsake of the one who had been a greater surprise than any other in her life. After the man had settled on a cost Specs could cope with, Gussie gave him a few of the coins from her reticule, wrapped the jar in her handkerchief, and tucked it away.

"You didn't have to purchase that," Specs said when the man walked away, a swagger in his step and the coins tucked into his palm. "It's in every bit of soap at the bungalow."

Gussie made a sound of acknowledgement in her throat. "So that's why you smell so divine."

She leaned toward him, pushing her nose into his neck, and inhaled. He responded immediately, his shoulders stiffening and throat working around a swallow. There. That should settle things. She wouldn't allow him to go around startling her into silence without repayment.

"Scrumptious." She grinned and pushed open the infirmary door.

But before she could walk through, he settled his hand at the curve of her back and leaned close. "Glorious."

She jerked her head around and found her face only inches from his, the scent of cardamom on his lips constructing all kinds of word games in her mind. "Astonishing."

What was this? A flirtation . . . with Specs?

Gussie fled inside. Absolutely not. She had a romance to orchestrate that had nothing at all to do with her and Gabriel MacLean.

"Dr. Paul," she called as they passed by the pharmacy, where he stood grinding something in a mortar. "I thought I would take some photographs."

He raised his brows but followed her and Specs into the examination room.

"Yes," she said, turning to take in the space, "this will do nicely. The light, you see, is quite good."

"Why are you taking photographs, Miss Travers?" Dr. Paul asked. He approached one of the cots, took the patient's pulse, and pressed his stethoscope to the man's chest.

Gussie tipped her head. "What are you listening for?"

"The patient's heart rate. His is strong and regular. This man had surgery last night, and if his heart beats very quickly, it can predict the beginnings of an infection." He waved Gussie over. "Come and listen."

She gave Specs a wide-eyed glance, lifted her skirts in her hands, and hurried over. She followed Dr. Paul's instructions and arranged the ivory earpieces in her ears. Then she bent low and set the bell-like end of the contraption to the man's chest.

At the steady *thrump-athrump-thrump*, Gussie's lips parted around a startled gasp. "I can hear it so clearly." She tilted her chin to look up at Dr. Paul and smiled.

"The heart tells us many things."

She remembered Specs holding her near the lake. She'd felt his heartbeat beneath her palm, galloping in a way that spoke of something more than fever.

She cleared her throat and straightened. "I'm sure it does. If you would position yourself just as I did, Dr. Paul?" She stepped back and slipped the camera from her satchel, then stepped to the right so that the entire scene fit in the frame. "I thought it would be good to document your work here," she said as she pressed the lever.

"Will you write about it?"

"Well, no. But there's value in keeping visual records, is there not?"

He shrugged. "I suppose so."

"Specs, come stand by Dr. Paul and pretend to do"—she waved her hand toward the patient—"doctorly things."

"Doctorly things?" He smirked. "I'm not sure I know what you mean. Should I stand like so?" He stood at the patient's head and, resting an elbow in his open palm, held a finger to his lips and stared up at the ceiling with a contemplative expression. "This is how they taught us to look doctorly in medical school."

Gussie straightened her spine and glared. "Dr. MacLean, do not test my patience."

He dropped his pose. "I wouldn't dream of it."

"Now, if you—" She caught sight of Bimla entering the room, her arms around a stack of folded sheets. "Oh." She shooed Specs. "Never mind. Go assist her."

He gave a little shake of his head but did as she'd asked.

"Bimla," Gussie called, "will you help me with this?"

Bimla stared after Specs, who'd taken the sheets from her and shoved them into the cabinet in the corner.

"Bimla?"

"Yes?" Bimla approached Gussie, her brows pinched.

"Can you stand there, right beside Dr. Paul?"

Bimla did as she was told.

"Very good. Now, look down at the patient and . . . I know, lift up his hand as though you're comforting him."

Bimla rubbed her forehead, and her scarf slipped a little. "He's unconscious, though."

Gussie waved her hand. "That's all right. You're not actually comforting him."

"No," Specs called from across the room, "you're pretending to do doctorly things."

Gussie frowned at him, then stepped nearer the bed. "Dr. Paul, will you look at Bimla? Yes, just so. Isn't she lovely?"

Dr. Paul murmured his assent, and Bimla, Gussie was gratified to see, swallowed hard and looked everywhere but at her superior. My, but Dr. Paul was looking at Bimla with as much intensity as . . . well, as Specs had looked at *her* during their verbal entanglement in the infirmary doorway.

Gussie lifted her camera, hardly settling it at her waist before Bimla scuttled out of the frame. "What's wrong?"

"I have work to do before we leave tomorrow." Bimla hurried toward the door and disappeared down the hall.

Gussie pressed one fist to her hip and tapped her foot. Then she gave Dr. Paul a pointed look. "Do you think you should see if she's all right? She looked upset."

"Gussie," Specs warned.

Dr. Paul smiled at her, awareness settling into the curve of his lips. "I think I'll return to my herbs in the pharmacy."

Gussie lifted her finger. "Wait, I have something for you." She glanced at Specs and hurried toward Dr. Paul, who had made it to the door before Gussie stopped him. She reached for the small photograph in her satchel and handed it to him. "I wanted to give you this before I left. I'd hoped to give you something . . . more, but that didn't work according to plan."

He stared at the photograph, his thumb sweeping across Bimla's shadowed, fuzzy image. "It is amazing, is it not, that we are now able to capture such images forever?" He gave her a crooked smile. "I will not give up if you don't."

Gussie laughed and waved him off.

"What were you hoping would happen here today?" Specs asked, coming upon her as she tucked her camera back into its case.

Gussie busied herself moving film, photographs, and an orphaned earring around in her satchel. He remained silent, though, which caused her no end of discomfort. He knew she didn't like it when he did that. Knew she would fill the quiet with chatter.

"Have you seen the way he looks at her? I thought they needed a little nudge. Bimla is so reserved, and Dr. Paul is just waiting. Sometimes you need to do something. We're leaving tomorrow for our trip, and she will be gone for a while."

"This is real life, Gussie. Not some romantic story where everything is about as deep as a *Lady's Weekly* article."

Gussie's hands stilled their fretting. "Oh."

He groaned. "I'm sorry. I didn't mean it like that." He touched her arm. "It's only that nothing will happen between them."

"Why? I don't see that anything needs to hinder it."

"She's a widow. That hinders everything here."

"That's such a small part of who she is. It doesn't define her. And Dr. Paul doesn't seem to care very much."

"You know as well as I do that the words society uses to define us are strong indeed. Etak's opinion about the entire subject is less important than Bimla's."

"Well, then . . . I shall just have to endeavor to speak louder than everyone else telling her she has no worth beyond her husband's death."

Specs shook his head, and an incredulous laugh caught in his throat. He reached for her cheek, his palm warm and reassuring. "I hope it turns out you're right. In the meantime, stay safe, Gussie Travers, for the world and I need your optimism."

13

After spending a day on the train, Bimla took over travel arrangements in Chittor, securing an excellent price on passage to Udaipur. From the ancient victoria, the landscape passed in a lazy river of quaint villages, clumps of date palms, and towering banyans. Gussie committed to memory all she saw on the road. The groups of camels whose long, spindly legs seemed hardly fit to carry such bulky loads. The mail carrier who sported a lacquered stick that dangled with his bags of letters and a cluster of bells. The colorful little shrines that appeared out of nowhere, boasting burning incense, garlands of flowers, and gilt-edged icons. And the laughter of her friends—old and new—tripping around their growing familiarity and reconnection.

From the tiffin packed by the Chittor-station baboo, they ate an assortment of breads, potatoes, chopped chicken, pickles, and lentils. Gussie couldn't say it was a comfortable ride, wedged into the back seat, but it was a lovely one and no more awkward than riding a horse through the Badlands with the fretful Miss Clutterbuck.

The sleeping arrangement was a definite improvement over camping in a tent. They spent the night in what Catherine called a dak bungalow—an inexpensive and basic lodging originally meant for Raj officials and mail carriers but now rented to travelers.

Just as the sun was setting on the second day, they arrived at a gate set into a wall.

"Where is it?" Gussie asked, peering at the thick ring of trees. Ahead, she could see temple spires poking through the canopy but little else.

"It will be a while yet," Bimla answered, waving them forward.

A *while yet* ended up meaning another two hours along a wide tree-lined street. But eventually, as they neared the city and cleared the trees, Udaipur greeted them. Like a bride at the altar, painted in white and studded with lakes that reflected the moonlight, she sat tucked into the hills.

The night had turned chilly, and Gussie wrapped her shawl more tightly around her shoulders as she leaned toward Catherine, who had nodded off, her head bouncing against the side of the vehicle.

"Catherine, we're here," she whispered, her limbs heavy with the sense of having entered someplace holy.

Catherine jerked and glanced around, her eyes widening at the beauty of it all. "Are you certain we'll be well-received?" She shivered and rubbed her arms. "I know nobody in this city."

"I have a letter of reference, and Lillian assured me the Resident of Mewar will welcome us. I don't see that two additional people will make a difference. Besides, I sent a telegram before we left Poona. They know I'm not traveling alone."

A moment later, the driver eased his horses down a street lined with grand mansions, all whitewashed and gleaming. They passed an armed guard and went through another gate that spilled onto a long drive. Up a small hill, the Residency, which combined the neoclassical style of Italy—tall columns and a portico—and India—domed *chatris*—made a welcome sight.

Servants slipped from the front door, and Gussie allowed a footman to help her down. As she waited for Catherine and Bimla, she took in the long verandah, striped rugs thrown over the tiled floor, and purple bougainvillea crawling up every available surface and perfuming the air. Around them, she could just make out the shadows of hills and, far in the distance, a palace glimmering in the moonlight.

Her breath, swirling from her throat in a silvery sigh, felt like a comma in the journey. A rest. A wait-and-see moment bound up in relief and anticipation.

How she loved India. It had invaded her thoughts and captured her heart. She could travel the width and breadth of it and still not have seen enough.

When the other two joined her, they followed the scarlet-liveried servants beneath the portico and through the door into a world that nearly replaced that comma with an exclamation point.

She stared with wide eyes at the splendor. Nothing in her privileged background had prepared her for this opulence. The large entry was set off by a series of arches that framed alcoves and tiled fountains. A black-and-white checkered floor flanked by walls the color of honey led directly to sets of glass doors on the other end of the house. Through these, Gussie could see a tangle of vines.

"That is the conservatory, memsahib," one of the servants said. "It is lovely any time of day, but Udaipur is called the City of Sunrise, and come morning, it will provide one of the most beautiful views in all of India."

"City of Sunrise. What a poetic name," Gussie said.

The servant dipped his head, and the movement—elegant and rustling, the gaslights turning the crimson of his turban and livery as luminous as her mother's rubies—combined with the sweep-hush of the punkah wallah's fan, lulled Gussie into a kind of enchantment.

"The Resident is unable to greet you but has had rooms prepared. Dinner has been laid, and I am at your service." He led them to a set of rooms connected by a small parlor, a table already set. Gussie's stomach rumbled at the scents creeping past the domed silver trays.

She fell upon the food, lifting lids and taking healthy sniffs of every dish. Ginger, ajwain, cumin, chilies . . . "Oh, this is divine."

Catherine sat beside her, and Gussie drew her brows together. "Bimla, aren't you hungry? Why aren't you eating?"

"I . . ." Bimla's sidelong glance landed on the man who had taken care of their needs. She approached on quiet steps and bent. "Surely they believe I am a servant. I will eat when you have finished."

"But you're not a servant." Gussie looked at Catherine, who shrugged. "Eat with us. Please."

Bimla moved around the table with a quiet elegance that would be the envy of any woman back home, but it was draped in fragile unease. She stood behind one of the chairs, her fingers kneading the wooden seatback.

Gussie turned to the servant. "You may leave. Thank you."

When he slid from the room, Gussie pushed at Bimla's chair with her foot. "Have a seat and eat with us." She scooped some rice and fish onto a plate and handed it over.

"Augusta, you have had advantages not offered to many." Uncle James's gentle reproof somersaulted into this gracious room, turning the food Gussie had swallowed into stone. Her world view shattered, its shards piercing the ignorant vanity she'd blithely wrapped herself in.

She set down her fork and rested her forearms heavily against the table. "I didn't realize it might be uncomfortable for you to stay here, Bimla. I'm sorry. I've never considered I might not belong somewhere. Anywhere, really. I've always felt as though the world unfurls a carpet before my steps, and I'm suddenly very aware of the pride that walks before me."

Catherine's fork scraped against the china, but before she could speak, Bimla poured balm over Gussie's shame. "We aren't responsible for where we have come from. Only where we go."

Gussie allowed that thought to settle into her spirit. Then, the conversation having grown entirely too serious, she cleared her throat and lifted her fork again. "Dr. Paul is a handsome man, is he not?"

"Gussie!" Catherine's fingers flew to her lips, and a nervous giggle escaped between them.

Gussie shrugged. "Have you not noticed his fine smile?" She gave Bimla a pointed look. "And his eyes? I couldn't come up with enough adjectives to properly describe them."

Bimla stared at her plate as though it contained something far more interesting than the attractive doctor of Ganj Peth. "I have not noticed."

A slow smile curved Gussie's lips, and she patted her mouth with a napkin. "Well . . . he has certainly noticed you."

Catherine gasped, and Bimla jerked her head up. Then Gussie waggled her brows, and both women dissolved into peals of laughter.

Gussie groaned and tossed her feet over the edge of the mattress the moment the sun crawled between the shutters she had left open in anticipation of that promised view from the conservatory.

A small grunt sounded beneath her feet.

"Oh, goodness. I'm so sorry." She knelt beside Bimla and patted the woman's arms, assuring herself she'd done no lasting damage. "I've been told I have rather large feet. What bad luck you had being put with me. Catherine has lovely small feet. And she wouldn't have leapt up with so little warning and so much enthusiasm." Gussie had offered the other side of the bed after dinner the night before, but Bimla had refused and unfurled a mat. "You should sleep in the bed with me tonight. There is no telling what will excite me at sunrise tomorrow. You'd best prepare for it by not staying down there."

Bimla pulled her braid over her shoulder and laughed, a small one that barely stretched her lips. "Maybe I will. I do not want a broken bone."

Gussie lifted her foot and held it up for Bimla's inspection. "Wise choice."

She washed up at the stand in the corner, then went to the wardrobe, where a servant had unpacked her clothes. After she chose a practical linen sunray skirt in chartreuse, coordinating mauve bolero, and white lace shirt, she shimmied out of her nightgown and into her undergarments and corset.

Humming, Gussie pranced across the room in stockinged feet and draped her clothing over the bed. "You will blend in with the buildings," she said as she passed Bimla wrapping herself in a length of white cloth. She pleated and tucked and wound. Between her legs and over her shoulder and around her waist. Her own toilet forgotten, Gussie watched with wide eyes. "Why don't you wear any color? Most of the women I see here wear so much of it."

"Once a woman becomes a widow, she is no longer permitted to wear color, for there is no more joy or beauty in her life."

Gussie's lips parted, ready to offer a rebuttal to the notion that a woman could claim no pleasure after her husband's death, but she shut them quickly. What did she know of such things? Life in India *could* prove joyless for a widow.

Bimla ran her hands down her midsection and stared at the thin fabric beneath her palms. Her eyes darted toward Gussie's vivid outfit laid out on the bed. "Some of the widows I live with . . . they have chosen to wear color again. They say if they are now allowed by law to remarry, then they might be able to find joy again."

Gussie lifted her skirt and let it fall over her head. She tightened the waistband and smoothed out the wrinkles. With practiced movements, she donned her shirtwaist, tucking and straightening. Something Bimla had said swirled to the front of her thoughts, and she cocked her head. "Bimla, I know I teased you last night at dinner about Dr. Paul—who is, indeed, very handsome—but why are widows unable to find joy outside of marriage? Do they need a husband, or even the law, to tell them they are worthy of happiness?"

Bimla's perfectly arched brows came together over her nose. The scars on her cheeks puckered as she drew her lips together. "I . . . I don't know. I never found happiness—even with a husband." She shook her head and lifted the end of her sari up over her head. Hiding like the joy she couldn't find. "And widows are mistreated everywhere they go." She finished wrapping the sari around herself, draped the scarf over her shoulder, and slid her feet into leather slippers. "There is no place in India, except Amma's Sharada Sadan, that is safe for us."

"And the infirmary. You've found safety there, haven't you?"

Bimla looked up from where she stood at the dressing table, shuffling through the vials that cluttered a teak tray. After a moment, her voice rose above the clinking and bustle. "Yes. The infirmary is safe. And I like my work there."

"Then there must be other places, as well. We just need to find them." Gussie shoved her arms through the sleeves of her bolero jacket, grabbed her camera bag from the trunk at the foot of the bed, and held out her hand. "My natural inclination to sleep as late as possible is always challenged when I awake early enough to experience the stillness of morning. I believe it is a most effective hour for bringing about joy."

Bimla offered Gussie a shy smile, and their palms met. Then they crept down the hallway, quietly passed by Catherine's door, and made their way toward the back of the house. Only a few servants scurried about, carrying baskets and brushing the floors with bundled twigs, the scraping noise oddly comforting.

Through the closed conservatory doors, Gussie could see a profusion of rainbow-hued blooms. Trailing vines and marble columns and pink sunlight. They pushed through and found themselves in the jungle, far removed from busy streets and ancient diseases. As near to heaven as Gussie had ever been.

She inhaled deeply, the air as spicy and thick as Christmas eggnog. Down a cobbled path hemmed in by palms and plants she couldn't name, another set of doors opened onto a wide expanse of lawn. Beyond, a fairy-tale palace, more daydream than reality, sat atop one of Udaipur's many hills.

Gussie unhooked her bag and lifted the Kodak from it. At the far end of the grounds stood a chest-high stone wall boasting urns filled with flowers. Her steps sounded heavy as she approached it, a discordant note against the chorus of trilling birds and buzzing insects. Against the very air itself that breathed like a folktale come to life.

Clouds obscured most of the sun, so she pulled the stop, setting it on the smallest one, and placed the camera atop the wall. After a moment of fiddling, she found her shot, depressed the time exposure lever, counted a second, and pulled it back into place.

"My readers will be taken far away, Bimla." She turned to wave her friend forward. "Will you sit up here? I can get your photo. This makes a beautiful backdrop."

Bimla's eyes widened, and she shook her head, fingers clutching her shawl more tightly around her face.

"It can be for your eyes only, if you wish."

"I wish even less than others to see myself."

"What if you faced away from the camera?"

Bimla's gaze fell to the ground, and she picked at the hem of her sari. Then her shoulders rose with a giant breath, and she nodded. Gussie saw the strength and courage stamped upon Bimla's seemingly inconsequential decision and had never admired anyone more.

"Stand here, with your back toward me."

Bimla did as she was told, her graceful, slim figure a striking contrast to the dark, solid wall. Gussie directed her to shift her hips, stretch out her arm, rest her hand beside an urn, lift her chin, until . . .

"Perfect. Don't move."

Gussie walked backward, keeping Bimla and the distant palace within the finder. The clouds had scuttled away, spilling light over the scene, and Gussie pulled the stop back to the correct setting. With a click, the image was captured.

She took a few more photographs of just the palace and wooded hills, and when she had exposed the last of her film, she joined Bimla at the wall, near enough that their arms brushed.

"I'm a landscape photographer. That is what my readers want, though they're happy with architectural photos, as well, if it's a particularly beautiful building." Gussie turned and leaned her elbow against the top of the wall. She fiddled with her fingers, not knowing if she was stepping into a cultural or personal mire. "But

I love taking portraits of people. Not the overly beautiful ones. I don't care much for perfect or proper faces. Kodak has created the Kodak Girl. She is modern and wears a fashionable dress. Her curls are always shiny and her cheeks always pink. But I think she's a little boring. I prefer interesting faces. I like the ones with wrinkles and scars best of all. They tell stories."

They were quiet for a few minutes, looking out over the splendor that was India.

Then Bimla spoke into the silence. "I never wanted to be beautiful. I thought, when I was young, that my husband would not touch me if I were ugly. And when my cousin took me in, I thought his wife would not be jealous if only I could make myself less than her. I thought my cousin might leave me alone at night when he believed I was sleeping if I didn't draw his attention. My beauty was a curse. But when it was gone, I missed it. Now I only see disgust and pity in others' eyes. I had everything a person needs for survival, but when my husband died, I became worthless. And when my family abandoned me and my beauty was taken from me, I was left with nothing but scars." Her accent had grown thicker the longer she spoke, her voice husky.

Gussie had never heard her say so many words in so short a time, and she held her breath, afraid that releasing it would blow away whatever magic had risen with the sunrise and that Bimla would turn back into a widow. Unnoticed. Without opinion.

Bimla touched the puckering skin on her cheek. "These are the visible ones. Those you cannot see reflect my true shame." She rearranged her scarf so that her face was once again hidden within its folds. "I like the idea of you seeing me, though. So many people do not."

She dipped her head in a little nod, then left Gussie standing there in the shadow of her spirit's beauty.

14

The day sparkled with promise as Gussie stood between Bimla and Catherine, their arms entwined. They made their way down a broad, sandy road toward the bazaar one of the Resident's servants had told them about. So much of India was found in the things not seen—in the shadows that the sun cast and behind the screens that protected women from view. In the things not said—in the words spoken by lowered eyes and the whispered shuffle of a servant's step.

This country was a paradox, so unlike New York with its candor and direct aggression. It was like the wrapping of a sari, round and round until the form was lost beneath gauzy layers.

Gussie took to pausing every few steps to admire whitewashed havelis. She noted the flashes of orange and scarlet and gold, brilliant saris made more vibrant by the colorless backdrop, like chrysanthemums strewn over a tomb. As they entered the bazaar, she pulled her Kodak from its bag, not able to decide where to focus her camera first. They were hemmed in by beauty. By baskets spilling over with produce, spices piled on wooden trays, and silver bracelets that drew curious fingers and envious glances.

The scene before her wasn't the arresting vista she normally photographed, but it possessed a charm she wanted to make immortal. A bustle and pulsing of life that taunted her with its constant movement and vibrant color. It challenged and mocked. *Can you catch me? Are you really able to do justice to my beauty? Do you think you are worthy of this?*

She would wrestle India until it etched on nitrocellulose all its beauty and chaos.

Gussie pulled out the lens, the bellows extending with a creak of leather, and lifted the Kodak to her midsection. She blinked at the image in the finder, noting the street's line directing the viewer's gaze toward the temple ahead. On either side, layers of pillars and ornately carved brackets and porticoes topped with fretwork offered an interesting backdrop for the man crouched inside the doorway to his shop, his mustache brushing his knees. For the woman wearing an embroidered scarf, unmindful of the picture she presented as it fluttered behind her. Of the stacks of baskets and mounds of brass pots and piles of garlands.

The frame was perfect.

Everything about the day was perfect, and Gussie wished she could capture every moment. Every color and sound and scent. But she only had six frames and one more roll of film in her bag. It had to be enough.

They walked for a quarter of an hour in silence, leaving the tangled maze of bazaar streets to spill out near the lake. Across the surface of the water, islands floated, each one boasting a gleaming white palace. They were like the *œufs à la neige* Gussie had once had at a restaurant—fluffy clouds of meringue atop custard. Beyond them, the Aravalli Mountains rose in brown pleats from the mist that hovered over the water.

The scene spoke of history and fables. Of childhood imaginations and bookish daydreams.

"Do you want to hire a boat?" Bimla asked. "They will take us across Lake Pichola to that island there." She pointed at an island nearly entirely covered with a palace. "It is called Jag Niwas."

Gussie nodded, and as Bimla went to negotiate the ride with one of the boatmen balancing atop the vessels near the shore, she allowed herself to be pulled into a hazy kind of languor.

She didn't want to leave India. It had been too long since she'd been so entirely pulled into the magic of a place. Maybe she had grown jaded as she traveled more than half the length of her own country, but somewhere between her first jaunt to Florida and her last trip to South Dakota, each destination had become a task to accomplish.

"Why must you be so starry-eyed? You know life isn't a game, right? It's meant to be overcome and conquered, much like your lack of judgment."

Gussie silenced her father with jerky movements that pulled her camera from the bag and readied it for work. She focused her attention on the scene before her, hoping to capture its enchantment. Hoping the proof of it would be enough to bring her back here in a month. A year. A decade.

What would her life look like in a decade? Would she still be writing for *Lady's Weekly*? Or would she have written books? Would she have conquered her lack of judgment . . . or the insecurity her family's disinterest and exasperation had bred?

And between these questions wove a siren song, drawing her in. Poona, with its twisting roads and wide boulevards. Poona, with its wealth and poverty. Poona, with its friends and . . . more than a friend?

Poona called to her.

Never had Gussie heard such a thing. *Come and stay with me.* Never had she wanted such a thing. *Stop and rest awhile.* Never had she considered such a thing. *Could it be home?*

Her heart collided with her sternum, sharp and startled. No. Absolutely not. It was only that Specs was in Poona. Specs with his endearing smile and tenuous grasp of control. It was only history calling to her. Nothing more.

Gussie shook her arms, finding that they had begun to tingle in a most peculiar way, then followed Catherine to the boat Bimla

153

had hired. She climbed in, holding her arms out to balance and keep from plunging overboard, then sat on the hard seat, facing her friends and Udaipur. Fragments of descriptions ran through her mind.

The great white palace of Udaipur . . . sprawls atop the hills . . . a fortification—

No.

. . . rises from the hills surrounding the city as though the rocky ground has given birth to . . .

Gussie rested her chin in her hand as the boatman pushed off, his square feet perched on either side of the bow, toes clenching, long pole braced against his hip.

Birth to a colossus? No, not descriptive enough.

Birth to a cluster of enchanting tumors? Gussie snorted. Maybe *too* descriptive. And not at all a positive image.

"What has you all knotted up?" Catherine asked. "You're frowning so intensely, your lips are slipping over the edge of your chin."

Gussie sighed. "What do you think the palace looks like from here?"

Catherine glanced over her shoulder, then back. "It looks like an overlarge fortress meant to keep people out."

Gussie rolled her eyes. Catherine had never been romantic. She'd always kept her feet firmly on the ground and her head out of the clouds.

"I think it looks as though the palace has always been here," Bimla said. "As though there was never a time when it did not exist. Even before the Maharanas came to Udaipur, it stood. Impenetrable and eternal." Bimla's eyes darted, then dropped to her feet as though she was mortified to have spoken.

. . . has given birth to an eternal monument meant to placate its conquerors, the ancient Maharanas of Udaipur.

Gussie sat upright and clapped her hands together. "You're an inspiration, Bimla. I wish I could shrink you down and tuck you inside my pocket so that you can come with me always."

Bimla stared at the boat's floor. "I wish for that also."

Gussie briefly met Catherine's concerned gaze. "Can you tell us why you needed to leave Poona?"

Bimla picked at the edge of her sari, drawing it between her fingers like she might worry a talisman. "My cousin has found me. He has been coming to Sharada Sadan—he doesn't know I have taken lodging above the infirmary—demanding I return to his home. Amma told me to stay away, but one day, missing some of my friends, I made a visit. He waited for me to leave and followed me to the market. He made threats about things he would tell my family. So Amma thought it would be good for me to leave for a while. To go far away from him."

"I thought you haven't seen your family since you returned to the city after your husband died."

"I haven't, but I love them still. I do not wish for others to think poorly of them. And I do not wish for them to think poorly of me."

"I'm not sure you can change their minds if they've already decided who you are." Gussie had long since given up trying to change her parents' and sisters' minds.

Their conversation dwindled as the boatman steered them over the glassy surface of Lake Pichola, and Gussie let it. Bimla's answer had stirred things in her own heart best not dwelt upon. Philosophical ponderings that teased open relationships fraught with all manner of disappointment.

From her vantage at the stern, Gussie had a view of Udaipur's white palace imposing itself into the sky. Hanging terraced gardens of green and scarlet and gold danced over the hills, twirling with showy blooms and tangled vines. At the steps leading to the lake, women in saris whose colors must have drawn the envy of every flower moved with grace, even while setting out to complete mundane chores.

The boat glided past the walls of the island palace, open doors revealing courtyards full of glossy leaves and lively blooms playing peekaboo. This was a moment meant to be immortalized in a photograph, hung forever on a wall or pasted into a book.

These images wouldn't be tucked away and hidden. They

wouldn't be buried beneath better memories. She slipped her finger beneath the flap of her camera bag and felt for the photograph she kept in the pocket. Its edges, softened from regular handling, held enough power to set Gussie's heart rocking like the boat. She closed her eyes and saw them again—her parents sitting on a studio settee, Gussie and her sisters perched on little stools at their feet. The lackluster striped wallpaper, fringed lamp, and dull carpet at odds with their smiles and clasping arms. No stiff dignity and sober expressions for the Traverses of Harlem.

The photograph had been taken only a year before Father became the man he'd always meant to be. Before they were the Traverses of Fifth Avenue. Before her parents decided there was little benefit in having a child as free-spirited as Gussie and set about shaming her into becoming Augusta, daughter of a man about to claim the world and jewel in her mother's tiara.

How unfortunate for them that Gussie remembered and *liked* who they'd all been before. She'd no notion of making a splash in society and would never condescend to being molded into something she hadn't been born into.

And here was proof that joy had been stitched into the fabric of her family once. In black and white. Forgotten by everyone but her.

***

After an hour exploring the palace—crossing a labyrinth of parapets and channels and tanks clogged with lotus leaves beneath crystal-topped domes—they took the splintered boat back to shore.

More than once, Gussie had pulled out her Kodak and striven to capture, somehow, the beauty of a spot. More than once, she knew it to be a futile attempt.

They bumped up against the crowded ghat and disembarked, pushing past women washing laundry, chasing naked children with strings tied around their wrists, and gossiping beneath the sun. A pair of elephants braced massive feet against the lake's shifting sand, and Gussie took their photograph while Bimla hailed a tanga.

Gussie tucked her skirt beneath her so it wouldn't become caught in the large wheel, and they set off, gripping the edges of the seat and laughing as the wind reached for their hats and scarves.

Bimla asked the driver to take them the long way back to the Residency, riding around the lakeshore and weaving up and down streets hemmed in by ornately carved temples that looked like stacked wedding cakes. Gussie slapped her hand over her mouth to capture a shout as a camel ambled past, its lanky legs bending in unnatural ways. Dressed as decadently as a bride, it wore a brilliantly embroidered red-and-gold blanket and silver bells around its ankles. She smacked Bimla on the shoulder, begging her to tell the driver to stop, as she pulled out her camera and attempted to capture the image before the animal disappeared around a corner.

"I got it!" she crowed, with a quick depression of the lever. "I got it."

"Gussie," Catherine hissed. "Shh!"

Gussie jerked her head around. "What is it?"

But Catherine only poked at the driver. "*Jao*."

They lurched forward, and a moment later, Gussie saw him.

He stared at her, his linen suit rumpled and a straw boater pulled low over his eyes. Her initial reaction—one that saw her heart swell with fondness and her hand lift in a wave—crashed into her first thought.

I've been found.

She looked away from Uncle James and urged the driver on. "Go faster. Go faster." A giggle bubbled up in her throat, warring with the tears clogging it. It had been too long since Uncle James had given chase. But not long enough.

The driver, either not understanding or not wanting to force his tired horse into anything more hurried than a plodding walk, continued making clicking sounds with his tongue and waving his head to silent music.

"Hurry!" Gussie chanced a look behind her and saw Uncle James waving for a tanga. Over Bimla's head, she met Catherine's gaze. "I cannot be caught so soon. I'm not ready to go home. I'm obligated to *Lady's Weekly* to finish my tour. Six months. I'm to be in India six months. How did he find me so quickly?"

Catherine reached past Bimla's startled face and gripped Gussie's shoulder. "He can't know where you are staying. Let's get back and leave. We will go to Jodhpur early. You have what you need from Udaipur. He might well chase you all over India, but if I know you, we will remain one step ahead of him. And that's all you need."

Gussie turned forward and willed the crush of people and carts and animals from the street. Wished for them to open like the Red Sea before the Israelites. "Bimla, tell the driver I will pay him double if he gets his mangy animal to at least give me a trot."

Bimla spoke harshly, and the driver, motivated by the promise of money or the frightening tone in Bimla's voice, sat up straight and urged his horse into what Gussie knew was the best she would get. Trot or not, it might be enough to spirit her away. She glanced behind them and saw Uncle James just scrambling into a vehicle—a cart pulled by a pair of donkeys—and grinned. She lifted her fist into the air and faced forward again with a relieved sigh.

"Who is that man?" Bimla asked, a tremor in her voice. "Is he dangerous?"

Gussie took Bimla's hand. "Oh no. Not in the way your cousin is. He would never hurt me. He is my uncle, and he's come to take me home."

"But you do not want to go home?"

Gussie shook her head. "I'm a disappointment to my family. And before I left, there was a scandal. They planned to send me to my aunt's in Chicago, forcing me to give up my work. They can't stand the censure I bring on them, so I escaped and came to India. I knew Uncle James would follow me. But I thought I had months left." She blew a puff of air from between her lips. "I underestimated him."

"So . . . you are running like me. You are hiding like me. You have brought shame to your family. Like me."

Gussie opened her mouth to reject the notion. Their situations weren't anything alike. Bimla had experienced trauma Gussie couldn't claim. Bimla had been abused and cast out. Gussie had only been mocked and sent to Chicago. But the expression on her new friend's face gave her pause.

Bimla leaned forward, fists clutching the fabric of her sari, her tongue darting to lick her lips, eyes focused and intent. "You are like me? You understand?"

Gussie recognized Bimla's need to be part of a shared experience that transcended nationality and class. They, both of them, were knit into a larger story—one where women were expected to conform and obey. To sacrifice dreams and hope for family pride.

While Gussie would never endure what Bimla had, she recognized the similarities in their stories. She and Bimla were alike because they were both women who had wanted something other. Something more.

Their differences could only be measured in degrees. Yes, Bimla and all of Ramabai's widows had suffered more—struggled more—than Gussie had. But that didn't mean there weren't similar pictures of rejected obligation. Each of them had tossed off cultural mantles meant to bind them to ideals not their own.

Bimla wasn't meant to live life wrapped in a shroud of grief— her days one colorless moment after another. She was called to joy.

And Gussie wasn't meant to be shackled to a future that had stolen the peace of her past. She was called to freedom.

Bimla had seen that when Gussie had only looked at the surface.

"Yes, I understand. We are alike."

15

After another two days riding a victoria back over the village-pocked landscape, chased by the fear that Uncle James would force Gussie home, they boarded a train and set off for Jodhpur. They spent three days in that desert fortress city, as different from Udaipur with its greenery and glistening water as a mountaintop citadel could be.

The days were sweltering, offering only brief respites from the intense glower of the sun for a few hours in the morning and a few in the evening, but something about the sparse land, the towering fort that looked over a sea of blue-painted houses contrasting with the red cliffs, the women with their richly embroidered head-to-toe coverings and dusty toes boasting silver rings, spoke to Gussie's heart. Quieted her spirit. She felt safe in that isolated, barren place.

But she could tell Catherine grew tired. The days of travel and living in a shabby dak house were too much for her expectant friend.

"I think I'm ready to see Jaipur. I would really enjoy staying in a home for a little while instead of living like a transient," Gussie said one afternoon over a meal of lentils and rolls called *dal bathi churma*.

Catherine lowered her eyes, but not before Gussie saw relief flooding them. "I'm not opposed to the idea. But I'm not promising to stay there with Morag when you are ready to move on. I know that is what Gabriel expects. I just . . . I love Poona, Gussie."

Me too. "I wouldn't dream of forcing you."

Jaipur was only a five-hour journey by train, and they were met at the station by a well-maintained carriage.

"Where does this friend of yours live?" Gussie asked.

Catherine allowed the driver to help her into the carriage and sat opposite Gussie and Bimla. "Oh, Morag is more Gabriel's friend than mine. She works for the Presbyterian Medical Mission here."

"She? What kind of name is Morag for a woman?"

Catherine smiled. "Scottish. That is what first sparked a friendship between her and Gabriel. He was one of her professors at the Women's Medical College. Morag thought with a name like MacLean, she'd be learning from a countryman and sought him out before her first class to introduce herself."

"And she got an American."

"Yes. But they've been friends ever since. Colleagues too. They worked together briefly in Poona when Morag first arrived in India. I've only met her once, but she and Gabriel write often, and he reads me her letters."

Gussie looked out the window and attempted to restrain a disbelieving grunt. So Specs's letter-writing habit extended past their own friendship. She had always felt singular beneath his attention. But she hadn't seen him in a decade, and this Morag had spent nearly a year with him while attending the college where he lectured. Had worked with him in Poona. Had Morag Balfour filled the place left by Gussie's absence? Her stomach churned, and her breakfast burned the back of her throat.

"Are you well?" Catherine asked. "You're pale."

"Green," Gussie muttered to herself. But she smiled and nodded. "Just looking forward to our arrival and a pleasant stay in Jaipur."

Catherine seemed satisfied with her response, but Bimla nudged

Gussie with her elbow and lifted her brows. Gussie wrinkled her nose and looked away. What an ugly emotion jealousy was. She would never admit to it. Not before meeting this rival, at least.

The driver directed the horse down a dusty street lined with fanciful temples and sprawling houses washed in pink. Ornately carved doors were flung open to reveal marble courtyards, and merchants had set up booths beneath the great trees that marched them toward a spitting fountain in the middle of a square.

Before reaching it, the carriage stopped in front of a narrow three-story haveli, green shutters shielding from view whatever stood behind the small windows lining each floor. A sign above the door proclaimed it a public hospital and home to the doctors of the Presbyterian Medical Mission.

Waiting on the bottom step was a person Gussie would never have dreamed could be a staid, dull doctor. She had expected someone as . . . well, as drab as she'd always thought Specs was. Instead, they were greeted by a woman wearing a delicious concoction of pink-and-blue-striped silk. Her black hair proved a startling contrast to her porcelain skin and warm eyes.

The woman came forward, hands outstretched, and met Catherine. "My sweet Catherine, how lovely to see you again. Gabriel has told me how beautiful you have grown in your condition. And beautiful you are. Positively radiant."

A sheen of sweat glistened above Catherine's upper lip and forehead, her face red from the carriage's warmth, but her expression relaxed beneath the compliment, and Gussie found herself liking Morag Balfour, if only for Catherine's sake.

Dr. Balfour turned, and Gussie could see a glint of amusement in her pretty eyes as Catherine made introductions. "Miss Travers, it's a pleasure to finally meet. I have heard so much about you."

Had she? Had Specs spoken of her to this seraphic woman? "It is lovely to meet you as well. Thank you for hosting our little group."

Dr. Balfour's lips curved into a smile. Full and pretty, bowed at the top. Shaped very much like a heart. Gussie could have hated her, but she seemed a pleasant sort.

"Tell me," the doctor began, "has Gabriel ever mentioned me in any of the many letters I know he writes to you?"

"Not once."

Catherine slanted a look toward Gussie, a question in the tilt of her head.

But Dr. Balfour only laughed—a lovely one, of course, full of tinkling bells and generosity. "As I thought."

And with that tidbit of cryptic information, she instructed the driver to fetch their bags and led them through the door and into an open courtyard filled with potted ferns and citrus trees.

"I have a surprise for you, Miss Travers," she said when they crossed into a long hall lined with heavy wooden doors.

"A surprise, Dr. Balfour?"

She grinned. "Gabriel wrote to me and asked that I arrange a particular adventure for you."

Gussie's pulse trilled an allegro. Whether at the mention of adventure or Specs, she didn't dare puzzle upon. "What is it?"

The doctor led them up a curved staircase, her heels clicking against the marble. "You will see. And please, call me Morag."

Gussie had always thought herself in possession of a unique character. Eccentric in the most adorable way possible. She may not have had Mother's deportment or Lavinia's beauty or Phoebe's sweetness—as superficial as Gussie knew it to be—but she owned a daring character that set her apart. Made her interesting.

Morag, however, challenged that in every way. And more disheartening, she seemed to possess the deportment, beauty, and sweetness everyone said Gussie lacked. Unfortunate because it meant possessing a grand spirit didn't in any way preclude one from also demonstrating the social graces Mother despaired of her ever achieving.

And what other excuse did Gussie have? All she had, it seemed, that surpassed the perfectly lovely Morag Balfour was a prettier name.

Gussie stood at her bedroom window the next morning. It overlooked the courtyard, and she had been woken early by the sound of scuffling feet and slamming doors. She spent a quarter of an hour watching a steady stream of people walk beneath her window: men wearing white tunics and pajamas, the tips of their shoes curved upward; women shuffling by, their heads bowed. Some walked bent over as though life had broken them with burdens too heavy. Others carried wiggling babies whose chubby wrists were circled with bands of silver and whose sweet chatter warmed her heart.

There was also an abundant supply of doctors—men and women whose expressions consisted of wrinkled brows and pursed lips. Europeans and Indians who had important places to be and important things to do.

And in the middle of it all, popping in and out of the courtyard from an examination room, was Dr. Balfour. Unflappable, eternally cheerful, waving at people, kissing children, and looking absolutely lovely doing it in a printed indigo gown and froth of foamy white lace that set off her coloring.

Gussie glanced down at her ready-made and ran her hands over the shirtwaist, itching to remove it and don a prettier dress. Something with frills and lace. Mother had always said white was not made for those with a sallow complexion and only made Gussie look bilious.

Perhaps she should have listened to her. There was not a hint of sallowness in Morag's complexion. But the doctor had told her the night before to dress practically. Gussie glanced at the wardrobe and considered changing. How could she compete with the darling Dr. Balfour when she herself was the very image of dull pragmatism?

Gussie huffed. "Of all the silly creatures in the world, you are silliest of all. Now, get to work."

She stalked to the desk in the corner of the room, where she took her seat. With a deep sigh, she closed her eyes and envisioned the beauty of Udaipur's lake. The island castles draped in mist and vines. Latticed windows and lush gardens. Her lashes flickered, and she put her pen to paper.

In nurseries across the country, there are illustrated fairy-tale books that boast ink renderings of faraway castles and magical glens. They are the daydreams and longings of childhood. I have come from just such a place.

Udaipur lies in the northwest of India and is known for its man-made lakes and royal palaces. Unlike metropolises in the United States and Europe, one does not simply stumble across the City of Sunrise.

You must want to go.

And, dear readers, there is no reason you should not want to go.

Gussie rubbed her temples. Most of her readers would never have the chance to go to Udaipur. Why should they want to when there were meals to be made and children to be tucked in and shirts to be mended? Gussie could spin words that would do her photographs justice, but what was the point?

An ache, deep and throbbing, settled somewhere between her sternum and ribs.

Vanity of vanities! All is vanity.

She batted away the words the way she would a mosquito. Pesky things that never ended their torment in this sun-drenched country. But they persisted.

Was it? All of her work . . . just vanity?

She scratched a few more words onto the paper. Her readers relied on her to help them escape the meals and children and thimble. They wrote letters to *Lady's Weekly* demanding further stories from Miss Adventuress. They needed her, didn't they?

She lay her forehead on her notebook. Smacked it down with a satisfying thump for good measure. "Focus, Gussie."

With a deep breath, she sat upright, the paper clinging to her face. Tugging it from her skin, she saw that she had crumpled the corner and smudged the ink, so she flipped to a new page and set about finishing her column.

But her fingers rebelled, producing something quite unlike her typical work.

I have always thought a life free of chance was one full of tedium. And what kind of story is that? Who of us grows up thinking, *If only I could live a dull, uninspired life, then all my dreams will have come true?*

So with that theory firmly in mind, I set out at an early age to live with risk and abandon. Unending escapades. Adventure. New experiences and merry chases and the deep-rooted understanding that I would rather be objectionable than expected.

Then, dear reader, I set off for India.

And I discovered that everything I had thought important . . . isn't.

Gussie stared at her neat script—the one aspect of her studies she'd actually excelled in—and hardly recognized the words and sentiment.

"No. This is ridiculous." She slashed across the page with a broad stroke, ink splattering from the pressure she put on the pen. Then she turned to a blank page and wrote what her readers expected.

Vanity of vanities! All is vanity.

Flattening out the crumpled paper, she pulled a few rejected lines from it and fit them into her updated column. She could share a bit of how India was shaping her. Growing her. Surely her readers didn't *only* want to read of whimsy. Lillian couldn't expect her to remain stagnant in her writing. She had to know there would be change along the way.

With her work complete, Gussie gathered her camera and exposed film and tucked it all inside her satchel. Before her promised adventure, she would find a studio and have the photographs developed. She could send Lillian the film along with her columns, but she liked to see what she had captured. Liked to remember those moments.

Not half an hour later—there were as many photographic studios in Jaipur as in New York—Gussie and Morag bumped their way through the city. In silence, at first, but that soon grew tiresome.

"Why did you come to India, Morag?" Gussie asked.

"I came for the same reason you did, I assume."

"Adventure and to escape a fate worse than death?"

Morag grinned. "Close—an irresistible call that showed up just in time to rescue me from an obligatory marriage to a family friend."

"You don't wish to marry?"

"I do. Just not to a man twice my age and half my size. Plus, my medical training would have been wasted back home in Scotland. My community is small and conservative. Even had there been someone who needed me, they would have never admitted it."

Morag's hair had been pulled into a severe bun at the nape of her neck, but tendrils escaped here and there, softening the look and framing her pretty face. Gussie could not imagine any man spending more than a few moments in her company without falling madly in love.

Had Specs considered the possibility? Gussie admitted that two doctors whose hearts turned toward service were a likely match. And they seemed equal in so many ways—both were intelligent and serene. Well-educated and kind.

A familiar lump took up space in her chest. She'd done everything she could to escape the inadequacy of being the least-loved sister. The one who could never do anything right. She had traveled halfway across the globe only to come face-to-face with another who did everything so much better than she did. Morag, no doubt, could embroider and dance a beautiful waltz, as well.

Very soon, they passed through the more populated part of Jaipur and rolled into what looked like an abandoned suburb. The carriage wheels bounced over rutted roads, and the horse whinnied at peacocks who pranced around them with feathers unfurled. There were decaying mansions and neglected gardens, forgotten tombs and overgrown walls, all choked by vines and flocks of brilliant parrots.

The desolation spoke to some secret part of her—shoved out of the way and hidden. Suffocated by neglect much the way this place was. "'Everything suggests a beyond,'" Gussie murmured.

"Hmm?" Morag asked.

Gussie glanced at her. "Isabella Bird. She was describing a Wyoming settlement, but the words seem to fit here, as well. There are stories in these moldering stones. Echoes of history. We see what's in front of us, but . . ."

Morag looked at her expectantly.

"It's pretty."

But that wasn't it at all, and Gussie couldn't understand why she just didn't tell Morag the truth—that she identified with the abandoned town on an elemental level. That *she* was the decaying place—smothered and forgotten in equal measure.

Morag studied her, her brilliant eyes as deep and indecipherable as an underexposed photograph. Gussie knew every emotion she'd ever experienced made itself known on her face. Her own eyes were the color and clarity of aquamarine. Easy to see through. Free from ambiguity. Uncomplicated. And Morag was no idiot.

The doctor shifted her knees so that they bumped against Gussie's. "I would like you to see me as a friend, not a threat."

Gussie could lie and pretend she didn't understand Morag, but neither one of them would believe it. "I will see you as a friend if you are not a threat."

Morag laughed. "I am no threat to you, Gussie Travers." The carriage stopped, and she gave a little clap. "I'm so pleased to be part of this surprise. Gabriel told me it is your fondest dream."

"My fondest dream?" Gussie tipped her head. And then came the tickling whisper of memory. Of summer and friendship and laughter.

"What is your fondest dream?" Specs had asked. They lay be-

neath sheets stretched between trees and bushes and chairs in the yard behind their snuggled houses. It was mid-August, and their hideaway had grown unbearable in the heat. They were twelve and too old for such childish games. Still, they stayed—Gussie, Catherine, and Specs—squished together and reading books and nibbling on sugar cookies.

"*I want to marry and have children.*" That was Catherine's answer to every question.

Specs looked at Gussie, his brows raised in question, and she had wrapped her arms around her legs and rested her cheek on her knees. "*I want to ride an elephant in India. Just like Cordelia Fox.*" She'd just finished reading *Clouds in the Desert* for the fifth time and couldn't dismiss the romance of such a notion.

Catherine stared at her with wide eyes, but Specs reached toward Gussie and touched her nose. "*I believe you will.*"

Awareness pierced her thoughts, and Gussie gasped. He remembered.

She shoved open the carriage door, and there, ahead of them, stood an elephant, gray and wrinkled, sporting a gold-embroidered red blanket that swept the ground. Atop that, a carved and canopied howdah. A mahout came from around the elephant's flank, his hand running along the animal in a touch both tender and firm.

He remembered.

Gussie clapped her hands over her eyes, then her mouth, then against her cheeks. Specs had done this. And then, murmuring against the excitement of the moment, his answer to the question came back to her.

He'd waited until Catherine had tumbled from beneath the blankets, gasping for fresh air and waving a paper fan in front of her face. "*I wish to be with you on that elephant, Gussie Travers, sharing in your adventures.*"

Gussie had laughed and told him he would likely be in some dusty library, reading books and sipping tea. She hadn't understood then why his eyes had shuttered, the little smile that teased his lips slipping. She wished she could go back to that moment, cup his face between her hands, and invite him into her daydream. She wanted him here now.

For he had always been part of her adventures.

"Oh, my sweet Gabriel." She inhaled deeply, then ran with light steps toward the elephant. "What is her name?"

Morag came behind her and translated, but the mahout shook his head and scratched at his bearded face with long, pointed fingernails. After he answered, Morag turned to Gussie. "He said she has no name, for it is an elephant, not a person."

Gussie leaned her head against the elephant's body, her arms spanning the breadth of it. "Then I shall call you Cordelia."

It was the start of an absolutely divine relationship. Miss Fox hadn't exaggerated the charm of riding an elephant. Gussie, gently swaying in the sky, thought Cordelia's plodding movements an excellent way to pass a couple of calm hours.

When they had seen their fill of the abandoned ancient neighborhood, Gussie slid to the ground, and as soon as her feet touched the hard-baked earth, she recognized that she had beyond any doubt gone and fallen in love with her childhood friend.

When they returned to the hospital, Gussie saw Catherine reading a book in one of the courtyard's cozy nooks. She looked so much like her brother—with her mound of vibrant hair, pointed chin, and shy smile—that Gussie paused and stared, an ache lodging below her breastbone.

"Did you have a good time?" Catherine set her book aside on the marble bench and stood. "Morag told me about the surprise before you left, and I've been waiting ever since to hear of it. I wish I could have gone with you." She said this with a slight trace of wistfulness, but then her hand found the swell of her belly, and it faded beneath a shining smile.

"Did you know it was Specs's idea?"

"Morag mentioned he suggested it in a letter. How thoughtful of him."

Gussie shook her head. "No, it was more than that." She glanced around and took Catherine's hand, then tugged her back toward the bench behind a cluster of leafy palm trees. "He remembered from years ago that my fondest dream was to ride an elephant like Cordelia Fox. How he remembered, I've no idea, because I only thought of it when Morag told me Specs wished for me to have the experience."

"He hardly forgets anything. Especially when it comes to those he loves."

Gussie's mouth turned as arid as a desert. Catherine hadn't meant anything by saying that, but what if it was true? "He doesn't . . . does he?"

Catherine looked at her, her brow furrowed. "Doesn't what?"

"Love me."

"Of course he loves you, Gussie. You are practically a sister to him. Hasn't today proven that?" She took Gussie's hands and squeezed them. "We both love you very much."

Gussie released a shaky laugh. "Yes. Of course. Like a sister. It is just that I have little experience with siblings taking my dreams seriously."

"Why, you're trembling. What is the matter?"

Gussie pulled her hands away—they *were* trembling—and covered her face. "You traitorous things." How her parents expected her to conduct herself with demure propriety, she didn't know. God had made her completely unable to conceal a single thought that made its way through her mind.

Catherine laughed. "You don't have to tell me if you don't wish to. But stop abusing yourself for a moment and take a deep breath."

Gussie did as directed, and her hands settled. "I was only worried that perhaps you meant Specs might have a greater regard for me than one would expect from a friend. Or a sibling. And that would be unbearable."

Catherine blinked. When awareness dawned, it came with a sudden stiffening and hitching breath. "Would Gabriel loving you be unbearable?"

"Oh yes. Most certainly. Because then I couldn't hide how I feel. And he would know anyway. Instead of laughing at me and pointing out how ridiculous we would be together, he would . . ." Gussie swallowed. "What would he do? Could I *marry* him? I couldn't. Everything would become hopelessly muddled. I cannot, after all, stay in Poona. No matter how it calls to me. I will not live a life full of regret."

Catherine frowned. "Nothing you are saying makes sense."

"No, I don't suppose it does." Gussie sighed. "Come, let's go. I need fresh air."

Catherine narrowed her eyes and pressed her lips flat, but she gathered her hat and gloves and followed Gussie out to the street. "Shall we ask to take the carriage?"

"No . . . unless you aren't feeling up to a walk." Gussie glanced at Catherine, who seemed robust enough.

"I am able to walk. In fact, it sounds rather nice." Catherine lifted a small parasol above her head, snapping it open with a flick of her hand, and Gussie did the same with her own.

Then they threaded arms and spent a quarter of an hour strolling in silence. Gussie pulled out her Kodak a couple of times, but mostly she tried to formulate words that would convince Catherine of her lucidity and sensibility. She wasn't so unaware that she didn't realize how peculiar her rationale was. Most women dreamed of the day they became a wife. Most women would find Dr. Gabriel MacLean a more-than-suitable catch. But that would require sacrificing a future as gleaming and daring as the one Cordelia Fox had created for herself.

It would mean . . . staying.

And was there freedom in that?

Gussie's gaze roved over the colorful scene, pausing here and there to blink as though depressing the shutter of her camera. Imagining the emotions each photo would elicit. They passed a booth vibrant with tumbling piles of fruit, and she stopped to admire it. An old woman, the contours of her face lost to the wrinkles crisscrossing it, offered a toothless smile, and Gussie couldn't help but respond in kind. "*Khamma Ghani*," she said, having learned the Hindi words when Morag took her to the photography studio.

The woman clapped her hands together and held them to her face, her round eyes brilliant with joy. She wore her purple sari over her head, a silver tassel resting on her forehead, and strings of glass beads around her neck. Lifting a knife, she made quick work of a yellow fruit and handed a slice each to Gussie and Catherine.

Gussie lifted the star-shaped fruit to her lips and poked her tongue toward it.

Catherine jabbed her side with a finger. "Do not be so tentative. It is only a carambola. It is no more terrifying than an apple."

"So many things here are spicy." Gussie laughed as she popped it into her mouth. "Oh, it's very good." She reached for another slice.

The old woman sat back on her stool and nodded with satisfaction, and Gussie fell a little in love with her.

"Can you ask if I can take her photograph?"

Catherine nodded. "My Hindi isn't very good, but I shall try."

A moment later, Gussie had arranged the woman's baskets and trays of fruit so they framed her slight form rather than hid it. Catherine had cleared the sidewalk directly in front of it so Gussie could step back a few paces, and the people milling around stopped to stare at the foreign photographer.

"There," Gussie said, centering the woman in her viewfinder and pressing the lever.

She trained her camera on Catherine, who was herding a dozen children out of the way, and snapped a photo. How funny she looked, holding her arms out and taking mincing steps left and right to corral the rowdy, shrieking, yammering group. She would make an excellent mother.

Catherine turned at the sound of Gussie's laugh and gave her a sheepish smile, then dropped her arms. The children swarmed around her, tugging at her sleeves and patting her arms until she shooed them away.

Someone bumped Gussie, and she stumbled, nearly dropping

to her knees. As she tried to regain her footing, she felt a yank, a push, and a twisting at her fingers.

Catherine's eyes and mouth dropped open in dismay, and she shouted, "He stole your camera!"

Gussie swooped to lift her parasol from the ground, and they were off, dashing through the crowds and pursuing the thief. Gussie pressed a hand against the top of her hat and pushed her legs past endurance. Then pushed even more. She couldn't lose her camera. Her half pay wouldn't cover the expense. Her parents had already, more than likely, cut her off.

And she needed the Kodak to continue working. Needed it to make sense of her world. Of herself. Her thighs began to burn, and her feet tired.

"Don't slow, Gussie! He's right ahead." Catherine reached for her hand and tugged her a few more steps. "Look, he's gone into that building."

They followed and found a dusty courtyard shadowed by the building rising four stories around it. Saris hung from the balconies that crawled up each wall, dripping water onto the ground. A goat, tethered to a sad little tree with drooping branches, bleated.

Gussie looked around, noting no open doors on the ground floor but a staircase in the corner. She started for it.

"Gussie," Catherine hissed, "is it safe to follow? There is no one here."

Gussie waved her hand. "Stay. I will be back quickly."

She marched toward the staircase, her parasol held aloft like a sword. The thief hadn't been large. More of a boy. She had experience dealing with headstrong boys. They'd forever tormented her in childhood. Specs had usually been around to take up her cause, though.

Catherine crept up the stairs behind her, her gasping little breaths stirring Gussie's temper.

"Catherine, just stay down there and rest. You probably shouldn't have run so far, and I don't want you becoming ill."

Gussie rounded a turn in the staircase and there, halfway between the ground and second floor, the thief crouched, her camera gripped between his hands. His throat worked a swallow, and he turned to flee.

Gussie took the stairs two at a time, and God intervened in the form of a scrawny cat. The boy tripped and twisted, her Kodak safe in his embrace as he fell. With a couple more clattering steps, she snatched it from him and lifted her parasol to whack at his thrashing arms and legs.

With a grunt, he thrust out his feet, barely missing her. He kicked again, and Gussie flattened herself against the wall.

His feet connected with Catherine's knees instead, sending her tumbling down the stairs.

16

Gussie lunged forward and reached for Catherine's flailing arms. Their fingertips brushed. And then, after a shriek and a sickening series of thumps, Catherine lay facedown at the bottom of the stairs.

Gussie shouted and flew after her, dimly aware of the boy sweeping past both of them and darting back into the street.

"Catherine. Catherine!" Gussie set down her camera and touched Catherine's shoulder. Her friend groaned. "Oh, thank God. Don't move. I'll find help."

Catherine made a great gasping sound and rolled onto her side, wrapping her arms around her belly. "Oh, my baby. My baby. Please, let my baby be all right. My baby."

Gussie had never heard such a tormented cry. Had never heard such grief. She choked on a sob and darted toward the door. "Help! Please, someone help us!"

Through the crowd pushed the little fruit seller, the purple scarf fluttering behind her. Gussie reached for her as she drew near, her eyes no longer smiling and her mouth twisted in concern. She followed Gussie into the building, her steps pausing as she caught sight of Catherine, who was sitting now, hunched over her stomach and weeping.

"Catherine," Gussie said as she rushed over. "Lie back down."

"It's too late. Oh no. My baby." She looked up. Her hair had fallen from its pins and turned into a cloud of silk and curls around her tear-stained face. She lifted her hands, and Gussie sank to her knees and stared at the slick of blood covering her fingers.

Catherine took shallow, rapid breaths and began muttering. "Please. Save my baby. Please. Please. Don't take her. Don't take her too."

The fruit seller came near, her gnarled fingers gripping Catherine's shoulders. She met Gussie's eyes, then gave a nod and disappeared.

Catherine grabbed for Gussie's hands, leaving them sticky with blood. "God can't take my baby. Not after taking my husband. It's all I have left of John. Please."

Gussie could only offer Catherine her arms to lean upon, words drying up and scattering like autumn leaves in the face of her friend's grief and fear.

A moment later, a noise at the door drew her head around, and she saw the fruit seller had returned, two men wearing white turbans and kurtas following her. They didn't have words either. Only strong arms that lifted Catherine and placed her in a waiting carriage with more gentleness than seemed possible for such rough-looking men. The fruit seller pressed her hand against Catherine's cheek, and Gussie told the driver where to go, shifting so that Catherine could lie straight across the seat, her head in Gussie's lap.

"Don't worry, Catherine. Morag will be able to help you. It will be all right." Gussie ran her hand over her friend's hair, pushing it back from her face and wiping the tears away with her thumb.

Catherine stared at the ceiling of the vehicle, fingers clutching her stomach, the same litany of pleas and questions spilling from her pale lips.

They hadn't wandered far from the hospital and arrived there in only minutes. Catherine didn't wait for help, instead choosing to push away from Gussie and step from the carriage as soon as the wheels stopped churning. Gussie shoved a palmful of coins at the driver and chased her into the courtyard, her heart squeezing at the sound of Catherine's cries echoing off the plastered walls.

"Morag! Help me!"

An inner door slammed open, and the doctor appeared. "What is it? What has happened?" A woman holding a child peered through the open doorway, her eyes wide.

"She fell down a flight of stairs," Gussie said, "onto her stomach. There's blood."

Morag's arms went around Catherine and guided her into the examination room. With a few soft words that sent the woman and child scurrying, Morag helped Catherine onto the table, pushed Gussie out of the room, and slammed the door.

Gussie blinked at it, noticing the whorls in the wood. The gouges and discolorations. From the other side came Catherine's cries, and Gussie stumbled back into the courtyard. She found the tucked-away bench where she had discovered Catherine reading only an hour earlier.

A chill found Gussie's limbs, which trembled so fiercely that she pressed against the wall to keep from falling. She rocked back and forth, her thoughts a jumble, spilling out in a mixed-up prayer she wasn't certain God could possibly untangle. "Please, her baby. Make it all right. I'm sorry. Don't punish her. I'm sorry. Keep her baby safe. Please. Help her."

A camera. It had all been for a camera.

Gussie touched her bag. When the men had lifted Catherine from the floor, she'd shoved it away, forgetting to snap the case closed. She'd never done that before. She closed it now, then lifted the strap from across her chest and tossed the bag against a nearby potted lemon tree. A fruit fell from a shaking branch and rolled toward her.

"God, please. Let her be okay. And the baby. Oh, God . . . the baby." Gussie pressed her hands over her mouth to catch her cry. She hunched over her knees and hoped God loved Catherine enough to overlook Gussie's carelessness.

Morag discovered her there a while later. She made no sound as she approached, but her fingers found the top of Gussie's head. "She is well. For now."

Gussie swallowed and looked up, her neck and back protesting the movement. "And the baby?"

Morag shrugged. "It's too soon to tell. There has been trauma, but the bleeding has slowed. All we can do is let her rest and see what happens."

Gussie nodded and stood. "Can I see her?"

"Yes. Bimla is sitting with her now. She's in her room."

With tired steps—how very old she felt—Gussie made her way through the courtyard, down the hall, and toward the staircase.

"Gussie, you left this."

She turned to see Morag standing in the doorway to the hall, holding her camera bag aloft. Gussie retraced her steps and took it from her with numb fingers. "Thank you," she whispered.

"What happened? How did she fall?"

"She was kicked. By a boy who tried to rob me. She was scared." Gussie sucked in a gasping breath. "But I followed him." All the words she couldn't say earlier filled her mind. "It was foolish of me. I didn't think. . . ." She slapped at the tears on her cheeks. "I'm very selfish."

Morag watched her with the same stillness Specs owned. "This isn't your fault."

Gussie shook her head. "I shouldn't have chased him."

"Or she shouldn't have. She said you told her to stay downstairs."

Morag's voice contained a note of assurance, but Gussie ignored it for the familiar. "You don't understand. I ruin everything."

"Because you cannot tell the future? Stop it." Morag gripped Gussie's arms. "Catherine is lying in her bed afraid *she* killed her baby. Because she didn't listen. Because she didn't stay back when you told her to. So you need to collect yourself, go upstairs, and

179

tell her it isn't her fault. And not by insisting it's yours either. Do you understand me?"

Gussie's fingers curled around the camera case, and she wanted to hurl it against the wall. To scream at the unfairness of it all. But she only nodded. "I will."

She knew the truth, though. She knew Catherine could lose her baby because Gussie was exactly what her parents and sisters and aunt and all of New York society thought she was.

There was no more running from it.

17

Catherine looked so small in the narrow iron bed, not much more than a wrinkle marring the blankets. Gussie pushed into the room, her heart thrumming wildly. When she was in Florida a couple of years ago, walking on the edge of a swamp looking for the perfect photograph, she'd stumbled on a nest of eggs and angered a mother alligator, who had snapped her great jaw and made ferocious noises. Gussie had found that frightening, but it didn't compare to this moment: facing her closest friend—her dearest friend—knowing she had, at least in part, been responsible for this terrible thing.

The room's windows had been closed, and drapes were pulled over them, allowing the heat no release. Perhaps Morag thought to make it so unwelcoming that the babe would choose to stay in the womb?

Bimla sat in a chair beside the bed, her hands folded in prayer, eyes closed. She'd swept her scarf off her head, revealing the violence inscribed on her face.

"Gussie?"

Catherine's call drew her across the faded red and blue rug.

Gussie winced as she knelt beside the bed, waiting for justified accusations. For anger and confirmation.

You were careless. You ruined everything. You always do.

But instead, Catherine pulled an arm free from the tangle of embroidered coverlets and cashmere throws, offering Gussie her hand. Sweat beaded Catherine's upper lip and dripped down her neck to collect in the dip of her clavicle. "I'm so glad you're here."

"I won't leave your side." Gussie cleared her throat when she heard the squeak in her voice.

Catherine nodded, her tongue darting over her lips. "Morag said only time will tell if the baby survived." A shudder ran over her. "She could already be gone."

"Or she could be perfectly fine."

"I want this child so much." Catherine's words trembled. "I have nothing else left of John."

Gussie's chest ached with the desire to offer comfort. To say something that would ease Catherine's fear. But she found her experiences wholly inadequate in preparing her for real grief. And Catherine had suffered so much from it already—first her parents, then her husband, and now this.

Bimla leaned forward, her words blanketing Gussie's lack. "You have memories."

Catherine's eyes shifted toward Bimla, and the pain Gussie saw in them undid her. She withdrew her hand, got to her feet, and went across the room to study a mediocre still life made interesting only by the flickering gaslight and the need to distance herself from the grief playing out across her friend's face.

Catherine's soft voice chased her. "I have never held my child. Or even met her. What memories, Bimla?"

Gussie focused her eyes on the tartan blanket scattered with jasmine in the painting—a strange juxtaposition of cold and heat, west and east—but she tilted her head so that the answer wouldn't be lost.

"You have memories of your husband, whose love helped create your baby. He is as much a part of her as you, and in your thoughts of him, you will find your child." Then Bimla's words grew too soft for Gussie to hear. She glanced over her shoulder and saw the two of them knotted in a hug, Catherine's shoulders quaking as Bimla whispered in her ear.

"You are completely useless, you know." That had been Lavinia, over some slight Gussie had inadvertently paid her sister's well-connected mother-in-law at a dull tea she'd been forced to attend. *"You say the stupidest things."*

Gussie folded her arms over her chest, hugging the shivers tightly, and refocused on the painting. What a hideous thing it was. Completely out of place and posing as a work of art.

After some time, Catherine's weeping eased, and she sniffed. "I want to go home."

"Dr. Balfour said you can leave as soon as the bleeding stops," Bimla said.

"No. I want to go home now. Tomorrow. I can lay on a train as easily as in this bed. You will be with me, Bimla. You are an excellent nurse. Dr. Paul has told me you are the very best. I cannot stay here, be here, when—if—I lose my baby. This place is too lonely. Too far from John's memory. And I want to be with my brother. I need him."

Bimla met Gussie's gaze. "I will accompany her, and you can continue on in your work. You were to leave us here in Jaipur anyway."

"What? No . . ." Catherine shifted her head on the pillow and pressed her palms to her eyes. "Please stay with me."

Gussie nearly tripped on the corner of the rug in her haste to reach the bed. "I will not leave you, Catherine. Not if you want me with you."

Catherine's chest bounced beneath gasping little sobs. "Of course I want you with me. But I cannot make that claim of you. I know you have obligations. Work to do. It was not in your plan to return to Poona so soon."

"None of this was in our plans. I will gladly accompany you." Gussie had enough photos from the previous couple of weeks to fill four or five issues' worth of columns. That would buy her time, and Lillian need never know that instead of traveling around India, Gussie had instead settled for another stay in Poona.

She would do this for Catherine. And perhaps, in some way, atone for her part in the loss.

Morag refused to allow Catherine to leave for four days. No amount of pleading or tears swayed her. It was only when Catherine's bleeding slowed to a trickle that she conceded, and only because Bimla traveled with them. She called out instructions even as they boarded the first-class train compartment Gussie had paid for out of her dwindling funds.

For three days, Catherine lay on her bunk, pale and quiet. Gussie and Bimla could neither pull her into conversation nor elicit even the slightest interest in the passing scenery.

They took turns disembarking at each stop to take in some fresh air and purchase food, but Catherine wasn't inclined to join them in either freedom from the train or eating. Gussie wondered if it might have been better had they stayed in Jaipur, where Morag could bully Catherine into at least taking a spoonful or two of broth.

It wasn't until the train pulled into Poona that Catherine showed an interest in what was going on around her. When they arrived at the bungalow, a servant opened the door, his face drawn into lines of shock. "Memsahib, you have come home."

Catherine limped inside. "Where is Dr. MacLean?"

"He is at the infirmary." The servant hovered, his eyes wide and darting. "Are you well?"

Catherine had begun to sway and reached out to steady herself. Gussie took her arm. "Let's get you into bed. I will leave Bimla to sit with you and go fetch Specs."

Catherine nodded and let herself be led into her bedroom. "I will help her change," Bimla said and waved Gussie off.

When Gussie arrived at the infirmary, she pushed through the door and found herself facing a crush of people. They filled the small waiting room, squeezed onto the benches and taking up nearly every bit of the floor. A slip of panic made its way through her confusion.

Beside her, a family in rags huddled together, their clasping arms twining around one another. A baby's reedy cry came from somewhere to her right, and when she turned to find it, she saw instead a man whose tears slipped down his weathered face and burrowed beneath the collar of his shirt.

Someone pushed in behind her, and Gussie stumbled forward, catching herself on her hands and knees. Around her, everyone shifted away, their eyes wide with horror. Mothers pulled babies to their chests, and men shouted and held up their hands. Gussie scrambled back to her feet and turned to see what had caused her fall, and there, behind her, lay a little boy, crumpled like a forgotten doll. A man rose from the floor beside him, watching Gussie with hard eyes that glittered with an almost imperceptible trace of pain.

She saw and recognized it, though.

Then he shook his head and backed through the door, turning and darting away.

Gussie approached the child, whose moan crept past the arm he'd flung over his face. She took a step back when everyone around her began to shout and wave their hands as though warning her away, but she couldn't leave the boy there, alone and hurt.

With gentle hands, she touched his head. He couldn't be more than four or five years old. And someone had just abandoned him in an infirmary. Had left him among strangers.

Gussie took his small hand, and his fingers twitched, curling around hers. They were black—even the nail beds—and shiny. "Do you need help?" She knew he wouldn't understand her words, but perhaps he would hear the compassion beneath them.

She pulled his arm away from his face and was rewarded with sweet round cheeks. Long lashes and smooth skin. A turned-up nose that shadowed full lips. Gussie pressed her palm to his cheek, and his eyes fluttered open. He stared at her, his gaze anguished and confused. Then he rolled over and spewed a stream of blood all over Gussie's skirt.

She gasped and scuttled back from the fetid vomit, but it clung to her. She reached into her reticule, withdrew a handkerchief, and, ignoring the mess, leaned forward to wipe the child's mouth. "It's all right," she said, her words tumbling together and making no sense in this place of fear and pain. She blinked away tears and lifted the boy into her arms.

Then she ran down the hall, past the pharmacy window, behind which a startled Dr. Paul stood measuring powder, and toward the room where she hoped to find Specs.

Before she reached it, he stood framed in the doorway, his expression harried. "Gussie?"

"Help him. He's hurt."

Specs took one look at the boy, and his expression turned stormy. "What are you doing here?"

"Please, Specs. The boy."

"He is not hurt. He has the plague. Put him down. Now. I will call someone to bring him to the plague hospital." His words were brittle. Hard. They sounded nothing like the boy she'd once known. The man she'd realized she loved.

"But he will die at the plague hospital." She knew that. Everyone seemed to know that. Was that why the man had abandoned him here?

"He will die anyway, Gussie."

She glanced at the child, whose eyes were slits. But still, tears clung to his lower lashes, and a shudder shook his small body. How frightened he was. "I don't want to leave him alone."

Behind his glasses, the skin around Specs's eyes tightened. His face went red. "Why do you never listen? Put him down!"

Her head jerked back at his shout. At the foreign sensation of falling into a rabbit hole where nothing made sense. Where up was down and right was left. Where Gabriel Maclean turned to anger when compassion was required.

Then a small cry made its way past Specs's throat—a sound that made the hairs on the back of Gussie's neck stand up—and she realized it wasn't anger girding his response but fear. For her?

"Please, Gussie. Put him down."

She nodded, and tears dripped from her nose and fell on the child's face, turning the blood staining his lips into a sunset watercolor. "But where?"

Specs lifted his hand, finger pointing, and she followed it, laying the boy on a charpai. The other beds were empty save one—and the form upon it had been covered by a sheet. "Where are all your patients?"

Behind her, Specs rustled through a collection of glass vials and jars. "There has been a surge of plague cases in Ganj Peth, and despite our pleas for them to go to the plague hospital, the people come here instead. They don't trust the officials, and there have been whispers that we won't call the plague commissioner on them. Which isn't true." He pulled a jar forward. "I don't blame them. But others who are ill or injured are afraid to come here now." He popped out the cork and motioned her toward the washstand. "You need to wash well."

When she lifted her hands, he poured a foul-smelling solution over them and instructed her to rub as he doused them in water from a nearby pitcher. He handed her a square of wrinkled linen to dry them, and when she finished, he gripped her shoulders and pressed a kiss to her forehead.

"Why are you home?"

Gussie glanced at the boy on the bed and out the door toward the hall that led to a roomful of frightened people. Specs could do nothing to help Catherine right now, who at the moment was likely still resting. "Take care of this, and I will explain it all to you."

His brow knit, and he chewed on his lower lip. Then he nodded and swept his hands down her arms, encircling her wrists in his fingers. "Very well." His gaze slipped to the boy. "Stay away from him. I will clear the infirmary."

She followed him down the hall and watched from the doorway

as he went to the middle of the room and turned in a slow circle, careful to avoid stepping in the bloody vomit. He scrubbed his hands through his hair, pulling the cropped curls until they fluffed open. His mouth tightened into a grim line. "Listen to me." He waved a woman over and pointed to the lump on her neck. "If you have any buboes like this anywhere on your body"—here he switched to Marathi, then back to English—"I cannot help you here." Marathi again.

He circled the room, giving each person a cursory exam. His barks of "go to the plague hospital" and "leave now" sounded nothing like him. His typical unruffled demeanor had been ransacked by jerky movements and a thin sheen of sweat that he mopped away with a rumpled handkerchief.

Gussie had never seen him in such a state, and her stomach clenched. Could the world function normally when Dr. Gabriel MacLean had lost control? Even oceans away, Gussie had felt safe just knowing Specs was there as always, steady and unflappable.

Most of the people filling the room left at his instruction. A couple tried to argue, but Specs just slashed his hand through the air and moved on to the next person. "Go to the plague hospital. We are not equipped."

Dr. Paul appeared, wiping his hands on a stained apron, and helped send people away.

Finally, the last patient left, and Specs shoved his handkerchief into his pocket. Dr. Paul clasped his shoulder. "Go home and rest. I will stay tonight—I don't want to leave the nurses to deal with all of this—and you can come in the morning."

Specs scrubbed his hands through his hair and sighed. "Very well. But I will stay with the boy until . . . until it's done." He turned to Gussie when Dr. Paul returned to the pharmacy. "You should go."

"Don't make me leave. He was so frightened."

Specs rubbed the back of his neck, stretching and cracking it as he took her measure, then he gave a short nod.

By the time they returned to him, the boy had begun thrashing, his spindly arms and legs flying, and his head tipped back as he wheezed.

"What will you do for him?" she asked.

He shook his head. "There is nothing to do. The infection has spread through his body. He would likely not survive transport."

She brushed her hand through the child's thick thatch of hair and began to hum the lullaby that had calmed Anjali. The simple tune made Gussie's eyes sting. The knowledge that this outcome would be far more sorrowful made tears spill over her lashes.

When the boy rested once more, Gussie turned and found herself in Specs's arms. "I'm sorry. I'm so sorry." She clutched at his shirt and buried her head against his chest.

"It's all right. I was startled to see you here when I thought you were safe up north. I know my reaction frightened you, but I was only scared for you. He is already here. He can stay."

Gussie sniffed and took a shuddering breath. He didn't know about Catherine yet. Didn't know Gussie's part in it. And she couldn't tell him, not now, while they kept watch over this dying child.

It wasn't the time to unburden her conscience.

She pulled away, but Specs pressed her against him, knitting them together. He had large, warm hands, and they brought her a measure of comfort she knew she shouldn't claim. But she did, for she didn't often find acceptance in the arms of another person, and it seemed wholly necessary at that moment.

They stood there for only a minute longer, and then by some unspoken agreement went to the bed and flanked the child so that if he happened to open his eyes, he would realize he wasn't alone.

He didn't open his eyes, though. He simply took in a deep breath . . . and was gone. Before Gussie could even make sense of this beautiful boy dying in front of her, Specs had him soaked in carbolic acid and wrapped in linen.

"I will have someone retrieve his body and take it to the morgue." He made her wash her hands again, scrubbing them between the rough pads of his fingers as she just stood there, staring at the wall. "Let's go home, Gussie."

He led her outside, and they walked half a block before finding a waiting tanga. Inside, he tucked her against him, taking her hand in his. They stopped by the plague hospital, and Specs spoke to someone through the gate. Finally, when they were only a street from the bungalow, Gussie regained her senses.

"Catherine . . ."

"What about Catherine?" A note of panic caressed his question. "Is she hurt?"

Gussie shook her head. Then nodded. "I don't know. There was an accident. She fell and bled. Morag made her stay in Jaipur until it stopped. But then Catherine insisted on returning home."

Specs blanched, and his jaw tightened. "You were with her?"

Gussie nodded, took a gulping swallow, and prepared to explain her part in the incident. Explain that she had run headlong after a thief. For a camera. That she had put his sister's life in danger without thought. *"So careless, Augusta. Why must you be so lacking in common sense?"*

But then he gathered her into his arms and rested his chin atop her head. "I'm so glad she wasn't alone. I'm glad you were with her."

And she couldn't tell him. Couldn't shatter his opinion of her. Because he had always been on her side. Had always believed in her. His faith in her was the only thing insulating her from sharp words that tore. And without it, she didn't think she could pretend to be anything other than what she'd been told her entire life.

When they entered the bungalow, Specs pressed Gussie's hand, then darted away to check on Catherine. Gussie pulled the pins from her hat and rubbed at the sensitive spots on her scalp where they had dug.

Bimla appeared in the hall. "She slept the entire time. Still is."

"Thank you for staying with her."

Gussie saw Bimla out, then hurried toward her room, where she changed out of the soiled skirt, pushing it into the corner with her foot. She glanced in the mirror, pinched her cheeks, then stepped back into the hall.

"Catherine is resting," Specs said, pushing off the wall where he'd been waiting for her. "I didn't want to disturb her."

A servant hurried toward them. "Sahib, someone came while you were out. He would not give his name or leave. I put him in the parlor."

Gussie followed Specs down the hall and into the room, her steps faltering when she saw, calmly sitting in one of the carved chairs, exactly the man she'd hoped not to see for a few months more at least.

Uncle James unfolded himself and stood. "Hello, Augusta. You've been caught. I think it's time to go home."

18

I'm afraid," Specs said, with a poke at his glasses, "that's impossible. At least for another seven days." He extended his hand and gripped Uncle James's. "Hello, Mr. Travers. Welcome to India."

Uncle James grinned. "Good to see you, Gabriel. I will admit that it has been an interesting journey thus far. I wasn't offered a warm welcome when I stumbled upon Gussie in Udaipur." He turned to face her. "I do hope you're happier to see me now that it has been a couple of weeks."

Gussie folded her arms over her chest and scrunched her nose. "I would be happier to see you come spring. How did you discover my whereabouts so quickly?"

A self-satisfied smile lifted Uncle James's lips. "I admit to a better-than-average ability for breaking into places. And Lillian Clare saw fit to leave me a trail of telegrams and letters spread over her desk."

Gussie's mouth fell open. "You broke into the *Lady's Weekly* office?"

Uncle James shrugged. "It's part of the game. It took me a minute to remember where you were staying in Udaipur, though. By the time I arrived at the Resident's home, you were gone. Now." He clapped his hands. "I don't know what Gabriel is speaking of, but you are not staying in Poona another seven days. We will travel to Bombay and take the first available ship to England."

Specs took Uncle James's vacated seat. "I think not. Gussie cannot leave the city yet."

"And why is that?" Uncle James looked at her, not Specs, as though expecting some outlandish explanation. "Your parents are beside themselves with worry."

Gussie snorted. "If by worry, you mean they are concerned about the harm this will do to my reputation, and by extension theirs, I'm sure you're right."

"That isn't fair, Augusta. They care deeply for you."

"Maybe they used to, but that has long since disappeared beneath their desperation to turn me into someone proper and acceptable."

"You are acceptable, Gussie," Specs said. "And propriety is dull. Isn't that what you have always told me?"

"Dullness keeps one from trouble," Uncle James said dryly. "Something Gussie might want to give a try."

Specs shook his head. "She shouldn't have to change to make others comfortable."

His words were a balm, and Gussie wanted to kiss him for it. Brush back his fuzzy curls and push those glasses up on his head and cup his darling face in her hands and kiss him. And kiss him.

Her face burned.

Uncle James raised his brows. "As interesting as that thought is, it will not prevent me from insisting Gussie return home. It is time. The game is up."

Gussie pressed her hands to her stomach. "But what if I don't want to play this game anymore, Uncle James?"

"You wish to stay? Here?" He squinted and tilted his head, staring at her as though attempting to puzzle out a challenging case.

"It matters little if she wishes to stay or not. She must. For at least the next seven days." Specs pulled his glasses from his face and squinted at them as he rubbed his temples. "She came into my infirmary today when it was nearly bursting at the seams with plague patients. Not only that, she handled a child in the latter stages of the disease, touched his infected flesh, and allowed herself to be vomited on." He replaced his glasses, pushed himself up from the chair, and stood in front of her, tilting her chin so that he could peer into her eyes. "It can take up to seven days to show symptoms of the disease—"

"Then why are you examining me now?" She huffed and pulled away from him. If he was going to stare into her eyes, she'd rather it be somewhat less clinically.

He stepped back and clasped his hands behind him. "While we are less affected here in the Civil Lines than the more populated areas of the city, there is a slight possibility she could, even now, be carrying the illness should the child have developed the pneumonic form of the disease. I don't want her leaving the country and being struck down in the middle of the ocean. I will not allow her to suffer if it's in my power to care for her."

And then Gussie did kiss him. Not on the mouth as she wished to, and not with all the other acts of affection she'd imagined, but on the forehead, above his left eye, the rims of his glasses biting into her chin. When she pulled back, his face had turned as red as the tartan in Morag's hideous painting.

"Thank you for that lecture, Dr. MacLean," she said. He rolled his eyes, and she turned back to her uncle. "Since it's settled, you'll likely want to do some sightseeing. I'm sure Specs can offer you suggestions. I hear the south is lovely. I will see you next week."

Uncle James smirked. "Amusing, Augusta. I will stay here in Poona. In fact, I will stay right here in this very house. I've already claimed a bedroom. Next door to your own, I've been told by one of the servants."

She opened her mouth to refute his plans, but before she could say anything, Specs stood and slid into the conversation. "You should probably wash up after what happened at the infirmary. I'll send a servant to your room with a tub."

"All right. But first, Gabriel, can I have a word?" she asked. Uncle James shot her a razor-sharp look, but Gussie ignored it, for Specs's eyes widened a little, and his tongue swept over his lips in a nervous gesture that drew her fascination more than her curiosity.

"Of course." Specs motioned toward the door, and they crossed the room together, he with an unsteady gait, arms hanging limply at his side. He stumbled over the fringed edge of the rug, catching himself before falling.

"What has come over you?" she asked when they finally reached the hall.

He glanced behind him toward the parlor, then tugged her into the library. "Gussie, you haven't called me by my name since we were children."

"That can't be true."

"Not once. So you're either about to make me deliriously happy, or you've some scheme you want to rope me into, and you're trying to soften me."

"I only wanted to ask if you are seriously concerned about my risk of contracting the plague, or if you said that to give me the opportunity to escape from . . ." She frowned. "How could I make you deliriously happy?"

His eyes slid to the ceiling as a groan slipped from his lips. Then he held up a finger, went to the cellarette tucked into the corner, and lifted the lid. He pulled out a bottle and a glass, poured something that smelled suspiciously hoppy, and took a long drink before turning to face her again.

"Since when do you drink ale?" she asked.

"Since when do you call me by my given name?"

Gussie rolled her eyes. "Are you going to answer my question?"

"About what would make me deliriously happy? No, I'm not. And though I'm not terribly worried you'll catch the plague from your one brush with it, I'm also not going to help you escape your uncle—if that was, indeed, what you were about to ask me to do." He took another swallow of his drink, grimaced, and set the half-full glass on a table.

"Why do you drink it if you dislike it so much?"

"I'm a glutton for punishment."

"Is that a metaphor?"

"Yes, Gussie, it's a metaphor. Go home. Put me out of my misery, please."

Catherine's words nipped at her thoughts. *"Would Gabriel loving you be unbearable?"*

And Gussie had said it would be because . . . She couldn't remember why now. She only wondered at his cryptic comments and the feeling she had when he was near. As though she were falling. Falling and tumbling in the most delicious, exhilarating way.

"Specs . . ." Gussie's voice sounded as though it came from far away. Not from her. It pushed through filmy layers of cloud dust and daydreams. Uncle James was forgotten. Leaving India was unfathomable, and not for reasons she'd considered only moments ago.

"Gussie, what is it? Are you dizzy? You look unwell." His hand reached for her, and she became very aware of his nearness.

She shook her head and focused on him. On his narrow chin and the little bump on his nose. He'd broken it once, a long time ago, when trying to best her in a tree-climbing contest. She had won.

But he had gotten a kiss for his efforts and, now that she remembered, had looked for all the world as though *he* had won, even as his nose dripped blood and his father scolded him until the doctor arrived.

"Does your delirious happiness have anything to do with me?"

"Who else would it have to do with?" He stepped away from her and lifted his glass again. He held it to his lips but didn't drink.

"Specs?"

With a sigh, he set it down and went to the window. "Just go take your bath, Gussie." And then he groaned and banged his head against the glass.

She tried not to think about what he might be imagining when he told her to take a bath. She pressed her hands to her cheeks. He wouldn't imagine anything. He was Specs.

But he was *Specs*.

He stood with his arms extended above his head, hands flat against the glass and hip cocked. His back rose and fell with breathing too deep to be automatic. He'd taken off his coat when they'd entered the bungalow. Handed it to a servant and told him to burn it. His sleeves were rolled up around his forearms, and a shiver ran down her spine.

Gussie stepped toward him. Could she? She'd never been afraid to pursue what she wanted before. But she'd never wanted a man. And not just any man, but Gabriel MacLean. The only man, she knew, who could hurt her. Hurt her worse than her parents and sisters ever could. She felt safe with him. Accepted.

And if he rejected her—rejected this—she could never escape the pain.

Her hand found his arm, and she leaned her head against his back. Wrapped her other arm around him and pressed her palm to his stomach. She was no coward. His soft gasp encouraged her.

"Gabriel."

He turned, and for the second time that day, she found herself in his arms. But this was no comforting embrace. His breathing was shallow. Rapid. His hands roamed her waist, spanned her back, gathered her to him so that there was nothing between them but a bit of fabric. "I cannot . . . I cannot move."

"Why? Move, Specs, for goodness' sake. Move your mouth closer to mine."

"This isn't real."

"It is. It is."

His eyes closed. "It isn't happening."

Gussie did all she could to convince him of the reality of the situation. It only took a firm touch against the back of his neck. The pressing of her lips to his. The opening of her mouth, and then . . .

"You cannot leave," he said, drawing her lower lip between his teeth.

"No, of course I can't."

"Not with your uncle." His mouth found the sensitive spot between her neck and her shoulder.

"No."

"Not at all." He made a trail of kisses back toward her mouth.

"Not at . . ." Gussie blinked and pulled away. "Well, I have to leave eventually, Specs. I have columns to write and photographs to take."

He dropped his arms to his side and stared at her. "Will you run again, Gussie? Truly? After this?" He pressed his thumb against her lips, then let it slide over her chin and into the hollow between her clavicles. "And this." His fingers spread and reached over her shoulder. Around her neck. Tangling in the little hairs that escaped her knot.

"I've already been paid, Specs. You wouldn't want me to—"

"And this." His lips found hers again. His hands sliding, sliding until they discovered the roundness of her hips, which seemed created for this very purpose, and pulled her as near to him as she had ever been to a person.

"You do," she said when he turned his attention to the surprisingly lovely-to-be-kissed place behind her ear, "argue most effectively." She could feel his smile against her skin. "But really. I really do need to meet my commitments. And, Specs, how could I just . . . stay? I'm not meant to stay. Not really."

He groaned and stepped away from her. "Upon all that is holy, Gussie, you torment me."

He crossed his arms, and she couldn't help but notice how nice they looked. How very unlike the gangly Specs she remembered of their adolescence. She'd had no idea being a doctor could change a man so much.

Beneath her stare, he smiled. Reached for her again, his fingers grazing her ribs, warm against her back. "Could I induce you to change your mind?"

She grinned. "I doubt it, but I wouldn't mind if you tried."

"Aren't I supposed to be quarantining?" Gussie asked Specs, her gaze tracking the athletes running up and down the field a couple of days after the kiss that had stolen her sleep and any ability she'd ever had to think rationally.

"You cannot spread plague before symptoms. And even then, you have to have contact with suppurating buboes."

"Oh. Like the ones I touched on the child."

"Yes, Gussie, just like those."

"Specs." Gussie turned from the sports game—cricket, Specs had called it—and leaned against the railing of the Poona Gymkhana Club's red-roofed pavilion. "When I said I wouldn't mind if you tried changing my mind, I was speaking of more . . . physical persuasions."

His lips tipped, and he chuckled.

She lifted her glass, relishing the delicate acidity of the sherry. "You clearly aren't going to reciprocate my flirtation." She waved toward the game transpiring before them. "I don't know what is going on out there. Can anyone possibly follow it?"

Specs squinted. "Not that I can tell. But isn't this nice? They have badminton, squash, polo. Regular parties and dances. The food is very good too."

She shrugged and placed her empty glass on the tray of a passing server. "I suppose so." She braced her hands against the railing.

"You don't like it." He sighed. "I guess I'm not surprised. I only wanted you to realize there is so much to do here in Poona. Especially once the governor arrives in the summer. Boating and racing and parties. I know you've spent the last few years traveling and having adventure after adventure, but there are things to keep you occupied here too."

She bit her lip and peered up at him from beneath the brim of her hat. "Oh, I'm quite aware of the things that can keep me occupied here in Poona."

Specs gave her a sidelong glance. "I see you have not internalized your uncle's comments about propriety."

She pushed away from the rail and looked out over the crowd

milling beneath the pavilion. Wealth everywhere. Turbaned men wearing satin and dripping gems. Tony British women in breezy gowns and ornate hairstyles. Soldiers, their heels clicking against the marble floor. "It is only that this reminds me of home." She looked up at him, ignoring the shouts coming from the crowd that gathered on the grass nearer the game. "I left home."

He glanced down at her and offered a sad smile. "As you shall leave . . . Poona."

She could tell he hadn't meant to say Poona, and her heart went still within her chest. Urged her forward. She placed a hand on his arm. It was a good thing, she knew, that they were in public. Because she would do almost anything to ease the sting of his realization.

"I am not ready to give up Miss Adventuress." Even as she said it, though, other things filled her thoughts. Bund Garden and the flowing river. The singing children at Mukti Mission. Bimla and Catherine, shrieking as their little boat bounced against the floating palace. A crumpled piece of paper that boasted sober words. Truth and promises and goodness.

But *Lady's Weekly* didn't want such things.

She took Specs's elbow and smiled. "Come. Let us leave and go to the infirmary. I don't want you to miss any more work on my account."

Specs and Dr. Paul had finally managed to convince the residents of Ganj Peth to seek help at the plague hospital instead of their infirmary. The doctors had worked themselves ragged, and Specs had only just that morning been given a couple of hours away.

He hired a tanga outside the gated three-story club, and they rode in silence to Ganj Peth, passing shops that sported garlands of marigolds hanging from eaves like rays of sunshine and sellers of gourds, painted pottery, and bundles of everything from pigeons to cinnamon sticks beneath tattered awnings strung from trees and poles.

"I do not think I will give up on you just yet," Specs said just as the tanga creaked to a stop outside the infirmary.

She buried her hand between his arm and jacket. "Good. I would hate for you to lose your position as the only person in this world who refuses to give up on me."

He swept a curl from her face, and the tenderness in his gaze nearly undid her. It made her want to sink into this dusty, devastating place. To stay.

That thought clapped manacles around her wrists. Caused her breath to become trapped somewhere between her throat and her sternum, smothered beneath expectations she would never live up to.

With jerky movements, she pushed away from Specs and walked stiffly into the infirmary.

"Gussie? What's wrong? What did I do?" He trailed her inside.

"Nothing. Nothing." *Run. Run.* She couldn't start doubting everything she'd always wanted. If she stayed in Poona, stayed with Specs, she'd lose her career. Would likely lose any opportunity at all of writing a book. And she might well lose herself.

"You must leave. You shouldn't be here. How did you find me?" Bimla's voice, thick with tears, drifted into the waiting room from the hall. It drew glances from the patients on the benches, and Gussie exchanged a look with Specs as they hurried through the room.

Bimla gasped, and the sound of something shattering against tiles echoed down the hall.

Dr. Paul stepped out of the examination room. "What has happened?"

"It's Bimla," Gussie said as they met outside the pharmacy.

Dr. Paul's eyes widened, and he pushed through the door, Gussie and Specs just behind him.

Bimla crouched in front of the long, scarred counter that ran down the middle of the room, picking up pieces of crockery. Herbs were scattered over the floor, and Bimla brushed her hands through them, trying to scoop up the mess. A man stood over her, his lips twisted into a tight sneer.

"Dr. MacLean," she said without looking up, "will you retrieve the jar of dried amla so I can make the *triphala* again? A young boy was just brought in with severe digestive . . ." She sniffed and cleared her throat.

Specs crossed to a floor-to-ceiling cabinet and took a small glass jar from a shelf.

Gussie clattered across the room and sat on her heels. "Let me help."

Bimla nodded, causing her scarf to slip from her head, and Gussie gasped at the red mark on Bimla's cheek.

"It is nothing."

"It is hardly nothing." Gussie's legs shook as she stood and looked at the man who had crept nearer the door. "Who are you? What have you done?"

Bimla lifted the jagged pieces of pottery to the counter. "He is my cousin."

"What? How did he find you?" Gussie surged across the room, her own hand raised in retribution. The man ducked and skittered to the side. Before she could correct her course, Specs's arm wrapped around her waist, and she found herself lifted clear off the floor. "Put me down."

"What are you doing?" he asked, disregarding her. "You can't attack people."

"That man," Gussie said, pointing her finger, "struck Bimla."

Dr. Paul sucked in a harsh breath. His nostrils flared as he took two steps forward.

Bimla's cousin fled, and they all started after him.

"Stop." Bimla's quiet command drew each of their heads around. "He has left. I don't know how he found me here, but I'm glad, for now I no longer have to look over my shoulder, wondering about it."

"Are you frightened he'll return?" Gussie asked. "You ran from Poona just to escape the possibility of encountering him."

"I know." Bimla looked at each of them in turn, a wry smile lifting her cheeks. She grimaced and pressed her palm against the red mark on her face. "But it seems I have an army of defenders, and

202

my cousin is a coward. He said what he came to tell me, and I don't think he'll return." She spooned some of the dried amla Specs had set on the counter into a small copper bowl. "Dr. Paul, will you pour some hot water and honey into a mug? A lot of honey. I am giving the child a large dose to help stimulate his bowels."

Dr. Paul stared at her, his eyes glinting with admiration. When Bimla glanced at him, he smiled and set about following her directions.

Gussie settled her elbows on the counter, chin in her hands. "I don't understand. How can you be so calm about this?"

Bimla's fingers tightened around the spoon, her knuckles going white. "This is my home. The only place I have found where I belong. And I won't allow him to steal my peace." She sprinkled some dried herb Gussie couldn't dream of identifying into the bowl. "Besides, I'm glad he came. He meant his words to harm, but they have brought me freedom. I now know what I must do. I had asked God for an opportunity . . ." She glanced at Gussie, and her lips clamped tight.

"You are an enigma." Gussie ran her finger through the dusting of powder coating the counter, then looked over her shoulder. "The noble doctors have left, and I want to point out that one, in particular, seemed eager to defend you."

"Gussie," Bimla warned, tugging her scarf down low over her hair.

Gussie held up her hands. "I'm only pointing out the obvious. It's clear he holds you in affection."

"No." Bimla shook her head. "It is impossible."

"Why? Because you are a widow? I don't understand why that should—"

"Because I am . . ." Her finger found the largest of her scars, puckered and cresting her cheek. "I am not enough."

Gussie had nothing to say to that, for she well knew how deep that wound could plunge.

"What are you going to do?" Catherine asked two days later. Her bleeding had stopped completely, but Specs insisted on caution and wouldn't allow her up except for necessary matters.

Gussie shifted in the seat beside the bed, set Isabella Bird's *Six Months in the Sandwich Islands* on her lap, spine up, and tapped her fingers against the cover. "I have no idea. This situation has me confounded."

"Flummoxed." A weak smile tugged Catherine's lips.

"Befuddled." Gussie threw her shoulders back against the chair and stared up at the ceiling. Specs's face floated into her mind like some dashingly tempting apparition. She touched her lips, remembering the kiss—the many kisses—from that day in the library. And the two others they'd stolen since. "Your brother has me tied up in knots."

There was a moment of silence, and Gussie lifted her head to see Catherine's scrunched expression. "My brother? I thought we were talking about your uncle and his insisting you leave."

Gussie bolted upright. "Oh, absolutely. That is exactly what I was talking about."

Catherine tipped her head. "Why are you thinking about Gabriel?"

"I'm not." Gussie flipped her book over and turned the page, her eyes scanning the words before her. Registering none of them.

"Most people don't willy-nilly blurt names in the middle of conversations that have nothing to do with them."

Gussie lifted the book. "'Waimanu had turned out to meet us about thirty people on horseback, all of whom shook hands with me, and some of them threw over me garlands of ohia, pandanus, and hibiscus.'" She peered over the edge of the pages only to see Catherine staring at her. "Oh, very well. I'm thinking of your brother because I kissed him, and when one kisses a man, they think of him occasionally."

"You sound out of sorts for having been kissed. Was it not a good kiss?"

"*I* kissed *him*, Catherine. Well, then he kissed me. And I kissed him again." And again. And again. Gussie sighed. She shook her head to clear the kisses from her thoughts. If that was possible. How *had* he become so very good at it? If she'd any idea when they were younger, she might have taken advantage of it. "Yes, our kisses were very nice. I'm out of sorts because he wants me to stay."

She shifted against the hard seat of the chair beneath Catherine's unrelenting stare. Her eyes were the same unnerving color as Specs's—golden with flecks of brown. Like an ancient piece of amber she'd once seen. An insect with long, graceful legs had been trapped in it, forced into a millennia-long ballet. Gussie hadn't been able to look away, so entranced was she by the sight.

"And that would be so awful?"

"I'm a writer and photographer. I have readers and a column. I would have to give up everything."

"Except him."

"But everything else. Every possible adventure."

"All of life is an adventure if you're spending it with the right people."

"But not enough of one. Not for me."

"Then why did you kiss him? If you had no intention of making it something permanent, why would you tease him? That was very poorly done."

"I . . ." Why had she? She loved him. She knew she did. But enough to stop traveling? Enough to give up her career? Enough to stay put and promise to find marriage a suitable replacement for . . . everything else? "It was. I'm sorry for it."

"You are my dearest friend, and I love you to distraction, but . . ." Catherine shook her head. "Ever since we were children, you've drawn Gabriel into your schemes." She raised a hand when Gussie opened her mouth in protest. "No, let me finish, for I know I will not be brave enough to say anything after I've had a nap and retrieved my normal inhibitions. Gabe was always happy to be your champion. But you have to know that this time, you've gone too far."

She had. Gussie knew it the moment before she went to him at the window. She should have listened. Should have exercised better judgment. "I didn't want to hurt him."

"But you have. You have to know he didn't just stumble into his feelings for you the moment you realized yours for him."

Tears pricked Gussie's eyes, and she dropped her head. "I hadn't thought of that." She hadn't thought at all. "I also didn't think about how this could hurt you."

"I won't deny that I've always wished for you to be my sister, but my feelings are less important in this than his. And yours. Just be sure you're chasing adventure, not running from fear. You and Gabriel have that in common."

An uncomfortable silence, one they'd never experienced between them, filled the room.

Catherine's ragged words slipped into it. "Will you continue reading?" Then she leaned against the pillows piled behind her back and closed her eyes.

Gussie, eager to move past the conversation, lifted her book. "'Where our cavalcade entered the river, a number of children and dogs . . .'"

After ten minutes, Catherine began to breathe deeply, her fingers jerking every so often in her sleep. Gussie continued reading because she knew the moment she stopped, she would have to consider what Catherine had said to her. She didn't want to hurt Specs—one of the only people in the world who knew her entirely and still thought well of her—but couldn't imagine a way not to. Was it possible to have everything a person wanted?

"How many times have you read that book?"

Gussie's voice dropped off, and she looked toward the doorway, where the handsomest doctor of her acquaintance stood. "At least two dozen."

"Do you not tire of it? You might consider writing your own."

"Perhaps I will."

"Will you dedicate it to me? I believe I was the first person to exhort you to write."

Gussie smiled. "There is no one else I would dedicate it to. I could have filled a book already with the letters we've exchanged."

Specs came into the room, pausing a moment beside Catherine. He laid the back of his hand against her forehead, then lifted the covers and tucked them around her, his movements gentle and firm. Kind and efficient. Practiced and concerned.

"I'm home for lunch, but I will be in the library for a time before it is served."

There was an invitation in his words, so she followed him down the hall to that room full of dust and books. He didn't sit down but instead leaned against the desk, his legs crossed at the ankles, feet bare.

"I will never get used to seeing you without shoes."

"It is much cleaner this way. I'm not dragging all manner of germs and filth through the house."

"So you've said." She raised her eyes and took in his familiar, angular face. How much she had missed in dismissing him all those years as lanky, studious Specs. "I'm sorry I kissed you."

"Was it so terrible?"

"No. But I was."

His chest heaved, and he rubbed beneath his eyes, jarring his glasses. "You weren't terrible, Gussie. I've known you a long time. You haven't acted out of character. I'm just glad I finally did." He gave her a rueful smile.

She went to the bookshelf and ran her finger over the spines, tripping over a bronze elephant tucked between a collection of medical manuals and a set of Shakespeare's plays. She settled on one with a supple red leather cover. *Through South India*. She'd not been south yet. There was so much of India to see. She flipped through the pages, drinking in the photographs of beaches and jungles.

Then she turned to face him, the book clutched to her chest. "Do you forgive me for it, though? I cannot stand the thought of us at odds."

His teasing grin softened. "I will forgive you anything because

I love you, Gussie. I have since I was young, and that isn't likely to change. I've grown used to your particular brand of impulsivity and enthusiasm."

She reached for the shelf behind her, patting the air in an effort to locate the one thing that might keep her from falling to the ground. Just as she began to sway, her hand found purchase, and she gripped the shelf with every bit of her remaining strength. Which wasn't much, for Specs's declaration had nearly knocked her insensible.

He crossed the room and took the book from her, tossing it onto the settee.

She squeezed her eyes closed. "I'm not staying in Poona, Specs. I can't. I have work. Obligations. Dreams."

"I'm not going to ask you to."

She flicked one eye open. "You're not?"

He shook his head, and she opened her other eye. His lips twitched. "You look terrified. I think I like finally having *you* wondering what's coming next."

"Don't get used to it," she said tartly.

"No. I wouldn't want to." He held out his hands, palms up, and wiggled his fingers. She released her stranglehold on the shelf and rested her hands in his. "Is it possible you care for me?"

"I do. It surprised me when I realized it. But it changes nothing, Specs. I cannot give up everything."

"Then don't. Not now. But when you are ready to stay somewhere, will you return? To Poona. And me."

Poona and Specs? The two things that had made her question the leaving and running.

She shook her head. "I can't make you wait for me. I don't know how long it will be."

He leaned his forehead against hers, and their noses touched. "I have been waiting years for you already, Gussie. I can wait a few more."

"If this is a proposal, Specs, it's not a very good one."

He brushed his lips against the corner of her mouth. "It's not a proposal. Only a promise."

"And if I decide to travel forever? What if I never want to settle down in one place?"

He pulled away from her, and his eyes glinted with something frightening. Something fiercely determined. "Eventually I will retire. I will grow too old to practice medicine. My vision will grow weak, and my hearing dull, and my hands will tremble so much I won't be able to hold a scalpel. Then I will chase you."

"Across the world?" she whispered.

"Even to the moon by cannon blast, if necessary."

"Dr. MacLean, you know allusions to adventure are the way to my heart, do you not?"

"I know you well."

"I won't kiss you again."

"That is a shame, for I did so enjoy it."

The space between them narrowed, but this time Gussie—quite uncharacteristically—showed restraint and pulled away.

And not a moment too soon, for Uncle James poked his head into the room. "A woman is at the door, demanding to see you, Gabriel."

Specs strode away, and Uncle James's expression turned thoughtful. He walked toward her. "Your parents want you to marry well."

"My parents want a lot of things for me I care little about."

"If you wed, they will stop insisting you return to New York. If you wed, I will no longer have to chase you." He raised his brows and nodded toward the door through which Specs had just disappeared.

Gussie crossed her arms. "Why, Uncle James, are you growing tired?" Something within her rebelled at the idea of him puttering around his house in New York. Poking about the little garden behind his terrace. Like her, Uncle James was meant for adventure. Meant to be around the corner, a clue or dropped note or train ride away. If she stayed, she would have Specs. But would she lose Uncle James? "I cannot wed if I am unwilling to stay in the same city as my husband."

"At some point, you are going to have to stop running, Augusta. It seems you've found reason enough to stop here."

"Maybe." Definitely. But there was risk in resting. In stopping. So much hinged on her proclivity for disappearing. "But there is still an enormous amount of the world to see."

"You can't see the entire planet. Not even in a lifetime."

"No. But I wish to see enough of it that I won't doubt my decision when I decide it's time to settle."

There was a shuffling at the door, and Specs reappeared, Ramabai behind him. His mouth made a grim slash, modeling the thick, straight lines of his brows.

"What's wrong?" Gussie asked.

"It's Bimla," Specs said. "She's missing."

19

Ramabai gripped the edge of the splintered cart, leaning farther out over the street, and strained to see down a narrow alley as they lumbered on. Gussie looked over her shoulders but saw nothing except a stack of crated chickens.

Gussie hoped Specs, Dr. Paul, and Uncle James were having more luck in their search for Bimla. Already they'd bumped and rocked over what seemed to be all of Poona. "What did her note say again?"

"Only that we shouldn't worry, and she would be well."

"And you don't believe that?"

Ramabai's face pinched. "No. Her cousin has been trying to convince her to go to his home. It doesn't make sense that she would."

"Did Specs tell you he came to the infirmary the other day?"

"Yes. I . . ." Her voice sounded like broken glass, sharp and jagged. "I recently lost one of my girls, and I do not want to lose another."

"What happened?"

"She visited her sister and was exposed to plague. They sent her to the segregation camp. The watchmen, who are meant to keep order, abused her terribly. She was so brilliant. And when she was released, her light had been extinguished, and she disappeared."

"Where did she go?" Gussie asked in a whisper, not sure she wanted to know. Needing to know.

"The river."

A chill swept over Gussie's arms and legs, prickling her skin. "Should we check the segregation camp?"

Ramabai shook her head. "She hasn't been exposed to plague, so I don't think they would have taken her. Perhaps we will look there and at the hospital if more time passes and we still haven't discovered where she has gone." She leaned toward the driver and murmured a command. He encouraged his horse to turn left down a street hemmed in by one-story houses that clung to one another like shivering children listening to ghost stories.

"I wish I'd taken a portrait of her. Then we could at least show it to people as we search." Gussie's words swept behind a heavy sigh. She had the photograph of Bimla standing beneath the tamarind tree, and the ones she'd taken in the infirmary and at the Resident's home in Udaipur, but none of those would help. They were merely shadows and forms.

Ramabai turned from her perusal of the street. "She would never allow you to take one. And it wouldn't help anyway, because she covers her face in public."

"I know. I don't understand why she hides, though. Once you get to know her, you hardly see her scars."

Ramabai gave Gussie a long look before leaning toward the driver and motioning down another street. This time, when the tanga clattered around the corner, she rapped her knuckles against the side of the vehicle, causing the driver to tug on the reins. They drew to a stop beside a great banyan tree, its many roots tethering the thick, horizontal branches to the ground. Gussie lifted her hand to her throat, easing the lump that settled there.

She hated banyan trees. She could never look at one without feeling as though she were choking. As though those parasitic roots reached for her too. Wanted to hold her down and pin her to the ground. Trap her.

Ramabai studied a three-story house across the street. The top two floors were fronted by windows, shutters flung open and bundles of drying herbs strung from a cord beneath the second-floor balcony. "That is where Bimla's cousin lives. He would not open the door to me earlier in the day, so I will sit here and wait until I am able to discover if he has her."

Gussie gazed at the house, studying the windows for any movement that would reveal Bimla's slender form, but all inside seemed still. "It might be a long wait."

A monkey scurried across the street, dodging great wheels kicking up dust and rolling carts piled high with radishes and spinach. The animal stopped when it reached a banana plant and chittered, drawing Gussie's smile. She reached for her camera, only realizing when her hand smacked against her hip that she'd left it at the bungalow.

She sighed and tried to take a mental picture of the scene. Knowing she'd forget it the moment their tanga crossed into another street. That was the problem with life—the good moments, the interesting and beautiful ones, were as fleeting as the dull ones. Unless you had the ability to imprint memory on paper, even important things faded.

The monkey disappeared up the tree. "I wish I had thought to bring my camera," she said.

"Because that is your *dupatta*."

"My what?" Gussie laughed.

"Dupatta. It's the scarf Bimla wears over her head and shoulders. You don't understand why she hides her scars, but you do the same with that little black box."

"I don't hide behind my camera, Ramabai. I use it for work. To take photographs. It's a tool."

"And also a dupatta." Ramabai shifted in the seat so that her body angled toward Gussie while still allowing her to keep an eye on the house. "Bimla has scars here"—she ran her knuckles over her cheeks—"and she says, 'I will not show my face because of these scars.' And you say 'I cannot do this or that because of my tiny black box, my work.'" Ramabai put her hand over Gussie's heart, her fingers warm and sure. "But the truth is that you are both afraid."

"I'm not afraid of anything." Gussie crossed her arms over her chest, forcing Ramabai's hand back to her lap. "You don't know me. I have everything Bimla doesn't—wealth and safety and family and—" She choked a little on the word and shook her head. "You don't know me."

But Bimla had known her. Had seen her that day in Jaipur when she recognized Gussie ran too.

"Fear is an easy thing to see," Ramabai replied. "Especially when it is rooted in rejection. But it is a hard thing to bear. You wear no dupatta, but still you hide."

Gussie had made a life writing articles that barely scratched the surface. Honeyed stories and landscapes touched by sun. Words and pictures trapped tightly beneath a veneer of blithe freedom. People didn't care about truth as long as you tickled their imagination.

"How do you know? How can you tell?" she asked.

Ramabai's hand found Gussie's cheek, and she offered a soft smile. "It is written on your face as clearly as a photograph." Her expression turned thoughtful. "It's also written into every one of your columns and bleeds into each of your photographs. There is a yearning, an expectation, in them. But you choose to restrain yourself, to avoid giving in completely to your gift. Rejection can hinder God's leading, if we allow it. You told me at Mukti Mission that you want to write stories that matter. Why don't you?"

Gussie didn't answer—she didn't think Ramabai expected one. She sat back in her seat, and while Ramabai watched the house, she stared at her hands knotted in her lap.

She'd made a habit of burying pain. And when plain old neglect hadn't been enough of a distraction, she'd filled her life with other things. With escape and chance. With seizing every moment and wringing from it all the excitement she could. With the accolades of a thousand strangers. And even with the outrage of a thousand more.

It hadn't mattered if she fell from a tree or ruined her reputation on a prairie. Those things were far less painful than admitting the truth, one she couldn't hide from now. Ramabai had lifted a flash sheet, shedding light on what had been hidden in darkness.

Gussie had said she couldn't stay in Poona because of her work. Her dreams. But the truth was, fear buttressed that decision. Life had proven itself untrustworthy and contemptuous, so she had run from it. Hidden. Spent her time arranging other players because she'd turned into a collector of memories, tucking them into pockets and books and drawers.

Instead of writing the things that whispered to her in dreams, she'd disappeared into stories that shackled her to sentimental banality. Because, as Ramabai said, she'd been rejected. Made to feel small. And there was safety in continuing to do what she had always done instead of risking more. More of her dreams. More of her heart. More of the optimism and joy she wore like a scarf. Hiding.

If she stayed, would Specs eventually reject her too?

Maybe. He might.

Was casting off the fear that bound her worth that price?

Beside her, Ramabai sucked in a breath and launched herself from the tanga.

Gussie pushed away the reflections and introspection and started after her. "Ramabai," she hissed, "what are you doing?"

But then she saw. Bimla's cousin and a woman had stepped from the house.

"Where is she?" Ramabai demanded, then launched into Marathi. She stopped only inches from the couple, poking her finger at them, her round, gentle face sparking with holy anger.

The woman squeezed behind Bimla's cousin, pressing against his back, while he looked at Ramabai, obviously baffled—and maybe slightly frightened.

Finally, he snapped something that appeased Ramabai. She straightened the scarf framing her face and lifted her shoulders. "He will let us in," she told Gussie.

They ducked beneath the low doorframe and into the house. It only took a few minutes, though, to realize Bimla wasn't there, and they found themselves back on the dusty street.

Ramabai stared dumbly at the tree the monkey had climbed. "It doesn't look as though she's been in that house at all."

Gussie glanced at the couple still standing near their house. "Let's go. Perhaps Uncle James and Specs have discovered where she is."

"Your uncle has never been to Poona. How would he find her?"

Gussie laughed. "He's never been to a lot of places, but that never stopped him from finding me. I will convince him to stay until Bimla is located."

And perhaps she would stay too. As attractive as the image of a shaking, wrinkled Specs was, she didn't want to wait until they were old to finally walk in courage.

A few days later, Gussie took a seat at the dining table and smoothed a napkin over the skirt of her striped green-and-white linen lawn dress. The fruit on her plate beckoned, and her mouth watered in anticipation. Maybe she would write about the unique and tantalizing offerings of an Indian meal. She could include a recipe . . . or not. Lillian might find that too common.

"I have a lead," Uncle James said. "A person of interest contacted me and suggested Bimla has been seen at the fish market in Nana Peth."

"That is near Ganj Peth. To think, she might not have gone very far at all." Catherine had insisted on joining them at the table, but Gussie noted the sheen at her temples and slow movements. According to Specs—whom Gussie assumed had already left for the infirmary—the child remained within her, but she still experienced sudden pains that left her shaky and pale.

"Perhaps, now that we've exonerated her cousin from any guilt, we should respect Bimla's wish and trust that she has a reason for disappearing," Gussie said, raising her brows. Uncle James grunted. She grinned and speared a slice of guava. "It seems to me that if she wanted to be found, she would be." She brought the fruit to her lips.

"But what if Ramabai is right, and she's been coerced into leaving?" Catherine said.

"She left a note. And there was no sign of her in her cousin's house."

"Then why didn't she tell anyone where she was going?" Uncle James lifted his teacup and wrinkled his nose at the weak brew.

"Perhaps for the same reason I never told. Maybe she knew no one would approve."

"All the more reason to make sure she's safe." Uncle James glanced down at his watch, patted his mouth with a napkin, and stood. "I'm off. You're able to leave now, you know. No sign of plague. I'm determined to find Bimla today and make arrangements to depart from Poona."

Gussie merely saluted him with her fork.

Catherine stared after him, then set down her fork with a frown. "I wish you could stay forever."

Gussie offered a distracted smile, as though she hadn't spent every moment between her conversation with Ramabai and now considering making a home in Poona, with its crumbling forts, placid river, and stalking disease.

She brought her fork to her lips, taking a bite of food, marveling at the peace invading her thoughts. Everything that had always buzzed inside of her, all the pressure and prickling, eased.

Her career? *Might grow in a different direction.*

Adventure? *Might look like something she never expected.*

Her family? *Might finally make peace with her.*

A servant entered holding a tray. "Memsahib, a message." He approached Gussie, and she took the letter.

"Who is it from?" Catherine asked, craning her neck to see the print.

"Ramabai. She says with the increase in plague cases, she'd like to see if Bimla has been brought to the segregation camp or hospital. She checked the camp this morning and saw no sign of her, and she wants me to accompany her to the hospital." She scribbled a note telling Ramabai she would be ready late morning and handed it back to the servant. "If I'm going to leave later, I need to work."

The overflowing garden and buzzing insects drew Gussie outside. She settled on a wicker chair beneath a flowering tree that drizzled petals. A little iron table made a suitable desk.

How can I describe to you the dichotomy of India? It is everything daydreams are made of—dazzling and sultry. The sound of women's bangles clinking together and monkeys chittering in palms overhead. But it also renders one almost mute at the sight of so much suffering. Famine and plague drift from the Arabian Sea to the Bay of Bengal, shrouding the land with desperation and grief.

I have seen the most beautiful and terrible things here and—

"Writing another column?"

Gussie lifted her head and lost all interest in the pen between her fingers. Before her stood Specs, clutching a handkerchief and snuffling, sending her heart into her throat. "How terrible you look."

He narrowed his eyes and scrubbed the handkerchief beneath his already reddened nose. He sneezed. Once. Twice. Three times. "I don't feel my best, that is certain."

She smoothed the ruffles lining her bodice, wondering if he admired the way the fabric draped her shoulders, tapering at her waist. It was a frothy thing, dainty and feminine, and much less practical than the day's duties demanded. But she hadn't had occasion to dress nicely since arriving in India, and while her ready-mades made her feel capable, they never made her feel pretty. She wanted so badly for him to think her pretty.

Which was the silliest thing. He had seen her covered in mud, nearly drowned, and facedown in the dirt after being jumped on by a nasty brute of a neighbor boy. He'd seen her tired and ill and angry. He'd even once seen her wearing nothing but a moldy rug stolen from a forgotten corner of the attic—it had made a wonderful prop when she played Cleopatra—but she had been only five years old then. She didn't imagine, if she appeared before him in only a rug now, that he would laugh until he wet himself again.

"Why aren't you resting?" she asked.

"I have spent too much time in bed." He poked at her paper. "What are you writing?"

Gussie slid a blank sheet over her work, unaccountably nervous. He had read and kept every one of her columns. He'd performed the part of villain and wizard and prince in every play she'd penned during childhood. But she didn't want him to see this—her first attempt at something serious. Lasting. It revealed too many of the things stirring within her breast. New things she wasn't comfortable revealing to others. Not even to Specs.

"It's only a tale. I sent five columns to Lillian a few days after we returned from Jaipur and will have to send another few next week so my readers' demands are met."

"You are leaving soon?"

"Uncle James wishes me to leave as soon as Bimla is found."

"So you shall run? Poona is not exciting enough for Miss Adventuress." His words slurred together, the congestion in his nose not allowing him proper articulation. He sounded adorable.

"No, certainly not." She stood and twisted her fingers around the full pleats of her skirt. "But it might be exciting enough for Miss Travers."

He sneezed into his handkerchief, then lifted his glasses and rubbed at his watering eyes. "What do you mean?" he asked, settling things to rights again.

She stepped toward him and cupped his face between her palms. "Only that I've found the place that makes me want to stay."

He stilled, stopping a sniffle midway through.

"I ran from what I knew I didn't want, but I had no idea where to find the thing I did. So I looked everywhere." She ran her fingers over the ridges and hollows of his cheeks and jaw. "I care little for wealth, for it turned my family into something unrecognizable. And I care even less for position, which makes me feel like an animal in a cage." Her thumb traced the pocket between the peaks of his lip, then slipped over his mouth. His eyes gleamed like the bronze elephant she'd seen tucked between the books in the library.

She pressed her thumb to her own lips, kissing it with the promise she was about to make. "I thought I wanted to share the world with my readers, but I wasn't doing that. Not really. I was only sharing bits and pieces of it—a version that looked good in a photograph. I was pretending to live the life they couldn't, but really . . . I wasn't living any life at all. I was trapped by fear."

She looked away from him. She would bare her heart but couldn't stand for him to see her while she did. She stepped to the side and made for the pebbled path that wove between trees and through plots of wild, tumbling plants. "Will you walk with me?"

They strolled, Gussie plucking a camellia and holding it to her nose. Stroking the velvet furls of a blood-red hibiscus. Listening to Specs sniff and snort and blow into his handkerchief.

"Would you rather have this conversation when you feel better?" she asked.

He gave her a vexed look. "I would have rather had this conversation ten years ago."

"When we were still in the schoolroom?"

His shoulder rose in a crooked nod to his absurdity. "Maybe if we had, you wouldn't have spent so many years chasing phantoms."

With a tripping smile, she took his hand. Tugged him toward the cluster of guava trees rimming the far end of the garden. She paused behind them, hidden from view of the house. "I needed to go after things without substance so I could recognize, eventually, that they aren't what I truly want."

"And what do you want? Have you discovered it yet?"

She nodded. "I believe I want you." She drew so near that not even a whisper could fit between them. Her skirt enveloped his legs, her arms his waist. "Among other things, but those escape me at the moment." His laugh rumbled. "I have spent so many years chasing experiences that made me feel alive. Hoping that just around the corner, I would find acceptance. That if I captured just the right scene and explained it in just the right way, my work would offer me a greater purpose than just being someone who could never do things the proper way. But I failed. In every regard, Specs, I failed."

A tear slipped by her defenses, and he lifted his thumb to catch it. "Don't you know you are enough in my eyes? In God's? Can you truly not see the plans he has for you?"

"I think I'm discovering them here in Poona. With you. So I'm wondering if you would give me three months."

"Three months for what?"

"To settle my affairs. I still owe *Lady's Weekly* months and months' worth of columns." She laid her free hand against his chest, but that seemed too aloof a gesture, all the fabric a barrier to the intimacy she craved, so she brushed aside his jacket and slipped free two vest buttons, and there she found his heart, evident beneath only the thin layer of his shirt. Fingers splaying, she closed her eyes and counted the beats, knowing each one was for her. Not quite believing it should be so. "I don't expect you to wait until you are gray and retired to have me, Specs. And as much as I like the idea of you chasing me, I don't wish to wait that long either."

"Is this a proposal, Gussie?" Laughter tickled his words.

A sneeze followed them, and she opened her eyes. "It's a promise."

"I shall be content with that for now."

And then even his heart wasn't enough, so she lifted her arms over his shoulders and cupped his brilliant head in her hands. "I could kiss you."

"You will catch my cold if you do."

"I rather like the idea of catching every part of you."

He tasted like peppermint tea, and she found she'd never wanted anything more. At first, his touch brought to mind the long, lazy summer days they'd spent as children. Playing games in the yard, sneaking into the kitchen for sweets, and feeding the ducks in

Central Park. Small, barely-there kisses that allowed him to rake his fingers into her hair, causing pins to fling about and her curls to spill over her shoulders.

But then he tilted his head, angled his lips, and pressed her up against the tree's trunk so firmly, all thoughts of childhood were scattered. She no longer kissed ungainly, studious Specs, but found herself captured entirely by Dr. Gabriel MacLean.

She tugged him closer. Closer still. Until a groan slipped past his lips and tangled with her tongue. She pressed her palms against his back, beneath his coat, and ran her fingers up and down the crease of his spine until she thought she would go mad from wanting him. "I suppose I love you."

His laugh vibrated across her lips. "I'm happy to hear it."

She hadn't meant to say it at that moment. In that way. But now that she had, she was glad, for she knew with the speaking of it, she'd been finally caught. And there was nothing within her that wished to run.

Gussie could have hidden there all day, letting Specs kiss the sense out of her, but the sound of soft footsteps sent them skittering apart.

A servant appeared, his watchful gaze taking in Specs's swollen lips and Gussie's tumbled-down hair, and his brows lifted. But to his credit, he said nothing. Merely inclined his head and reported, "Pandita Ramabai is here to see you, memsahib."

Gussie nodded and cleared her throat, her gaze staying firmly on the pointed toes of her patent leather boots. She didn't look up until the servant's steps receded, and when she did, she refused to meet Specs's gaze. She heard his laugh, though, made throaty because of his cold.

"Will this promise lead to an engagement, Gussie? There will be gossip among the staff," he teased.

"I hardly think I would kiss a man like that whom I hadn't promised to become engaged to." Gussie crossed her arms.

"You have kissed me before, but not quite so . . . exuberantly."

She bit her lower lip and lifted her face. "Can I kiss you again?"

He reached for her, closing the gap, but only rested his chin atop her head. "It is tempting, but Ramabai will wonder at your absence. Why is she here?"

"Oh!" Gussie disengaged from his embrace and started for the table to retrieve her notebook and pen. He followed at a respectable distance. "She sent me a message this morning, asking me to accompany her to the plague hospital."

"The plague hospital? Why?"

She tossed a glance over her shoulder and stepped through the doorway. "To see if Bimla has been brought there."

Specs stared at her, unblinking and throat working. And Gussie knew fear had spiraled and consumed him.

"Specs." She ran her hand down his arm and knotted her fingers with his. "Would you care to accompany us?"

A shudder passed over his shoulders, and he exhaled. "Yes, I think I would."

Dear Specs. Perhaps, in time, his aversion to risk and her penchant for it would meet in the middle, and they would both find balance.

***

Gussie stood across the street from the plague hospital, watching the British soldiers, smart in their khaki uniforms and pith helmets, guarding the gate. A long fence, rusted sheets of iron hanging from the rails, kept curious eyes from seeing what lay beyond, but she could see the corrugated iron roofs of rows and rows of buildings.

"Did you secure permission for this visit from Dr. Hunter?" Specs asked.

"I did not see the need to." The hardness in Ramabai's voice drew Gussie's attention. "She would have refused. Hopefully, with you and Gussie accompanying me . . ." She crossed her arms and glared at the fence attempting to confine Poona's plague.

"Rama!" Specs sneezed his way through the rest of his reproof. "Are you using Gussie as a means of gaining access?"

"There is no other way," Ramabai said. She glanced at Gussie, and when she looked back at Specs, her voice softened. "You know Dr. Hunter runs the plague hospital with . . . uncommon discipline. She likes things—all things—to be done correctly and with decorum." There was a strange tightening of Ramabai's lips and around her eyes, as though she wasn't being completely forthright.

"I don't mind," Gussie said, eager to smooth over the tension between them. "I will be on my best behavior." She gave a resolute nod and determined to pretend to be Lavinia, who never put a wrong foot forward. Never did anything even remotely scandalous.

"How disappointing that is," Specs muttered.

Gussie kicked him, and he pressed his lips flat. Then he sighed. "They still might not let us in."

"I know." Ramabai squeezed Gussie's hand. "But we will hope for the best."

They crossed the street, dodging carts and weaving around piles of horse and elephant dung. Gussie's camera bag bounced against her hip, and she patted it, finding reassurance in its solid weight. She stopped feet from the gate and pulled out her Kodak. It made a compelling picture—the formidable fence, corrugated roofs peaking above, and the soldiers, with their handsome mustaches and easy posture, keeping guard.

A woman dressed in no-nonsense white linen, crisp and bright despite the dust, passed the open gate, and her gaze caught on Gussie's camera. "You there."

Gussie glanced around. "Me?"

The woman sighed. "Of course. You are the photographer from the magazine? We expected you tomorrow, but today is just as well."

"I *am* a photographer from a magazine."

"Well, come in." She strode away, and the soldiers stepped aside.

Specs came up beside her. "What was that about?"

"No idea." Gussie shrugged but followed the woman, Ramabai and Specs on her heels.

The woman entered a rickety shack. Gussie peered around

the doorframe and saw her sit down at a makeshift table, hands smoothing her brown hair, which was parted severely into a knot.

"Come in. What are you waiting for?"

Gussie entered, and the woman's eyes went wide when Specs and Ramabai crowded in behind her. "Dr. MacLean? How are you affiliated with our photographer?"

"We are childhood friends." His gaze met Gussie's and said everything he'd left out of that explanation. "Gussie, this is Dr. Marion Hunter. She is the assistant physician here at the hospital and is on the plague committee. Dr. Hunter, Augusta Travers."

Dr. Hunter looked over Ramabai but said nothing before turning back to Specs. "Your work has been noted in Ganj Peth during this last outbreak."

"Has it?" His words were as tightly wound as an out-of-tune piano.

"Of course. We hope we can rely on you if the need arises."

"That would depend on what you expect."

Dr. Hunter gave him a stiff smile, then turned to Gussie. "I was surprised, but not negatively so, when Dr. Adams informed me a photographer would be coming."

Gussie glanced at Specs, who shrugged. "Dr. Adams is the hospital medical officer. He isn't currently in Poona, though." He frowned. "Did your editor tell you to come?"

"No." Gussie turned back to Dr. Hunter. "I'm sorry to tell you there has been some confusion. I don't typically take photographs of"—she motioned out the door—"things of this nature."

"You aren't working on a story for *The Sketch*?" Dr. Hunter asked, her eyelid twitching a polka.

Ramabai stepped forward. "She is a photographer with *Lady's Weekly* and writes the most popular column in the United States."

Gussie stared at her. "Yes, that's true, but—"

"And she is looking to share a story of a more serious nature. She could write about the hospital." Ramabai met Gussie's eyes, and there was a plea in them. "How it demonstrates the efficiency and"—she swallowed—"productivity of Poona's medical system."

Dr. Hunter sat back and watched them each in turn. "Is that so?"

Gussie scratched her head. Not precisely, but there was enough truth in the sentiment that she could acknowledge the story without making herself a liar. She could *write* about the plague hospital. What she would do with it, she didn't know. "Yes."

"I suppose it's all right you're here, then. If Dr. Adams saw fit to allow a photographer for *The Sketch*, I don't see why we can't have a photographer for *Lady's Weekly*." She tapped her neatly trimmed nails against a stack of paper, then gave a short nod. "Come with me."

Dr. Hunter led them down a narrow dirt path toward the largest of the structures making uniform lines over the stamped-down grounds. She pointed out the various wards, separated by gender and, in some cases, caste. "The pneumonic cases are kept separately, giving our other patients a better chance of survival."

"What happens to the pneumonic patients?" Gussie asked.

Dr. Hunter kept up her brisk pace. "They die."

"Oh." Gussie glanced at Specs, who offered his arm as they passed a circle of children. She allowed her gaze to settle on them, their sweet smiles and wide eyes easing the frantic pace of her heart. A girl of about ten watched over the smaller ones, who stuck dimpled fingers into piles of rice and lentils mounded on platters. A few older girls, wrapped in threadbare saris of faded red and blue, grinned at Gussie. They lifted their hands to their mouths, chiming bangles and hiding giggles.

"These are some of our convalescing children. Their mothers, female patients, are in that ward." Dr. Hunter waved at the tent-like structure. From the corner of her eye, Gussie saw Ramabai slip away. "But today I will show you our male Portuguese and native Christian ward. It is quite full at the moment. Here we are."

She swept through the doorway and ushered them into a nightmare.

Rows of charpais marched across the room, each one boasting a patient. The plague victims lay supine, covered in thin, scratchy-looking blankets that must have trapped the heat against their bodies. In fact, the tent billowed with heat, and Gussie soon found herself surreptitiously swiping at the back of her neck.

As they walked down a row, the afflicted reached for them with blackened fingers. Many spit up blood or vomited into buckets held beneath their faces by impassive nurses who, once finished assisting one patient, would set the bucket on the floor and turn toward another.

There were those whose faces were wrapped in fabric and some who looked hardly human at all, with purple-shadowed eyes and noses and lips falling victim to necrosis. Some were covered in bruises, and nearly all of them displayed those terrible buboes beneath their jaws or arms.

Dr. Hunter must have seen Gussie staring because she drew near and said, "The ones with buboes on their groin have higher rates of survival. Unfortunately, many of these patients have progressed to septicemic plague, and all of those will die."

Gussie swallowed and tried very hard to avoid meeting their eyes. How could she look at them, knowing they might not see another sunset, hear a baby laugh, enjoy a meal?

They took a few more steps, and Specs came up beside Gussie, attempting to shield from view a man being ministered to by a harried-looking doctor wielding a savage needle. Stripped bare to his waist, the patient's hands clenched at his chest as the doctor plunged the needle into his groin. Gussie gasped and clapped her hands over her mouth.

"Are you well, Miss Travers?" Dr. Hunter paused her tour. "If it is too much for you, we can leave." She glanced around. "Where did your servant go?"

Gussie didn't correct her regarding Ramabai. Couldn't have anyway, because a lump had settled in her throat, and she was trying, unsuccessfully, to breathe the foul air around it.

But Specs, understanding Ramabai had gone in search of Bimla and needed time, spoke in Gussie's defense. "She is well. She has helped me at the infirmary and proven herself a capable assistant."

"A nurse as well as a photographer." Dr. Hunter tipped her chin, her gaze sweeping Gussie's impractical gown. Then she shrugged and set off down the aisle before Gussie could respond.

Pushing after Dr. Hunter, Gussie stiffened her spine and set her gaze ahead. She was not a fearful, trembling thing. She would not hide in the corner.

Life was made up of the lovely and the ugly, just as she had written earlier that day. And there was nothing so special about her that she deserved to live entirely in the former. Had being so sheltered been a privilege? Had ignorance resulted in anything other than superficial insight?

She unlatched her bag and removed her camera, taking comfort in its familiar weight. Light streamed through the open spaces where the lifted roof allowed air that didn't do much to ease the stifling heat. Wandering between cots, her gaze initially skipped over them—those patients who moaned and reached emaciated hands toward her and gripped thin blankets over concave chests. She forced herself to look at them. To see them. And she instructed the nurses to ask permission that she capture their images. These people weren't landscapes and buildings, waiting to be admired. They weren't fearless athletes determined to capture imagination. And she wouldn't exploit them.

"Will you bring me that table over there?" She waved toward the corner, and when Specs put the table before her, she pulled out the camera's bottom support and set it down sideways so she could capture the entire room. "Can I have your pocket watch?"

He handed it over, and she laid it on the table. Then she pulled out the camera's stop slide, allowing it to capture every bit of light, steadied it with a firm hand, and pressed the lever. With an eye on the watch, she counted. *One, two, three, four.* And pressed the lever again to close the shutter.

"I'm done." She packed up her camera and, without another glance, left.

She made it out of the building and around its side before her trembling knees softened like the *kheer* that had been served after dinner the night before. Sinking to the ground, Gussie stared straight ahead, seeing nothing. Seeing everything. Pain stabbed at her heart, and she grasped at her bodice with pinching fingers, wishing she could tear at the hooks. Pull the ribbons that kept her chemise drawn. Drag down the corset that pressed too tightly against her chest. She couldn't breathe.

Air wheezed in her throat. She couldn't breathe.

"Oh, God." She couldn't breathe.

She leaned her head against the rough wall and ran her hands over the dirt. Counted the swipes she made on the dusty ground. *One. Two. Three.* Closing her eyes against the spinning picture made of metal and mud and anguish. *Four. Five. Six.*

But then there were the people. The buboes and lancing and moans. How had she not known? Why had she not realized?

"Gussie?" Ramabai's voice, normally as solid and strong as the fort that refused to give itself to the sea, was tempered with empathy. "It is a hard thing to see. And Bimla isn't here. That is a good thing."

She settled on the ground and said nothing more. Only reached for Gussie's hand and sat while Gussie attempted to claw her way free of the agony brought on by awareness.

It was only when Gussie could suck in a deep breath of clean air that she allowed herself to think, really think, on all the pain and suffering. All that a photograph couldn't capture.

And she wondered how many stories she had missed because she had been too focused on seeking the prettiest view through the finder.

20

Y ou look as though you're up to something."

Gussie had tried to sneak past Specs, who sat in the parlor, but she'd shortsightedly chosen to wear a particularly swishy skirt that morning, and it made all kinds of happy sounds as it brushed the hallway wall.

She paused and considered pretending not to hear his accusation. He wasn't her keeper, after all, and their one-day sort-of-engagement offered him no great authority over her actions.

Of course, Specs had never once tried to exert authority over her. But he'd always, even as a child, been obnoxiously correct about everything.

Footsteps clicked behind her. "Gussie? What are you doing just standing there?"

"More than likely avoiding me, Catherine," Specs called.

Gussie arranged her expression into one so angelic no one would consider her capable of tomfoolery, and turned on her heel. "Catherine, how well you look today!"

"I feel so much better." Catherine wore a high-necked amethyst morning gown that spilled lace over her shoulders and chest. "Will you accompany me into the parlor?"

Gussie sagged but went to offer her friend support. She couldn't allow Catherine to crumple to the floor just to avoid Specs. Once in the parlor, she settled Catherine on an upholstered chair with spindly legs and managed to get halfway to the door before Specs finished fussing over his sister and turned to her.

"You've received a telegram."

Gussie paused in her escape and eyed the card Specs had lifted from the table.

"From New York."

She reached for it and looked down at the yellow envelope. "It's from Lillian." She removed the card, and her cheeks burned as she scanned it. "It seems a scolding was in order."

Stories doing well. Many new subscriptions. Gossip and outrage continue. Last story sent was too sober. Remember who you are.

Miss Adventuress.

She'd written a little too much of Gussie Travers into her thoughts on India. She read the telegram twice more and winced. *"Many new subscriptions. Gossip and outrage continue."* She could read between those lines—her fall from society had only helped *Lady's Weekly*. She tossed the telegram back onto the table.

Catherine reached for the message, and her eyes scanned it. Her jaw tightened, and the card bent in her clenching fingers. "Your editor is incredibly vexing. She does not appreciate you, Gussie."

"Thank you for your support, but it isn't necessary. I forgot for a minute who I was." Gussie bent to kiss her cheek. "I should go now, or I'll be late."

"You don't want breakfast?" Specs asked.

"I had some toast and tea in my room."

"I should think you would need more sustenance than that. You have a busy day ahead of you."

Gussie rolled her eyes and crossed her arms. "Really, Specs, if medicine fails you, consider following Uncle James to the Pinkerton Agency."

He took a few steps toward her, which she countered with a few shuffling steps backward. "Where is your uncle?"

"He has gone again in search of Bimla. I believe Ramabai has made a favorable impression on him, and she has convinced him of his moral obligation to use his skills in locating her. He told me he won't leave until they discover what has happened to her."

"You didn't care to join them?"

"I would have, but as you seem to know, I have a prior engagement."

"The plague hospital."

Gussie raised her brows in a challenge. When he didn't say anything, she smiled sweetly and turned to go.

"Have you had an argument?" Catherine asked.

Gussie turned. At this rate, she would never make it out of the parlor, let alone back to the hospital.

"We haven't argued," Specs said.

He would never be the first to tell of their recent promise to each other. Gussie could hardly understand what it was they'd decided, so she certainly wouldn't be the one admitting they had declared intentions. Theirs was an unconventional understanding, which left them feeling peevish and unsettled.

Of course, with Specs standing not a foot from her and looking so appealing with his hands on his hips and his glasses slipping down his nose, Catherine might also recognize the attraction between them.

"Will you at least have breakfast with me?" he asked Gussie, holding his hand toward the door. "Catherine?"

His sister shook her head and sank deeper into her chair. "No, thank you. I've already eaten."

Gussie rubbed the tension from the back of her neck. There would be no getting out of examining her *episode* at the hospital with him. He'd tried the day before, while he rubbed her hands between his and ordered her to breathe deeply, but she'd refused to discuss it. Perhaps it *would* help to talk about it.

"Very well," Gussie said. "But you must promise not to upbraid me."

"When have I ever?"

Gussie ignored his question and the hurt contained in it and went to the dining room, where she took a seat. Specs filled his plate at the buffet and sat beside her instead of across the table.

She made a point of lifting the watch pinned to her breast and peering at it. "I promised to be there by ten."

"We have been friends a very long time, and in all the years I've known you, through all your escapades and fanciful notions, I have only ever supported you. I've never done a single thing that would cause you a moment's thought otherwise. And yet you don't trust me enough to confide in me your plans." He looked at his plate, his fork hovering over it.

Gussie realized with swift insight that he wasn't looking to scold or refuse her like a recalcitrant child. He wasn't searching for an opportunity to lecture. She held on too tightly to the rejection she'd experienced at others' hands. Never his.

And she had hurt him.

She unknit her fingers and reached for his hand on the table beside her. How many times had she held it? She thought through a catalog of childhood memories playing ring-around-the-rosy, chasing ducks in Central Park, skating circles upon a frozen pond, or hoisting each other up trees.

Never had she noticed how long his fingers were. How freckles covered the backs of his hands like cinnamon dusted over a cake. How his nails made perfect crescent moons, short and even. How his skin felt brushing over hers, and how her pulse throbbed beneath his palm, and how, more than anything in the world, she wanted never to let go.

"I'm sorry I didn't tell you," she said. "I was afraid you would disapprove. So many people do, you know? It's hard to imagine a different response."

"I understand that. But I don't disapprove of you, Gussie." His thumb swept the inside of her wrist, and his lower lip softened. "I'm only concerned. After what happened yesterday, why would you want to return?"

"It was nothing. Only a minor episode. It has never happened before and will never happen again."

"Minor episode? Gussie, when Ramabai found you, you were sitting on the ground, trembling and gasping for air."

Gussie withdrew her hand and sat back against her chair. She could again feel that crushing pain in her chest. Her heart clenched in a fist so persistent, the only answer to it could be death. She could again feel the dust beneath her fingers as she grasped for a stranglehold on reality. Kept herself from slipping into the darkness that whispered, *You are such a useless creature. What purpose do you have? You think of nothing but your jaunts and photographs and flouting every expectation.*

Darkness sounded much like her mother. Her father and aunt and sisters and every journalist who had chastised her.

"You have a tender heart, and Poona is bursting with pain and death." Specs's words disrupted the memory.

Gussie shook her head. "It wasn't only the death and pain, though that was hard to bear. It's that I realized my entire life meant nothing. I take pretty photographs. I write pretty things. And I've missed the fact that life isn't some grand game of chase. There is real suffering. And I want to do something about it. I want to write about it." She leaned toward Specs, needing him to see. To understand. "I need to do this."

Specs tucked a strand of hair behind her ear and rested his hand on her cheek. "Gussie, you are one person. What could you possibly do about the world's suffering?"

Pain came swift and consuming. It filled her limbs with lead and her eyes with hot tears. That Specs, her ever-present champion, would dismiss her now . . .

That his voice would join all the others who had denied her purpose . . .

She pulled away and sniffed. With an angry swipe of her fingers, she removed all trace of tears and straightened her shoulders. "I must be off."

Then she stood and left, all those words she hated lying in a tangle at his feet.

———

Gussie stomped down the street, sidestepping a hairy black pig rooting in a nicely manicured bush. This part of Poona, with its sprawling bungalows and wide expanses of lawns, boasted an abundance of trees and a lack of vehicles for hire.

She had nearly reached the crossroads when steps sounded behind her. Expecting the pig, she tossed a wary glance over her shoulder only to discover a much more astonishing creature.

"Catherine, what are you doing out here?"

Having obviously changed out her morning gown for a walking dress in a hurry, Catherine tugged at her jacket, which couldn't be straightened, given that she'd done up the buttons crookedly. "You were so upset when you left the house that you didn't even hear me call to you. I'm worried about you going about the city in such a state, and Gabe has been so distracted lately."

"It's nothing, Catherine. Don't worry about it. You should return to the house and get back into bed."

A blush crawled up Catherine's neck and filled her face. "I am so tired of people thinking I'm too weak to know what is going on. Just because I don't feel entirely well doesn't mean you must shelter and protect me. Just because I have suffered loss doesn't mean I'm made of glass. My entire life has been one loss after another, and I've yet to shatter."

The pig, poking about the brush across the street, snorted and lifted its head at the sound of Catherine's voice, which had risen as she spoke.

Gussie took her friend's elbow and led her away from it. And as they walked, she recognized her hypocrisy. "You are right, of course, and I'm sorry. I'm angry at your brother because he pretends to support me in my endeavors, but when it comes down to it, he has very low expectations of me. Just like everyone else. I guess I can't blame him too much for that, as I haven't given him or anyone else reason to believe I'm capable of more, but I *am* capable of more. And when I told him of my plans to *be* more, he said, 'What could you possibly do about the world's suffering?' That tells me he believes me incapable of doing anything."

She dropped her hand and wrapped her arms around her waist, attempting to hold in everything that threatened to pour out. It wasn't just this incident, of course. It was incident upon incident. Being written off by everyone—family and strangers alike. But at the moment, it seemed an impossible thing to contain.

"I cannot marry a man who believes I'm useless. I can't. I've heard it my entire life, and I didn't think he would add his voice to all those that torment me."

Catherine blinked. "Marry? Why . . . have you an understanding?" Her smile bloomed.

"Had. We *had* an understanding."

"Oh, Gussie." Catherine grabbed Gussie's hand and pressed it between her own. "I'm so glad! I dreamed of it, but I didn't dare allow myself to hope. And now you will be my sister!"

"Sister? Augusta, have you taken my advice, after all?" Uncle James walked up to them, lifting his hat and offering Catherine a polite nod.

"I *considered* it, Uncle James. You'll have to excuse me, though, because I'm late."

Gussie set off, but she was soon joined by Catherine on one side and Uncle James on the other.

"I don't know why you feel as though Gabriel doesn't support you, Gussie, but you needn't worry, for he has talked of nothing else but you and your successes and daring spirit since you began writing as Miss Adventuress. He is proud of you." Catherine sounded very sure, and it would be easy for Gussie to allow the words to sway her had she not heard him say otherwise.

"Where are you going?" Uncle James asked.

"To the plague hospital so I can do something worthwhile." Beside her, Catherine sucked in a sharp breath, and her steps slowed.

"Catherine, please go home. I would feel terrible if the exertion of this outing proved dangerous to you and the baby."

"I will, but this isn't the end of our discussion. I won't give up on you." Catherine turned and made her way back up the street.

Gussie's throat tightened as she watched, and she pulled at the high neck of her blouse to release the pressure. But it did little to dislodge her guilt. Despite Catherine and Morag claiming it hadn't been her fault, she'd spent too long being accused of every calamity to pretend inculpability.

She turned and found Uncle James watching her.

"Tell me what happened," he said in his no-nonsense way, and it felt so familiar that Gussie wanted nothing more than to explain everything.

As she divested herself of her disillusion over Specs's response, she discovered the frightful truth behind her reaction. "He is all benevolence and intelligence. Sacrifice and giving and martyrdom. I will likely never be a good enough person for him."

"Hmm." Uncle James waved down a tanga. He helped her inside, told the driver where to take them, and settled beside her. "I've just spent a couple of hours in Pandita Ramabai's company. She's an incredible woman."

"She is."

"She had kind things to say about you. Good things."

Gussie tipped her head. "Did she?"

"She told me that you took a week to go to Mukti Mission and take photographs for her. You hardly knew her and had other things to do, but that didn't stop you from meeting her need. She also said you thought nothing of taking along this woman we're looking for—Bimla—even though you had no forewarning. Not only that, but you befriended Bimla—"

"That wasn't difficult. Bimla is a delight."

"Yes, but you didn't need to, and that's the point. You didn't need to do many things that you've done. Because you're not a terrible person. You aren't selfish because you have dreams. You aren't lacking because you don't want the same things your parents want for you. Yes, you're impulsive. And yes, you have an adventurous streak that has put more than one gray hair on your mother's head." He winked. "You get that from me. But you're also willing to grow. You're talented and courageous and adaptable and creative. You are so many good things."

Gussie swallowed hard. She picked at a loose thread on her cuff, worrying it until it unraveled and made a small hole in the fabric. "But everyone says I'm—"

"Who cares? Do you know what people said of me when I became an agent? Do you know what *my* parents said of me? They were hugely disappointed. Your father was the successful one, and I never escaped his shadow. I know how you feel."

"What about Specs?"

"I have no great advice when it comes to romance, but I'm pretty good at observation. He loves you. Maybe he said something obtuse and that hurt your feelings, but I have watched him since you were children, and what he feels for you isn't something that will go away. You owe it to him to talk about it."

The tanga rolled to a stop just outside the plague hospital gate. Already, Gussie could smell the peculiar rotting scent of death that permeated the place. Her heart began to throb, and she pressed her hand against it. Uncle James came around and helped her to the road. Before she could turn away, her head full of too many thoughts and questions, he stopped her with a touch.

"Don't let what people say define you. Stop repeating their lies. You are called to a different sort of life, Augusta. That can be a hard thing for others to understand." He cupped her hand between both of his and smiled, his mustache bristling like the back of a porcupine. "God has big plans for you, my girl."

When he left, Gussie nodded at the soldiers guarding the gate and followed the dusty path to the women's ward. Inside, she wove between charpais, seeking Bimla in every ravaged face. Hoping to find her. Glad when she didn't.

When she finished her search, she pulled her notebook from her satchel and glanced at the rear of the building, where a cluster of senior nurses sat at a long table cluttered with piles of bandages. Dr. Hunter had arranged for Gussie to interview them, believing her readers would find their experiences interesting. Gussie would speak to them, of course. But she didn't know what she was going to do with the information, since it was clear from her telegram that Lillian had no tolerance for anything of a more serious nature. And that was only responding to the little bits of solemnity Gussie had woven into one of the columns she'd sent. There would be no opportunity to explore in *Lady's Weekly* the plague and injustice infesting every corner of Poona.

Still . . . it was a story worth telling. And barring that, worth knowing. She considered the collection of essays she'd already written in her journal since that trip north. She couldn't seem to stop the words spreading across the pages. Between her typical merry observations and droll snippets for her column, Gussie could see the flexing and spreading of Augusta Travers.

A thin cry threaded into her thoughts, halting her steps. She jerked her head around, looking for the person who had made such a heartrending sound.

A woman groaned to her right. A child whimpered to her left. Before her, a fat, naked baby banged a tin cup against the chest of his mother, who looked as though only gossamer threads tied her to earth. All around, suffering.

Gussie tucked her notebook away, and as she walked, she noticed that no one held their hands. No one sat by them and read to them from books or letters. No one comforted them, but for the brisk ministrations of the nurses. And that was the real tragedy of Poona's plague.

A hand reached for her, fingers black and swollen. "Help." The woman took a wheezing breath, and then a string of Marathi rasped from between her swollen lips.

Gussie reached for a nearby nurse. "Excuse me. Can you help translate?"

The nurse nodded and listened carefully as the patient repeated her words.

"She wants you to help find her son. But he is not here. She has been repeating the same question since arriving two days ago."

Gussie touched the patient's cheek. "I wish I could help you."

The woman spoke something that sounded more like a moan than words.

The nurse translated. "The boy was taken to the American doctor from Ganj Peth. She saw you here with him yesterday, but she didn't have the strength to call out. She says it was the Monday before last."

Gussie blinked. She had just arrived in Poona, Catherine unwell, their trip cut short. She had gone to Specs's infirmary. And there had been a boy.

Gussie swung around, intent on leaving—she'd only come to work, not to break a mother's heart—but the woman reached out and gripped her wrist. "Where? My son." She had beautiful, deep-set eyes that drooped at the corners. They were rimmed by long, thick lashes much like the little boy who had died with strangers.

"It might not have been your son. It might have been another boy."

The nurse translated, and the patient's expression froze. Hardened. She spoke—a couple of words strung together with savage awareness.

"She wants to know what happened." The nurse, until this moment, had spoken with detached professionalism, but even she could not remain impassive in the face of this poor mother's grief.

"He died," Gussie said.

The woman did not need translation to understand. Her lovely eyes shuttered, and she wrapped her arms around her head and wept.

21

Gussie left the hospital as the sun peaked.

When she arrived at the infirmary, she found it full not of patients but of soldiers. "Pardon me," she said as she elbowed her way through. But the men closed ranks before she reached the office.

"You cannot go in there, miss," a young man said. He sported the fuzz above his lip of someone who had barely left his youth.

"And why is that?" He shrugged, and Gussie narrowed her eyes. "Will you stop me?"

He gave her a startled look and licked his lips in a nervous gesture that disclosed how recent his posting was. With a smirk, she ducked between two other men and continued her search. She needed to explain to Specs why his words had stung her so badly.

"I will not join the Searchers. I am not beholden to the British army."

Specs's angry shout made her pause. She had only ever heard him shout once—when she held the sick boy. Otherwise, she doubted he had ever raised his voice.

"What are the Searchers?" Gussie asked the nearest soldier.

"They search an area for plague victims, sending the sick to the hospital and the rest of the household to the segregation camp for quarantine."

"That sounds dreadful. Why are you here for Dr. MacLean?"

"With the recent outbreak in Ganj Peth, we need to search the area, but the residents have been particularly resistant to us. Dr. Hunter, who runs the plague hospital, has decided Dr. MacLean should join the party in this area. His presence might induce compliance."

"You will find him no great defender of the plague management methods employed by the British. And he is a stubborn man."

"He can be as stubborn as he wants. No one stays in Poona who isn't welcomed by the army. If he resists, he will be forced out."

"He will resist."

The soldier shrugged.

Gussie's lips tightened, and she pushed past him. After a few more minutes of grunting effort, she found herself in the office doorway. Specs stood nearly chest to chest with an older man whose face was as red as a strawberry. He had narrow-set eyes and a fleshy nose tightly wound with fine purple strands of burst veins. He did not look like the type of man one could disobey without recourse.

"Dr. MacLean?" Gussie called.

Both men turned to look at her.

"Gussie? What are you doing here?" Specs had removed his glasses and was gripping them so tightly that they looked about to snap in two.

She crossed the room, skirting the chair set before his desk, and took them from him. "I came to speak with you and encountered a barricade of soldiers."

"I am being conscripted," he said bitterly.

"Come now, Dr. MacLean, this isn't a war. No need to act so gloomy." The red-faced man, who Gussie now realized had a red face not from emotion but because his skin was mottled by a nasty-looking rash, propped his hands over his generous belly.

"Isn't it, though, Officer Greene?" Specs took his glasses from Gussie and slapped them back onto his face. "You force yourself into these people's homes with no understanding of their culture. No care for their modesty and privacy. You burn their belongings, separate husbands from wives, children from parents, and deposit them in inhumane conditions at camps. You refuse them the dignity of dying at home and do it all with force. It sounds like a war to me."

"And what would you have us do? Allow the disease free reign? It would disrupt supply chains across the country."

"Your methods motivated the Lokhande brothers to kill the commissioner. To kill my brother-in-law. I cannot condone it, let alone be part of it."

"You will regret refusing us."

"What can you do? I'm an American citizen, not beholden to Crown rule."

Officer Greene's mouth twisted. "Maybe not, but what about Dr. Paul? He *does* answer to Raj rule. Would you risk his infirmary? Where would you work if it was shut down? Could you continue on if he left Poona? Dr. Hunter has insisted you join our team. She holds a powerful position."

Specs's eyes, always as warm and inviting as a cup of tea, went hard, and the vein in his forehead throbbed. His fists clenched, and Gussie remembered a similar stance, a similar look, when she'd been knocked down by an older boy. She and Specs had only been eight years old, and he was smaller than average. Yet he defended her. And lost a tooth—thankfully not a permanent one—in the process. He stood to lose much more in this case.

Gussie pinched Specs's side and cleared her throat. "Will you give us a moment, Officer Greene?" Specs didn't respond well to manipulation and threats. The red-faced officer was going about it all wrong.

Specs sighed. "What is it, Gussie?"

She ignored him until she had ushered the other men from the room. They stood just outside the doorway still, so she pulled him into the corner and whispered, "You should go with them. If you go, then you will be able to manage how they treat the people who live in Ganj Peth. Those are your patients, Specs."

He rubbed his forehead. "I don't want to give any credence to their methods."

"They're going to do it whether you like it or not. Why not be a part of it so you can guide them in their actions? The people of this neighborhood know you. They trust you."

"That's precisely why I don't want to do this. I do not want to be the one who sends them to a segregation camp. The conditions are deplorable. It's such a vile way of treating people."

"I know." Her arms felt heavy at her side, remembering Ramabai's story and her lost widow. "This is what you do about the world's suffering." When she saw he recognized the twist she'd made of his words, she took his fingers between hers. "Your part. My part. It makes a difference to the ones you're able to love."

Specs shifted from foot to foot and absently scratched his cheek as Gussie silently urged him to listen to reason. Finally, he groaned and pressed his hands to his head. "Very well. I hope I won't regret this."

"You will not. Ganj Peth needs this infirmary. Who else will care for the needs of the people here if it is forced out?"

She waved the soldiers inside, and Specs told them his decision.

Officer Greene smiled, and Gussie noted his straight, white teeth. Perfectly square and not one missing. Strangely incongruent, given the mess of the rest of his face. "Very good. Nice work, miss." He turned to Specs. "We will go out tomorrow afternoon." He started for the door, then turned back. "And your nurse will attend, as well. Dr. Hunter told me about her, and each search party requires a female attendant. Yours seems particularly adept at managing you."

***

"I hate that you were pulled into this madness." Specs sat beside her in the tanga and rubbed his eyes, which were red-rimmed from lack of sleep and the lingering effects of his cold.

They had departed soon after the soldiers, and now, when

Gussie would rather have been apologizing for her rash behavior that morning, she instead found herself parroting Catherine's words from earlier. "I'm not a wilting flower, ready to fade away at the least bit of ugliness. I have seen and done more than the average woman."

His hand found hers. "I just want to protect you."

"You cannot possibly keep me safe every moment. I won't live my life constantly worried you're going to smother me with your anxiety. Will you wrap me in cotton and force me to choose the path of least danger every day we're together? You should know by now that will never work. When have I ever done the safe thing?"

"Never."

"Never. And look, even when you think you're making the safe decision—like sending Catherine away from Poona to protect her from the plague—things still happen. She still got hurt. You can't account for all the variables."

Gussie hadn't meant anything other than to point out the futility of trying constantly to protect the ones he loved, but his stricken expression drew attention to the unintentional accusation hidden beneath the surface.

His next words worsened Gussie's guilt. "I *put* her in danger. I never meant to." He covered his face with his hands, and his shoulders slumped.

"No. No. That isn't what I meant. If anything, it was my fault Catherine was hurt. I followed the thief, and she followed me."

Specs jerked upright. "What thief?"

"The one who stole my camera." He stared at her, and she pulled her hand from his grip to fiddle with the pretty lace spilling over her wrist. "The one who ran into the building and up the stairs?"

Still he stared.

"I didn't realize Catherine had followed me, and when he kicked, I moved aside, and his foot hit her instead." Her gaze darted away from his, and she finished the story in a whisper. "She fell down an entire flight of stairs."

He finally spoke. "She never said. *You* never said. Why wasn't

I told? No wonder she had so much trauma. It didn't make sense when she told me she'd simply fallen. How could a trip or stumble cause such injuries?"

He pulled away from her, and Gussie felt the distance just as surely as if he had jumped out of the tanga. His jaw tightened, and he stared straight ahead.

"I'm sorry," she said. "I didn't mean for anything to happen."

"How could you keep it from me?"

"I . . . I felt guilty."

"Was it your fault?"

She shrugged and picked at the clasp of her camera bag, her nails clicking against the brass. "No, I . . ." *I told her to stay back. I did.* But she'd also gone forward. Hadn't bothered to make sure Catherine had stayed safely on the ground floor. She had been careless. Reckless. And while she hadn't purposely put Catherine in danger, she had valued her Kodak over wisdom and caution.

She pressed herself more firmly into the corner of the cart. The driver had hung a scarlet fringe from the canopy, and it danced and bounced with their bumping movement. Gussie kept her eyes on it, her mouth clamped shut.

They stopped outside the bungalow, and one of Catherine's servants appeared. He helped Gussie onto the walk, and Specs rounded the vehicle. When she reached the lower step leading to the verandah, she waited for him to draw near.

"Gussie?" Specs looked at her, brows raised in expectation. She hadn't answered him. Didn't want to now.

She put her hand on the stair rail, her fingers rubbing the polished wood. "I cannot deny my part in Catherine's accident."

Silence. Had there ever been so thunderous a sound?

Catherine appeared in the doorway. Upon seeing them, she hurried across the verandah and toward the steps.

"Do be careful, Catherine," Specs called. "You've already had one fall down a staircase. Your child will not survive a second."

Catherine's face blanched, and her steps slowed.

Gussie turned, not anticipating how close Specs was. Not realizing his nearness would steal the breath from her throat. She fastened her eyes on his chin. "That was cruel."

"It's the truth. Something you seem to have little regard for." With that, he sidestepped her and went inside.

"Have you come home for luncheon today?" Catherine asked. Gussie didn't turn. Not until she'd schooled her features—she'd had plenty of practice hiding hurt feelings. A lifetime of vicious barbs that tore at her spirit. All hidden wounds that would never see the light of day.

But nothing—not one word anyone else had ever spoken—could compare to the gaping emptiness she experienced at Specs's savage accusation. It wasn't true. She hadn't kept her part in Catherine's accident from him out of deceit, but because of . . .

Because of what?

"Gussie, will you eat with us?" Catherine asked softly.

Gussie turned and shook her head. "I'm not feeling well. I think I will rest for a while." With the loss of Specs's regard came a gnawing emptiness in her belly that promised nothing but pain.

Catherine narrowed her eyes. She whipped her head around. "Gabriel, stop." Her command caught Specs just as he was about to disappear through the dining room door.

He paused and slowly turned. "I'm hungry."

"Come here."

Gussie had never thought Catherine possessed a strong will. She'd always been happy to pursue Gussie's plans, trailing behind and willing to take whatever bits of leftover adventure were thrown her way. But the steel in Catherine's words caused Specs's eyes to widen.

Catherine glowered at her. "Gussie, if you please."

Gussie swallowed and took the steps slowly. One foot in front of the other, until she stood in the entryway beneath the brass coffered ceiling, Catherine looking between her and Specs.

"What happened?" Catherine demanded.

"I don't know what you mean by this foolishness, Catherine, but I want to eat."

"Don't try to cajole me into submission, Gabriel MacLean. You can pretend to be as calm as a duck with your cool composure and even tone, but I see something snapping in your eyes. There is too much tension between the two of you to allow this to continue. And I am done standing by silently while everyone else around me lives, and destroys, their lives."

Gussie met Specs's gaze, and he gave an almost imperceptible shake of his head.

"I'm only upset because Dr. Hunter has insisted I join a search party," he said.

Catherine stared at him. Her hands went around her belly, and she swayed. Specs and Gussie both wove an arm around her simultaneously, their limbs twisting.

"Come," Specs said. "Let's go sit down."

He led Catherine to the dining room, releasing her back, and Gussie's arm, to pull out a chair.

When Catherine had been settled upon it, she rested her elbows on the table and her head in her hands. "You cannot go. You cannot."

"I've already agreed." Specs waved over a servant and murmured for him to bring tea.

"But why? It's too dangerous."

"It is safe enough." He patted Catherine's hand. "John was not killed while on patrol, but when it was wholly unexpected. We will be fine. The people of Ganj Peth know me. They trust me."

"We?" Catherine's attention had stuck like a burr to Specs's slip. The servant placed a cup before her, and the steam lifted, drawing her fingers.

"Officer Greene asked that Gussie join us." Specs turned to look at the sideboard, where a casual lunch had been set in silver chafing dishes and upon platters.

But before he could rise from his seat beside Catherine, she set down her cup with a sloshing of tea and grabbed Specs's arm. "Do you mean," she said, each word spat out, "that not only have you been convinced to join this terrible venture—one that you have railed against for a year—but also my friend?"

"It will be fine," Gussie said. "I'm unlikely to be accosted in the street in the company of soldiers."

Catherine turned to her, and Gussie's mouth snapped closed. "You have no idea what it is to lose someone you love to violence. No idea."

Catherine pushed away from the table and brushed past Uncle James, who was just stepping into the dining room, without a word.

"Is everything all right?" Uncle James asked after he had filled a plate and sat across from Gussie.

She gave him a bright smile. "Fine. Just fine."

He chewed his food, and Gussie tried not to look at Specs, who sat beside him after filling his own plate. She tried not to wish her uncle away so they could be alone. But then she wished he would stay forever, not knowing how she could bear another moment of Specs's heavy disappointment.

"Was your visit to the plague hospital this morning fruitful?" Uncle James asked.

Gussie poked her fork at a congealing bit of chicken and dragged it through the gravy. "I thought I could write about it, but Lillian's telegram made it clear that *Lady's Weekly* won't publish anything of the sort I have lately considered writing, so . . ." She shrugged and set down her fork. "I have an idea of what I'd like to write, but I don't know what I would do with the piece."

Uncle James patted his mouth with a napkin, tossed it down, and reached into his jacket pocket. "I have been waiting for the right time to give this to you. You have been otherwise distracted." He leveled a look at Specs. "But it seems now would be an opportune moment to reconsider your professional association with Lillian Clare."

Gussie sniffed. "What is it, Uncle James? I know you don't care for her."

"Very likely you won't, either, once you see this." He handed her a sheet of paper. "It turns out Dora Clutterbuck had nothing to do with the maligning of your reputation. I discovered her happily ensconced as Aunt Rhoda's companion in Chicago. She refuses to give up your hat, by the way, and Rhoda told me it was just restitution for her having to put up with you."

Gussie rolled her eyes, but when Uncle James tipped his chin toward the note between her fingers, she unfolded it.

I believe this arrangement will prove beneficial to both of us, Miss Clare. Tomorrow, New York will know who stands behind Miss Adventuress's inimitable pen and camera. The rest of the country's papers will disseminate the information, helping your subscription rate, but we will be the first to tell.

Sincerely,
Irving Porter
Editor
New York Daily News

Her fingers tightened around the paper, crumpling and tearing the edges, and her chest burned. She set the note beside her plate, took a sip of water, the glass slipping in her sweat-slicked palm, and stood. "If you'll excuse me."

"Gussie?" Specs called as she walked from the room, his chair scraping the floor.

But she ignored him in favor of the privacy of her room. Father had been right after all. Lillian Clare was no friend. Gussie stood at the desk and stared at her notebook—evidence of her great wrestle. Miss Adventuress and Augusta Travers.

She hadn't realized when she'd begun the journey toward herself that it would be such a painful process. One with no clear answer.

She sat in the desk chair and cradled her head in her arms. After a few minutes, she lifted a pen and wrote her name on a scrap of paper. *Augusta Constance Travers.*

Little good it did. No one seemed to want her.

22

Gussie sat on the edge of her bed, staring at the trunk she'd asked a servant to retrieve from some tucked-away storage room. She had packed half the contents of the wardrobe, folding and wrapping in paper and stowing away, until she remembered they still hadn't found Bimla. Every other time Gussie had run, she only had to worry about herself.

And anyway, she had no idea where she would go. No idea if she even wanted to write for *Lady's Weekly* anymore. Did Lillian deserve her loyalty? No idea if she would stay in Poona, with its ancient river. Its stories baked into stone fortresses. Its afflicted people. Its angry doctor who felt as betrayed as she had when reading Mr. Porter's note. No idea if she should just return to New York with Uncle James. Go to Chicago. Be molded into the image of respectability.

But she wanted to stay. To rest.

To attach herself to one place. One people. This place and this people.

She threw herself back against the mattress with outstretched arms. Her stomach rumbled, and she pressed her hand to it. She'd skipped dinner the night before, sending away the tray and ignoring Specs on the other side of the door, asking her to please let him in. Now it was time for breakfast, and she wished she could be like one of those fainting women who ignored their hunger and lamented life's grievances. But she was too coarse—too earthy—to skip more than one meal without real regret.

"Remember who you are," Lillian had written.

Miss Adventuress, photographer of pretty landscapes, barren landscapes, exotic landscapes—but definitely always landscapes. And author of nonthreatening columns as light and airy as candy floss.

But Gussie was more than that. She wanted more than that.

How very obnoxious that no one would *let* her be more than that.

She bolted upright and tossed a baleful look at the pile of shirtwaists threatening to topple beside her. Then she pushed them onto the floor. Kicked a stray one from her boot.

"Remember who you are."

"Well, I'm tired of everyone else telling me who I am." She licked her lips, and her chest hitched.

"Talking to yourself?"

Gussie jerked around and saw Uncle James standing in the doorway.

"You missed dinner yesterday and breakfast this morning. Is your diminished appetite a result of Lillian's treachery?"

"I'm not upset about it at all." Gussie wrapped her arms around her waist. "I'm not."

And then tears betrayed her.

Uncle James sat beside her and held out his arm the way he always had when she was a child. Gussie caught a sob behind her palm and leaned her head on his shoulder, letting him hold her.

After a few minutes, she took the handkerchief he'd produced and rubbed it over her nose. "I don't understand what is happening. I'm all out of sorts. I don't even know who I am anymore."

"You are the same person you were before you boarded that ship and snuck off to India."

"I'm not. I knew that Gussie. I understood her. But everything is different now. Being here has made me see that the world is so much bigger than I imagined. I never realized how coddled I was. How sheltered. I thought because I traveled by myself and saw grand things and had adventures other women could only read about in magazines, I was worldly. I was just a child, though." She blew her nose into the handkerchief, making a great honking noise her mother would certainly disapprove of. "I wish I hadn't come. Because now I want different things, and I'm not sure it's possible to achieve them."

"Why is that?"

She shrugged. "What if I'll only ever be Miss Adventuress? Perhaps I'm not capable of writing anything but cheerful pieces meant to offer a bit of distraction."

Uncle James sat back and stared at her. "You're not seriously considering continuing to work for them after what Lillian did?"

"What else can I do?"

Catherine had suggested Gussie write what she wished. But she couldn't do that for *Lady's Weekly*. She didn't think anyone in New York would overlook her ruined reputation and print her story about the hospital. Maybe a British paper would be interested?

"If you ever decide to write things of a more serious nature, I will be happy to take a look."

Gussie's arms prickled with the reminder of Mr. Epps's words. When he'd refused her work, she'd thought that the end of it, but what if it only meant the start of something new? What if she could be Gussie Travers?

"I thought you were going to marry Gabriel," Uncle James said.

She sighed. "I think he has discovered I'm not suitable."

Uncle James looked away, but she could see the smile twitching his lips.

She tossed the moist handkerchief at his head, and he flicked it to the floor, where it fell atop her shirtwaists. "I didn't say anything amusing."

"I thought you didn't care about suitability."

"I don't, except when it comes to Gabriel MacLean."

Something about abandoning his nickname for his given one made a fairy-tale prince of her childhood playmate. He became unattainable. Almost too wonderful to be living and breathing beneath the same roof as someone like her.

She groaned and buried her face in her hands. "I don't like the person I've become—all deep thoughts and insecurity." Her words were muffled, but Uncle James heard them still.

"Augusta." He touched her arm, gently pulling down her hands. "Listen to me carefully. You have only changed inasmuch as maturity changes people. You are right—you have been coddled and protected, and now you have seen things your parents would never have wished for you." At her protest, he held up his hand, and she fell silent. "They were wrong. They think you frivolous and reckless, but you were merely a woman of deep thought trapped by expectation and convention. And when you discovered what set a fire in your belly, what made you *want* to do grander things, your experiences weren't able to support it. Your entire worldview has been turned inside out. Of course you are going to struggle with that. Of course you have questions." The hard lines of his jaw softened, and the observant gleam in his eyes mellowed. "I'm proud of you, niece. Growing up is not an easy process. You could have chosen to continue on in your ignorance, but you're doing the hard work of becoming the woman God has always planned for you to become."

Warmth spilled through Gussie's middle, spreading through her limbs and making them limp with gratitude. "I love you, Uncle James."

He kissed her forehead and stood. "I love you too." With a curious swipe of his hand against his eyes, he took a few steps toward the door before turning back toward her. "Ramabai will be here soon. We are looking again for Bimla."

"Will you be alone? How scandalous!"

Gussie had meant to joke, but Uncle James's shoulders straightened, and his brows lowered into a glower she knew had intimidated criminals and convicts across the United States. "I would never do anything to harm her reputation. She is a woman of uncommon strength, dignity, and goodness. We will take some of her widows with us."

Gussie blinked as awareness settled. "You care for her." How had she not seen that? "Will you do anything about it?"

He rubbed the furrows the years had carved across his forehead, and for only a moment, Gussie caught sight of a much younger man—handsome and eager and ready to prove his mettle. But the image disappeared, and Uncle James gave a rueful shake of his head. "Pandita Ramabai is meant for much greater things than life with a codger like me. Much like you are. And I don't think your parents could bear losing both of us to India."

His words registered just before the door clicked shut, and she jumped from the bed. Wrenching it open, she saw Uncle James halfway down the hall. He turned with raised brows, and Gussie launched herself at him, throwing her arms around his neck and pressing kisses to his cheek.

When her exuberance had been exhausted—or rather when Uncle James had been exhausted by her exuberance, for Gussie had never in all her twenty-five years come to the end of her supply—he set her down and gave her a stern look. "When Bimla is found, I will go home alone. But I would feel much better about it knowing you had the protection of a husband."

Gussie crossed her arms and glared. There had been no formal agreement. Only promises. But promises were made up of hope and dandelion fluff. "That is unfortunate, for I'm not sure where to find one in so short a time."

"I believe," Uncle James said, jerking his chin and giving a pointed look over her shoulder, "there is one standing behind you."

Gussie whirled and discovered Specs leaning against the wall outside her bedroom. "Have you been there this entire time?"

"Yes. I've come home for lunch."

"Well . . . I . . . it's rude to listen to a conversation you weren't invited into."

He raised his brows and blinked innocently, his glasses magnifying those beautiful eyes. How unfair that he maintained his hold on complete adorableness when she was made a sputtering mess in his presence. Vaguely aware that Uncle James had left them alone in the hall, she watched with wary caution as Specs took a few steps toward her.

"I hate that we argued," he said. "And I hate even more that I was the dunce who allowed this division between us. I miss you."

Gussie's heart crashed into her feet, then melted into a puddle of regret and longing. "Me too."

He came even nearer, his hand reaching for hers.

"I'm so sorry," she said. "So very sorry about what happened to Catherine. If I could go back and ignore that thief—let him take my camera and run—I would. I hate that I was responsible for hurting her."

From the parlor down the hall came a thump and a clatter. Catherine appeared, her hair mussed and red creases cutting across her cheek.

"I thought you were resting in your room," Specs said.

Catherine shook her head. "I feel asleep on the settee while I was reading. I awoke when Mr. Travers came into the room." She turned to Gussie, her eyes shimmering and her words twisting with panic. "Have you thought my accident was your fault this entire time?"

"I should have never followed him. It was careless. And you were hurt in the process."

"Oh, Gussie, no." Catherine crossed the hall and gripped Gussie's upper arms. "It wasn't your fault, but mine. You told me to stay downstairs where it was safe, but I didn't want you going after him alone. And I wanted to be brave like you."

"You are braver than anyone gives you credit for." Gussie pulled Catherine into an embrace.

Specs cleared his throat. "This is lovely, but I really must insist you release Gussie to me, Catherine. We were in the middle of a . . . sensitive discussion that requires privacy and, on my part at least, courage that I cannot claim in front of an audience."

"Oh." Catherine glanced between Gussie and Specs, chewing on her bottom lip. "Very well. I will disappear, but I should like an accounting of everything when you are through."

Specs laughed as his sister disappeared back through the parlor door. "You have been good for her, Gussie. She was brought low by John's death and became a whisper of herself. But your visit has helped her rediscover life. More than that, she once again seems like the woman who existed before our parents' deaths." He reclaimed her hand. "I think it would be good if you could stay. Here in India. In Poona."

"Good for Catherine?"

"Good for me too."

"I think it would be good too." She brought his fingers to her lips. "But . . . I will always want adventure. And in India, there are so many things begging to be photographed and written about."

"I have no doubt. Poona is host to a well-established photography club, and even though I think Lillian Clare an awful person, I will not stand in the way of your work."

"But I no longer want to write the kinds of things you believe I should."

His brows drew together. "I don't have any presumption where that is concerned. What do you mean, the things I believe you should write?"

His speech and the sentiment dancing across Lillian's telegram poked at her thoughts, harsh and demanding, scattering any certainty that she could accomplish her goals. That she was even worthy of them. How powerful words were. And how much more powerful because they belonged to friends.

"You told me I couldn't possibly do anything about the world's suffering."

"I was worried for you. I know how sheltered you are, Gussie.

You've seen little of the brutality of life. Your heart hasn't been touched by hardship and grief. So why should you expose yourself to it if it isn't necessary? I would hate for you to lose the vibrancy and joy that make you up."

Gussie shook her head. "But isn't it better to understand the world we walk through? I'm happy to give up a portion of my innocence if that means I'm aware of what's going on around me."

"I only want to protect you."

"You can't do that, Specs." She touched his face, and he turned to nuzzle into her palm. Pressed a firm kiss against her skin. "Since coming here, I've learned things about myself I don't like. And I want to grow. I want to do something that matters."

"Your work does matter."

"But it isn't enough now. I've watched Ramabai's work and yours too. I've seen how Dr. Paul has offered an entire community care. And Bimla, who is a balm to all who meet her. I want to do more. I want to be part of a bigger purpose. More than being a launching point for others' dreams, I want to use my talent for something good. And I think, once I've fulfilled my obligation to *Lady's Weekly*, I'd like to see what I can do with it."

He laid her hand over his heart, which beat an even, steady tempo. So reliable and steadfast. So calm and composed. One day she would lay her head against his chest and fall asleep to the thumps beneath her ear.

"I understand, though it frightens me a little. What if you change so entirely that I do not recognize you anymore? You have been a friend since childhood, keeping my fear at bay and reminding me that buried beneath the grief, there is joy as well. I don't want your vitality to be quenched by life's cruelty."

"It will not be. I'm not changing so much as growing."

He scooped her toward him, pulling her as close as possible, his hands cradling her lower back. Nothing but cotton and silk between them. And even that seemed insubstantial in the face of the heat his touch inspired. It would burn away, surely, leaving them able to become more than childhood friends. More than the vaporous things promises were made of. More than spirit and matter.

His mouth found hers, and she settled into the kiss the way one might find oneself cossetted by a well-loved armchair by the fire. All warmth and softness.

She pulled away, though, for there was something else she must say. She asked, hope tantalizing and terrifying, "Do you forgive my part in Catherine's accident?"

"Catherine herself said there is nothing to forgive." His eyes darted from her, though, as he offered her absolution. It was a Lilliputian movement, one that might have no significance at all. So when he again met her gaze and she saw only love in it, she pushed away the ferocious seed of doubt and disappointment that had sprouted when he couldn't look at her.

It didn't take more than a few words to convince her she had misread him.

"Will you marry me, Gussie? I find myself in need of something more concrete than promises and possibilities."

After another kiss, this one much shorter than Gussie cared for, they joined Catherine and Uncle James in the dining room, where lunch was being laid out. Catherine sat in a seat facing the door, her hands conducting a symphony with a napkin.

"You are to marry?" she asked, coming to her feet when they appeared.

Gussie and Specs exchanged a glance, and the next few minutes were filled with squeals and hugs and exclamations of delight.

"But will you live here, Gussie? In India?" Catherine had lifted her water glass and held it aloft now, midway between the table and her lips.

"Of course. Where else would I live?"

"Won't you miss New York? Your family?" Her voice caught on *family*, and Gussie knew Catherine could never understand that some families didn't work quite as well as her own. The MacLeans had embraced one another. There was never a harsh word spoken that wasn't later atoned for. And their snug home, while empty of valuables, had been full of kindness.

"I have spent the last two years doing everything in my power to escape New York. I shall not miss it a whit. My family . . . Well, they shall be happy I have finally found a place I wish to settle." And perhaps they would embrace the missionary doctor as her husband in lieu of continued gossip and scandal.

Catherine cried a little, making hiccupping sounds into her napkin. When she managed to gain control of her happy tears, she turned her attention to the food before her, but a wide and irrepressible smile made eating a challenge.

Halfway through the meal, a servant appeared, Ramabai trailing behind. "She insisted, sahib," he said with a bow of his head.

"Of course, she does not need an invitation." Specs waved Ramabai into the room.

Ramabai's sharp steps kicked up the pleats of her sari, and her generous mouth twisted in tight acknowledgment of Specs's welcome. "I'm sorry to disturb your luncheon, but I want to tell you I must leave Poona for the time being."

"Leave?" Gussie stood. "Bimla hasn't been found yet."

"There has been an outbreak of mumps at Mukti Mission, and they are in desperate need of my guidance and help. It isn't ideal—I wanted to remain here until Bimla was safely home, but it cannot be helped."

"Do you need me to accompany you?" Specs asked. "I'm happy to see to the children."

Ramabai shook her head. "No. You have your own work here. We have been through mumps before, and I feel better leaving knowing that Bimla will have friends to turn to once her whereabouts are discovered . . ." Her words trailed off.

"Come," Uncle James said, standing and offering Ramabai his elbow. "There is something I must discuss with you."

Specs watched them leave the dining room, and his forehead wrinkled. "I'm growing more concerned every day. Even if Bimla did leave of her own accord, I don't believe she would abandon her job without a word of explanation for so long."

"Hopefully Uncle James is successful in locating her, if only to set everyone's mind at ease." Gussie well knew the things one could walk away from if there was a strong enough reason.

Specs glanced at the watch pinned to his vest. "Time to go, Gussie," he said. "The Searchers await."

23

Thirty minutes later, Gussie scanned the crowd gathered outside the infirmary as Specs helped her from the tanga. "I didn't realize it would be such a large group."

He looked over the gathering, and his jaw clenched. "They aren't going to like this."

"Who?"

"The residents of Ganj Peth. Imagine having your entire neighborhood overrun by foreign soldiers who know nothing about your culture or religion, forcing themselves into your homes, insisting on examining every inhabitant without—"

"Come now, Dr. MacLean. You make us out to be villains in a penny dreadful. We are only trying to halt the spread of this disease." Officer Greene pushed between two native soldiers wearing billowing white pants and long black coats. "And we have made allowances for the females. Look." He waved toward a cluster of women—a European wearing a somber dress stitched in linen and grief, and two Indians dressed in white nursing uniforms. He turned a charming smile Gussie's way. "Miss Travers will accompany you, of course. The division will be split into ten search parties, each one containing three British soldiers and a native gentleman. When inhabitants insist on the attention of a female, one of the nurses will be called. I will be accompanied by the man with the yellow flag so that, if plague victims are discovered, I am easy to find."

"And my role?" Specs asked.

"You will start with a particular party, but if there is issue with a house, you will be called upon to handle it." Officer Greene scratched his head and shifted his considerable bulk. "When the day's work is over, you will return to your infirmary, which we are using as a holding center, and examine each patient to make sure they do, indeed, present with plague symptoms. Then the ambulance will deliver them to the plague hospital, and everyone else who has been in the infected houses will be sent to the segregation camp." He waved at someone. "If you'll excuse me."

"Explain to me again why we are doing this?" Specs asked Gussie after he left.

"You are protecting Dr. Paul's work here. *Your* work here. It also offers you a modicum of control, and you will be able to oversee the process. You can ensure only people who are truly sick are sent to the plague hospital."

"Unfortunately, the segregation camp isn't much better."

"Yes, but there, at least, people will not be separated from loved ones and can leave in a week." As long as they weren't widows. "It's the best you can do for now."

"You're right, of course, but I hate everything about it."

There was a shout, and the crowd began to form groups, each boasting a trio of soldiers carrying a pickaxe, lantern, and pot of paint.

"It looks as though we are about to step into an illustration of Snow White's dwarves," she said.

Specs's expression was grim. "Except this is no fairy tale."

"No, I suppose it isn't."

Until Gussie arrived in India, life had always seemed straightforward. It was about one thing—escape. Escape from her parents' expectations and Uncle James's detection and the words that followed her. Stung her with sharp, biting censure.

Then she came here. And life became much more complicated. But also richer and deeper.

"Dr. MacLean." A soldier approached with crisp steps, his uniform straight and blond hair tucked beneath a topee. "You and Miss Travers are to join my search party. We will all fan out from here and head east. Are you ready?"

"Very well. Let's get this over with." Specs glanced at her as they followed their small contingent down the dusty street. "I will have to leave the house. Etak suggested I stay with him."

Gussie grabbed a fistful of skirt and stepped around a pile of horse dung. "What do you mean?"

"I can't very well live with you if we are engaged to be married. It isn't seemly."

"I guess so. Where shall we live after we wed?"

"Catherine has already asked if we would live with her in the bungalow. At least until we need more space."

He gave her such an endearing look that she was tempted to kiss him right there in the middle of the street. She wouldn't, of course, but resisting was a frightful feat.

"Are you sure this is what you want?" he asked, stopping. "I have no intention of leaving India. Ever. Everything I want is here."

She touched his arm and smiled. "So is everything I want."

They resumed their walk, and Gussie experienced a moment where everything was right in her world. A shiver ran across her shoulders. There had never been a moment when she felt as though things were as they should be. Had never been a moment when she felt as though she was where she belonged. She'd never known a time when she was entirely satisfied with stillness.

Something dark, wrapped in a lifetime of condemnation, mocked her joy, but she tightened her hold on Specs's arm. She wouldn't listen. She would claim the peace and belonging.

Following the other members of their group, Specs guided her up a short walk that ended at what appeared to be a crumbling brick wall.

Her brows knit. "What are we doing here?"

One of the soldiers—the one who held the pickaxe over his shoulder—pointed, and there, hidden in the shadows of a peeling woven screen, stood a door halfway off its hinges. He knocked.

They waited.

After another knock and the Indian soldier calling a greeting through the crack where the door tugged away from the wall, a small child answered. Dressed in a dusty tunic and baggy pants, he peered up at them with eyes as wide as the plains Gussie had crossed on her way to South Dakota. His beauty struck her fiercely. How lovely people could be—more than the highest mountain peak or deepest ocean. And how much more interesting. There were stories to tell *about* places, but they were *in* people.

The boy hovered halfway behind the door. He looked over their group, his chin quivering. One of the soldiers stepped forward, and the boy stumbled away with a cry.

"You're scaring him!" Gussie shoved past the soldier and knelt on the threshold. She couldn't speak to the child, but many things could be said without uttering a word.

Specs bent beside her. "Namaskara, Isar."

He spoke in a low, soothing voice—the same one he used when he was trying to convince someone to make different choices. Gussie had spent a lifetime ignoring it, but now she wished to listen to him speak just like that until she fell asleep tucked within the soft, dependable folds of it.

With a skittering glance at the soldiers, the boy took a tentative step toward them and said something. Specs nodded, then turned to Gussie. "I have seen Isar at the infirmary. He says his mother is home but his father and older brother are working."

One of the soldiers pushed forward. "Then we shall examine the mother and search the house."

Specs stood up so suddenly that Gussie was knocked off balance and smacked her hand into the wall to keep from toppling over. "You will not examine the mother. They are a modest family. I have never even met the mother. She likely doesn't leave the house." He reached down for Gussie and hoisted her to her feet.

"Miss Travers will examine the mother. I'm sorry, Gussie. I know you aren't trained for this, but Officer Greene has put us in an untenable situation."

He knelt in front of the boy again, and Gussie loved him more in that moment than any other since coming to know Dr. Gabriel MacLean. He was a dichotomy of kindness and resolve. Compassion and justice. There was nothing straightforward about him. Gussie knew she was uncomplicated. She held her emotions and thoughts close to the surface, finding solace in keeping those deep places free from clutter.

And yet he loved her.

"I will do it. I can. I promise you," she said.

He finished speaking with the boy and turned his face toward her. "I don't doubt it."

Had anyone ever believed in her like Specs? Had anyone ever thought her capable? She didn't think so. He made her want to be more than she seemed. Made her want to dig and plow and pull up the weeds that had sprouted with lack of attention and care. Made her want to fill those tilled spaces with things that mattered. Like this little boy and his fear and family.

"What should I do?"

Specs sighed and shoved his fingers beneath his hat, scratching and grimacing. "You'll have to look for buboes here"—he pressed his neck and beneath his arm—"here, and . . ." He stood abruptly and waved toward his pants. "And here."

His eyes didn't meet hers, and she found herself in the distinctly peculiar position of seeing Specs flustered, his color high and voice even higher.

She bit down a grin and forced her expression into one of earnest comprehension. "I shall do my best."

"You're enjoying my discomfort," he grumbled.

"So much."

He rolled his eyes. "All right. You men, you have permission to search the house but for the kitchen and idol room—Dhaval will check those areas—and the room where Isar's mother is. Gussie, follow me."

With that, he led them inside, the little boy shuffling beside him and casting dark looks at the men trailing Gussie. They crossed a small open space, empty except for a carved sofa against the wall and dust motes that cavorted in the light squeezing through the slats of the shutters. A gecko slithered between them, able to break through where air couldn't.

A few doors, closed tightly against prying eyes, led off the central room. The child pointed to each one in succession and said something in the language Gussie was beginning to equate with sun-dappled streets that smelled of overripe fruit.

The sepoy, Dhaval, who had remained silent in the face of Gabriel's satisfactory comprehension of Marathi, spoke up. "That door leads toward the kitchen. And that room is where the mother has gone."

"Follow Isar, Gussie. He will tell his mother what you are to do." Specs squeezed her shoulder, then jerked his chin toward the door through which the boy had disappeared.

A dozen steps and she found herself standing within a puddle of sunlight. It spilled through an ornate wooden screen and created a marquetry of geometric patterns across the floor. Gussie closed the door softly behind her and leaned against it.

In contrast to the one through which she'd just come, this room boasted enough furnishings to fill an entire New York townhouse. Carved settees piled high with pillows embroidered in gold and silver rimmed the perimeter except the space that was occupied by a bed set low to the ground and featuring a curved headboard. A plush blue-and-red rug peeked out from beneath it, its wool pile swirling together a garden of botanicals sure to make the ones in Central Park jealous.

But most surprising were the walls. Painted with ocher, they were covered from arm's reach down with figures done in white. Gussie crept nearer, vaguely aware of a conversation cloaked in soft vowels and gentle murmurs. All around her, a swirl of triangular people went about life—harvesting rice, carrying water, pulling carts. A woman sat in a simple house, tending to a baby who rolled on the floor. A coconut palm, heavy with fruit, dipped a curtsy toward a circle of dancers beneath it. Gussie's breath caught at the elegant simplicity of it. At the playing out of life in the day-to-day. What would have looked like a depiction of drudgery only a couple of short months ago called to her like a lovely, faraway song.

The silence crept nearer Gussie's consciousness, and she realized Isar and his mother had ended their conversation. She licked her lips and turned. "Hello."

Isar's hand went to his mother's, which lay on the armrest of a gilt chair tucked beside the screened window. She sat like a queen about to receive court, her smile broad and displaying straight teeth but for the right upper canine, which tilted toward its neighbor as though leaning in for a hug.

When Gussie stood a few feet away, she saw that Isar's mother wasn't much older than she herself. She had a long, thick braid of shiny black hair draped over her shoulder. A blue scarf fringed with glass beads draped her head and displayed a wide forehead free from lines and round cheeks that bunched beneath her eyes. Gussie couldn't help but smile in return.

Isar spoke, and the woman shrugged, then stood and pointed her chin toward the ceiling, revealing the smooth expanse of her neck, bubo-free. She dropped her head, waved at Isar, and spoke a few sharp words. The boy scurried from the room and shut the door behind him. Then, almost before Gussie realized what she was doing, his mother pulled at the long end of her sari, made quick work of the snaps, and dropped her blouse to the floor. Before Gussie could even make a sound of surprise, the woman lifted her arms, one at a time, and patted each fuzzy armpit. She grabbed Gussie's hand and pushed her fingers into the slick hollow.

"Oh." Gussie's eyes widened, and the woman nodded in satisfaction.

"No sick," she said. Then she bent over, grabbed the hem of her sari, and drew it up.

Gussie's mouth dropped. She knew what was required of her, but she had expected a greater lead up in deference to the sensitive nature of the situation. The woman's fingers poked at areas meant only for the eyes of a husband or doctor. At the sight of the reaching hand, Gussie sidestepped to avoid complete mortification.

"Wonderful. You are obviously completely healthy. I see no sign of plague here." Gussie turned back to study the paintings on the wall, allowing the woman to dress.

A knock came, and with a glance at the woman, now fully dressed and again sitting in her chair, Gussie went to the door.

"Yes?" she asked, peeking out.

Specs stood there, his brows knit and his teeth working the inside of his lower lip. "Dhaval must look inside the kitchen. The door leading to it is locked, but he believes there might be another one through here. I don't want them destroying the property if they can avoid it."

He had put his face as close to the opening as possible without seeing inside and began to speak to Isar's mother. His words were calm, as usual. Even speaking in Marathi, they had a singular effect on Gussie. Wrapping her in their mellow way, as warm and cuddlesome as a winter fire.

They did not, it seemed, have the same effect on Isar's mother. For the moment Specs finished speaking, she jumped from the chair and ran toward the far wall where, Gussie noticed for the first time, there was a small doorway not even as tall as a man.

The woman stood before it and shook her head, and though Gussie understood none of what she said, she easily perceived the terror behind her words.

"She seems overwrought. Could it be she doesn't want a man in the room? I could look," Gussie offered.

Specs shook his head and sighed, his hand wrapping around the back of his neck. "No, you cannot. You aren't Hindu." He muttered something to someone behind him, then turned back toward her. "She doesn't have a choice. They must check every room. Dhaval will be respectful and not look in her direction."

Dhaval stepped forward, spoke a few terse words in Marathi that encouraged the woman to begin wailing loudly, then pushed into the room and headed toward the door.

The woman sank to the floor and flung her arms over her head.

Dhaval uttered a harsh command, but the woman didn't obey, so he grabbed her wrist and yanked her away.

"Stop!" Gussie cried. "You're scaring her."

"He must see inside that room. If her behavior is any indication, her husband and son aren't at work." Specs kneaded his forehead with firm, sure fingers. "This isn't right, how they do this. But there is no other solution."

The door to the kitchen bounced against the wall, and Dhaval's shout called Specs forward. His eyes drooped at the corners, and he crossed the room with faltering steps. Gussie followed, and when he ducked to see through the kitchen doorway, she crouched beside the woman.

"Did you see any buboes on her?" Specs asked.

"I didn't."

"Then she and Isar will be taken to the segregation camp. Her oldest son, who is very ill, will be taken to the plague hospital. Go, tell one of the soldiers to fetch Officer Greene. He will need to come and see to the body."

The woman's cries had chased Gussie from the house. She couldn't witness it. Couldn't wrap her mind around so much suffering. Officer Greene arrived in time to instruct two soldiers to disarm Isar's mother. Where the knife had come from, Gussie had no idea, but it had appeared in the woman's hand before Specs had turned from Gussie and she had fully absorbed the fact that there was a corpse on the floor.

Based on the sounds that came from the woman, she hadn't realized it either.

Officer Greene had completed his own examinations of the body and the older boy crouched in the corner of the room, feverish and sporting telltale plague signs. When Officer Greene motioned to his men to remove her husband, the woman had made a guttural cry and slashed the blade in a wide arc, catching Dhaval's arm.

Chaos had erupted—men shouting, Isar crying, blood dripping—and Specs had pushed Gussie from the room. "Get out of here. Wait for me back at the infirmary."

Gussie had just stared, stupefied by the violence—the soldiers, angrily smashing the woman's hand against the wall. Smacks that left red handprints and yanking that revealed a tumble of hair as polished as the mahogany desk in Father's office.

Specs had gripped her shoulders. "Go, Gussie. Now."

And she had run.

She ran until she reached the end of the street, where a man leaning against a wall, smoking, watched in interest as she clutched one of the kerosene streetlamps, her fingers scraping at the wooden post, splinters digging into her palms.

Gussie pushed away and pressed her hands to her mouth, her breath coming in deep, gulping gasps. "How could they?" That poor woman. To be handled so carelessly after such a shock.

The son would be taken to the plague hospital, where Gussie knew most went to die. And the mother would be sent with Isar to the segregation camp. The very same camp Ramabai held in such disgust. And all while grieving her husband. It was too much to bear.

Horrific awareness slammed into Gussie's thoughts. Isar's mother was a widow. Being sent to the same place where Ramabai's friend had been treated so terribly. A widow who would now belong nowhere.

Smoke, musky and smelling faintly of pine, coaxed its way down her throat. Gussie coughed and hurried on. The streets were a tangled mess, narrow alleys spilling out onto broad avenues. Crushed with palanquins and tangas and ox carts and carriages pulled by fine horses. She crisscrossed Ganj Peth, passing by dimly lit shops and stalls hemmed together like a patchwork quilt, as she made her way back to the infirmary.

An elephant lumbered by, its mahout swaying atop the grand animal, legs splayed and knees gripping. She reached for her camera, hands patting the spot it normally hung, and she consigned the sight to memory.

Take a picture.

Gussie slowly blinked, much like a shutter depressing. Imprinting upon her mind the moment. The utter wonder at such a sight. There was still beauty undergirding the sorrow and heartache.

A woman walked by, her hips swaying and arms reaching in a graceful pose to hold a jug upon her head. Gussie blinked. And remembered.

Take a picture.

There were stories behind every heavy brow and filmy scarf.

A man crouched in the tiled doorway of a three-story building that looked about to topple over. He guided a young boy's hands at a flat spinning wheel, one end spitting out a line of fine white floss. *Take a picture.* Gussie closed her eyes.

So many things could be said through photographs. Life could be hard, but it still retained beauty. And in the darkness behind her lids, words blinked like stars spangling the night sky.

A Photo Adventure through India.

A title?

She opened her eyes. Lifted her hand when she saw the boy had noticed her standing there. Smiled at the old man.

A title.

Now she only needed the courage to finish writing the things that spoke to her. Things that Miss Adventuress couldn't claim. And even though Lillian didn't want it, perhaps Mr. Epps would.

Her thoughts were filled with words, spilling and bubbling, and they were everything they should be. Grand, purposeful, encouraging. Sentences strung—gleaming, perfect pearls forming a necklace so divine, so deliciously simple that nothing else was needed to embellish them.

Not witty allusions. Not naïve proclamations. Not saccharine descriptions.

Perhaps no one would want to read it. Lillian might scoff, and Mr. Epps might reject it. Perhaps no one would care for the photographs and stories of this bewildering, disarming, astonishing country. But she knew . . . her words were enough.

As she turned from the spinners, a shout caught her attention. "Miss Travers? I've come to bring you back to the infirmary."

Officer Greene hurried up the street she'd just traveled, mopping his face with a wrinkled handkerchief. "This is beastly work, I tell you. That woman put up quite a struggle."

"She'd just discovered her husband was dead and her son would be taken away from her."

He waved his hand, dismissing all that pain. Had he become so immune to suffering that he felt nothing in the face of it?

"I'm able to see myself back," she said.

Officer Greene offered a patronizing smile. "There's no reason I can't escort you. You have wandered into Vetal Peth, and we have already been through this area. Anyway, it seems your work with the Searchers today has been prematurely ended. Dr. MacLean has been called upon to help the victims of an accident at the ammunition factory and asked that I see you back. You will help us another time."

The man holding the yellow flag trailed them, along with a group of soldiers who kept a respectful distance, their eyes sweeping house after house, probing for signs of the disease that gave meaning to their effort.

"This area is free of plague, then?" she asked.

"For now, though it spreads with the rats that infest the area and will come back, no doubt. The plague here seems to have originated with that house"—he jerked a thumb toward the building across the street—"and spread from there."

Gussie strained her neck to see around the crush of traffic. The remains of scaffolding and still-brilliant whitewash attested to the house's recent disinfection.

"We had heard that a boy was borne away in the night and had not returned. A week later, we searched the property and came upon a woman, who was removed to the plague hospital. The husband, it seems, abandoned his wife and hasn't been seen since."

"And the building next to it?" It had been handsome once, three stories high, with carved balustrades and arched windows, but it seemed to be creeping toward the earth, its color the same dingy yellow as the street.

"Abandoned for some time now."

A movement—only the shifting of light and shadow—in the second-floor window belied his statement. Gussie squinted up at it, resting her hand above her eyes to throw off the sun's glare.

There. Another flash of white. A curved arm. A palm lifted in greeting. And then a familiar face swathed in fabric. Dark eyes. The fall of a scarf meant to hide.

"Bimla?" Gussie whispered.

"Pardon me, Miss Travers. Come . . . there is nothing to see here. The house is empty. No need to fear."

Officer Greene drew her down the street, and Gussie let him, for she could see Bimla's taut expression. The firm shake of her head. And the fear in her eyes.

24

Gussie woke, quite uncharacteristically, before the sun. One moment, she was clothed in black senselessness, and the next, her eyes popped open and she saw Bimla's stricken face in the darkness.

After Officer Greene had escorted her back to the infirmary the day before, she'd helped Dr. Paul and his nurses with a few patients. Not only out of charity but because she'd hoped Specs would show up and she could speak with him about Bimla.

But Specs never showed up. And by the time she returned to the bungalow, long after dinner, Catherine and Uncle James were already in bed.

Sunlight turned the sky outside the window a startling shade of orange. Unrefined. Reckless. Irrepressible. The gecko she'd affectionately named Lizzie scuttled from her place in the corner toward the window and darted over the sill.

Gussie pushed off the blanket, wrapped herself in a dressing gown, and went to the ornately carved rosewood writing desk.

In the top drawer, she found her notebook. Her nerves popped and sparked like logs in a fireplace. The moment felt weighted.

Heavy with possibility. The possibility to succeed. To see her dream come to fruition. Or to fail. To fall on her face and affirm the words that twisted like living things and snapped at her spirit.

She could reach for a clean sheet of paper. There would be no failure in writing what was expected of her. And of course, she would. Soon. She'd leave Poona for a time and finish penning the Miss Adventuress columns still owed to *Lady's Weekly*. But this moment called for courage. All the courage Catherine thought she possessed. Risking everything was no easy thing.

Pulling the ribbon from her hair, she scrubbed her fingers through the thick braid and wrestled it free, then sat in the chair, opened the notebook, and began to scan through the two months' worth of entries.

Experiences and thoughts, ideas and prayers crammed its pages. She flipped through, noting at which point her thoughts had turned significant. Questions that probed deeper. Ideas that were entirely too intense and poignant for *Lady's Weekly*.

There . . . after her talk with Bimla in the Resident's garden in Udaipur. That was where Miss Adventuress had begun the transformation of turning into Augusta Travers.

> . . . I set off for India.
> And I discovered that everything I had thought important . . . isn't.

Gussie found the crumpled page tucked between descriptions of a camel and details of the train ride back to Poona. She drew her finger down the lines of script, tracing the ugly slash she'd made to cross away her uncommon thoughts, pausing halfway down the page where they ended.

No, they hadn't ended. She had forced them away. But she only had to close her eyes to recall them again. They twirled through her mind like weaving dancers at a ball. They spun round and round, filling her head with ideas that would have been unimaginable only a few weeks earlier.

"You are like a flash of your powder, Augusta. So brilliant and eye-catching, but with very little substance."

"It's not true."

"You write about places, not people. Remember who you are."

"I know who I am." She wouldn't be defined by what others said of her. She flipped through the notebook to a clean sheet of paper, lifted her pen, and wrote.

As the hours swept by, other words, those spoken by Uncle James and Specs and Catherine and Ramabai and Bimla, bathed her spirit.

"God has big plans for you, my girl."

"I wanted to be brave like you."

"You do not need to be enough for everyone."

"Can you truly not see the plans he has for you?"

"Even Christ told stories, Gussie. There is power in them."

A knock at the door interrupted her, and she blinked up at it, noticing, for the first time, how her fingers cramped around her pen and her shoulders ached. "Yes?"

Uncle James peeked inside her room. "Are you going to join us for lunch?"

"Is it lunch already?" Gussie glanced out the window, where sunlight bathed the garden. She ran her palm over her dressing gown's satin collar "How lazy I've been. Has Specs returned?"

He shook his head. "We had word, though, to keep him and the victims of the accident in prayer. Doctors all over the city have gone to help. He likely won't be back until tonight or even tomorrow."

Gussie tossed her pen onto the desk and sighed. "Then you are lucky enough to be the first to know that I have found Bimla. Do not tell Catherine. I'm not sure what is going on, and I don't want to burden her."

Uncle James raised his brows, his mustache curving above his smile, but said nothing.

"Dumbstruck?" she asked. "Maybe I should hang out my shingle and establish myself as Poona's first female detective."

He crossed the room and leaned over her to read her writing.

She resisted the urge to cover it with her hand. She could trust in her safety with Uncle James. He had never mocked her. Never made little of her dreams.

His fingers squeezed her shoulder. "Maybe not. I discovered Bimla's whereabouts three days ago."

Gussie jerked her head up, and his chuckle spilled the scent of tea and cumin over her. "What? How? You said nothing."

"She didn't leave the house, and I couldn't figure out why she was holing up in a place that had been abandoned at the start of the outbreak. I only ever saw a couple of street children enter it. She seemed safe enough, though, and I've been keeping an eye on her."

"You told Ramabai?"

"Only yesterday when she came. There was no sign Bimla was there against her will, and someone taught me a while ago that it's best to allow people to do their work in peace, even when no one else understands it. Bimla has a reason for disappearing, and I didn't see any reason to betray her. But I also didn't want Ramabai worrying needlessly. She was leaving for Mukti Mission, anyway."

"I have to go. I need to see that she's okay."

"I think you should."

Gussie tipped her head. "This means you could have left Poona days ago. Why did you stay?"

"You weren't ready."

She shook her head. "It doesn't matter how long you wait. I'm not going to return with you."

"You misunderstand. I wasn't waiting for the right time for you to leave. I was waiting for the right time for me to leave." He tapped the notebook. "It seems that time has come."

"You should wait here," Gussie told Uncle James. "It's not your fault, but Bimla might think you're dreadful. I'm sure it has nothing to do with the fact that I implied it when you chased us in Udaipur."

"Of course not," he said dryly.

Gussie stared up at the house. It looked vacant. No laundry hung from the second-floor verandah. No servants sat outside, pounding spices and chewing betel leaves. No crying babies or playing children or singing grandmothers.

She crossed the street, glancing both ways not only to assure herself of a clear path but to check that no one too official-looking lurked about, and knocked on the door.

A man crouching before a potted curry leaf tree at the house next door looked up at the sound and flapped his hands. "They left. House is empty."

"But I saw someone here yesterday."

He shrugged, pinched a few vibrant green leaves from the plant, and shuffled away.

Gussie knocked again.

The door flung open, and Bimla pulled Gussie inside. "Were you followed?"

"Of course not." Gussie examined her friend and patted her arms. "You seem safe and in good health."

She glanced around. Directly across from where she stood, a courtyard boasted lemon trees, herbs, and a small pool meant to collect rainwater. Brass-studded doors led to rooms around the perimeter, and their steps were sharp against the marble floors. It had once been a fine house, but now neglect whispered in its corners.

"Where are we?"

"My childhood home."

Gussie dragged her attention from a trio of pierced bronze lamps hanging from the ceiling and searched Bimla's face. She wore her scarf over her shoulders instead of her face, and Gussie's gaze pinned to the scatter of scars. Her fingers went to her own cheek, and she frowned. "You returned to your family?"

Bimla nodded.

Gussie tossed up her hands. "Are you going to say why? Ramabai has been so worried. We've spent the better part of a week scouring the city. You left your work."

"They hired a new nurse when I went with you to Udaipur, remember? I did not leave them without enough help. And I left a letter. I knew it wouldn't be permanent, but if I had told Amma where I was going, she would have convinced me against the idea. And I *needed* to come. I wanted to come." Bimla crossed her arms with stiff resolve. "I thought you would understand. Sometimes you need to do what you feel called to, even if it makes everyone else angry. It is what you have done."

Gussie's breath expelled from her lungs in a puff of disbelief. "But I leave because my family despises me. I don't tell them where I'm going because they don't understand. You did the opposite! You left people who love you for those who sent you away—twice. You returned to the ones who rejected you."

Bimla's arms fell to her side, and she reached for Gussie's hands. Pressed them against her cheeks. Against the proof of all she had suffered. "We are not the only ones who have suffered rejection and scars. And I will not be what they have always said I am."

"They don't care about you, Bimla!"

"There is beauty in loving those who cannot love you back."

"Or will not."

Bimla shook her head. "Cannot. No one chooses not to love. Their own scars, their own brokenness, prevents them from sharing what God has given so freely. Come. I will show you."

She tugged Gussie's hand and led her through the house that was a labyrinth of twisting corridors and curving staircases.

"This was once the home of someone rich, but then it was turned into smaller apartments. Most of the people who lived here left when the plague broke out in Poona, but my family had nowhere to go. My nephew was the first to get sick, and my brother took him . . . somewhere." She glanced over her shoulder, sorrow shadowing her gaze. "It happened before I arrived, and he would not tell anyone."

"How have you escaped the notice of the Searchers?"

"We have kept quiet. No one but a couple of neighbors know we're here, and they would never tell."

Bimla led Gussie to the second floor, where a lattice-carved partition allowed the courtyard's dappled sunlight to paint the marble room in gold. She pushed through a heavy door, and they passed into an open room boasting only sunlight and shadows. Dust coated the indigo-tiled floor, sloppy footprints a ghostly reminder of life.

"I didn't come to clean," Bimla said when Gussie swept her foot over the floor, scuffing her own mark.

"Why did you come?"

"The day my cousin found me at the infirmary, he told me my rebellion had brought a curse upon my family. They were suffering because I had rejected all that was good and right. I had caused my husband's death. I refused to live in humility. And I had embraced a foreign God who called me *beloved* instead of *it*. My cousin meant to discourage me. To break my spirit. All he did was call me home to share what I've discovered—that nothing anyone else says or believes of me can diminish my value. That my worth is found in Christ. And that he is meant for everyone, even for those who mistreated me." She spoke confidently, her certainty lending poetry to the beauty of her words.

Bimla swept aside a moth-eaten tapestry, which Gussie could tell had once boasted as many colors as a summertime meadow. It now hung limp, tattered, and gray. Small and absent of windows, the next room stood in stark contrast to the previous one. No light. No air. No color. Nothing of comfort. Only a mat shoved against the wall, upon which lay a woman as small as a child, wrapped in a white sari.

"My father died in an accident a month ago—something my cousin laid at my feet, as well. My brother has all but abandoned her. I will not."

"Even though she abandoned you?"

Bimla took a deep breath. "Even though."

She crossed the room and crouched to touch her mother's shoulder.

Gussie crept nearer, repelled by this woman who had treated her

281

friend in the cruelest way possible but drawn by Bimla's gentleness. Her forgiveness and quiet certainty.

The woman gasped and turned. She batted at Bimla's hand, and a moan slipped from her lips, turning into a keening wail that filled the room, every dark and dusty corner. She saw Gussie, then, and reached clawlike hands toward her. Gussie was unable to understand the words she spoke but grasped the desperation beneath them.

"She says she must die, but I won't let her," Bimla translated. "It is true. I won't. Not yet."

Gussie allowed the woman to take her hands and swallowed the bile that rose to her throat at the feel of papery skin and bony fingers.

"She believes my being here is punishment for my father's death." Tears slipped down Bimla's cheeks, the scars acting like dams and sending them scuttling in zigzag fashion toward her chin. "But look." Bimla pointed toward the shiny bubo swelling her mother's neck. "There isn't much time to share the truth with her, and I won't leave, no matter how much she insists or insults."

The door behind them opened, and they both turned toward it.

"*Bhā'ū*," Bimla said. "My brother Vivek."

He gave Bimla a dark look and turned toward Gussie.

She gasped. "You. You are the one who left the boy at the infirmary."

"Did he die alone?" His voice was rich and smooth, like honey spread over buttered toast.

Gussie shook her head. "I was present. And the doctor."

Bimla reached for Gussie's arm, her fine-boned fingers clasping. "Then my nephew died with friends."

"But your mother needn't die at all. Take her to the hospital, where she will receive care." Bimla's expression shuttered, so Gussie looked at Vivek. "It isn't any worse an environment than this closed little room. And you took your wife, did you not? I met her there."

"The Searchers took my wife to the hospital. When I saw she was sick, I took her to the house next door, which had already been cleaned. I knew they would find her there when they came to treat the floors with quicklime." He flung his hand toward his sister and mother. "We stayed here."

"You abandoned her?" Gussie looked at Bimla, whose gaze dropped to the floor.

She lifted her scarf and draped it over her head, taking the edge in one hand and pressing it against her cheek. "I didn't know where he'd taken her. And what could I do? If I followed, I would have been taken to the segregation camp. I cannot go to that place."

"No, of course not." Gussie looked at Vivek. "Your wife is very frightened."

"My wife is dead." His eyes were cold as he looked down at Gussie. "They put her body in a shed with others. There has been no respect shown." He clenched his fists, and his jaw twitched.

"Respect?" Bimla laughed. "You left her to be found by strangers, yet you speak of respect?"

Vivek slashed a dismissive hand toward her.

Bimla's mother groaned, and Gussie pulled her fingers free of the woman's grip. "Should we tell Dr. Paul or Dr. MacLean to come? They will help you."

"No, you must not tell them where we are. She is not ready."

The old woman pushed herself up and repeated the same worn phrases from before. She slapped at Bimla, but Gussie saw it was the things she spoke that found their mark.

Bimla's chest heaved, and she met Gussie's gaze. "She says I must leave. I must let her die. That I am bad luck. *Vidhva.*"

Vidhva. Widow. An outcast. Cursed. The scapegoat of every sin, every misfortune. Abused and abandoned and unwanted. That one word meant so many ugly things in this place where Gussie had finally found acceptance.

Bimla didn't defend herself. Didn't deny her mother's accusations and abuse. And Gussie no longer stood in this sad little room full of brokenness and dust. She sat in a parlor chair, crafted by a skilled worker, meant to be a place of comfort and rest.

"Sit in that chair, Augusta. Yes, right there."

And that first time, Gussie had gone.

"You are nearly grown now, and we have entered a different type of society. You must behave. You must repress your undisciplined nature, your passions, your silly pursuits, and make sure you do nothing, say nothing, that will reflect poorly on us. Your sister is about to marry. You wouldn't want to ruin that for her. You have, for too long, ruined things."

She had been sixteen, rebellious against her parents and their need to paint her into a portrait of a young woman raised in a Fifth Avenue mansion. Hating that they had torn her from everything and everyone she loved. Despising who they had become. Who they wanted her to become.

"You are a silly thing. Perfectly useless."

When had they decided harsh words and unkindness was a better way than love? What had it gotten them but a fractured relationship with their middle daughter?

"Stupid, stupid girl." Same chair, another time. "You have made a complete mess of everything."

"I do not see an end to this foolishness. We have very nearly given up on you."

Bimla's mother continued her tirade, heaping insults cloaked in a beautiful cadence that did nothing to hide their ugliness. Their pointed jabs found their mark. Drew blood.

And Bimla just stood there. Shielding herself from the abuse with only her filmy scarf and solid faith. Defending herself not at all. Saying nothing.

But Gussie had words. So many words. They poured out from her pen at night when no one was looking. They wound around her mind like a vise, gripping and squeezing and demanding release. They settled at the base of her throat, choking her with their insistence.

"That is enough." She hadn't meant to shout, but perhaps it was for the best, for Bimla's mother stared at her openmouthed and shaking, her contempt slipping from her tongue in a twisting whisper. "You do not deserve your daughter's love."

Then, before guilt could gnaw at her resolve, Gussie fled from the house and the ghosts chasing her.

25

Before Gussie reached the front door, she took a moment to compose herself. A gentle tug on the hem of her jacket, a wiggle of a pin threatening to come loose and send her hair tumbling over her shoulders. She pinched her cheeks, arranged her expression into one that would draw no attention, and took a deep breath to force her racing heart to steady.

All for naught.

The moment she stepped outside, Uncle James pushed away from the wall, took one look at her, and pulled his brows together. "What's wrong?"

"Nothing." She waved her hand in a breezy fashion and stepped toward the street as though waving down a tanga was her only thought.

He reached for her fingers, stopping their nervous ascent. "You are many things—exasperating things—but you are not a liar. What happened?"

Her answer came at the tail end of a long exhale, a mere whisper on the tip of her tongue. "Bimla chose to return to her family—she is currently caring for her mother."

"And why would she do that?"

Gussie threw up her hands. "I haven't any idea."

That was partially true. Gussie couldn't begin to untangle Bimla's undeserved devotion to her family. But she knew that wasn't what Uncle James was asking.

With no tangas in sight, she started down the street. Uncle James stayed with her, saying nothing, just tugging her elbow when she veered too closely to a slumbering cow and making a clucking sound when a small child approached him with outstretched hands. She did note that he glanced her way before sliding a coin into the little palm.

He was a good man. And his work as an agent had equipped him with an admirable ability to keep a confidence. She scratched her head, shifted the pin digging into her scalp, then chose to trust him.

"Bimla's mother is ill with the plague. At first, it was her nephew. Then her sister-in-law." Gussie glanced behind her, as though those around them, on their way to work or home or the market, were at all interested in what she had to say. As though their protruding clavicles and wary gazes and trudging steps didn't take precedence over yet another person hiding from the Searchers.

"And no one else knows?"

"No." They exited the narrow alley, and she found, with the widening of the street and distance from the example she had no hope of living up to, breathing came easier. So did her words. She hailed a passing tanga. "And you can't tell anyone about it either. Bimla doesn't want her mother taken to the plague hospital, and as little grace as I think that family deserves, she herself cannot be sent to the segregation camp. Terrible things have happened to widows there. I won't betray her. She's already suffered too much from life."

Uncle James helped her into the vehicle, and when he sat beside her, he pinched and rolled the tip of his mustache, brow wrinkled. "Ramabai told me her family rejected her. Turned her out and left her alone. It doesn't make sense. Why would she care for such people?"

Why indeed? Gussie still couldn't work that out entirely. But there was the beginning of understanding, a teasing of truth that tantalized.

"Did you know Bimla once said we were the same, she and I? I didn't agree with her, not really, because all I saw was that she had obviously suffered more. But—"

The driver turned with an impatient clap, but Uncle James only held up his finger. He didn't even take his gaze from hers. "You do now?"

"I think I've realized our story, though the particulars are different, is one shared by many women. We've suffered from words spoken carelessly over us. We've been defined by what we're not— married, acceptable—rather than by who we are."

Gussie wove her arm through his. She'd always relied on him— even when he was chasing her and she was certain she didn't want to be caught. She knew he would eventually be there—seated across from her on a train or catching up with her in some dusty town of suspect decency—and he would be her soft place. When gravity made itself known, Gussie could land upon his kindness. His acceptance. When the words that were said destroyed her, all the things he didn't say built her up.

"And who are you?"

"I'm only now beginning to understand that. Bimla has done it much better. She was so timid when I first met her. So frightened. But she's realized it doesn't matter what people say of her scars. It doesn't matter what they said of her husband's death because she knows the truth of who she is. And she's discovered that in listening to a different type of Word altogether." Gussie ducked her head. "I never thought to turn to God for truth when everyone around me was spinning lies."

"Because you don't believe it?"

She shook her head. "I was so angry at Mother and Father for disrupting my life, I cared only about disrupting theirs." Realization dawned, and Gussie pulled away from her uncle, shame not allowing the comfort of affection. "I stopped listening to God when they stopped listening to me."

The driver turned again and spoke in a rush—nothing they understood, but the tone was clear. His gesturing made it even clearer.

Gussie swiped at the tears pricking her eyes and gave Uncle James a wavering smile. "We should go."

"Why don't we do some sightseeing? I'll be leaving soon, and it would be a shame to visit India without seeing anything except the cloud of dust kicked up by your running feet and the inside of a nicely maintained British bungalow."

Gussie gripped the side of the vehicle as the horses were urged into a trot—an inadvisable speed, given the crush of vehicles, which Poona's drivers seemed to ignore. "I'm glad you have made peace with my staying."

"You would never be happy in New York, as much as it pains me to say it." His voice caught a little, and he sniffed and scratched at his temple, but she still noticed the gleam in his eyes. The quiver of his chin. "I'm proud of you, Gussie. This hasn't been an easy journey, I know. It has taken you all over your own country. All over this one." He gave her a sad smile. "You've found home, haven't you? Maybe, all those times you ran away, you were looking for a place that would so capture you that nothing could induce you to leave." He cupped her head and pressed a kiss to her cheek. "Stay, Gussie. You can live a lot of life in this place."

❧

Gussie's gaze glanced off her journal, tucked between Cordelia Fox's memoir and a paperweight of a bronze peacock. Her fingers itched for it, and she pulled her lip between her teeth. No.

She needed to work, and she'd again stayed up too late spinning stories. Filled another two dozen pages with essays. She clenched her pen and put it to paper.

> . . . graceful Italian arches perfectly blend with the Islamic architecture, and twelve acres of lawn and gardens offer a peaceful way to spend an afternoon. There is nothing more to do but roam the

halls, dappled with sunlight, and enjoy Poona's pleasant breeze whistling through the verandahs.

Uncle James, in his thoughtful offer to take her sightseeing the day before, had provided her with a subject for her next column, which would be sent with him, along with a few others, arriving in Lillian's office before her deadline. Gussie had taken a photograph of Aga Khan Palace's verandah as the sun spilled beneath its graceful arches. This was the type of thing Lillian, traitor though she was, wanted to see—all cheerful descriptions and playful pictures.

Gussie's lips tightened. She only owed ten more columns. She would say nothing until she'd met her obligation and gathered her due pay. She wondered how long it would take for *Lady's Weekly* to lose their new subscribers once the public learned of Miss Adventuress's retirement.

. . . but should responsibility keep you tethered to hearth and home,
I will be your ears. My trusty Kodak your eyes. And I hope, for a
few moments at least, you are swept away.

Three more months of travel. She could write faster—proven by the tens of thousands of words spilled out in her journal over only a few days—but she needed to crisscross the country, and that would take time.

Three more months pretending Miss Adventuress hadn't been transformed by India.

Three months away from Poona. She'd come to love this city in the hills. She didn't want to leave it.

Three months away from Specs.

Gussie leaned her elbows on the table, heedless of the ink, and cupped her face in her hands, rubbing her temples and pinching the bridge of her nose. Perhaps that was what had dislodged the spark of brilliance. Or maybe it was the thought of being away from his sweet face and not-so-sweet kisses.

Whatever it was, just as a knock came at the door, Gussie realized how to solve her problem.

"Come in," she called, twisting in her seat.

Catherine pushed open the door. "Gabriel has finally come home, if you'd like to see him. He is hoping to get some sleep and then relieve Dr. Paul, who has spent day and night at the infirmary while Gabriel attended to the ammunition factory accident."

Gussie bolted from her chair. "Yes. Wonderful." She darted across the room, dragged Catherine into a quick hug, then went in search of her intended.

"Gussie," Catherine called, "don't you wish to tidy up? Your hair is falling free of its pins and you have—"

But Gussie waved her hand over her shoulder.

He stood in the library, waiting for her. Waiting for her.

Despite the dark crescents beneath his eyes, despite the lines creasing his forehead, despite his rumpled coat and stained shirt—was that blood?—his entire face lit up, and the sun no longer seemed as bright in comparison.

He held open his arms, and she flung herself into them. He tucked her head beneath his chin and inhaled deeply. "How I enjoy this."

"Good. Let's marry in two weeks' time." She pulled away to seal her stroke of brilliance with a kiss but found herself approaching a mouth hung open in surprise. She cocked her head. "I suppose I can work with this." She leaned toward him.

"Gussie, what are you talking about?" He set her away from him and took a step back.

"It's the answer to our dilemma."

"Which one?"

"The one that will separate us for months." She ticked a finger. "The one that is forcing you to move in with Dr. Paul for an extended time."

Specs shrugged. "I've already had most of my things taken from the bungalow. I only came here because it is closer to the factory. But I will not stay beneath this roof another night. After

I rest, I will go to Etak's." He swept his arm around her back and dipped her low.

She flicked another finger. "The one that . . ." She stared at the ceiling beams. "No, that's it. Do we have any other dilemmas?"

He laughed and righted her. "Not that I'm aware of, but I'm certain you'll create one soon."

She pouted, but his kiss melted it away.

Until he said, "Gussie, we cannot marry so quickly. We need a period of engagement."

"Why? If we marry in a couple of weeks, then we can leave for our honeymoon, tour the country, and I can write enough columns to fulfill my obligation to Lady's Weekly. It's perfect. Stop being such a stodgy old man." She drew near enough that she could hear the uptick in his breathing as she played with one of his vest buttons.

"You are extraordinarily convincing." He gripped her waist. She didn't have a fashionably tiny one, even with a corset, but Specs's hands were broad and long-fingered, and the way his touch settled in her curves, so warm and perfect, nearly undid her thoughts. "But it is too soon."

"Too soon?" she murmured, lifting onto her toes. His words registered, and she dropped back down. "No, it isn't. I've known you my entire life. If anything, we have waited too long."

"There is too much to think about, and . . ." He glanced away and rubbed at his face, bristling with two days of crimson growth.

"And?"

"I just want to be . . ." He cleared his throat. "Let's talk about this later."

Her thoughts froze, and words turned to icicles in her throat. Waiting to be knocked down and shattered. "I—"

But then he pressed his lips to hers, his gaze polished like lacquer, and everything within her melted.

"Just kiss me," she begged. "Until I am senseless." Until the niggling doubt that had sprung up wilted.

And he did. With an adroitness she couldn't credit. Was it because he was a doctor?

"Have you kissed many women?" she asked after he had stolen her breath. Stolen her heart. Stolen every part of her. "Because you do it so well."

"Never. Only you. There has only ever been you."

At the door, a scuffling sound sent them jumping apart.

Catherine entered the room. "I'm sorry to interrupt, but you've received a message." She handed him a note and glanced at Gussie, her lips pinching a smile.

He unfolded it, eyes scanning. "It's Officer Greene. They've heard of a few families in Vetal Peth who have been hiding from the Searchers. There are whispers of some residents having fallen to plague, and they are going to do another search." He groaned and crumpled the note. "I'm so tired. But he asks that we meet him there. They've already set up a cordon of soldiers to keep anyone from escaping notice."

A desperate knowing filled Gussie's mouth with bile. "Where is this area?"

"North of the infirmary. Officer Greene says it's where he stumbled upon you."

Oh, Bimla. She would be caught and sent to the segregation camp. Separated from her mother, if she hadn't died yet.

Specs rubbed his face, then tossed the note onto a table. "I'm going to eat something. Can you be ready to leave in twenty minutes?"

Gussie nodded, and when he left, Catherine gripped her arm. "What's wrong? You looked about ready to pass out when Gabriel read the letter."

"I will tell you, but Bimla made me promise not to tell your brother or Dr. Paul."

"Bimla?"

"Come with me to my bedroom. Help me get ready."

After she confessed the entire story, Catherine crossed her arms. "How could you have kept this from me?"

"I didn't want to burden you. You've not been well, and you started bleeding again."

"Hardly. It was only a very little bit and almost not worth noticing." But Catherine's chin trembled as she said it. She reached for the wardrobe, her knuckles whitening as she gripped the door, and swayed.

"For goodness' sake, Catherine, please go lie down. You have only just recovered. You need rest."

Catherine turned, yanked a skirt from the shelf, and shook it with more violence than the creases deserved. "What I need is everyone else to stop making decisions for me. I'm not a child."

"I never said you were." Gussie took the skirt from her, grabbed a shirtwaist, and tossed both onto the bed. She looked at Catherine, whose face had gone white, and motioned toward the richly upholstered chair in the corner of the room. "Please sit down. I only want you to be safe."

"Yes. You and my parents and my aunt and Gabriel and my husband. You all want me safe and therefore believe what I do is entirely your decision. As though I'm incapable of deciding things for myself."

Gussie had undone the buttons of her bodice and now struggled with the tight-fitting cuffs. Catherine stalked toward her and pulled the sleeves over her wrists, sending a spray of small pearl buttons jumping over the tiled floor.

"Catherine!"

"That color doesn't suit you anyway."

Gussie stared at her, and Catherine had the wherewithal to redden.

"I'm sorry. It's just so infuriating. All my life I have followed others. I have done what is expected of me. I have been meek and mild and tried not to cause problems. And I hoped when I moved to India, even though my aunt thought it was a terrible idea, it would prove how capable I am. Except Gabriel took it upon himself to protect me from . . . from everything! And then I met John, and I thought after I married him that people would finally think me competent. After all, I would have to manage a household, and he was important here in Poona. But John, as much as I loved him, never allowed me to exert myself in any way. 'You are too gentle,' he told me. Weak—that is what he thought of me. I have never experienced life. Not as you have, Gussie. I am tired of being shoved into a chair and told to behave myself."

Gussie stared at her friend. She brought her hands to her chest, the torn cuffs flopping around her wrists. "I had no idea you felt this way."

"No, you wouldn't." Catherine's voice had softened, and when she moved around Gussie and unpinned her skirt, her touch had, as well. "I followed you around all those years because I hoped your courage and life would somehow spill out over me. And then, as we got older, I wished for your competency and the respect others gave you."

Gussie snorted. "Respect? You must be delirious. No one respects me." The skirt puddled around her feet, and she stepped out of it.

Catherine lifted the shirtwaist from the bed and helped her into it. "Everyone who matters does. No one tells you to sit in the corner. No one expects you to be content with days full of embroidery and quiet activities. I've lived in India for two years, and until you came, I'd never set foot outside Poona. I've known Ramabai since I arrived and haven't developed the relationship you have in just a couple of short months. You're a doer, Gussie. And I want to be one too. But how can I, if no one allows me the freedom to do so?"

"Well, then do, Catherine. I'm not stopping you."

Catherine lifted her chin. "Do not let them send Bimla to the segregation camp. Whatever else happens, you must not let them. And you mustn't tell Gabriel either." She gripped Gussie's shoulder when Gussie opened her mouth to protest. "You can't. He despises the way they have managed things, but he is a doctor, and he believes in the method, if not the implementation. If Bimla is discovered in an infected house, he will insist she be taken to the camp."

Pain stabbed at Gussie's heart and spread to her chest, her throat, her head. She hated keeping things from Specs. Hated that she had to choose between what Bimla wanted and what he hoped for—honesty and mutual respect between them.

"I won't," she finally said. Because in the end, she couldn't allow her friend to be sent to that terrible place where widows were abused and used. After all, Bimla had just found freedom from the scars inflicted upon her.

26

A re you all right with doing this again?" Specs asked as he assisted Gussie into the tanga. "Your uncle is leaving tomorrow."

She settled onto the seat and avoided meeting his gaze. He wouldn't like her silence. And she didn't like the guilt that tore at the smooth edges of their new relationship, turning it ragged and grubby.

But she smiled and nodded, knowing she couldn't choose between Bimla's safety and Specs's trust. "I spent all of yesterday with him."

They were soon passing through Ganj Peth on their way to Vetal Peth, and it became clear that extricating Bimla would take a bit more ingenuity than she possessed. There were soldiers everywhere.

"They have guarded the peths well," she said as they rode past yet another street monitored by a khaki-garbed soldier.

"Yes. They discovered that people would leave the peths when the search party arrived, then return after they left. The Searchers would find empty houses with obvious signs of disease and no way to find the occupants. Now they set up a cordon and detain anyone who tries to slip past. If Vetal Peth indeed proves to have plague cases again, they will have set up a cordon there, as well."

"Why can't people recover at home if they wish?"

"There is no way to maintain any kind of quarantine." He waved at the crumbling buildings they passed, clinging together as though nothing but their neighbor held them upright. "How could they isolate? We know vermin are a vector in disease transmission. Rats care little about flimsy walls. And when there are so many people crowded into one apartment, once the plague gains a toehold, it spreads rapidly. Like fire."

He withdrew his hand from hers and stared straight ahead, his gaze unblinking, thinking of, she knew, more than metaphorical flames. The memory of that terrible night had seared itself into his consciousness, and he was never more than a carelessly spoken word away from it.

"Specs?"

He raised his eyes, and her breath caught at the naked pain turning them into burnished bronze.

"There's nothing to be done here," he said. "Nothing that can fix it. No easy answer. I despise the plague commission and the hospital. The segregation camps and forceful searches. They cost Catherine her husband and have caused untold pain. But I also recognize that this disease is vicious, and it targets the most vulnerable. I only wish I could do something about it, or at least hadn't been dragged into all of it. Perhaps we should get married sooner rather than later. We can escape for a little while. I'm beginning to understand your penchant for disappearing."

She only had a moment to smile because the driver turned off the main street, and they began to bounce over a rutted, narrow lane hemmed in on both sides by windowless shops and houses.

"Two weeks is the longest I will wait," she said, only half joking. The tanga stopped with a jerk, and Gussie found herself pulled from the cart by a harried-looking soldier who ushered her toward a house that sported the painted date proving it had already been searched. In front of it, a cluster of soldiers congregated, but they pulled apart like an overstuffed bun as Gussie approached, revealing a stooped old man tucked into a white dhoti. His chest caved in, sticking to his ribs as he struggled to breathe. Beside him, crumpled on the ground, sat an equally old woman who reached for his hem with trembling fingers. Blood dripped from a wound on her temple.

"There, a woman has come." The soldier thrust Gussie toward the couple, who only stared up at her blankly.

Gussie slapped the soldier's hand away from her arm and glared at him.

"What is going on?" Specs asked, and there was more authority in his quiet question than the entire group of soldiers, with their uniforms and angry glances and guns, could command.

The one who had manhandled her stepped forward. "We were waiting for you to arrive, per Officer Greene's instructions, when we realized this house was inhabited. When we last went through it, we discovered three plague cases, two already dead. These two," he practically spit, "were not in the house during our first inspection. They hid—to escape being sent to the camp, I suppose. They returned after the house was cleaned."

"You suppose right," Specs said, "and can you blame them? That place is a deathtrap, and they are elderly and obviously weak." He approached the couple and crouched down in front of the woman. "Have they been examined?"

"The man. The woman refused for want of a nurse."

The soldier stepped away from Gussie, and she joined Specs. She watched as he probed the old woman's head, carefully avoiding the cut. "What happened to her?" he asked. He spoke evenly, his voice pitched low. But Gussie knew him well enough to detect the wrath stewing beneath his words.

"She attacked us when we began examining the old man," the soldier said. "She needs to be locked away in an asylum. She's lucky she wasn't hurt worse."

"What she needs," Specs said, "is to be treated with respect and care." He stood, and when he turned, his nostrils flared white and his jaw twitching, even the brash soldier seemed cowed. "You will stay here."

Then, with infinite tenderness, he cupped the old man's elbow and spoke in Marathi. "Gussie, come with us."

She followed them inside the house, taking note of the numbers scrawled over one of the newly whitewashed walls. 3, 2.

Three patients with plague. Two deaths.

The old woman tottered and leaned heavily against Gussie's arm. In a couple of steps, they reached the only additional room in the house. The man pushed the door open, revealing . . . nothing.

No furniture, no rug, no mats for sleeping, no clothing or baskets. Nothing.

"Where are their belongings?" Gussie asked.

"Once a house has been contaminated, the Searchers disinfect it and remove everything. The bedding and clothing, they burn. Everything else is cleaned and either given to a neighbor for safekeeping or sent to a warehouse."

The old woman lay on the floor against the wall and curled onto her side. With hands tucked beneath her head, dusty feet curving together like nestled kittens, she stared blankly across the room, her gaze fixed on the barren wall opposite. Weariness draped her form, slipping over her shoulders and hips like the sari she wore.

"What should I do?" Gussie asked.

"I will take Mr. Holkar into the other room. You only need to examine his wife. I don't think she is ill, though. Merely tired."

The two men disappeared, and Gussie approached the woman with slow steps. She sat beside her, thankful Catherine had insisted she change, for the hard floor, bare of carpet or cushion, rubbed roughly against her skirt and bit into her hip.

Unsure where to start and unwilling to frighten Mrs. Holkar any further, Gussie held out her hand and waited. After a moment, the woman reached over and laid her wrinkled fingers atop Gussie's.

"I'm so sorry," Gussie said. "It isn't fair, is it?"

She'd never realized how much of life groaned with injustice.

These were things a bright smile and a train ticket couldn't fix. She blinked, her lashes growing wet, but once she considered the pain that rose from this city, this street, this house alone, she couldn't contain her grief, so she just quietly conducted her examination, all the while letting tears splash onto the floor.

When she finished, she helped the woman sit up, and they clasped hands. Gussie drew them to her chest and ducked her head to press a kiss atop the twisted knuckles. Then she stood, brushed her skirts, and left the house.

"The woman isn't ill. There are no buboes and no sign of the plague."

The soldier who had taken charge nodded. "Good. We will send them to the segregation camp."

And because Gussie had no control over the situation, no say over what happened or didn't, she said nothing. Specs joined them a moment later, and together they watched as the elderly couple was escorted into a cart that would take them to the camp.

Perhaps they would survive the terrible conditions and be home in a week. Perhaps they would escape contracting the disease they'd managed to avoid so far. Perhaps they would one day feel as though they had autonomy over their own lives.

When the cart rumbled away, the soldier pointed to the house across the street. "That one is next. There are no women inside, so you may wait here."

Gussie acquiesced, but when Specs disappeared inside with the rest of the men, she began to creep down the street, her eyes on the house where she'd last seen Bimla.

She only had ten minutes. Fifteen at the most. Gussie didn't bother knocking. She pushed the door open and slipped inside.

"Bimla," she called, her voice bouncing around the empty, windowless room. She stepped toward the staircase. "Bimla?" Panic caused her to call louder than she'd intended, and she clapped her hands over her mouth. Then she began picking her way up the steps, her heart in her throat as she cast glances over her shoulder to make sure no one followed. She hurried through the room, whose tile floor danced with bits of light shining through the screen, and pushed through the heavy, carved door.

A strange sound slipped from the little room behind the tapestry, and Gussie followed it. "Bimla?"

"It is done." Bimla's mother lay flat on the mat, her gray face a still mask. Arms bearing the black spots of the disease lying still at her sides. "She is gone from this earth. And I'm so very tired."

"Oh, Bimla, I'm so sorry, but you must leave. Hide. There is a search party going house to house. They have discovered that some of the people of Vetal Peth hid during the earlier searches. They will find you and send you to the segregation camp. You cannot go there. You must not."

"It is worse than that." Bimla lightly touched the left side of her groin. "They will send me to the hospital." With a groan, she pushed herself to her knees. "I cannot go to the hospital. I will not die alone. I will not. There are people who care about me now. Help me up. There is a shed behind an empty house three doors down. I will hide there until I can leave."

Gussie skirted the mat, avoiding touching the body that lay so near. She hooked her arms beneath Bimla's and lifted with a grunt. "Are you sure you cannot trust Dr. Paul?"

"No." Bimla twisted from Gussie. "No, you must not tell him. I don't want him to see me like this."

Bimla shuffled forward, taking one excruciatingly slow step after another. She swayed, and Gussie looped her arm around her friend's waist.

The door flung open, and Bimla's brother stepped through. His gaze swept the room, rested for a moment on his mother's small, stiff body, then met Gussie's eyes. "We must get her out of here. They come." He crossed the room in three steps and lifted Bimla easily into his arms. "The bread baker's shed?"

Bimla's expression softened, and she nodded. "The house is empty now, and no one will think to look in that place." There was meaning behind those words. The bread baker. The empty house.

Vivek didn't look at Gussie as he bore Bimla away, and she clattered down the staircase after them. He went to the back of the building, easing past a dry fountain. Huddled against the marble base, a boy with pinched features and knobby wrists stared at them from beneath a fringe of shaggy hair.

Gussie smiled at him, and he held out his hand. "British?" he asked. "Doctor?"

Gussie shifted her camera in its bag and retrieved a few coins tucked beneath it. She handed them over, her fingers glancing against his rough palm. "American." He reminded her of the boy in South Dakota. "Photographer."

Bimla was being carried through a narrow door hidden in the corner, and Gussie patted the boy's cheek and hurried after them.

"Why did you come back?" Vivek stared straight ahead. Not at Bimla but at the tumbling stone wall that separated them from the narrow alley behind the building. "Why return, knowing how we felt about you?"

"Love." Bimla's voice was soft. Fading as her pain increased and her arms fell limply from his neck. "'Beareth all things, believeth all things, hopeth all things, endureth all things.'" She laid her head against her brother's shoulder, and her gaze met Gussie's. "It never fails."

They picked their way over dried grass toward a small shed that had once housed something that smelled vaguely of goat. It had almost completely slumped into the mud in a heap of plaster and splintered planks. Bimla's brother eased open the door hanging off its hinges and carried Bimla to a straw pallet in the corner.

"You can't leave her here!" Gussie eyed the decomposing bed. "She'll be crawling with lice in moments."

"There's nowhere else." He set Bimla down with more gentleness than Gussie would have credited him.

"Amma?" Bimla gasped and groaned, her head flopping to the side as though she had not enough strength to hold it up.

"She's at Mukti Mission. Is there anyone else at Sharada Sadan who can care for you?"

"No. Do not ask them. If I'm found, they will all be sent to the segregation camp, and it is not safe for them there."

Gussie pressed her fist to her stomach and looked at Bimla's brother. "I must go, or I'll be missed. Stay with her until I come back tonight." She squeezed through the door and peeked back inside. "Do not leave her. I will return."

27

Good-bye. I'll miss you. Good-bye. I love you.

The next morning, after Catherine had insisted Bimla be brought to the bungalow, and Uncle James had lifted her from the shed and sat with her in a carriage he'd hired to bring her to the relative safety of the suburban municipality, Gussie sat in a tanga and stared straight ahead. Stared at the driver's red turban and counted the tucks of it winding around his head. She couldn't make sense of this—sending Uncle James away. Not joining him in his return.

When will I see you again?

She kept her words hidden away like the driver's dark hair, not willing for Uncle James to think she had doubts about her course. Doubts about her ability to pull off a book, let alone a romance with someone who might be entertaining his own doubt. She didn't want to think about that.

"Uncle James, I . . ." She looked at him sitting beside her, and the gentle understanding on his face undid her. "I'm going to miss you more than you can imagine." She tossed her arms around him, the jostling of the wheels against the dusty road setting them off balance. But his embrace held her firm. Held her safe. She sniffed.

"I can imagine a great deal, Augusta."

She laughed and sat back. The tanga rumbled to a stop near the train station, and the driver went to buy a ticket and search for someone to help with the luggage.

"I'm glad you've finally found somewhere to settle," Uncle James said. "I hated thinking of you wandering your entire life. I understood it, but I wanted more for you."

Gussie cocked her head. "But your life has been full of adventure and excitement."

"And I would have given up every moment of it to have what you've found instead. When I went after you that first time, I'd just retired from the agency. I had no idea what to fill my days with but knew I couldn't continue chasing those of the criminal persuasion. It's a job meant for a much younger man. And perhaps there was a small part of me that saw, in going after you, a way to continue my running. I've spent my entire life running, you know. Filling the quiet spaces with those things you just mentioned. Hushing the words that gave me chase." He ran his hand over his mustache, twirling the end between his fingers. "We have much in common. But you . . . you are considerably brighter than I am."

As he spoke, Gussie remembered what he'd whispered to her months ago on that train to Chicago.

"You are fearfully and wonderfully made. You are the daughter of my heart, knit from my own dreams and hope. There is nothing wrong with you. Nothing that makes you broken."

And all the remaining shadows that had wrapped themselves around her heart dissipated.

"'Perfect love casteth out fear.'"

"Hmm?"

"Something Ramabai said. I think it means there cannot be love where there is fear. And, Uncle James, your love has set me free of all the things I let define me. I didn't have to go very far to know it's always been you."

He smiled, unashamed by the tears that slipped down the crevices and creases of his face and burrowed into his mustache. "Listen and believe, Gussie. You are loved by the Creator. The One who spun the clouds and swept the oceans aside. You are strong and capable, made so by his embrace. You are forgiven for every misdeed in the past and every one you've yet to commit. You are whole, entirely enough. You are not bound by fear but made free through God's love. You have been adopted by a perfect Father."

Gussie sank against the seat and pressed her hand to her stomach. "It seems almost extravagant."

"That, my dear, is the point."

The train's whistle blew, and a bevy of activity erupted. People spilled from the station house and boarded in haste. The middle class, having shut up shops and homes, desperate to escape the plague that stalked the city. Officials in fine suits swinging walking canes on their way to misty hill stations and clean water. The poor, carrying children and not much else, in search of another place to make enough for food and shelter.

They climbed out of the tanga, and Uncle James directed the porter to his luggage. He pressed enough coin into the driver's hand to see Gussie home. "I leave you now to your grandest adventure."

She clasped his hands between hers. "Thank you for chasing me all these years. Even though it was at Father's direction and you meant only to bring me home, I am grateful for it. I never felt alone because I knew you would soon be there."

His mustache dipped, and he retrieved his hand to touch her cheek. "My girl, I never chased you because your father asked me to. Not even to bring you home. I only ever wanted to make sure you were safe." He bent to kiss her temple, his eyes wet and bright.

When he disappeared into the first-class cabin, the irony was not lost on Gussie that she had spent years leaving him staring after departing trains, and now it was she waving and reaching. And staying.

At last, she hopped back into the tanga, brushing the tears from her cheeks and pasting a bright smile upon her lips, and told the driver to take her to Shaniwar Wada. She didn't particularly care to see the destroyed fort, but Specs had sent a message that he was only working in the morning and would meet her there.

Guilt gnawed at her the entire trip, but when she arrived and saw Specs buying a bag of dates from a vendor in the market that sprawled around the old fort's walls, her guilt conceded to the delight bubbling up within her.

He turned and saw her, and the smile that tipped his delicious lips promised relief from her festering worry. "I don't like that we're living in different houses now." He split a date and held it out to her.

She took it between her teeth, eyes not leaving his until she slapped her hands over her chest and let her lashes drop. "Oh . . . oh, I could write an entire column about this fruit alone."

"Better than candy corn?"

She popped one eye open and screwed up her nose. "I was twelve. I could hardly be expected to show restraint around such a delight." He'd given her a bag of the penny candy for her birthday, and she'd consumed the entire thing while he scolded her. Then she'd promptly vomited all over his shoes.

"Just pace yourself." He laughed and handed her the bag, which she expected would be empty by the time their excursion was over.

They crossed through the market, weaving around baskets of eggplants and onions, and reached the capitol building that had once been the pride of the peshwas. Her throat ached with the loss stamped across its stone façade. Its granite ramparts, arms spread wide to protect the nothing that was left, and massive studded doors promised it had been great. Had been impressive. It was the old lady at the ball, once a belle but now nodding off against the walls, her snores the only thing reminding people she lived.

"It seems a very tragic place," she said.

"Come on, Gussie. You have the heart of a storyteller. Imagine it as it was, the peshwa approaching atop his elephant. The court coming alive." He pointed to the arched doorway, as wide as four men and at least as tall. "That is the *Dilli Darwaza*. The Delhi gate."

They started for it, Gussie taking the opportunity to eat another date. And another.

Specs cast her a sidelong look. "You're going to get a stomach-ache."

She shrugged. "Why would you buy them for me if not to eat?"

"I can't argue with that, although I did expect you to share them with me."

"Based on history, that was a very misguided assumption." She stared up at the teak door.

"The metal spikes were meant to prevent elephants from battering it down."

He put his hands on the smaller door cut from the larger and pushed it open, and they crossed over into a time long gone. One that boasted warriors on elephants and rajas dripping with rubies. The stones echoed a lament. Pages torn from a storybook, imprinting the worn floor with larger-than-life tales that now told themselves in whispers.

"Gussie," Specs whispered as his feet traced a path up the stairs to sunlight.

"Yes?"

He paused his ascent and pressed himself against the stones, tugging her hand as she started past him. They were alone. Hidden in the embrace of ruined dreams. She fell against his chest and smiled up at him. Waited for his touch and taste.

But instead, he offered words. "I sometimes wonder if this is wise."

"What?"

"Us."

Her hands stilled their exploration of the dips and planes of his chest and shoulders. He became impenetrable, like the walls that hemmed them in.

"I'm afraid you'll never be happy here," he said.

"What do you mean? I've already told you I want to stay."

"But for how long? How long before . . ." His eyes skittered from her, landed somewhere beyond. "Before something happens to . . ."

"To what, Specs? What are you trying to say?"

"I just don't know if you're ready . . . I'm ready to risk every-thing." He shoved his fingers into his hair and groaned. "Gussie, you haven't exactly been reliable. And you always seem to find yourself stumbling into trouble."

Her throat ached. *Perfect love casteth out fear?* She stepped away, giving him space. Giving herself space. She took three steps closer to the light that spilled down the staircase. Closer to the view that would show her all of the city. But then she turned back and studied him. Saw the shadows in his gaze. The memories of flames and loss.

"I want this. I want you," she said. "And I want it to last the rest of our lives. But we cannot have it if you insist on strangling our love beneath your fear."

I have spent half my life running after one adventure or another. I believed I would find joy just around the corner, purpose over the hilltop, validation with the perfect shot, acceptance through my scribbles. I came to India to escape someone else's dream for me and discovered my own had changed along the way.

I have learned many things as I've journeyed through this coun-try. But it was only when I stopped traveling that I fully began to understand. India captured my imagination, but Poona claimed my heart. I enjoyed my time as Miss Adventuress, but I cannot fool myself anymore into thinking I had any real impact on anyone. I thought that was all I could aspire to be and do. But there is so much more to be had and done. There is a world out there needing your touch. Desperate for your affection. Thirsty for your compas-sion and understanding. You do not need to board a train to find it. It might be in the desperate child exiting an alley. Or the lonely widow in your building. Or the neighbor suffering from illness.

Do your part, wherever you are.

I have long aspired to join the ranks of those great intrepid female travelers. My childhood was spent reading their stories. And you discovered when you began this book that I very nearly accomplished that goal. But then, somewhere between Jodhpur and Ganj Peth, I found my way.

Dear reader, I assumed I would capture lovely vistas and interesting faces. It would be the making of my career, you see. But in the end, it turned out to be the making of me.

Gussie drew the title page from the bottom of the stack of papers and stared at it.

A Photo Adventure through India.

Then she put pen to paper, tapped a colon, and wrote the words that had been tumbling about her thoughts since her conversation with Uncle James at the station.

Wandering No More.

Resting her hand on the desk, she blew out a breath. It was done. She'd spent nearly the entire two days since that disappointing date with Specs at Shaniwar Wada finishing her story of running and resting. Seeking and finding.

Sitting beside Bimla, watching her chest rise and fall beneath pain-laced breaths, Gussie had written about trial and grace.

Thinking of Uncle James heading back to Bombay and the ship that would return him to a life he now regretted made her weave together the disparate stories of finding her place where she least expected to.

Shuffling through the stacks of photographs she'd taken and developed, she wrote of beauty and depravity, joy and loss.

She patted the stack of paper, knowing she'd given it her best. Knowing it would be in Mr. Epps's hands once she dropped it off at the post.

Then she went to check on Bimla.

"How is she?" she asked Catherine, who sat in a chair at the side of the bed.

"Resting. She managed to have some jelly."

Gussie touched Bimla's cheek. "She's so warm. I wish we could do something else."

"There's nothing else to do. Linseed meal poultices, nourishing food, and sleep. She has survived the first forty-eight hours. That is good. She might well live. Inguinal buboes have the highest rate of survival." Catherine absently rubbed at her middle and shifted. "I know you feel guilty about not telling Gabriel, but he would send her away. He would worry if he knew she was here. Ever since our parents died, he's clung to the belief that if he accounts for all possibilities and chooses the one with the best outcome, he can be certain of safety. For all his education and intelligence, he understands very little about life."

"I know. I hate lying to him, though. When he discovers our duplicity, he will be furious."

"Please . . ." Bimla's ragged voice teased into their conversation. "I lived too long alone. I do not wish to die alone, as well." She lay perfectly still, only her lips moving, and she shook with the effort.

"You aren't going to die. Not here or anywhere." Gussie brushed Bimla's hair back from her face and turned to Catherine. "I don't see how we can keep this from him. What if he comes for lunch? We've been lucky that he's been too busy at the infirmary to visit, but he will come. And what about the servants? Will they not tell him?"

"The servants answer to me, not Gabriel," Catherine said. "It is my home and my inheritance paying their wages. They will say nothing. And when he comes, he has no reason to visit this wing of the house."

How the roles had reversed. Gussie couldn't remember another time when Catherine stood firm, and she quivered with fear. But Catherine had already lost nearly everything. Gussie had only just obtained her happiness.

"I must run an errand," Gussie said. "I will be back before dinner."

Just before she closed the door behind her, Catherine called her name. "Bimla *is* much safer here than at the hospital. You know that, right?"

"I do know that. But is it safer for everyone? What if you contract the disease? It will kill your baby."

Catherine's eyes filled with tears. "Oh, Gussie. That doesn't matter anymore. I think the baby is already dead."

"What? Why?" Her errand forgotten, Gussie rounded the bed and slipped to her knees. She pressed her hands to Catherine's belly, prodding with her fingers as though she could feel life stir.

Catherine's hands grasped hers, stilling the frantic movements. "I haven't felt her move since my fall. Before, there was a fluttering. Gentle, but there all the same. I *sensed* her with me. But now . . . there is nothing." She tripped over her final word, but she sounded so certain. And a mother should know, shouldn't she? A mother would be able to tell when life was pulled from her child.

But Gussie's mother had missed so much. She had never known much about her daughter at all. There might still be a chance Catherine's baby lived. "I refuse to accept it. You fell weeks ago. Surely you would have miscarried by now if the baby was lost."

"Do you think so?" Catherine looked at the ceiling and exhaled as though a prayer had settled in her lungs.

"Absolutely." Catherine's baby was fine. Had to be fine.

Catherine kissed Gussie's forehead. "I do love you. Thank you. I had all but given up hope. Now, go finish your work. You have important things to see to. I promise to be very careful and sanitize everything."

"Will you tell Specs about your concern for the baby?"

"No. He is so busy. I don't want to worry him."

"But, Catherine . . . I know you want to prove yourself capable, and I completely understand that, but he's not only your brother, he's your doctor, as well. And he would hate to know you're suffering alone with this fear."

"I'm not alone anymore. I've confided in you."

Gussie left her and made her way to the storage room that had been converted into a darkroom, chewing on her lip and worrying over this new thing she couldn't tell Specs. She could envision the foundation of their relationship crumbling beneath the secrets. It wasn't right that she should have so many.

But these weren't stories she could claim. They belonged to

Bimla and Catherine. She pulled a photograph from where it dried on a clip, frustration making her movements jerky and rough and tearing the paper at the corner.

"You seem upset."

Gussie whirled, dropping the damaged print. "Specs! What are you doing here?" Goodness, with her voice cracking and pitching, it was a good thing she hadn't chosen to follow Uncle James into detecting.

Thankfully, Specs didn't seem to notice. "When I fell asleep measuring medication and hit my head on the edge of the table, Etak insisted I leave and rest. I have been working too many nights and mornings."

Gussie's eyes widened, and she poked at the scrape and bruise she'd just noticed peeking from beneath the hair flopping over his forehead.

He winced and grabbed her fingers. "I'm fine. Only a little sore of pride. But I slept for an hour at Etak's and decided seeing you would do me more good than rest, so here I am."

"Here you are."

In this house full of secrets she wished to untether herself from. But Bimla's desperation felt like so many stones. *I do not wish to die alone.*

"Gussie, I must apologize for what I said at the Shaniwar Wada. It was unconscionable. Sometimes my fear gets the best of me, and you're right, I can't allow it to strangle our love."

She reached for his cheek, her smile soft and encouraging. "Thank you." She took a deep breath. "And now I must run an errand, if you wouldn't mind joining me."

Away from the house. Away from Bimla. Away from the knowledge that she was trapped between honoring her friend and honoring this man she loved.

28

Why are we here?" Specs looked up at the sign above the shop. "You have a perfectly good camera hanging from your shoulder."

Gussie had heard there were a number of photographic studios in the Sadar Bazaar area and had hired a tanga to deliver them to P. S. Bhasin and Son Photography Studio, which looked the most promising.

"I'm missing a photograph for the book I'm sending to Mr. Epps."

"One you can't take yourself?"

"I cannot take this one."

She pushed through the door, sending the little bell above it dancing and singing. A table stood against one wall, boasting a stack of thick photo books, and a large carved screen partitioned off a portion of the space. Below their feet, a thick carpet muffled their steps.

Photography in Poona seemed to be a lucrative business.

A man circled the screen, his hair, teeth, and clothing white and gleaming. "Welcome. Welcome."

314

"I need a photograph taken," Gussie said, responding to his smile with her own.

"Yes. An engagement photo, perhaps?" He looked between them.

"Oh." Gussie blinked and looked at Specs. "I didn't even think of that."

Specs held up his hands. "I'm not dressed for it anyway. We'll come back."

Gussie nodded and turned back to the photographer. "Not today. I only need a photograph of myself."

"Of yourself?" Specs scratched the spot where his glasses curved over the bridge of his nose. "Don't you have some already?"

She reached into her camera bag and slipped out the one she'd kept tucked away for over a decade. She gave it a lingering look— her laughing father and poised, smirking mother. Her playful sisters. No one poisoned by desire for social success. A family. Happy and secure in one another's love. Unaware of the storm brewing on the horizon. "This is the only one."

"What do you mean that's the only one? You have *no* others?"

"None."

"But why?"

She smiled at Mr. Bhasin, who watched their conversation with the studious interest of a scientist examining slides beneath a microscope. He held up one finger. "I am nearly done with my current customer. Please continue." He disappeared behind the screen, popping his head back around it to add one final request. "But . . . speak loudly enough for me to hear."

Gussie laughed. "He is amusing."

"Very." Specs tipped his head. "So why do you have no photographs of yourself? That seems an odd thing for a photographer."

She shoved the photograph back into its hiding place, not yet ready to fully release it to the dappled sunlight of the past. "This image reminds me of everything that used to be. Nothing that came afterward compared, and I never wished to capture another moment with myself in it."

"But something has changed?" Specs reached for her, his fingers brushing her waist. Stealing thoughts from her mind and words from her lips.

She nodded.

"Are you going to tell me what?"

"*Everything* has changed. I've found peace. And I've written a book. A book, Specs. A book I've been dreaming of writing since I was a child tucked in bed with Cordelia Fox's stories. I've proven to myself that I'm more than what others say of me. I've fallen in love with someone incredibly dear and familiar." She stroked his cheek, stealing the advantage. Her finger tripped over his lips.

He captured it with a quick nip of his teeth. "You should be careful, Gussie. You're in a rather public place."

She grinned and retrieved her fingers, curling them inside her palm. "Everything has changed, and not only do I need to send a photograph of myself to Mr. Epps with all the others, I'm ready to move on. I'm ready for life to continue. Instead of looking back at what has been, I want to remember this moment because it's when I began looking forward."

A strange squeaking sounded from behind the partition, followed by a sharp command. Gussie glanced toward it, but Specs's next words drew her attention once again.

"And your parents?"

A stone lodged in her throat. "What about them?"

"Have you forgiven them?" He handled the inquiry as though she were cut glass. About to shatter at the slightest pressure.

She loved him for it, but she also didn't intend to be prodded into a conversation she wasn't ready to have. "Have you forgiven Mrs. Templeton?"

"Years ago."

"Truly?" Her brows knit. "I thought you hated her for what happened to your parents."

"I did. For a time. But then I recognized who was really at fault and shifted the blame and hate to where it belonged."

"And where is that?"

"Right here." He poked his thumb against his chest.

Before she could formulate a reply, Mr. Bhasin appeared again, leading two handsome men in embroidered hats and curled slippers. And a dancing monkey tethered to a golden chain, which proved distracting enough that it wasn't until the photographer had settled her on a rattan chair that she turned back to their conversation.

"What do you mean by hating yourself over what happened?" she asked Specs as Mr. Bhasin reappeared, dragging an ornately carved column behind him.

"Now isn't the time, Gussie. What is he doing?"

Mr. Bhasin positioned the column beside Gussie, settling an overflowing basket of vibrant flowers atop it.

"Oh no. That is too much, Mr. Bhasin." Gussie waved her hand toward the arrangement. "I want something simple."

He rocked back on his heels. "Simple?" His gaze traveled from her head to her feet, and he tapped his full mouth. Then, poking a finger into the air, he jumped up and disappeared into a room at the back of the studio, from which they heard a great deal of shuffling, clinking, and grunting.

"He must keep his props back there," Gussie said.

"I can't wait to see what he returns with." Specs winked at her.

But Mr. Bhasin returned with only a scarf. A long green one embroidered with gold. He handed it to Gussie, and she touched the fabric, which was as fine and light as spun sugar. "It's lovely."

"And it is simple." Mr. Bhasin motioned her to arrange it over her shoulders, then held his hand out for her camera bag, which she had been clutching in her lap, easing her nerves by clicking the clasp open and closed. *Click click click.*

Why she was nervous, she didn't know. She'd taken thousands of photographs over the years. The process was as familiar and natural to her as breathing. Yet . . . *click click click.*

"It is important to you?" Mr. Bhasin asked, motioning toward her bag.

Gussie nodded.

"Then you shall have it in the photograph." He took the bag, withdrew her Kodak, and handed it over. "There. It is perfect."

And with that, he went to the larger studio camera, which stood on a tripod.

"Are you all right?" Specs asked. "You're pale."

"I'm not sure. This feels like a big thing. I don't even fully know why." She fussed with the tie at her collar. She'd worn a ready-made. It seemed the most obvious choice, even though it wasn't as stylish or as pretty as her other dresses. No frills or froufrou. Just a woman with her camera, recording images of life and love and loss.

"It is a big thing." Specs knelt in front of the chair, his hands warm and comforting on hers. "It's a statement. This is the final piece of your book, which is the culmination of your dreams. You're saying with it that you are someone to take seriously. More than Miss Adventuress taking off on a jaunt. More than pretty scenery and airy editorials. More than the well-off daughter who never fit. And with all of that, there's room for rejection, isn't there?"

She swallowed and nodded. She'd faced rejection her entire life—never good enough, never correct enough . . . never enough. But that was when she hadn't aspired to be anything more than what others already thought of her.

And here she was reaching. Hoping. Desperately wanting. Failure seemed an even closer companion in this moment than any other.

"It's worth it," Specs said. He lifted her free hand and kissed her knuckles. Then he removed himself to the other side of the space and motioned to Mr. Bhasin.

"You are ready?" Mr. Bhasin smiled, then fiddled with his Petzval portrait lens—how Gussie's mouth watered over it—and she cupped her palm around her camera.

"I am ready."

Clutching the envelope that contained a few prints of her rather elegant portrait, Gussie stepped out of the studio feeling as though she had emerged from a chrysalis. As Mr. Bhasin snapped photographs, rearranged her arms and chin, and convinced Gussie to allow the appearance of a small potted plant in the arrangement, she shed the old.

She released Miss Adventuress.

From here on out—or at least once she sent her remaining stories to Lillian and ended her relationship with *Lady's Weekly*—Gussie intended to write under her own name. She would claim her own adventures. And that deep, yearning wish to write truth and use words to change lives—change perspectives—would be free.

Perhaps, one day, a young girl with too-big dreams would clutch Gussie's books and imagine how her own words could one day be sent into the world.

"Are you ready to return home?" Specs asked, holding out his arm.

"Yes." And then she remembered Bimla, ill in the guest room. She pulled away from Specs. "But you don't have to escort me. I know you must have work to return to."

"I do, but there is enough time for me to escort you back to the bungalow." He stopped beside a tanga that waited at the roadside.

She allowed him to help her inside it. She could just tell him. Blurt it out like she did so many other things. But Bimla had been so desperate to stay out of the plague hospital. And Catherine along with her. What if Gussie did tell him? And what if he insisted on sending Bimla away? What if Bimla died from lack of care? And died alone. She'd been doing so well.

Gussie settled into the tanga. She worried the envelope, pleating the edges and rubbing the corners.

"You're going to ruin your portrait," Specs said. "Truly, Gussie, sometimes your moods are as changeable as springtime weather."

Setting the envelope on her lap, she clutched her hands together.

The tanga jolted and made its way down Taboot Street. Trees shaded pedestrians, and the gutters here, unlike in Ganj Peth, were covered with stones. It wouldn't do to expose the wealthy to disease and filth.

The buildings, while still copious, were fronted with windows and boasted signs declaring an array of merchandise and services—haberdasheries, European imports, tea and coffee, clocks, and coach builders. Even a factory that produced ice cream, which annoyed Gussie endlessly, for she hadn't realized ice cream could be had in Poona.

"Gussie? Are you well?"

She couldn't get away with a lie. "Will you tell me now what you mean by hating yourself over the fire?"

Perhaps it was the gentle swaying of the tanga as they rode through this pretty area of the city, or perhaps it was the desperation in her question, but he opened up to her in the most stunning way possible.

"It's my fault my parents died."

Her first reaction was one of disbelieving laughter. But the sound died as soon as it escaped her lips. "You can't be serious. It was Mrs. Templeton. Everyone knows that. She set the house on fire."

"But I gave her the cigarettes."

Gussie paused. "Why would you do that?"

"She'd been with us since I was a baby. I felt quite loyal toward her. And when my parents told her she wasn't allowed to smoke in the house, it seemed very unfair. She was old—should really have retired but couldn't afford to be out on her own—and the smoking calmed her nerves. The longer she went without her cigarettes, the more agitated she became. I could see that and couldn't understand why my parents would take the poor woman's one consolation. So I bought her some and told her only to smoke in her bedroom, after everyone had gone to bed. It seemed a good solution at the time." He removed his hat and dropped his head into his hands. "Obviously, the end result changed my opinion on that."

Gussie remembered the terrible day when she learned of the fire but not if her friends had escaped. She remembered the sight of the house, rubble and ash and smoke. The fire brigade with their soot-covered faces and slumped shoulders. And the police officer who had told her there were deaths. Multiple deaths.

Gussie had returned home in a daze. She sat on the seat built into her little window nook, where before she had brought Cordelia Fox and spent hours daydreaming. Toward evening, a messenger arrived. Three deaths—Mr. and Mrs. MacLean and the housekeeper, who had fallen asleep while smoking. The younger MacLeans were safe at a friend's house.

After that, Gussie's mother hadn't the heart to diminish her friendship with Specs and Catherine, and Gussie spent every moment she could with them. Until they left to live with an aunt in Pennsylvania a few months later, breaking up their tightly wound cord.

"It was an accident, Specs. You can't blame yourself. You had no way of knowing what would happen."

"There are no such things as accidents. All disasters are preceded by choices."

Specs's choice. His parents' choice. Mrs. Templeton's choice. Who was to say which choice was most responsible for the fire that took so much from them? Gussie only knew that life wasn't worth living tied up in fear—whether one's own or someone else's. Fears rarely came to fruition anyway.

She was about to say so when the driver guided the horse onto the street where Catherine's bungalow and a dozen others snuggled against oleander, spider lilies, and fig trees.

"What is going on?" she asked when they came in sight of the house. Half a dozen soldiers stood in a knot on the steps leading to the verandah.

Specs leapt from the tanga before it even rolled to a stop, and Gussie waved him away when he waited to assist her down.

"Go. Go. See what is wrong."

He hurried across the grass, heedless of the delicate clusters of flowers that scattered the lawn. Gussie pressed a coin into the driver's hand and scurried after him.

"We heard there's a case here," a soldier was saying, his Scottish accent as thick as cream.

"A case of what?"

"Plague, Dr. MacLean."

Gussie gasped. No. No one else knew. They couldn't be here for Bimla. She pressed the envelope containing her portrait against her stomach and hurried up the steps.

"Why, that's ridiculous." Specs's words trailed after her. "I'll have this cleared up in a moment."

They reached the door side by side, and she barreled ahead of him. Maybe they hadn't found Bimla. She could get to her first and . . . what? Carry her out on her shoulders? Push her through the window? Hide her in the wardrobe? Soldiers clustered inside the front hall, blocking the way forward. There were so many.

Who had told them?

And then she remembered the scrap of a child huddled in the corner beside the dormant fountain. So eager to accept the coin she slid into his hand. So desperate. What would a starving boy do for a meal?

Gussie had been the catalyst for this discovery. *"American,"* she had said when the child questioned her. *"Photographer."*

She shoved at Specs in her haste to press between a couple of soldiers. "Let me through." She had to get to Bimla. Had to figure something out. Had to make it right.

"Gussie, for heaven's sake, stop pushing me." Frustration painted Specs's words.

The soldiers parted, and Dr. Hunter stood there, her mouth pressed in a tight line.

Specs straightened his jacket. "Dr. Hunter, what is the meaning of this?"

Gussie tried to sidestep him. Maybe she still had time. But Dr. Hunter held up her hand, eyelids twitching. "Where are you going, Miss Travers?"

Gussie's throat clenched, and she tugged the ruffle at her neck. "I . . ." Her glance bounced off the doctor and stumbled against the soldier blocking the hall that led to the bedrooms.

Dr. Hunter turned to face Specs. "After all our work trying to rid the city of plague, you pull this bit of folly. I am furious with Miss Travers, but so disappointed in you, Dr. MacLean, and you can be sure that I will be discussing it with the health commissioner."

Specs crossed his arms. "What are you going on about?"

Dr. Hunter took a few stalking steps toward them, her finger raised. "Because of your necessary work in the most disadvantaged areas of our city, you might still have a future here, but I cannot promise it."

Specs looked at Gussie, his stare incredulous. "Catherine," he whispered before turning back to Dr. Hunter. "Is it Catherine?"

"Your sister is fine." A duo of soldiers carrying a stretcher between them appeared in the hall behind the soldier blocking the way, and he stepped aside. Dr. Hunter waved toward the group. "But this one . . ."

"No!" Gussie cried. She darted toward Bimla, who lay still. "Bimla." She touched her friend's cheek, nearly crumpling to the ground at the warmth she found there. "She's still alive. Oh, thank God."

"Gussie!" Catherine appeared, clutching the edges of her dressing gown together. "I was feeling so poorly, and I only lay down for a moment. Just a moment. I was woken by Dr. Hunter, who insisted they take Bimla away." She gasped, and her arms rounded the gentle bulge of her belly.

Bimla's eyelids fluttered open, and she stared up at Gussie with eyes as wide and wet as the ocean. "I can't go." Her tongue darted out to swipe at the cracked corners of her lips. Gussie grasped her hand.

"No. No, you can't take her away. We are caring for her here." Gussie turned toward Dr. Hunter, whose expression brooked no rebellion. But Gussie had spent a lifetime rebelling, and the doctor was a sight less intimidating than her mother.

"Plague victims belong in the hospital."

"Where she will be alone. I won't allow it. We're caring for her here. She will stay."

Dr. Hunter's expression turned incredulous. "You don't get to determine medical policy, Miss Travers. She will not stay."

"Then I will go with her. I will care for her in the hospital."

"What is going on?" The roar filled the crowded hall, and all eyes turned toward Specs. Studious, thoughtful Gabriel who never raised his voice. Never shouted. Never said an unkind thing.

Gussie flinched. "I can explain."

"Do," he said with all the warmth of an icebox.

"Uncle James and I discovered Bimla at her mother's home in Vetal Peth. Her family had been struck by plague, and when she learned of it, she went to them. The boy in the infirmary who died was her nephew. Then her sister-in-law—"

"I do not care to hear the entire sorry tale, Augusta. Please just tell me why you brought a plague patient into our home, exposing yourself and Catherine to the disease."

"Bimla couldn't go to the plague hospital," she whispered. "It's a terrible place—even you said that—and she didn't want to die there alone. And I didn't want her to die at all. I thought we could help her survive it here, where she could have nutritious food and plenty of attention."

"Gabriel," Catherine said with a gasp, "it isn't all . . . oh. Oh no. No. Please, no."

Gussie released Bimla's hand and turned to Catherine, who had gone white, her mouth gaping. Short, labored huffs of breath raised her chest.

"My baby, Gussie. My baby. You said she would be all right. You said . . ." Catherine lifted her skirts to reveal a dark brown puddle. She slid down the wall and groaned.

"Specs! Help her." Gussie shoved Dr. Hunter out of the way so he could get through.

"Take her out of here," Specs demanded with a nod toward Bimla. He bent to lift Catherine into his arms.

The soldiers, quiet and wide-eyed, began moving Bimla down the hall.

"Stop. No, don't take her." Gussie grabbed for one of them, her fingers brushing only a coat sleeve.

Bimla whimpered. "Let me stay."

"Please, God, my baby." Catherine buried her head into Specs's shoulder, her fingers clawing at his back.

Gussie looked between her two friends. Shouts and blood and cries for help. Her hands began to shake. Then her arms and legs. Her chest heaved, twisting and stealing her breath. But there was no dirt to run her hands through. Ramabai wasn't around to ease her through the fear. And all the thoughts in her head, the words in her heart, leaked out with her tears and fell like stones to the floor.

29

The library offered Gussie her only solace. In the hours following, she found in its books, cushioned chairs, and shafts of light distraction and hope and comfort. She didn't fix her attention on any one book overlong—and if questioned, she wouldn't have been able to answer any inquiries on their subjects—but it kept her thoughts off Catherine and Bimla. Filling her mind with other people's words prevented the others—those cruel, vicious, repeated ones—from taking hold once more.

It didn't, however, prevent her friends' desperate cries from playing a perverse kind of duet that underscored her frantic study. It bounced off leather spines and Catherine's wedding portrait encased in silver. It echoed in Gussie's mind, opportunistic and avaricious.

She shoved yet another volume on some inscrutable medical condition back into its place and withdrew *Through South India.* Standing near the bookshelf, Gussie flipped through the pages, dotted here and there with photographs of stacked temples and tropical backwaters. She should go south.

The lazy thought bobbed and floated into her consciousness, and she pressed the book to her chest, eyes unfocused. Should she?

Would Specs forgive her? Catherine and Bimla? Would she even be welcome in Poona, this place that had become home and eased the itch in her feet?

"You said she would be all right."

"Let me stay."

"My baby."

She shuffled through the book until she discovered a yellowed waxed paper negative. Etched onto it, she saw carvings that breathed life into stone. Rumors of an ancient civilization spreading across a city turned to dust.

Hampi near Hospet—1857 A. Greenlaw

This place called to her. It eased the burden of the possibility of being cast out. Sent away, this time—not leaving of her own volition. But perhaps she could find meaning and purpose in Hampi . . . if the worst came to pass. And her readers would enjoy the photographs. The witty observations. She hadn't yet told Lillian this six months in India was Miss Adventuress's last adventure. Hadn't told her she knew of her correspondence with the *New York Daily News*. Her column was more popular than ever. She could continue on with *Lady's Weekly* until she heard from Mr. Epps.

Where would Miss Adventuress go next? China or Japan? The South Seas?

The idea didn't make her heart trip with excitement as it once would have. Didn't nudge her steps onward toward things undiscovered. She thought of her readers, snug in little houses, surrounded by sleeping children, and found her previous determination to provide a spot of amusement anemic.

It was worthy. It was good. It was enjoyable.

It wasn't Poona. Or Specs, Catherine, and Bimla. It wasn't her blood spilled out on paper. It wasn't going to inspire young girls trapped by convention. It wasn't able to change hearts and minds.

It wasn't what she was meant for.

"It might all come to naught." Gussie gave a decisive nod. Catherine could very well, at that moment, be resting comfortably.

The blood—well, sometimes pregnant women bled and ended up delivering perfectly healthy babies. And Bimla . . . she had been doing very well. People survived the plague, and the plague hospital, every day.

And Specs would forgive her. He always had.

She took the book and the photograph and settled onto the settee, determined to indulge in a frivolous daydream or two. Maybe she and Specs could travel through Hampi on their honeymoon. She lost herself to the fantasy.

And then Specs came into the room. He didn't see her sitting in the corner. He removed his glasses and rubbed the bridge of his nose, his shoulders heaving with a suppressed sob.

"Specs?" She stood, and the book fell from her lap.

He froze. Then, so slowly she aged a year, he replaced his glasses and looked at her. There was no warm familiarity in his gaze. No words of understanding on his lips. For long moments, he just studied her with a kind of wary curiosity.

Until she could no longer bear it. "Catherine?"

"Resting."

"The baby?"

"Dead."

"No. Oh, Catherine." Gussie sank back onto the settee. *"It's all I have left of John."* "She knew. She told me and I . . . I only wanted to give her hope."

"She knew? You knew?"

"Only that she hadn't felt the baby move."

"You knew, and you didn't tell me?" He took a few stumbling steps backward. "You knew about this too."

She stared at him, thinking of all she hadn't told him. Her hands lifted to her face.

When her tears had finished, Specs approached. She expected a touch on her shoulder. A gentle word. Instead, he spoke with such coldness, she hardly recognized his voice. "It was the fall, of course."

She jerked upright. "The fall? But that was weeks ago! The bleeding stopped, and she has been feeling fine."

He looked down at her, all rigid aloofness and glacial judgment. "The child was dark and soft, the amniotic fluid dark and minimal, and the placenta produced a clot."

"I don't know what any of that means, Specs." At the sound of his nickname on her lips, his expression darkened. "Please, Gabriel, tell me."

"When Catherine fell, she suffered a partial abruption of the placenta. The baby couldn't survive and died either immediately or soon after. Thank God she miscarried now, or she would have gone septic. *She* could have died. And you didn't tell me."

"It was an accident." Gussie's throat closed around her defense. "Only an accident."

"There are no accidents!" he shouted, his hands fisting at his side. She jerked against the seatback, and he dropped heavily into the chair across from her. "Only choices."

She stared at his feet, his brown leather walking shoes polished and pointed inward. She always thought it endearing when she managed to catch him sitting like that, as though his toes were kissing. Now she recognized the position as one of impotency and grief. Fear. A retreat from the chaos of life. And he was wearing shoes in the house. He didn't like that.

"Just go."

"But, Gabriel, please . . ."

"How can I ever trust you? I told you I was worried something like this . . ." He lowered his head into his hands, tugged his hair through insistent fingers. "You are not safe. Never have been. I knew. I've always known. Just leave."

"Very well."

There was nothing left to be said. She had her answer.

A fly, trapped inside the room when a servant closed the shutters, buzzed and bounced in its search for freedom. Gussie glared at it from where she kept vigil beside Catherine's bed. She'd been sitting there since leaving Gabriel in the library. Wishing into the silence all the things she would change. All the things she could have done to prevent tragedy.

But she kept circling around to the same conclusion.

Life sometimes hurt. And she wouldn't creep through it, peering around every corner before taking a step.

She followed the movements of a pink gecko as it skittered across the wall. Poor fly. Only a piece of painted wood kept it from safety. The gecko tipped its head in a parody of contemplation, and, with a scuttle, the fly was no more.

Gussie sighed and turned her attention back to Catherine. Moved to the edge of her seat when she noticed her friend's gaze on her.

"It was a girl." Catherine's voice broke. So did Gussie's heart.

"I know."

"Where is she?"

"I'm sure your brother has taken good care of her."

"I want to see her."

"Oh, Catherine. That isn't a good idea."

Catherine's face crumpled. "I shouldn't have gone with you. I only wanted to prove myself capable. Strong. But I'm not you, Gussie, and I killed my baby. John's baby."

"No." Gussie pushed off the chair and knelt beside Catherine's bed. "No. That isn't true. It was an accident." Whatever Specs said, accidents happened. He couldn't avoid grief just by willing it. Couldn't control the world by stiff adherence to rules wrought in fear.

When Catherine fell asleep once more, Gussie left the bungalow. She took her Kodak with her, tucking it safely into its bag and slipping a couple of extra rolls of film in beside it. She would soon leave Poona, and she wanted to take as many photographs as possible to remember it by. In those moments when she stepped into a new city or found herself in yet another unfamiliar place, she could pull these photographs from her camera bag and remember the place that had become more than a story.

She crossed the narrow lane, trimmed in tidy bungalows and wild gardens, and captured Catherine's house. Then she walked to the crossroads and took a photo of the dozing tanga driver lying across the two-wheeled carriage, legs stretched out in front of him.

After she nudged him awake and tempted him with a few coins, they made their way through Poona, Gussie calling to him when she wanted to hop down and capture another photograph. Bund Garden, with its graceful bridge and statues. The calm brown water of the Mula-Mutha River, along which walked European women carrying umbrellas and into which violated widows threw themselves. The white walls of Aga Khan Palace, erected in a bid to give work to the starving. Shaniwar Wada's ruins, where overgrown brush and peddlers shared room with Poona's ghosts. Ganj Peth, with its twisting streets, rooting pigs, wide-eyed children, and tumbled-together buildings.

The sun hung low by the time the tanga approached the plague hospital. Gussie sat for a few moments, lost in thought and regret, until a voice called out, "Beautiful memsahib, you wish for perfume?"

Approaching the tanga was a man who looked vaguely familiar. He grinned crookedly, and she recognized him.

Gussie tipped her head toward the attar seller. "No, I'm sorry. I don't wish to buy perfume." She lifted her wrist to her nose, her eyes closing briefly as she inhaled memories of Specs—his embrace, his sober voice, his restrained passion. She would allow herself the indulgence of wearing this patchouli attar over the next few months. By the time the little pot emptied, her heart would be healed, and she could move through life without Gabriel MacLean. "I have found one I like."

"Ah . . . you are the same lady who paid little for something important."

"What riddles you tell."

The merchant's eyes were very dark beneath his white turban, his brows slashes that lifted and shifted and dipped with alarming frequency. His face was arresting. Beautiful to look at. Full of emotion. Then he lifted a wooden tray cluttered with various tins, pots, and vials. "A lady needs many perfumes."

Gussie laughed and clambered down. "I will look."

She poked through the various containers and lifted a simple glass jar with a gold cap. Twisting it open, she held it to her nose and remembered—

A late spring rose garden spilling over with flowers. Two children playing at being grown-up. *"We shall marry for real one day, you know?"*

Winter frost stealing life, branches offering thorns instead of beauty. Tears falling on the fabric of a ball gown. *"They shall never understand me. Not the way you do."*

A house turned to sticks and stones, ash scuttling across the street with autumn's fallen leaves. *"I found this late bloom. Your mother's favorite, right? I am here for you."*

She'd trimmed her hat in summer. Roses to remind him of all they had shared. *"Must you go? What will I do without you?"*

"You will live, Gussie. Breathe and see and explore. Write to me of your adventures." He plucked a bloom from the brim of her hat and held it to his heart before leaving her on the station platform.

She had written. To thousands of American women, but mostly to him. Something she hadn't even recognized until India changed her.

"It is attar of rose."

Gussie looked at the man over the rim of the jar, her heart tangled with memories and words and scents.

"It is very important, this scent. I can tell. More valuable than coins." He dipped his head, his silky grin replaced by something almost tender. Then he slipped away before Gussie could even reach into her reticule.

With a final sniff, she recapped the jar and nestled it beside her Kodak. She took a deep breath as she approached the guards at the hospital gate.

"I'm here to see a patient."

"No visitors," one barked.

"Please. I will speak to Dr. Hunter first, then."

They exchanged a glance, then shrugged and ordered a small man bent beneath the weight of a bag of laundry to retrieve the doctor.

She arrived moments later, a scowl twisting her lips. "What is it? I'm very busy." Then she noticed Gussie, and her expression softened—only slightly, but enough that hope flared. "Miss Travers."

"Dr. Hunter. I was hoping to visit with Bimla today."

"We don't allow visitors. You know that."

"But you have allowed me entry in the past."

"As a journalist. Someone who promised to share all of this." Dr. Hunter waved her arm toward the matting sheds that housed hundreds of dying people in wards meant to heal. And divide. Ease death. And protect.

"Please. I'm leaving Poona."

Dr. Hunter sighed. "It's out of the question."

"You would have her suffer alone? When she has discovered love and friendship?"

Dr. Hunter threw her arm out again, encompassing the rows of squat barracks-like structures behind her. "*All* of them suffer alone. Bimla isn't special in that."

"I understand." Gussie was one of many people suffering the absence of someone she loved and feared for. All across the city, Indian mothers and husbands and children wept for those behind the plague hospital gates. She was not special in that. She was nothing.

"*You are fearfully and wonderfully made.*"

Perhaps not nothing, then.

"Will you give this to her?" Gussie reached into her camera bag and pushed aside the little glass jar. She pulled at the corner of the photograph she had hidden away in the pocket with her memory of a happy time. A happy place.

It was Bimla at the garden wall, looking over the gleaming city of Udaipur. Her white sari wrapped around her like a talisman meant to keep her safe. Unnoticed. She stood in angled profile, only the tip of her nose and a portion of her cheek and chin visible. A scarf draped her head, hiding more than her dark hair.

Dr. Hunter looked at the picture. "We do our best. It isn't perfect, but then, nothing is."

"I know."

The doctor stroked the photo, her thumb tracing the long lines of Bimla's sari. "There are few things in life painted in black and white. Everywhere I look, there is only shades of gray." She met Gussie's gaze, then took a deep breath and lifted her chin. "Goodbye, Miss Travers."

Gussie watched Dr. Hunter walk back through the gate. Then she turned, and her gaze swept over the street, snagging on the women's silver-threaded saris, the gold rings circling nostrils and arms and toes, the banana plants' emerald leaves, and the birds resting between clusters of fruit the color of sunshine. The attar seller with his jeweled bottles.

"No. It is more than gray." When she looked up from her camera's finder, she had discovered life was washed in color.

30

For a week Gussie stayed in the bungalow. She could have left. Could have boarded a train and escaped Catherine's grief and Gabriel's dark scowls. He had moved back in after Catherine's miscarriage. There was no reason now to worry about scandal when everything between them had shriveled beneath her silence and his fear.

She could have set out for another city. Somewhere exciting and pulsing with life. Somewhere not blanketed by grief and regret. None of the station doctors, she was sure, would stop her. Not someone who clutched a first-class ticket.

And she'd been very careful around Bimla. Hadn't touched the buboes. Hadn't been vomited on. Hadn't entered or left the room without scrubbing her hands clean.

But she stayed.

Because so many in her position didn't have a choice. So many women exposed to the illness were forced into a place that stole their agency. Stole their dignity. Sometimes even stole much more.

Now, though, the week had tapered to an end. Her trunks were packed. Her ticket purchased. Her book done. Her time in Poona over.

How she hated leaving. She'd spent half her life bound up by fear, though. Fear of never measuring up. Fear of becoming exactly what others thought of her. Fear of smothering beneath the weight of her own choices.

She couldn't take on Gabriel's.

Her steps were quiet as she walked into the library and laid the manuscript on the table. She read through the page she'd set on top of the stack, which was really the last page. The end. Then she lifted the photograph she'd retrieved from the copy of *Through South India*. Hampi. She would stay for a week. Give him time to consider what he wanted. One didn't actually need to leave a place to run away.

And one didn't need to stay put in order to feel settled.

Poona—with all of its complexities, its sprawling palaces and crooked peths, its progressive people and aching rules, its tossing off of injustice and hiding behind walls spun of silk, its joy and death—had somehow, in a stunning act of implausibility, become home.

And no matter where she roamed, Gussie knew she would forever be resisting its call. Unless Specs chose freedom. Unless he chose her.

But she wouldn't demand it. She had no right to force anyone to bend to her will. Even the man who was so much a part of her—a part of her history—that she couldn't be sure where he ended and she began.

He came into the library then, just as he had every morning since Catherine's miscarriage. He was a creature of habit. It was what made him so dependable. So appealing. He would find more than medical journals waiting for him today, though.

"My train departs at nine," she said.

He had seen her the moment he walked into the room, but at the sound of her voice, he startled as though not expecting her to speak. "Where are you going?"

"South, I think. First Hampi and then on to Cochin. I have months yet to spend in India, and I hate to waste an adventure."

"Is it safe?"

Gussie smiled. "Just as safe as setting off for the Wild West."

"Yes, well . . . I breathed a sigh of relief every time I received a letter."

"I'll write, if you wish."

He scratched his head and padded over to the bookshelf, browsing the titles he had no doubt already memorized. He wore no shoes, of course, and when she rounded the desk, she made one final, lingering study of him, ending at his feet—narrow and long, crisscrossing blue veins standing out in relief against his skin.

"Will you have this mailed for me today? The post office won't open until after I leave. It's the book I'm sending to Mr. Epps. I took the liberty of using Catherine's address for correspondence with him. I will keep her apprised of my whereabouts, and she can forward me his response."

"Of course." He still hadn't turned to face her.

She crossed the room, the sound of her steps swallowed by the rug. He turned when she came near.

"Gussie, I . . ." He dropped his head. "I don't know if I can allow myself to love you. To trust you. The risks you take . . . and will you ever be happy staying in one place? What if you get the urge to run again?"

She didn't try to convince him. Didn't tell him that Poona made her want to stay. That *he* made her want to stay.

It wasn't really about that anyway. He needed to recognize the truth of it on his own. Needed to realize his love couldn't be knit to his fear.

"I want you to know," she said, "that you have taught me more about love and sacrifice and honor and trust and family than anyone else on earth. I could travel from one corner of the globe to the other and find no one more deserving of my regard. There isn't one man in all the New York ballrooms, mining towns, or Maharashtra palaces who comes close to measuring up to you. I have hurt you. I have betrayed you. I have taken you for granted. I have kept silent when I should have trusted you. And I'm sorry."

She took up his hands, and they were cool. She stared at them. At the long, tapered fingers that brought comfort. At the palms that wrought healing. She didn't look at him. Couldn't bear to see unforgiveness or distrust in his gaze. "I'm sorry. I will carry my love for you wherever I go."

It took every bit of courage to leave him there. Every bit of her resisted this departure.

But she left.

Two hours later she sat on a train, face pressed to the window, her heart in her throat, as she watched Poona's station grow ever smaller.

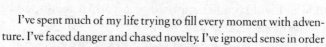

I've spent much of my life trying to fill every moment with adventure. I've faced danger and chased novelty. I've ignored sense in order to capture a photograph and winked at ruin so I could get the story.

I've traveled over much of the United States, photographing and documenting and writing amusing little anecdotes about my life. My, I was clever! Ignoring the whisper of discontent, pretending everything I saw and did was enough to give my life meaning.

For a few years, I've told women they must escape the tedium of their everyday. Be gone, washing! Farewell, cookstove! Adieu, nursery! And if they couldn't flee, I would for them. Here a column on an enchanted evening in the Everglades. There a photograph of the otherworldly Badlands. *My work is making a difference in the lives of these poor, bored housewives,* I told myself.

My life has meaning.

And then, India.

What a surprise it has been! I came here expecting a merry excursion. With my notebook and Kodak in hand, I meant to chase the horizon, flinging off caution—not that I ever had much—and the voices trailing me halfway around the world.

It was only when I left everything familiar that I came to understand what a foolish thing I'd been pursuing. Life is in the moments! It is in the everyday. It is in the washing and cookstove and nursery. It is in loving a friend well. It is in the quiet, when there is nothing but a conversation or a thick book or an afternoon picnic to fill the hours.

Before India, I loved the idea of travel because it gave my life— my name—prestige. It validated me. Made me believe that I had meaning. Now, having discovered there is, after all, a place I wish to rest, I have learned it isn't where I wander that gives my life purpose, but the people I love. The things I fight for. Who and what I believe in.

I leave you with this final thought, my dearest reader. No matter where you are in your journey or where your travels take you—near or far or somewhere in between—appreciate those little, seemingly insignificant things that fill your everyday. In the chasing of something significant, you might very well miss the fact that you already are.

31

Hampi was everything Gussie had imagined.

Only lonelier.

Something about the rock-strewn, ravaged city sang an elegy that knit itself through the Tungabhadra River, which poured life into the rice and sorghum fields worked by lean men with dark eyes and unfathomable thoughts. It echoed up the hills, crying out for restitution. Remembrance. It clanged against the ruined temple complexes and stone carvings of chariots, towers, and elephants.

That brittle negative Gussie had discovered in the travel book hadn't done this place justice. It hadn't expressed the grandeur. Nor the aching sadness. She had never thought to be struck dumb by a sight. Never sat with her notebook in her lap and been unable to describe what she felt. No pithy labels would suffice.

Hampi required words. Lots of words. And photographs. Many more photographs. And even then, she didn't think she could capture the sense of it.

She spent six days exploring, poking through abandoned bazaars, climbing monuments that seemed to be set in place by gods or giants, and walking over brush-covered red soil. Each evening, before the sun began to descend, she walked the few miles to the little village she had arranged lodgings in. It was so small, she didn't know if it even had a name.

At the Hospet train station, the railway agent had instructed her to stay in the city, even offering her the name of a suitable guesthouse. Gussie, thinking it likely he made a commission from the referral, chose instead to hire a driver to take her closer to the archaeological site first made known to the outside world nearly a hundred years earlier.

She wanted the freedom to come and go as she pleased without suffering the disapproving clucking of a house mother or grappling with the language barrier posed by hiring a driver twice each day.

But she knew it was foolish to stay out alone past dark, so she made sure to arrive at the village before sunset, where she would eat whatever one of the local women cooked for her. Then, by gaslight, she would spend hours in a mud and thatch-roofed structure, staring at her paper, pen in hand, unable to compose anything coherent.

Tomorrow she would return to Hospet, where a train would take her toward Cochin, so tonight she wanted to watch the sunset over the mountains and ruins. Over the river that twisted and curved around outcroppings of stony ground.

Specs had influenced her, though, in the short time she had become reacquainted with him, and she had hired a couple who lived in the village to wait for her with an ox and cart near the Achyutaraya Temple. They had spent a few hours exploring the ruins around it, weaving in and out of the pillars that lined what used to be called Courtesan's Street, where merchants sold exotic goods and dancing girls flicked their lashes, fingers, and hips. The temple alone, where people had worshiped long before the Vijayanagara empire had been built and long after it had been destroyed, exhibited life.

For a while, Gussie had made suitable noises of interest as her guides pointed out the crevices where the temple elephants had stood, the carvings of figures twisted into Ashtanga poses, and goddesses with their round breasts and bellies. But less interested in religious monuments than finding the words she felt certain would come with the dipping sun, she left the couple to their worship and walked the four hundred meters toward Matanga Hill.

She didn't climb very high, despite wearing a practical ready-made, now grimy and stained with sweat and dirt, for she found the perfect spot. A cozy seat made from the jutting of a flat-topped boulder that even offered a table of sorts—rock set upon rock—to rest her camera on.

She took her camera out, wanting to capture the mountains and hills, softened by the early evening light, a backdrop to the tiered temple rising from a carpet of palm fronds and tamarind trees.

She set the Kodak on an even place and pulled out the bellows, then pressed the lever that released the shutter. Shifting her camera, she caught the view from a different angle. Four more times, until she reached her final exposure.

She knelt and peered through the finder, smiling when a family of macaques scampered over a ruined sculpture, then squinting when a particularly large one clambered to the top of the pavilion halfway fallen into rubble and began waving its arms.

Gussie stood up straight and shaded her eyes with her hand. That was no monkey but a man. And no ordinary man but a rather extraordinary one.

She lifted her arms, nearly knocking her camera off its perch, and waved with complete abandonment. Had her limbs ever felt so light? Had her heart ever danced with as much joy?

He had come. He had run after her. He had remembered.

She laughed when a macaque, curiosity spiked by the madman stumbling from boulder to tumbled pillar to pile of stone, began to chase him. Specs slapped at the animal, jabbed at it with his foot, then set about running after it up the hill.

The monkey reached her first, but with an annoyed grunt, it darted away. Then came Dr. MacLean, looking undoctorly but so very dashing in a travel-worn suit, scuffed shoes, and crooked glasses.

These Gussie straightened when he finally stood before her. "You came."

"I did."

"Bimla?" Every moment since she'd left Poona had been teased with thoughts of her friend. She was terrified to know. Had to know. Couldn't ignore the fact that someone was more likely to die of the plague than survive it. She had lifted hope above a mountain of prayers. "Did she . . . ?"

Specs smiled. "She's recovering. Ramabai is back in Poona, and they've moved Bimla to Sharada Sadan."

The breath Gussie had held between her heart and her throat freed itself, and she dropped her head and pressed her fingers to her eyes. *Thank you. Thank you. Thank you.* If she received nothing else from God's hands, Bimla's life was enough.

"I read your book."

She blinked away the tears and looked up at him. "The whole thing? I only meant for you to read the final page."

"I read that first and then turned to the beginning."

Gussie sucked her lower lip between her teeth and turned her attention back toward the camera. She fiddled with the lens, then shoved the Kodak into her bag and pushed it behind her back. "I'm so sorry I didn't trust you enough to tell you about Catherine. And Bimla."

"I'm sorry I didn't trust you enough to make the right decision." He pushed at his hat and wiped the back of his hand across his forehead. "Catherine told me bringing Bimla to the house was her idea. And that she asked that you not tell me about her fear over the baby. Why didn't you explain that?"

Gussie shrugged. "It wasn't my place. And you weren't angry with me over those things, anyway. Not really."

"I was afraid." He reached for her, his expression hopeful, and she went to him. "Afraid I would love you and lose you. You can be so reckless."

"Only because I was desperate to prove myself worthy. That isn't something I plan to continue. I even hired guides to see me home this evening. You would approve of my choices."

"I approve of you." He kissed her forehead in a terribly proper way. She sniffed. "Catherine is consumed with guilt. I didn't really believe that you encouraged her to stay off the stairs, but I've learned a lot of things about my sister I wouldn't have thought possible even a few weeks ago. She's decided she wants to go to Pondicherry to stay with friends, after all. She wants to recover and isn't sure she can do so in John's house."

"She's stronger than you think."

"Yes." He was quiet for a moment. "You are too. I . . . I never really let you grow up, did I? I always saw you as a headstrong girl who needed protection. Instruction. I was a dreadful bore."

She laughed. "You were. But you are also one of the only people who encouraged me in my dreams. Who believed in me. You and Uncle James."

"Do you forgive me?"

She lifted her hands to cup his dear, adorable face. How she loved him. "Of course."

She kissed him then, not at all properly. She kissed him until they were both breathless.

"You will still marry me?" she asked.

"I did ask you seventeen years ago. Nothing has changed."

"We were children."

"My heart has only ever belonged to you."

She wrapped her arms around his waist and laid her head on his chest. "Look."

The sun, cradled in the dip between two peaks, dared not go to sleep cloaked in modesty. It draped itself with the spices of India and bathed the ruins, so small and insignificant beneath the brilliant sky, in golden light.

"Specs," she said.

"Yes, my love?"

"How very glad I am that you caught me."

344

So you see, dear reader, this shall be Miss Adventuress's final column. If you wish to know what happened to her, C. S. Epps and Company will be releasing Gussie MacLean's first book, *A Photo Adventure through India: Wandering No More*. Within its pages, you will discover that she may have changed her name and grown a bit more verbose, but she hasn't given up on adventure.

Epilogue

Poona, India
January 1899

Gussie finished pinning the *gajra* to Bimla's hair. The flowers scented every corner of the small antechamber off Mukti Mission's chapel.

"I'm so glad you're having an evening wedding, Bimla." Gussie reached up to poke her finger into one of the blooms. "It's lovely to go without a hat in favor of flowers."

Bimla turned, her face as white as the jasmine buds tumbling over her thick braid, and Gussie dropped her hand.

"Whatever is it?" Gussie asked.

"How can this be happening?"

"Are you having second thoughts? It's probably normal, given all you suffered in your previous marriage."

Bimla shook her head, the gold bells hanging from her ears making the lightest tinkling sound, as though fairies played about her lobes. "I wasn't meant to remarry. And to have a love match! What have I done to deserve this?"

"You have done nothing to deserve it, and yet God has blessed you anyway. Etak loves you entirely. What have any of us done to deserve the goodness in our lives?"

Catherine bustled into the room, her middle heavy with child. She had been married only nine months, but she and her French college-superintendent husband were mad for each other. They had surprised everyone with news of the baby when they traveled to Poona from Pondicherry for Bimla's wedding. "François and Gabriel have seated the final guests. The children are ready. Are you sure this is what you want? Because I'm not certain it will sound very nice."

Bimla laughed, and color returned to her cheeks. "Yes. I want the children to be part of this new beginning. They have seen too much loss and grief in their lives. It is good to give them a glimpse of joy."

Catherine shrugged and disappeared again.

Gussie straightened the pleats of the *pallu* draped over Bimla's shoulder. The red silk slipped between her fingers, so fine was its weave. Gold embroidery circled the arms of her blouse, with more creating a repeating palm frond pattern over the length of the fabric.

"It is too elegant," Bimla said, running her hands over her hips as though reading Gussie's thoughts. She lifted her hands and stared at the ornate Mehndi art staining them, as though trying to make sense of the circles and swirls and dips.

"Etak loves to lavish you with beautiful things."

After Bimla had recovered from the plague and returned to work at the infirmary, Dr. Paul had confirmed what Gussie had already seen. He'd watched Bimla grow in love and capability caring for his patients as he'd grown in love for her.

It had taken some convincing, though, before Bimla conceded to marry him. *"He is too good for me. He deserves a wife who is pure. One who doesn't bear such terrible scars."*

But Etak had persisted. Lovingly and with the patience of Job. His fondness for Bimla was a beautiful thing to watch unfold, and Gussie often found herself filling blank pages with their story. It might be that her next book would explore the depths of grace and love.

"Are you ready?" Catherine asked, poking her head through the doorway again.

Bimla met Gussie's eyes, then nodded, slowly but without hesitation. "This is much different from my first wedding ceremony—in a place I love, surrounded by friends, and I'm not weeping." She smiled, and Gussie draped the sheer silk chiffon dupatta over her friend's head.

"As a sign of humility, not concealment," Bimla had said. And in truth, the covering was as diaphanous as a daydream. It hid little.

Gussie kissed her friend's cheek, praying, as she always did, that God would finish the work of healing as her lips touched the puckered skin. "I will see you in a moment."

She left Bimla to her prayers and found her own husband.

"This is so exciting," she said as she slid onto the bench beside Specs. She reached for his glasses, straightening them.

"Do you regret not having a wedding like this of our own?"

She thought back on their hasty trip to Hospet, where Specs had secured the services of a Dutch mission pastor, bouncing in the back of that oxcart all the way to his little Lutheran church. So much laughter. And afterward, a sticky meal of mango and rice. And after that . . .

Gussie's face burned. "I regret nothing."

The children of Mukti Mission stood at the front of the room, lifting their voices and handmade instruments. Gussie covered her mouth with her hand. "Oh dear."

Specs chuckled.

They sang in Marathi, and she could only pick out a few words—her language tutor despaired of her ever speaking it with any kind of mastery—but she had learned that more important than the words themselves was the spirit in which they were said. Or sung, in this case.

And all Gussie heard was the sound of voices once lost, now found.

Author's Note

I originally intended to set *Every Word Unsaid* in a different Indian city. But when I discovered I had to move my timeline up so Gussie didn't have to travel with a suitcase full of equipment, I realized the story would coincide with when Pandita Ramabai Sarasvati, one of my heroes, was living and working in Poona. So Gussie was shifted hundreds of miles and a decade into the future to accommodate my desire to share with you a bit of Amma's story.

Ramabai was an early feminist. She worked tirelessly on behalf of India's widows, child famine victims, and Christ. I tried to stay as true as possible to what I've read in biographies and her own words. I know I've failed, though. There's no possible way anyone can demonstrate how incredible she was in a novel. I only hope you—and she (watching from heaven)—can see how much I admire her. It was challenging to find specific dates and descriptions when it came to the work she did at Mukti Mission. If I'm wrong in how I presented it, I take full responsibility and apologize.

Gussie and Cordelia Fox (both entirely figments of my imagination) are modeled after the intrepid adventurers of the late nineteenth century. Women like Isabella Bird and Nellie Bly, who paved the way for female travelers. Today, it's as easy as getting a passport and jumping on a flight. That wasn't so in the nineteenth century, when travel required substantially more effort and courage.

Many of the places mentioned in *Every Word Unsaid* exist—including Shaniwar Wada, Hampi, Jag Niwas, Dorabjee & Sons, the Poona Gymkhana Club, and even the abandoned suburb in Jaipur (a nineteenth-century traveler wrote about it).

The Lokhande brothers and the incident with Catherine's husband is modeled after the Chapekar brothers, who were involved in the assassination of W. C. Rand, the British plague commissioner of Poona. Catherine's husband, John, is entirely fictional. The real event was tragic—as were the terrible things done to Poona's citizens leading up to it. Depending on whose account you read, you get different narratives of how the plague was handled during this time. I can't begin to untangle all of it from my little house in Ohio 125 years later, so I've tried to paint as realistic a picture as possible given the information I have.

Dr. Etak Paul is loosely based on Dr. Yashwantrao Phule, the adopted son of Savitribai Phule (another of India's early feminists), who lost his life serving Poona's plague patients. Dr. Paul unexpectedly became one of my favorite characters in this book. Like Gussie, I enjoyed watching his tender and patient love for Bimla grow.

Dr. Marion Hunter really was a plague medical officer, and a photographer for *The Sketch* did take photographs at the plague hospital. The people who searched for plague victims were called The Searchers. (It sounds like something out of a speculative novel, doesn't it?) One of Pandita Ramabai's widows was assaulted at the segregation camp, after which she disappeared. And I had a gecko in India named Lizzie that kept the spiders away.

For years, I ran from words spoken over me. Even words I spoke. I let those things define how I saw myself, instead of embracing who God says I am. I think a lot of us do that. Despite what we're told in childhood, words are powerful. They may not be able to break your bones, but they can certainly break your heart. Break your spirit. The Bible speaks to the power of our words. They can heal or destroy. Lift up or tear down. Let's use ours to speak truth. To restore and love and praise. Gussie discovered her true worth is found in who the Word of God says she is, not in the ugly accusations cast over her by other people.

That is my hope for you—that you hear God's whisper in the shuffling of the Bible's pages. You, beloved, are valued. You are loved. You are His.

Acknowledgments

There's not enough room on the cover to fit all the names of the people who helped make this book a reality. First, as always, I want to thank everyone at Bethany House Publishers. I have enjoyed every moment working with you. Special thanks go to my editor, Jessica Sharpe, whose ability to transform my drafts into something worth reading is magical. If you're a fan of romance, you can thank her for the particularly swoony kiss in the library.

Thanks to my OWL ladies—Kristi, Hope, Leslie, and Lindsey—who helped me plan this story, as well as kept me connected to life outside my head. Thanks especially to Lindsey Brackett, who pulled me back from the edge *so many times* during the writing of *Every Word Unsaid*. When I called her, sobbing (seriously . . . sobbing), she said, "Send it to me. We'll figure it out." And we did.

Thanks to Rachel Fordham, who helped me craft a stronger first few chapters, and to fellow 2020 debut author Ashley Clark, who is my kindred spirit and has become the friend I didn't even know I needed.

To my in-person friends who have been supportive and encouraging from the beginning: Stephanie Gammon, Cassidy Staver, and Alicia Baum. I love you!

To my family. There are too many of you to list, but don't worry . . . you're not the reason I ran away to India.

A special thanks to Todd Gustavson at the George Eastman Museum in New York, who explained to me how the Folding Pocket Kodak camera worked and even let me handle one (and channel my inner Gussie).

To Madhu, my sweet sensitivity reader and friend. God was in our meeting.

To Anjali, the sweet girl with the deep dimples, and her beautiful sister Savitri. You were only two of the children I fell in love with, but you've managed to fill my heart these twenty-three years. I pray you have found your place in a world that isn't always kind but is always full of possibility.

Thanks to Breny Maurtua (@brenyandbooks on Instagram) for reading through *Every Word Unsaid* in its pre-published, mostly pre-edited stage with an eye toward the doctorly stuff.

To my children: Ellie, Grainne, Hazel, and August. You are loved. You are wanted. You have purpose and meaning in this life. Whether you stay close to home or travel far away, you'll always be my four greatest accomplishments. I'm so proud of who you are.

And finally, to Shane. For every time I wake you up in the middle of the night, needing reassurance I'm not a complete hack. For the weeks at a time I go missing with my laptop. For the last-minute graphics I insist you make. For every dollar I spend on random research books that I use to glean only a sentence or two of information. And for every second of the last two decades we've spent together. I know I've yet to dedicate a book to you, but in truth, you are the framework upon which I write every word and craft every hero.

Kimberly Duffy is a Long Island native currently living in southwest Ohio. When she's not homeschooling her four kids, she writes historical fiction that takes her readers back in time and across oceans. She loves trips that require a passport, recipe books, and practicing kissing scenes with her husband of twenty-two years. He doesn't mind. You can find her at www.kimberlyduffy.com.

Sign Up for Kimberly's Newsletter

Keep up to date with Kimberly's news on book releases and events by signing up for her email list at kimberlyduffy.com.

More from Kimberly Duffy

When a stranger appears in India with news that Ottilie Russell's brother must travel to England to take his place as a nobleman, she is shattered by the secrets that come to light. But betrayal and loss lurk in England too, and soon Ottilie must fight to ensure her brother doesn't forget who he is, as well as stitch a place for herself in this foreign land.

A Tapestry of Light

You May Also Like . . .

Determined to uphold her father's legacy, newly graduated Nora Shipley joins an entomology research expedition to India to prove herself in the field. In this spellbinding new land, Nora is faced with impossible choices—between saving a young Indian girl and saving her career, and between what she's always thought she wanted and the man she's come to love.

A Mosaic of Wings by Kimberly Duffy
kimberlyduffy.com

After a deadly explosion at the Chilwell factory, munitions worker Rosalind Graham leaves the painful life she's dreamt of escaping by assuming the identity of her deceased friend. When RAF Captain Alex Baird is ordered to surveil her for suspected sabotage, the danger of her deception intensifies. Will Rose's daring bid for freedom be her greatest undoing?

As Dawn Breaks by Kate Breslin
katebreslin.com

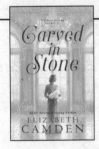

When lawyer Patrick O'Neill agrees to resurrect an old mystery and challenge the Blackstones' legacy of greed and corruption, he doesn't expect to be derailed by the kindhearted family heiress, Gwen Kellerman. She is tasked with getting him to drop the case, but when the mystery takes a shocking twist, he is the only ally she has.

Carved in Stone by Elizabeth Camden
The Blackstone Legacy #1
elizabethcamden.com

BETHANYHOUSE

More from Bethany House

After Pearl Harbor, sweethearts Gordon Hooper and Dorie Armitage were broken up by their convictions. As a conscientious objector, he went west to fight fires as a smokejumper, while she joined the Army Corps. When a tragic accident raises suspicions, they're forced to work together, but the truth they uncover may lead to an impossible—and dangerous—choice.

The Lines Between Us by Amy Lynn Green
amygreenbooks.com

After an abusive relationship derailed her plans, Adri Rivera struggles to regain her independence and achieve her dream of becoming an MMA fighter. She gets a second chance, but the man who offers it to her is Max Lyons, her former training partner, whom she left heartbroken years before. As she fights for her future, will she be able to confront her past?

After She Falls by Carmen Schober
carmenschober.com

After promising a town he'd find them water and then failing, Sullivan Harris is on the run; but he grows uneasy when one success makes folks ask him to find other things—like missing items or sons. When men are killed digging the Hawk's Nest Tunnel, Sully is compelled to help, and it becomes the catalyst for finding what even he has forgotten—hope.

Finder of Forgotten Things by Sarah Loudin Thomas
sarahloudinthomas.com

◆BETHANYHOUSE